A Fable-Parable-Fairy Story for our Children's Children
and Future Historians . . .

ALL LIES IN TRUMPERLAND

(BoJo Through the Looking Glass)

a.k.a. BE CAREFUL WHAT YOU WISH FOR!

by

TSB

Trevor Stott-Briggs

ABOUT THE AUTHOR

Leaving a cold, wet and gloomy Lancashire on 1 March 1976, he set out from the UK on a journey across Africa, not realising that he would eventually work in 34 countries across a span of 44 years. Along the way he married and somehow found the time to engineer four kids - all boys – as he only has one formula.

Always competitive and loving cars, he was involved in karting, rallying, circuit racing and anything with engines and wheels. And when he wasn't racing, he was playing, organising, coaching or refereeing rugby. Eventually, he found himself in the UAE and in possession of a body that did not work too well after breaking his neck in a sporting accident. So, he thought it would be a 'jolly good idea' to start writing books about life, the universe and everything.

He considers himself apolitical and has never voted Labour, Conservative, LibDem, Republican or Democrat – or even for anyone else – including Screaming Lord Sutch of the Monster Raving Loony Party, despite the obvious temptation to do so on principle.

Unlike most authors, he has never lived in Chipping Norton or Surrey, but did once own a time share in a resort, on a tiny island called Boracay, in the Philippines.

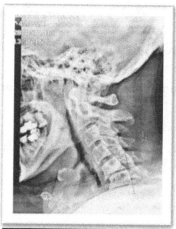

The Author

A Fable-Parable-Fairy Story

BY THE SAME AUTHOR

TSB – Confessions of an Ex-Hooker (Aged 66 And a Half)
a.k.a
DON'T STOP BELIEVIN'

OTHER BOOKS (STILL TO BE WRITTEN)

TSB – Confessions of an Ex-Lancashire Lad (Aged 26 And a Half)
a.k.a.
EE' BY GUMM!

TSB – Confessions of an Ex-Nondescript Nomad (Aged 56 And a Half)
a.k.a
RUCKIN' 'n ROLLIN' 'n RACING

TSB – Confessions of an Ex-Grumpy Old Man (Aged 76 And a Half)
a.k.a
KEEP ON KEEPIN' ON!

DEDICATION

I would like to dedicate this book to Paul Scriven at London Heathrow Passenger Assistance Office. Without Paul and his help, this book probably would not exist. Agnes and I arrived at LHR in the early hours of 20 February 2020. We were tired and unfocussed after an overnight flight and did not realise that my carry-on bag did not get taken off the tray under the seat of the airport wheelchair. We drove away from the airport carpark in the taxi after leaving the wheelchair behind - just dumped with all the other baggage trolleys.

But, in the bag was my laptop and the external drive, both of which had the only copies of about three quarters of this manuscript! A few calls by Olivia, my son Elliott's wife, got through to Paul and he personally went looking for the dumped wheelchair and the computer. What relief when he found it! Words cannot describe the feeling . . .

We met him when we flew out of LHR and he is such a nice guy. So, THANK YOU Paul. I could never have re-started writing this book.

Of course, I have to thank my wife Agnes and all my children, Elliott, James, Kyle & Colby for making me endless cups of tea & biscuits as I sat cocooned in my home office/family room writing this stuff.

The book is full of songs, YouTube videos, movie and TV clips etc. which have, hopefully, some relevance to the topics in the chapters. Therefore, I shall start as I mean to go on, with a very funny explanation, by a father to a question from his nine-year-old son, "What is politics?"

I think this says it all. It may be funny, but it's undeniably true . . .

WHAT IS POLITICS?
https://www.youtube.com/watch?v=3cUYmH7g30s

A Fable-Parable-Fairy Story

TABLE OF CONTENTS

A Fable-Parable-Fairy Story

ACKNOWLEDGEMENTS

As they say at the Oscars, Golden Globes, Tony Awards and BAFTAs – "I wanna thank . . . blah, blah blah . . ." followed by a list of everyone that breathed anywhere near their movie or TV show, right down to the guy that delivered the pizza. Well, that is unless you are Robert de Niro at the 2018 Tony's, in which case you might just say "F*ck Trump!"

I used to laugh at that but now I sort of know how they feel. Actually, the people I want to thank are the ones that ignited my desire to write this book in the first place. For most of my life I have considered myself totally apolitical. I have actually never voted in any election and, although I am British, I currently do not live in the UK. Nor do I live in the USA. It really started off as a reaction to the 2-3 years of nothing ever, ever happening with Brexit. Compared to that, the crazy stuff going on in the USA was jaw dropping – and continues to be so. I started by watching the late-night talk shows which were royally taking the p*ss out of Trump every night. People like Stephen Colbert, Seth Meyers, Trevor Noah, James Corden, John Oliver, Bill Maher etc. Then I realised it wasn't just funny – it was also a terrible hit on democracy, law & order, colour, race, religion, the Constitution, life, the universe and everything. So, I also began to watch the nightly cable news shows of Rachel Maddow, Lawrence O'Donnell, Chris Hayes, Ari Melber, Joy Reid etc. and daily videos by Glenn Kirschner. I personally like Rachel Maddow's investigative style as she digs really deep into topics for the back story. But everyone mentioned above has been a daily source of info and inspiration. A huge THANK YOU to you all – please keep doing it!

I must also mention all the people who post videos on YouTube, write reams on Wikipedia and place images on Wikimedia Commons for everyone's use. Thank you to all those contributors – particularly DonkeyHotey for the fantastic caricatures - that have added dimension to my words. Remember: "To steal ideas from one person is plagiarism. To steal from many is research". That will always be my defence.

But also, I do wanna thank the pizza delivery guy for the pizzas that fuelled my brain to get all these crazy ideas down on paper . . .

THANK YOU, JARED KUSHNER

On 9 September 2020, just a few days before this book was due to be published, the Washington Post reported on an extract from Bob Woodward's new book, *Rage,* about Donald Trump. In the book, Woodward writes that Jared Kushner advised people that one of the most important guiding texts to understand the Trump presidency was *Alice in Wonderland.* What more can I say, except that it looks like my crazy hypothesis was right 'on the money', to use a typically American terminology.

I always say TINSTAAC – There Is No Such Thing As A Coincidence.

So, thank you, Jared Kushner. Thank you very much!

FOREWORD - FOREWARNED IS FOREARMED

Dear Reader, the following book diverts from my usual style of telling stories about things that happened to me along the Rocky Road of Life. I grew up in UK from 1949 – 1976, when we were brought up with Prime Ministers like Winston Churchill, Antony Eden, Harold Macmillan, Alec Douglas-Home, Harold Wilson and Ted Heath. And, likewise, the USA had Presidents like Truman, Eisenhower, Kennedy, Johnson, Nixon and Ford. All of whom were fine upstanding gentlemen and real "politicians". One could even say "statesmen". Well, OK. Maybe Nixon failed on the upstanding bit. But what if we fast-forward to the present time and into the future? To the period from 2016 and to beyond 2020. What will politicians be like then?

The story in this book is somewhere between a Fable, a Parable and a Fairy Story and features a couple of political buffoons – "BoJo" and "Trumper". Sort of a "Dumb and Dumber" of the political world in the 21st Century.

As you know, fables are generally aimed at adults and cover religious, social and political themes and, usually, centre the stories around animals, plants or even inanimate objects.

| 1. | Every Day is a No-Brainer |

So, if it were just an Aesop's Fable it could perhaps be a variation on the Ass and the Pig (I leave it to you to decide who would be which) or the Tortoise and the Hare (or perhaps in this case – The Tortoise and the Hair).

Similarly, a Parable is usually a short, didactic story that illustrates a universal truth or a moral lesson or principle. So, if it were just a parable it could perhaps be The Blind Man and the Lame. If you don't know it, in that story a lame person is being carried by a blind one. Unfortunately, the blind man pays no heed to his lame guide until, after various mishaps, they fall over a precipice and die.

2. Lame Leads Blind

And, last but by no means least is the simple Fairy Story. Colloquially, the term "Fairy Story" can also mean any far-fetched story or tall tale. It is used to describe any story that not only is <u>not</u> true but could <u>not possibly</u> be true. A good example of this is the well-known classic, Alice in Wonderland, in which Alice falls down a rabbit hole and

3.   Alice is No Dodo

encounters all sorts of very weird people, plus bizarre and odd anthropomorphic animal characters that try and explain things to her. But, besides being far-fetched, most Fairy Stories usually have a real underlying moral, and, especially in the case of Alice in Wonderland, there are many clever literary twists to redefine logic and fantasy.

As this story combines all of the above, I arrived at the title All Lies in Trumperland (BoJo Through the Looking Glass) a.k.a. Be Careful What You Wish For!

Also, just to add a certain surreal flavour, I couldn't resist metamorphosising some of the words to take into account the out-of-this-world, catastrophic political situations in this glimpse into what could happen when things you usually take for granted – like honesty, fair play, working on behalf of the country that elected you etc – somehow don't seem important any more to the politicians that you voted for. Some words have been altered by adding, subtracting, or changing one letter, and giving a new definition. Others are neologisms, which simply have alternative meanings for familiar words. All of these are referenced and explained – somewhat tongue-in-cheek - in footnotes, so it's a good idea to read them to understand the story better.

Music and movies have played a big part in my life. Consequently, I have included the titles and many references to songs, lyrics, TV shows movies and relevant political clips in the chapters so that you, the reader, can share an additional mental image or musical memory that either prompted or was evoked by the story. I am hoping these will add mood, colour and depth to the chapters in the same way a soundtrack gives additional emotion to the story unfolding in a movie!

Many of you will already have seen, heard or remember some of them. But if you don't, you can watch and listen on YouTube by using your smart cell phone and scanning the QR Code with a code reader app, such as NeoReader. It's a free download if you don't already have it.

If you are using a Kindle e-Reader like Kindle Fire or an Android App you can access the YouTube video by just clicking on the URL link in the box. If the URL or QR code does not work – sometimes the video has been blocked or removed for various reasons – then just type in the title of the video from the text box on the page into the Search window on YouTube and usually several other versions will come up.

Also, this book is intentionally trans-Atlantic. Some of it is about BoJo the Brit PM and some of it is about Trumper, the POTUS. So, I have used British English and American English spelling for their respective dialogues. You're all smart, I am sure you can translate.

But, remember dear reader, that none of what follows is true. How could it ever happen? It's just a Fable-Parable-Fairy Story and, like all fairy stories, it begins with those magical words "Once upon a time . . ."

A Fable-Parable-Fairy Story

Based on a ~~True Story~~ Bunch of Lies.

Inspired by the magical, timeless prose
of Lewis Carroll and the erudite, satirical, political
meanderings of the small, but perfectly formed,
Ian Hislop of Private Eye.

4.   Inspiration Through the Ages - Lewis Caroll and Ian Hislop

CAST OF (DUBIOUS) CHARACTERS
- The Usual Suspects -

McDonald J. Trumper................President of Trumperland and the Leader of the Free World, or at least what's left of it. Practicing xenophobe, misogynist, egoist, narcissist. Full-time pathological liar.

Boris de Piffle Jockstrap..............Prime Minister of United Kingdom and Leader of Conservatory Party. Many similar traits to the Trumper.

Melonia Trumper....................Queen of Queens. Wife of the Trumper. A tough, Slavic cookie who takes no sh*t from the McDonald.

Bolt-On the Walrus..................Former National Security Advisor, disgruntled former employee, author and someone with an axe to grind.

Moscow Mitch the Mock Turtle....Ripofflican Senate Majority Leader, Grim Reaper and general all-round scary politico. Totally committed to backing the Trumper come hell or high crimes and misdemeanors.

Mick Malarkey........................Ex-Chief of Staff and Budget guy. Made the mistake of telling the truth – just once. But once too many times.

Gordon 'Egghead' Sunderland.....Ex-Ambassador to the UN. Paid $1 million to get involved in one of the Trumper's biggest messes. Nice guy but incredibly naïve. Was No. 1 of the 'Three Amigos'. Likes cell phones.

Roody-Doody Joolianose.............The Trumper's personal lawyer for many years. Loves messing about in Ukraine and getting paid by his employees. Has interesting clientele.

Levee & Ignor......................... Ukrainian hit men and good record keepers. Paying Roody-Doody for the privilege of working for him.

Mike 'Silverback' Penice.............Vice President without a single vice. Now in charge of and/or fall guy for coronavirus debacle. Has one face mask for all occasions.

Mikey 'The Fixer' Cohort.........The Trumper's very, very, personal fixer. Knows where all the stories are buried and what the burial cost was.

Mike 'Koch Addict' Pompeyo.......Secretary of State but cannot quite stick to the job description. Loves the Koch Brother(s) to bits.

Bill 'No Collusion' Barf.............. Attorney General, allegedly in charge of the Department of Justice but prefers 'private practice' for Trumper

Kurt 'The Hair' Volkswagen........ Ex-Special Envoy to Ukraine, No.2 of the 'Three Amigos' and permanent walking advert for hair gel.

Rick 'The Crotch' Perrier........... Ex-Secretary of Energy & famous for wearing tight jeans. Was No. 3 of the '3 Amigos'. Sparkling personality.

'Nervous' Nancy Palooka........... Speaker of the House and master tactician. Tough puncher. Not at all nervous and not likely to back down from the Trumper.

Colonel Alex Vindalooman......... Ex-Director - European Affairs, NSC. Served & testified without bone spurs

Fiona 'Hawaay the Lads' Hillbilly... Ex-Russian Affairs Specialist, NSC. Had 'True Brit Grit' when testifying.

David Pickapeckov-Pickledpecker..Publisher and Keeper of Secrets – as long as the Price Was Right.

Stormy Jack-Daniels.................. Adult Movie Star who said The Price Wasn't Right.

Karen McDoughnuts.................Playboy Centerfold who didn't play ball despite Heff's Happy Hour.

VP 'Sleepy' Joe Bidet................. The 2020 Presidential Candidate, O'Bama's VP and the reason the Trumper made that 'perfect call'.

B.A.R.A.C.K '44' O'Bama............Former President, Senator, Lawyer & eloquent speaker of many slow words

'Crooked' Hillarious Clingfilm......Dimocratic Presidential Candidate in 2016. Got 3 million more votes but lost to Trumper in Electoral College.

Vladimir 'The Invader' Pututin......President of Russia and former FSB Director. Alleged Trumper puppet-master & custodian of Pee-Pee tapes.

Kim 'Rocket Man' Jung-Ones.......North Korean President/Dictator. Likes rockets and writing 'love letters'

Jeff Bozo............................. Richest Man in the World and hated by the Trumper, just because of that.

Jeffrey 'The Kid' Schleppstein.......Peter-Pan Party-Animal, preferred to be popular with the younger crowd.

Randy Dandy Windsock.............. The Piss-Artist formerly known as Prince.

John Berrrccoww...................... Ex-Speaker of the House who was permanently on full volume.

Dominic Cummandgo................ BoJo Advisor. Suspected Russia links, landed gentry complex & wanderlust.

Jarhead Kushynumber.............. Son-in-Law and Presidential Advisor on everything he needs to know.

Spicy Sean the Gryphon............. Dancing Queen & Press Secretary.

A Fable-Parable-Fairy Story

1

BOJO DOWN THE RABBIT HOLE

Once upon a time in a galaxy far, far too close, the *Bozone Layer* [1] was thickening. The mist was clouding everyone's vision. What could BoJo do to avert the near disaster of him actually having to admit that he made a mistake about BREXIT? This had never, ever happened to him in his entire political career. BoJo, like his *American Idol* [2], the Trumper, was more used to relying on the *Dopeler Effect* [3] to get him through. That tactic was always better than actually telling the truth, which would be very un-PC.

---

[1] BOZONE LAYER: The substance surrounding politicians in the Conservatory Party that stops bright ideas from penetrating. The Bozone Layer, unfortunately, shows little sign of breaking down in the near future and is likely to cloud all sensible vision into what might actually happen if the UK does a No-Deal Brexit.

[2] AMERICAN IDOL: A so-called talent show where ne'er-do-well hopefuls parade their wares and hope that they get enough votes to win a million dollars and a recording contract. It's very similar to political elections except that in those, the million dollars comes as donations and the implicit contract that comes with it means that the politician does the bidding of the donor for the length of his term in office.

[3] DOPELER EFFECT: The tendency of stupid, fact-checkable lies to seem more believable when they come at you rapidly. Politicians on both sides of the Atlantic are very good at this. They spout ideas and opinions so fast and often so contradictory to the last time they spoke. As of the fourth quarter of 2019, The Trumper has made over 18,000 false or misleading claims - and counting. BoJo, as the new PM, was just getting going, but he will catch up soon based on past performance.

It had all started the morning before a speech to the local Conservatory Party members in Guildford, to the south-west of London.

BoJo had gone out for his usual not-so-early morning jog in his usual totally dis-coordinated, baggy, old, 'BREXIT Forever!' t-shirt and fraying public-school tennis shorts. He was enjoying his daily *innoculatte* [4], but, unknown to him, someone had spiked it with a triple expresso shot. BoJo suddenly started feeling lightheaded and got completely disorientated. He turned left. He turned right. He turned left. Left again. Right again.

5.   BoJo 'Mr. Brexit' Jockstrap

He was way off course, totally out of his comfort zone and suddenly ran into a big park that had never previously existed on his morning run.

"How odd," his over-caffeinated brain cell mused. He was also thinking about the Conservatory Party members' meeting that he was going to speak at later that morning. "Bah, humbug!" he thought. "I wish the UK had a presidency, like the US, then I wouldn't have to deal directly with all those other Ministers in the House and the damn Speaker shouting 'ORRDDERRR! ORRRDDERRRR!' all the time! I could just cite Article II, like the US President, and do whatever I want."

As he ruminated about being a President instead of 'just' a Prime Minister, he kept jogging along the path and, eventually, he saw that he was coming to a tunnel in the park. But, as he got closer, he realised that it wasn't a tunnel at all, but what appeared instead to be a very, very large rabbit hole. He momentarily considered what a huge rabbit it would take to build a rabbit hole so big. But that fleeting thought vanished when it went dark, very dark, there was a clap of thunder and a deep echoing voice said, "BE CAREFUL WHAT YOU WISH FOR!"

---

[4] INNOCULATTE: BoJo taking coffee intravenously when he was out jogging or running very late for his hairdresser's appointment.

BoJo was so shaken that he tripped and fell into the huge rabbit hole. Everything was suddenly spinning, and he was falling, falling, falling, down, down, down, down into the darkness.

Then, out of nowhere, there was a tiny, bright light shining in his face. That light got brighter, bigger and brighter, bigger and brighter . . .

Suddenly, he went kerplunk! BoJo's little rotund body found itself laying on the floor and he was staring up into the bright, white sunlight or what he mistook to be sunlight. But what BoJo didn't fully appreciate at that moment was that he was in Trumperland, a place where nothing is quite as it seems, anything is possible, and nothing is remotely like what was previously known as normal.

The first thing that BoJo gradually became aware of was that it wasn't sunlight. It was the glare from millions of watts of floodlights on towers that were strategically placed around the high, barbed and electrified perimeter wall.

He also noticed that the tower had some large gold letters on them and, as his eyes gradually re-focussed and became used to the glare of the floodlights, he could see that they spelt the words TRUMP TOWER . . .

6.   Trump Tower – New York Council Estate, Trumperland

And that wasn't just any wall. It was the perimeter wall to a Council Estate in one of the roughest areas of Trumperland.

What BoJo was soon to realise was that, in Trumperland, it is always important to keep any group of allegedly undesirable people carefully isolated behind a wall – or even a beautiful fence – so that they don't infiltrate the nice bits of your empire and dilute the breeding stock.

And, of course, you make them pay for the wall. Or at least that's what you tell everyone else during your election rallies

Despite what he said during his own rallies about being a 'Man of the People', BoJo had never been on a Council Estate before. His parents had told him stories about them at bedtime. You know how kid's bedtime stories are always about frightening things like wolves dressed up as grandmas who wanted to eat you and witches with poisoned apples, etc.? So, his well-off parents told him about the scariest thing they could think of - being poor, jobless and living in a Council Estate.

Hence, he knew that they existed but had never seen the slightest political need to visit one.

But, maybe now was an appropriate time to check as the Labial Party Election Manifesto had included a promise to build 150,000 of the damn things - and the Conservatories hadn't promised to build any.

"Hmmm!" thought BoJo, "What does the Labial Party know that we don't?"

Maybe, just maybe, it had something to do with the fact that many Labial MPs grew up on Council Estates in some grimy northern industrial city. Whereas most Conservatory Party MPs, like BoJo, Jacob Re-Smogg and others, had grown up on their parent's estates in the country.

2

PEOPLE OF COLOR

Suddenly, despite the floodlights, it went dark, very dark indeed. BoJo blinked and realised that he was totally surrounded by a whole bunch of faces. And they were all staring down at him. But what made it seem even darker than just 'very dark indeed' was that all those faces belonged to people of color. OOOoooooh!

And even worse – for BoJo at least – was that it was a gang called the *CHAVs*[5]. In fact, he had no idea what a CHAV even was. If he had, he would have probably been afraid. And rightly so - very, very afraid.

Unfortunately, the fact that Boris had benefitted from a significantly elitist upbringing, attended fancy English *public schools*[6] like Eton, and enjoyed a 'Shining Spires' Oxford education, had not given him any kind of preparation as to how to deal with the CHAVs.

---

[5] CHAV: An acronym for Council House And Violent. And if you are American and have no idea what a Council House Estate is, just think if the big inner city 'Projects' in the US. Enough said!

[6] PUBLIC SCHOOL: In England, a Public School is a very, very expensive Private School and Government Schools are called State Schools, even though we don't have any States like they do in America, because we call the regional political areas, Counties. Whereas, in America, the name they have for State Schools is Public Schools and their very, very elitist High Schools are called Academies and the exclusive universities are called Ivy League Schools. Simple isn't it?

xxx

So, in his total naivety and bumbling ignorance, he started trying to tell them that he was a Very Important Person. He was the Prime Minister of England and he lived at No.10 Downing Street. But, in the same way that he did not know what the CHAVs were, the CHAVs had no idea who he was. They were not in the slightest interested in politics and, unless someone voted to increase their weekly Unemployment Benefit handouts, they didn't know a politician from a poke in the eye.

To them, BoJo was just babbling away like the crazy, tousled haired, unkempt, homeless hobo that he appeared to be. What the CHAVs did not realise, of course, was that because BoJo really was a politician, he was actually suffering from a very severe case of *rectitude* [7]. As a result, despite his best efforts to the contrary, he just could not help sounding like he was babbling away like a crazy, tousled haired, unkempt, homeless hobo because that was what he did in Parliament every day.

"Wots up wiv you, innit?" said the Asian one from Essex.

"Nnnnnnothing, my dear chap" said BoJo, pretending to be brave.

"Whoo yuse callin a 'dear chap', innit? Mees not an *LGBTQ* [8]"

"Nnnno-one! Nnnnooo-one! Wwwhere am I?"

"Yuse in New York, innit"

"Ohhh! Yyyou mmean Nnew Yyork, Nnew Yyork?

"Naaah! I means New York Council Estate in Trumperland!"

It was starting to dawn on BoJo that something very strange indeed had happened to him. He had set off that morning in the historic market town of Guildford, Surrey, south-west of London, England, for a jolly jog in the park. He had fallen down a large rabbit hole and now was being accosted by a gang of CHAVs. But they were telling him he was in Trumperland, which he assumed was some sort of local gangland nickname for an area of America, where his 'boss-buddy' McDonald J. Trumper was President. Well, at least he had been President when BoJo set off jogging that morning. Who could tell what the situation was now and how could BoJo foresee what was going to happen next? It was a bit like trying to predict the outcome of BREXIT . . .

---

[7] RECTITIDE: The medical term given by proctologists for the widespread affliction of most politicians for invariably talking out of their asses.

[8] LGBTQs: A fairy-tale acronym for Lovely Good Boys, Tootsies and Queens

Although BoJo was confused about where he was and what sort of place he was in, he was slightly - well, ever so slightly - relieved that the CHAV gang members were speaking with English accents rather than American ones. Though, compared to BoJo's plum-in-the-mouth-upper-crust Eton/Oxbridge diction, it was hard for him to concede that an Essex 'innit?' at the end of virtually every sentence counted as a real question.

Nonetheless, somehow, strangely, even an Essex 'innit?' rather than an American 'yeah man!' at the end of every sentence was comforting as it meant that the gang members were not gangland's scariest *Crips or Bloods* [9] and probably did not have guns and, therefore, his chances of being shot were minimal.

Then, he suddenly remembered the massive cuts that the Conservatory Party had made in Police Force budgets – particularly reducing the numbers of coppers on the streets – and he realised that his chances of being saved were zero to none if a fight broke out and he was stabbed, which was becoming a common occurrence on UK city streets.

"Wwell, I, I, I am the Ppprime Mminister and you nneed to tttake me tttoooo your Lllleader" stammered BoJo.

He had heard it in a science-fiction movie, and it was the only thing he could think of at short notice.

"Hey maan!" said the Jamaican-looking one. "Aye reckons we takes him to de *Pokémon* [10]. Yeah! De Pokémon will know wot to dood wid 'im."

"The, the Ppokémon?" said BoJo. "Whhhats he ggggoing tttoo ddoo ttoo mmme?" Something about the name unexplainedly making his sphincter muscles tighten.

---

[9] CRIPS OR BLOODS: The largest and most well-known street gangs in the USA. They are arch-rivals with presence in most cities. Crips like the color blue and Bloods like red. Crips are generally well organized and form better networks. Bloods are generally more violent. The parallels between the Dimocrats in blue states and Ripofflicans in red states are not hard to imagine.

[10] POKEMON: A well-known gangland Rastafarian proctologist. He was the first to discover that most politicians are suffering from severe cases of rectitude as a result of trying to convince their constituents to 'Don't worry, be happy' and that everything will be OK despite BREXIT.

"Yeah maan! De Pokémon wills check out youse body parts ter sees whys yuse jus feld down in de floor laik dat. Maybees coz yuse a pulitchian, or a PM or whotevers, yuse got dat nasty *Hipatitis* [11] disease an wees doan wanna de *'Chosen One'* [12] toos catch dat".

"The, the Chchosen Onnne?" asked BoJo, who couldn't decide which sounded scarier. The Pokémon or The Chosen One? He was soon to find out.

"Yus, youse knows! Da Dear Leader, da Great Dictator, da King Kong of da Tower, da Boss, da Chosen One – da Trumper!"

"The, the, the Tttrrrumper?" stammered BoJo.

"Yeah! Hes's da Big Cheeseburger around here. An if he doan laik youse chubbies little chops, then he's gonna jus say '*You'se Fired*' [13]. And you'se jus doan wan dat. Believes me!!"

---

[11] HIPATITIS: Terminal coolness. Like when Theresa May-B'lieve gyrated onto the stage, sort of dancing to Abba's "Dancing Queen" and the rest of the Conservatory Party died of embarrassment.

[12] CHOSEN ONE: A self-aggrandized title bestowed upon himself by the Trumper. Also, refers to himself in the third-party as The McDonald, The Man with the Best Words, A Very Stable Genius and, probably soon, as The Savior of the Universe. Others tell the truth.

[13] YOU'RE FIRED: The Trumper's favourite catch-phrase in his Reality TV show, The Sorcerer's Apprentice. It appears that he still thinks he is in a Reality TV show as he has fired more staff and political appointees than the previous three Presidents put together.

3

MEANWHILE PART 1 – WHO ATE THE TARTS?

Meanwhile [14]...

Meanwhile, across The Big Pond. And, in this case, it does not refer to the colloquial name for the Atlantic Ocean. It's actually just a big pond - not quite a small lake and definitely not a tiny ocean - in the middle of the Trumperland in a district called Queens. There, the Trumper's wife, Melonia, also known locally as the *Queen of Queens* [15], was giving the Trumper a hard time.

"McDOONNAALLDT! You haff been playing wiz zose *tarts* [16] again!"

"It wasn't me," was the standard Trumper response. "Which tarts?"

"Yuse know wots I mean!! Don't 'Which tarts?' me. Yuse haff been screwing around wiz zose Playboy center-creases and prawn stars again!

---

[14] MEANWHILE: A fairy-story idea stolen from The Late Show with Stephen Colbert. While the main characters are doing their usual best to screw up the world's politics, democracies, alliances and economies, other things are happening at home between the Trumper and his wife Melonia, which are scraped together in a mish-mash of word-bites.

[15] QUEEN OF QUEENS: Melonia should really have been called the Queen of Hearts in this fairy-story but, with her quasi-Russian accent, it would have sounded like Queen of Farts and that would have upset the Trumper as, by association, he would have been the King of Farts. But that's not improbable given the British slang meaning of Trumper.

[16] TARTS: Like many words in English, they can have two totally different meanings. In the bakers shop they are small round bits of pastry covered in raspberry jam. But, between the boys, 'Picking up a couple of tarts' means getting some action with two girls.

Vy are so *Willy-Nilly* [17]? Andt how much vill it cost ziss time to keep zere pouty mouths shut? Anozzer $130,000 each beetch?"

"But, but Melanomia! I'm going to get my best lawyer/fixer/fraudster to sort it all out – even though I didn't do anything that the Flake News is saying . . ."

"Don'tch you dare 'But Melanomia' me! Yuse mean you vill get zat crazy wonker *Roody-Doody Joolianose* [18] tsu fix it?"

7.	Roody-Doody – Attorney Out-Law

"No, not Roody-Doody. He is busy screwing up other things for me."

"Tzo, if za Roody iss busy, how are yuse goink to making zese prawn-stars keep zere mouthzs shut closed?"

"I will use Mikey 'The Fixer' Cohort for this one. It's more his kind of thing – even though it wasn't me, I wasn't there, and I didn't fancy her anyway".

---

[17] WILLY-NILLY: The psychological need of the Trumper to prove he is not a misogynist by sleeping with as many Playboy centerfolds and porn stars as possible.

[18] ROODY-DOODY JOOLIANOSE: Former Southern District NY State Prosecutor, former NY City Mayor. Now seen running errands for and making crazy statements on Fox News to protect the Trumper. Usually, falls asleep in the middle and wakes up making completely opposite statements to the ones he made before he went to sleep.

"Ha! Zat iss vot you alvays say 'It vasn't me, I vasn't zere andt I didn't fancies her anyvay'. Bullshoot!"

"But Melaminia . . . "

"Andt 1 know zat anyvays, givink half a chance, you vould really prefer zat daughter Iwanka, from your first wifes, more zan me anyvay!!! You iss alvays talkin' abouts dating her, even zo she iss now Jewish, ha!"

"But Meelymenia . . ."

"Von more 'But Meelymenia' andt it vill be 'Off vizz yours head!!'"

THE QUEEN OF HEARTS – OFF WITH HIS HEAD
https://www.youtube.com/watch?v=CtCQHCOls2E

Fade to Black . . .

POSTSCRIPT

If you haven't already figured it out, it is the Queen of Queens who absolutely rules the Trumper household. Her constant vituperative barrage at him never lets up. She is totally critical of everything he does and has an incredibly low opinion of his mental capacity and his capabilities. The Trumper is utterly terrified of the Queen and once confided to Roody-Doody that she had the ability to "kill a man at ten paces with one blow of her tongue." A good example of this situation is Sybil & Basil's relationship in Fawlty Towers or was that Trump Towers?

FAWLTY TOWERS – BASIL & SYBIL
https://www.youtube.com/watch?v=60WVDnfY-_w

4

SEVENTY-TWO VIRGINS

BoJo was not enjoying his time with the Pokémon. He had not had such an invasion of his privacy and his private parts since getting a number of scathing reviews about his book *Seventy-Two Virgins: A Comedy of Errors*[19]. In fact, the most virulent criticism came from many Dimocrats who said, "Why the hell did you save him?". While the Pokémon was rooting around in BoJo's anal regions he was asking lots of difficult questions about BoJo's ideological views on BREXIT and other burning issues. At the end of the session BoJo wasn't sure which was burning most – his buttocks or his brain.

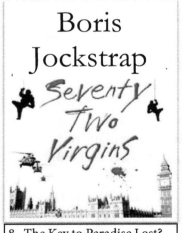

8. The Key to Paradise Lost?

[19] SEVENTY-TWO VIRGINS: The plot line goes like this. The President of the USA is scheduled to visit the UK Houses of Parliament. A Lebanese-born terrorist plans to assassinate him. A hapless, bicycle-riding, tousled-haired MP (Guess who?) foils the attack. The 72 virgins, of course, are the ones promised to Muslim terrorists when they blow themselves up along with many infidels. Or it could just be a story about Conservatory MPs having a wild party in the 1960s. Or one of Jeffrey Schleppstein's Manhattan penthouse dinner parties. Or just an ordinary Randy Dandy shooting party.

But at last, BoJo was cleared of carrying any nasty infections. Well, at least any more than the Trumper had already. As everyone knows, there is no cure for *rectiprocity*[20].

"Hokay" said the Pokemon "Youse are good ter go!"

So, the CHAVs threw BoJo in the back of their *USSR Moskvitch Moscow Mitch Mk3*[21] and set off down the road.

9.	Russian Demonstrator Crusher?

It was a bit slow going as they had to keep stopping to shovel coal onto the fire for the steam boiler. In Trumperland all forms of transport are banned unless they emit large volumes of smoke and CO2 and keep the Pennsylvania coal miners in a job. At the same time, this significantly assisted *global waming*[22] and climate change – even though climate change officially does not exist in Trumperland.

---

[20] RECTIPROCITY: Two politicians talking out of their asses and both nodding positively while knowing full well the other one is talking a complete load of claptrap.

[21] MOSCOW MITCH MK3: Russian street vehicle. Has huge tires but is very light as its built entirely out of aluminum from the Russky Plant in Kentucky. Can roll straight over pro-democracy demonstrators without slowing down to ask why they are demonstrating.

[22] GLOBAL WAMING: According to a (mis-spelt) Trumper tweet, it's a myth spread by scientists and Dimocrats to frighten coal miners into believing that they will drown or be eaten by sharks in their own mines when they are flooded due to the rise in sea level.

It's also part of a long-term plan to melt so much of the snow in Greenland that the Danes don't want it anymore and finally agree to sell it to the Trumper.

10.	Global Waming = Greenland ala' Trumper

Then suddenly a *White Rabbi* [23] ran into the road in front of the vehicle and the driver was so surprised that he had to suddenly screech to a halt. In the back, BoJo was thrown out of his seat and unceremoniously dumped on the floor.

Unaware of how close he had come to being someone's stew, the White Rabbi ignored them completely and just stared at his watch.

"Oyvey! I'm late. I'm late. For a very important date! I'm late. I'm late. They're going to close the gate! I'm late. I'm late. I'm late. I'm late. I'm late. I'm late. I'm late!" And then quickly ran off into the bushes muttering to himself.

---

[23] WHITE RABBI: In Trumperland it seems to have grown increasingly necessary to delineate the color, ethnicity, sex and religion of each person. It's apparently a Ripofflican thing when they talk about Dimocrats. They don't have to do it for their own party as everyone is a white, Caucasian, male, evangelist. Simple and easy to spot.

The driver and his CHAV partner had absolutely no idea what had just happened. But they weren't the brightest crayons in the box, so they just looked at each other, shrugged their shoulders and decided it looked like a good opportunity to dump BoJo and get on with their next nasty job.

5

MEANWHILE PART 2 - CHUBBY HUBBY

Meanwhile . . .

Meanwhile, back in the Colored House kitchen, the Queen of Queens was reading the riot act to the Trumper. She was blaming him for eating more than one kind of tart and getting fatter.

His tame personal doctor, Rear Adm. Michael 'Thriller' Jackson, was saying that the Trumper was in "excellent health" and even joked that he "might live to be 200 years old" if he made improvements to his diet. (Oh no!) But he still had to be careful about his bone spurs!

But Millymona had a different opinion. "Looks zat you! You are tzso overveight zat the media are all *flabbergasted* [24] and zey are snookering behind your big, fat backer-side after every *Choppertalk* [25]."

---

[24] FLABBERGASTED: The US news media being appalled over how overweight the Trumper is due to eating cheeseburgers (and no doubt a few tarts) in bed and, at the same time, the British press being amazed by how little effect BoJo's jogging and cycling has on his chubby body.

[25] CHOPPERTALK: Dispensing with the purpose-built press room, podium and microphone, the Trumper prefers to stand on the lawn, with Marine One noisily chuga-chugging away, while he shouts and waves his little hands and arms at the press. It's a scene reminiscent of an old man standing on his lawn and shouting at the neighborhood kids to "Get off my lawn!". All the Trumper really needs to complete the picture is a bathrobe, slippers and a hosepipe

There were numerous pictures in the media of the Trumper playing golf and looking significantly less than svelte and they were driving the Queen of Queens crazy.

| 11. | There's a McDonald's at the 9th Hole - Anyone for a Big Mac! |

"You are fetter zan zat cardboardt cut-out wannabe BoJo, in England. Yuse are goingk tsoo do ze *decaflon* [26] efery day for ze next six veeks."

"But, but, but, Mealymania! I can't survive without my Hamberders."

"I don't cares! But youse hadt better not take ze sneaky peak at ze *lunch codes* [27]. If I comes back in ze Oral Orifice an can smell zat McDo smell it vill be 'Off vizz your headt!!'. Gottit?"

"Yes dear!"

Fade to black . . .

---

[26] DECAFLON: The grueling event of getting through the day consuming only things that are good for you. To counteract to this, McDonald's have just developed a decaffeinated cheeseburger and expect home delivery sales in the Washington area to skyrocket.

[27] LUNCH CODES: Special codes that only the Cummerbund-in-Chief can know. They are needed to open a special locked case which has two big buttons inside. One green and one red. He can press the green button to launch a delivery of ballistic hamberders & fries. And the red button will cancel the order and the delivery boy will stand down.

6

THE CHESHIRE PUSSY

Back in the USSR Moskvitch Moscow Mitch Mk3, BoJo was trying to pick himself up off the floor when the door was flung open.

"Oy, gerroutervit!" shouted one of the CHAVs. "Weeese gorra go an harass sum owl age penishoners. We'll steal der Zimmer frames an kick der crutchis. Yuse can goan fine d' Trumper yerself!"

"Bbbbut, bbbbut, bbbbbut where will I find him?" said BoJo

"Jus' asks ennyones where da Colored House is! You stupid?"

"Cccolourred Hhouse?"

"Yers. Da one wid all does big pillocks and da flag at da top ov Trumpsylvania Avenoo"

"Bbbig pillocks? Er, do you mean big pillars?"

"Wotevers. Dat place is fulla big pillocks az far az I'm consigned!"

As the vehicle steamed and belched away, BoJo noticed the brand name on the back of it - USSR Moskvitch Moscow Mitch Mk3 - and some long-forgotten, subliminal connection in his mop-headed brain reminded him of those other four original mop-heads, The Beatles, and he started humming a tune.

BACK IN THE USSR – THE BEATLES
https://www.youtube.com/watch?v=nS5_EQgbuLc

What was the connection? What was it about this place that made BoJo think about the USSR? As it was too difficult to figure out, BoJo wandered off along the path into the woods, humming away, and soon found himself in front of a tree that had lots of signs on it saying things like *Up is Down* and *Down is Up* and *This Way* and *That Way* and *The Other Way* and *Some Way,* and one that said *No Way, Jose!* [28].

"Oh, golly gosh, goolies and gollocks!!" said BoJo to himself and no-one in particular – which was actually the same person. "Where is the bloody Coloured House?"

"Can I be of particular or peculiar assistance?" said a deep purple, purring voice from above.

BoJo wasn't quite sure why the voice sounded so deep purple until he looked up and, sitting on a branch, was the largest purple striped cat he had ever seen. In fact, it was the only purple striped cat he had ever seen, but it was definitely also the largest. He was having difficulty resolving that flawed conundrum as well as trying to assimilate the fact that not only had the cat just spoken to him, but also that it definitely had the

| 12. | A Hairy Purple Pussy |

widest and really stupidest grin he had ever had the misfortune to see.

"Er," whispered BoJo as he wasn't really sure he should be talking to a cat in case someone overheard him and thought he was crazy or a politician, or both. "Who are you and why are you up that tree?"

"Ahh, I am sooo glad you asked that question! I'm the Cheshire Pussy. My friends call me Galore . . . Pussy Galore. Someone just grabbed me, so I hid up this tree."

"Who was it?"

"Oh, it was that Trumper guy. He thinks he can grab any pussy, any time he likes, and get away with it just because he is famous and pretends to be a rich bigshot."

---

[28] NO WAY JOSE!: A sign that appears all over Trumperland, especially to make Mexicans and other Hispanics feel unwelcome.

"Oh, really that's terrible!" exclaimed BoJo while internally trolling through his memory banks to check if any of his own extra-curricular liaisons had ever included any similar acts. Concluding that *laudable deniability* [29] was probably the best course of action if any journalists started digging deep, he filed any alleged incidents under 'F' for Forgotten and turned his attention back to the Cheshire Pussy.

"But wait," continued BoJo, "your face is starting to change to look like the Trumper. How come?"

"Well," said the Cheshire Pussy, "everyone that is associated with the Trumper somehow becomes one of his *avatars* [30] and they slowly start to metamorphosize to actually look like him. Then they become an alter-ego and start acting like him, lie about everything and cover up things he does, It's terrible! Look at my face!!!"

| 13. | Grin and Bare It |

BoJo started to scrutinise the Cheshire Pussy but, as he did so, it started to slowly disappear until only the grin was left. And that alone was truly gruesome.

"Wait! What is happening to you? You are disappearing!!"

"Yes! It's OK. I just got confirmation that I have a $130,000 credit in my bank account as a pussy pay-off. So, now I am going to disappear until some smart-ass lawyer convinces me that I can get more for my story from a different news-rag than the National Enquirer. Byeeeee!"

"But that's absolutely craaazy," said BoJo in disbelief.

"I'm not crazy," replied the Cheshire Pussy, "my reality is just different to yours."

---

[29] LAUDABLE DENIABILITY: Yet another politician's favourite ploy which involves twisting the facts of any story about erroneous, and usually erogenous deeds, such that the acts of the perpetrator appear to be praiseworthy while the story of the complainant sounds like a lot of sour grapes or a cooked up ploy to be awarded a big pay-out for damages. Monica Lewinsky was an early victim of this when she made the mistake of claiming on her White House Staff expense account for her outrageous dry-cleaning bills for the blue dress she wore in the Oral Office.

[30] AVATAR: A different image of yourself for use in another or virtual reality. Ask kids!

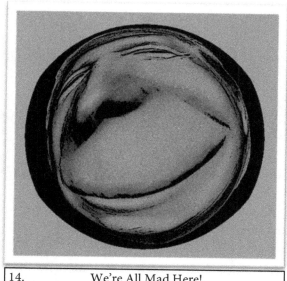

| 14. | We're All Mad Here! |

"Well! I've often seen a cat without a grin," said BoJo, "but a grin without a cat! It's the most curious thing I ever saw in all my life! And that's a fact!"

"Actually," opined the grin of the Cheshire Pussy, "I prefer some *alternative facts* [31] rather than the truth, which is usually so boring and often misconstrued into *flake news* [32] by all those *enemas of the people* [33], the socialist, left-wing press."

"That sounds a bit confusing and I feel like I am going mad," said BoJo somewhat tremulously.

"Oh, you can't help that," said the Cheshire Pussy, "we're all mad here. I'm mad. You're mad."

---

[31] ALTERNATIVE FACTS: A phrase famously coined by Kellyanne Conwoman as a way of trying to sugar-coat actual lies and distort the truth so much that the Ripofflican base would be dumb enough to believe them.

[32] FLAKE NEWS: Generally used to describe any news, provided by Dimocratic flakes, which is considered by the Trumper to be negative or detrimental to himself i.e. all of it.

[33] ENEMAS OF THE PEOPLE: Real news by real reporters working for real media outlets – other than Foxy News – that made the Trumper sh*t himself because it was really true and really bad for him.

"How do you know I'm mad?" asked BoJo.

"You must be," said the Cheshire Pussy, "or you wouldn't have come here."

"Would you tell me, please, which way I ought to go from here?" asked BoJo hesitantly, thinking to himself that it was way past time for him to move on.

"That depends a good deal on where you want to get to," retorted the Cheshire Pussy.

"I don't much care where –" BoJo started to say.

"Then it doesn't matter which way you go," cut in the Cheshire Pussy, or rather all that was left of it, which wasn't very much.

And with the words "We're all mad here!" echoing spookily in the forest – *pooof* [34]- the Cheshire Pussy was gone, leaving BoJo pondering what exactly to do next.

"Curiouser and curiouser!" he said to himself as there was now no one else to talk to. Not even a crazy, purple Cheshire Pussy.

So, he wandered off along a Yellow-Brick Road that had suddenly appeared at his feet, without even considering how that could possibly have happened or why it might be significant.

But he would eventually find out . . .

---

[34] POOOF: A phrase coined on The Rachel Mad-Dog Show to indicate the withdrawal of one of the many, many Dimocratic Presidential Candidates from the race. Seems also very fitting for the disappearance of the Cheshire Pussy from the tree as it was similar to the disappearance from the media of any attention given to the Hollywood Access tapes when, 'just coincidentally', Wikileaks released the 30,000 emails of 'Crooked' Hillarious Clingfilm, twenty minutes after the Trumper's "Grab them by the p*ssy" remark. Just a coincidence, of course. Maybe, we are all mad here . . .

7

MEANWHILE PART 3 – THE PEE PEE TAPES

Meanwhile . . .

"McDONALDT!!" screamed the Queen of Queens. "McDONALDT!"

"Yes dear?" cringed the Trumper

"Vot iss all zis abouts sum 'Pee Pee Tapes' ven youse vas in Moscow cuddlink up to zat nastiez Russky, Vladimir Putitin?"

"But, Millynoma, it's all flake news by the Dimocratic Party media."

"I'm don't belief zat! I know vat zees Russian Presidentz and zere buddy-buddy ogligarkz are doings all ze time. Zey giff you ze free Russian girlz andt take lottsa picz so zat zey can blueball you laters."

"Blueball? Don't you mean blackmail, darling?"

"Vots de different? Za blueballs or za blackmails it's all cums to the same very stickies endingk. Woteffers! Andt chust donts 'darlink' me you chitting, excuse-me for a husband!"

15.	The Queen of Queens!

"But Mellamonia. It wasn't me! And I didn't fancy those girls anyway. So, it doesn't count, even if it had been me. Which it wasn't."

IT WASN'T ME – SHAGGY
https://www.youtube.com/watch?v=2g5Hz17C4is

"Vottt!!!! Andt vy do you need to go bonkink Russian girls anyvay? Vot do you sink I am? Vere do you sink I am cummink from? Do I look Chinesess or Koreeun? Look at zeese chickbones! Look at zeese eyes! I know zat your geography sucks, butt vere do you sink Slovenia iss?? Iff you vant someons Russian to pissz on you, you don'td need to go all ze vay to Moscow. I am szo pisst off viz you dat I vud pissz on you ennydays!!"

"But, don't you believe me...?"

"Viz you McDoonaldt, sometimez I haff believedt ass many ass six impissoble thingks befores za breakfadst."

"But, Melamine..."

"Andt you betters did not catch *Osteopornosis* [35] ziss time..."

"But..."

"Not anozzer 'but' or its 'Off viz your headt!'"

Fade to black...

---

[35] OSTEOPORNOSIS: A degenerate disease. Frequently found in politicians and businessmen after staying in Russian Hotels. Very contagious. Usually passed on via body fluids.

8

HUMPTY TRUMPTY

BoJo wandered along the *Yellow-Brick Road* [36] not actually thinking that the road had any relevance to himself or the Trumper. But that was typical of both BoJo and the Trumper. They rarely thought of anything very far beyond the context of themselves.

WIZARD OF OZ – JUDY GARLAND
https://www.youtube.com/watch?v=b3DD3vDyuog

BoJo suddenly realised that he had come out of the forest and into a sort of no-man's land with no trees, no bushes and nothing at all in it.

---

[36] YELLOW-BRICK ROAD: Famously featured in the movie The Wizard of Oz and the song by Elton John. The Yellow-Brick Road symbolizes, in Buddhism and Kabbalah, what is known as The Golden Path - the path of the Soul from Egoism to Enlightenment. Both BoJo and the Trumper know everything there is to know about Egoism and, contrariwise, very little to nothing about Enlightenment.

Well, there was nothing at all in the empty space except a huge wall running east and west as far as the eye could see. To anyone who had fought in the Vietnam War or the Korean War it would have made them think of a DMZ, a De-Militarized Zone. Likewise, it was also reminiscent of the open space surrounding the perimeter fences of POW camps in WWII. That might have been a sobering thought, but BoJo, like the Trumper, hadn't been in any wars – apart from the political ones he fought on a daily basis – so, to him, it just looked like an empty space.

The Yellow-Brick Road ran straight up to the wall and then split left and right along its base and disappeared over the horizon in both directions. As BoJo got closer to the wall he saw a small sign. It said EGOISM with an arrow to the right and ENLIGHTENMENT with an arrow to the left.

"Hmm!" he thought, "What now?" He didn't have long to wait for the answer.

"Hey, blondie! Can I sell you a hair-brush and some Super Glue Hair Spray?"

"Whhatt ddo yyou mean? Cheeky blighter!" BoJo retorted and looked up to see a rotund figure sitting on top of the wall. In fact, the figure wasn't just rotund, he was completely egg-shaped.

"What's your name?" asked the 'egg'.

"It's Boris Jockstrap, but people call me BoJo for short," he replied somewhat *frumpily* [37].

"Ha! BoJo for short. I like that. You look a bit short, especially in the leg department – and maybe others. You know, I'm good with words. In fact, I have all the best words. Do you know what your name means?"

"No! Must a name mean something? It's just an English family name," retorted BoJo, testily.

"Well, isn't 'Jockstrap' a slang word for penis supporter? And, if you prefer BoJo, that is probably a reference to your short penis. LOL."

"Wwwwhat!" spluttered BoJo. "I'll have you know that my penis . . . Er. Well. Never mind! What's your name anyway?"

"Me? I'm Humpty Trumpty, of course!"

---

[37] FRUMPILY: A combination of *'frumpy'* and *'grumpily'*. Being someone who is a bit old-fashioned and proper in his ways and in a bad mood at the same time.

"Ha! Well, my dear chap," chirped back BoJo smugly, "for your information, 'Trump' is an English slang word for lots of hot, and usually putrid, air leaking out of someone's anus."

"You are wrong, of course," Humpty Trumpty said poutily, "my name means the shape I am — and a good handsome shape it is, too. With a name like yours, you might be any shape, almost, but more than likely, short, soft and with a large round head."

16.	Humpty Trumpty Had A Great Fall! (Please)

"It sounds to me like you are describing an egg rather than anything with a 'good handsome shape'. And, by the way, you do realise that eggs come out of birds bottoms?!?" retorted BoJo.

"When I use a word," Humpty Trumpty said in rather a scornful tone, "it means just what I choose it to mean — neither more nor less."

"The question is," said BoJo, "whether you can make words mean so many different things?"

"The question is," said Humpty Trumpty, "who is the master-debater? I don't have to give you an *esplanade* [38] of what my words mean."

"What are you talking about?" responded BoJo. "You just keep throwing words into sentences without any logical meaning or order. They don't make any sense – like most things around here."

"Who can say for sure what is sense or nonsense?" hooted Trumpty.

"OK!" shot back BoJo. "If you are so good with words, and if you have all the 'best words', tell me what *Oringis* [39], *Lawmarkers* [40] and *Foistered* [41] mean. And where is the *United Shhtates of America* [42]?"

"Er, well. There always have to be some special words for special occasions. Sometimes you have to make up a new one that fits the task or the situation exactly," weaseled Humpty Trumpty.

"Hmmm! That sounds like a load of bullpucky to me. Or like someone is *wurring his slurds* [43] because their false teeth don't fit, they are drunk, or they've been listening too much to Archie Bunker." ("Or," BoJo said to himself, "demential brain-fade is starting to kick in.")

"You see, it's like a *portmantoe* [44]— there are two meanings packed up into one word. Like, for instance, where *slithy* means 'slimy and lithe'," said Humpty Trumpty somewhat defensively, and significantly unsuccessfully, in an attempt to clarify matters.

---

[38] ESPLANADE: Humpty Trumpty trying to attempt an explanation of his new made up words like they really existed and were not just a mispronunciation on his part.

[39] ORINGIS: The orange glow that appears at the beginning of something and then slowly fades as time goes by. Similar to the Trumper's fake orange tan. It's bright just after he comes off the sun bed - except for the white circles round his eyes – then fades.

[40] LAWMARKERS: Special Sharpie pens used to by lawyers to show the connections between all the crooks, bandits and grifters in the Trumper's many nefarious activities.

[41] FOISTERED: The attempt by the Trumper to force upon, or fraudulently impose on the American public, lots of unjustifiably weird words in order to confuse them.

[42] UNITED SHTAATES OF AMERICA: A place that used to be the land of the free and the home of the brave. But now the President is so drunk with power that he is constantly wurring his slurds and is blaming everyone else for his predicament.

[43] WURRING HIS SLURDS: Just try to get someone who is drunk – with alcohol or power – to admit that they are slurring their words. They just won't.

[44] PORTMANTOE: A large suitcase made by former Vice President Dan Quayle for putting together, and carrying around, lots of Spelling Bee words

"And so, I suppose that *gerrymandering* [45] means Ripofflicans cheat a lot to win elections, otherwise their complete *House of Cards* [46] would collapse!" spat back BoJo, getting into the spirit of the master-debate.

"Hey! That's unfair!" whined Humpty Trumpty. "I heard that you also have a lot of special new portmantoe words relating to Britain leaving the European Union - and how badly its being handled."

"Hhhey wwait a minute! That's a bit OTT," jumped back BoJo. "OK, we started off with *BREXIT* [47] with all the jolly *Brexiteers* [48], then we got *Brexiety* [49] plus a load of *Remoaners* [50] who wouldn't stop whingeing and now lots of them are showing signs of extreme *Cakeism* [51]."

"Well, there you are," said Humpty Trumpty, "that's exactly what I meant. You are making up words just as fast as I am."

"Bah! Humbug! Change the subject!" said BoJo like any politician when cornered. "What is this wall for, why are you sitting on top of it, who will pay for it, and why is there a big empty space in front of it?"

"Whoah there, boy! Easy, tiger! That's way too many questions," said Humpty Trumpty. "I can only handle one sound-bite at time and my staff usually show me lots of pictures so I can absorb things quicker. If I get hit with too many things at once, my very thin shell starts to crack. And, if that happens, even all the Queen of Queen's horses and all the Queen's men, couldn't put Humpty Trumpty together again."

"Duuuh!" said BoJo. "OK, for you, one by one. What's the wall for?"

---

[45] GERRYMANDERING: A combination of the last name of Massachusetts' Gov. Elbridge Gerry and Salamander to mean politically contrived redistricting done to the benefit (primarily) of the Ripofflican Party. The first time it was done, the perimeter of one of the districts that was created resembled a very curvy salamander. Go figure!

[46] HOUSE OF CARDS: TV series with a cunning, dishonest, manipulator, tyrant who wants to be in power so he can go beyond law, humanity & conscience. Sound familiar?

[47] BREXIT: Britain's exit from the European Union. The start of all the problems . . .

[48] BREXITEER: A supporter of Britain leaving the EU. Usually a Conservatory or Russian

[49] BREXIETY: A state of heightened anxiety in non-Brexiters - and in most intelligent people - triggered by concerns about the imminent withdrawal of Britain from the EU.

[50] REMOANERS: People who continue to moan and argue that Britain should remain in the European Union despite the result of the referendum of 2016 that was fixed by Russia

[51] CAKEISM: Trying to have your cake and eat it - is also recognised as having been used by Remoaners and Brexiteers to describe their rivals. Defined as 'A wish to enjoy two desirable but incompatible alternatives'.

"It's to keep everyone safe by making sure all the CHAVs and people of color can't get out of this Council Estate and mingle with, terrorize or inter-breed with the real people on the outside."

"But why would they do that?" asked BoJo innocently.

"Well, there are a lot of bad people in here, drug dealers, criminals, murderers, *rapperists* [52] and politicians. It's a Swamp!" advised Humpty.

"Hmmmm . . ." responded BoJo. "I have met some odd people in here, but they can't all be bad, surely?"

"Ha! It's better to be safe than sorry! Some of those young, socialist, liberal, colored, non-Christian politicians are such a pain in the butt. They are all so smart and wanting a *Green New Deal* [53] or whatever. I have no idea what that really means. Probably to put more salad on McDonald's Big Macs to make them healthier, or something. Yuk! I just tell them all to go back where they came from."

"But aren't they all American citizens and most of them born here?" said BoJo innocently, inquisitively.

"Maybe, but they are still immigrants!" retorted Humpty.

"But, apart from the American Native Indians, you are all descended from immigrants who came from somewhere. Even you and your family!" retorted BoJo. "I hate to be the bearer of bad tidings, but America was discovered by an Italian whose voyage was funded by a couple of those Hispanics that you hate so much!"

"Yes, well, that Christopher Columbo was good at finding things and solving mysteries – I liked that TV series. But that was a long time ago and now the country is full up," countered Trumpty, an excuse that sounded very *mimsy* [54] to BoJo.

"If you think the USA is full up you should see the North of England. They have tiny little terraced houses where there isn't room to swing a dead cat in. And at least some of us Brits are actually British."

---

[52] RAPPERISTS: People who sing and point at the ground while attempting non-consensual intercourse.

[53] GREEN NEW DEAL: Proposed US legislation to address climate change and economic inequality. Ripofflicans are politically opposed to it, strongly denying climate change is real and that other people should have anywhere near as much money as they do.

[54] MIMSY: A portmantoe of *miserable* and *flimsy*. In other words, it was a very thin excuse from a very unhappy person.

"So, those that are, really do believe they are entitled to grumble about immigration. You should come and visit us some time." suggested BoJo.

"No, thanks! Last time I came, people in London weren't very nice and that Duchess Meghan Markle made some 'nasty' remarks about me," grumbled Humpty in a sulky, baby voice. "Doesn't Prince Harry realize that she is colored? Plus, he is a 'Ginger'. What sort of color is the kid going to be when he grows up? Maybe you will have a colored King of England someday, like we had that Kenyan, Barack Obama."

17.	This Is One Baby That Should Be Behind Bars!

"But at least they named the kid after *Archie Bunker[55]*," said Trumpty. "He was my kinda guy. Well-spoken, lots of really good words, smart, very PC, lived in Queens and a real family man. Just like me."

"When I went to France for the WWII D-Day 75th anniversary - unlike in UK - all the people there loved me. They were lining the streets and cheering me as I went by," bragged Trumpty. "It was just a pity it kept raining. So, I missed a couple of events. I don't think they were important. I heard everyone in those cemeteries was dead. Real 'losers'."

---

[55] ARCHIE BUNKER: Star of the TV show 'All in the Family'. He had a gruff, overbearing demeanor, and was famous for his bigotry towards a diverse group of non-WASP individuals. Blacks, Hispanics, 'commies', gays, hippies, Jews, Asians, Catholics, 'women's libbers' & Polish-Americans were usual targets. Sound like anyone you know?

ARCHIE BUNKER – BLACK AND WOMEN PRESIDENTS
https://www.youtube.com/watch?v=ffh09f4TdM8

"Sorry to say, old chap, I think that was 'jeering' not 'cheering'. There is a difference, you know. And I heard you have a bit of a problem with your hair in the rain and umbrellas . . ." BoJo sarcastically replied.

"Really? Maybe cheering sounds like jeering because of their French accents," defended Trumpty. "But those London demonstrators write all that weird British *giraffiti* [56] on their posters. I just don't get it!"

18.	So Much Wrong. So Little Cardboard!

"Anyway, the USA is never going to have an open border policy like the European Union with your Shanghai go-any-where-you-want-without-any-checks Visa," said Humpty Trumpty matter-of-factly.

"I think you mean Schengen Visa, actually," responded BoJo. "And that's one of main things that I will change when we are out of the EU. All that open border stuff will stop. Unfortunately, while the British public is OK with closing borders to non-Brits – and many openly relish that prospect - we are having other problems because of BREXIT."

[56] GIRAFFITI: Anti-Trumper statements written on placards at anti-Trumper rallies that are so subtly clever that they go way, way, way over his head.

"Really?" said Trumpty, eager to learn of others' border problems.

"Yes! BREXIT will also close the borders to the importation of goodies from Europe. That's what all this 'cakeism' is about. Everybody wants to have their genuine imported French croissants and wine, yet still get their British sausage rolls from Greggs - but only if they are served by a 55-year old Anglo-Saxon lady, who can trace her lineage back before the Magna Carta," grumbled BoJo vociferously.

"Sausage rolls? Mango Tarts? I don't know what you are talking about. But it sounds like you have the same feelings about borders as I do. Do you want to use one of my contractor buddies to build a wall for you? They could do you a nice one between Northern Ireland and Ireland or between Scotland and England," offered Trumpty.

"Er, herumph! Don't say that too loud. Someone might overhear," whispered BoJo. "Ah, but at least I don't put people in cages and camps while they are processed like you do."

"That's true," smirked Trumpty. "You let the French do it for you! And then I heard that lots of immigrants sneak into UK in refrigerated container vans because no one checks them at ports when they drive off the ferry. I also heard that you have upset the Vietnamese government with that one. Be careful you don't start a war with those people – you will never win it. Trust the American experience on that one!"

"I say! That's a bit much!" said BoJo trying to defend the indefensible. "Anyway, what do you know about the Vietnamese? I heard that you apparently, allegedly, 'suffer' from 'bone spurs'"

"Yes, I do, and I know a good doctor that can diagnose some for you too – for a fee. But all that open border stuff is a disaster waiting to happen. I know. I'm just saying . . ." said Trumpty, wagging his little fingers at BoJo. "But what was your second question?"

"Why are you sitting on top of it?" repeated BoJo.

"Ah, that's an easy one. It's so I can see when the *Car-a-van* [57] is coming!" smiled down Trumpty from his perch.

---

[57] CAR-A-VAN: A group of poor, persecuted and frightened families from the Central American Trailer Park trying to walk miles to seek asylum on the other side of the wall in the free world. The Trumpty hyped up and escalated the whole thing into an 'un-invasion' by hordes of 'very bad people' just so he could get money for his beloved wall.

"You mean like a British *caravan* [58]? The homes on wheels that Brits and Europeans tow behind their cars to go on holiday?" queried BoJo.

"No! We call those mobile homes. I mean the un-invasion of un-refugee, low-lives from the Central American Trailer Park who are trying to get past my wall and into my beautiful Trumperland." explained Trumpty.

19. Brit/Euro Caravan En-Route	20. Trumper Ca-ra-van Checks Route

"What on earth do you mean? 'Un-invasion' and 'un-refugee'. I don't understand" queried BoJo.

"Don't you know, the Ca-ra-van is a national emergency? Those people are doing an un-invasion to get out of the Council Estate because they are always threatened by the CHAVs. And they want to un-refugee themselves, so they are real people again." Trumpty sort of explained.

CARAVAN CHALLENGE – TOP GEAR/JEREMY CLARKSON
https://www.youtube.com/watch?v=kNTnrpL1Uw0

---

[58] CARAVAN: Brits pay many thousands of pounds to buy caravans so that they can save £30/night not staying in a 2-star hotel. All other road users hate them as they are so slow. They send Jeremy Clarkson of Top Gear/The Grand Tour abso-bloody-lutely apoplectic.

"But how can you stop them all?" queried BoJo.

"I will just make this beautiful wall taller and bigger and longer than any wall has ever been before," bragged Trumpty.

"OK. But that is going to cost a huge amount of money. So, that was my third question. Who is going to pay for it?"

"Well, that's easy! The Mexicans are going to pay for it. Everyone knows that!" boasted the Trumpty.

"But, I heard that you shut down the Government for a couple of months in a literal *Mexican Standoff* [59] where you wanted the money from the budget to pay for the wall that you said the Mexicans were going to pay for. Duuuh! It was just like the last scene in Reservoir Dogs. Oops sorry! Belated 'Spoiler Alert'," chortled BoJo.

21. I Shoot You, You Shoot Him, He Shoots Me – Ad Infinitum. Everyone Dies

"Well, it would have worked if all those one million Government staff hadn't grumbled so much about needing the money to live on. Why didn't they just go and borrow money from their Dad's? It always worked for me," whined Trumpty, like the spoiled brat that he was.

---

[59] MEXICAN STANDOFF: A confrontation in which no strategy exists that allows any party to achieve victory. Any party initiating aggression might trigger their own demise. Famously used in Quentin Tarantino movies. Doesn't work in Trumpty real life. Ever . . .

RESERVOIR DOGS – QUENTIN TARANTINO
https://www.youtube.com/watch?v=GLPJSmUHZvU

"Well, I heard that you and Nancy had a bit of a personal Mexican Standoff and that she had bigger *cojones* [60] than you. Not half bad for a 79-year old woman. Ha! LOL!" chortled BoJo.

"It wasn't that!" retorted Trumpty. "It was those Dimocrats in Congress saying that spending all that money on my Beautiful Wall was *inappropriate* [61] for some reason."

"Well, you were stealing it from all those military projects that were supposed to protect the National Security – real-war stuff, like fighting against Iran, Syria, ISIS and Russia - and then spending it on a so-called 'Beautiful Wall', just to stop a bunch of poor, defenceless, homeless, unarmed Hispanics with women and kids and babies, who just wanted asylum from a gang of thugs," pointed out BoJo, somewhat obviously.

"Ho! You can talk!" jabbed back Trumpty. "You tried that sneaky *pro-gyration* [62] of your Parliament so that you could stop your opponents from checking on you and spotting how bad your BREXIT agreement really was."

"No, no, no, noooo! It was a very reasonable request to prorogue Parliament so that all the MPs could have a longer break and come back fresh and fluffy faced when the BREXIT deal was all done and dusted."

"Exactly what I just said!" chirped Trumpty excitedly.

---

[60] COJONES: An appropriate Mexican word, literally meaning testicles. But more generally used to denote courage. The bigger the cojones, the less likely the person is to back down. Nancy beating Trumpty says a lot for her and not much for his cojones.

[61] INAPPROPRIATE: The action of Trumpty syphoning off money that was appropriated, constitutionally by Congress, which has 'The Power of the Purse', for something legitimate and necessary, in order to spend it on his stupid 'Beautiful Wall'.

[62] PRO-GYRATION: BoJo put a totally untrue spin on what he told the Queen as the reason that Parliament needed to be shut down. Yes, Ma'am. Thank you, Ma'am.

"Well, it was all that Irish 'back-stop' business that created the problem. Ireland will still be part of the EU and Northern Ireland will not when it BREXITs with the rest of UK. So there has to be a 'border' again even though the Irish on either side don't want one," fumed BoJo.

"Look, just build a wall like mine. I will get you a good, honest Irish-American contractor and only take a 10% commission. It's only £20 million per mile. That's a bargain," schmoozed Trumpty like a used car salesman at an Edsel Ford dealership in the 50's.

"Oooer!" grimaced BoJo. "The Irish border is 300 miles long, so that means £6 billion for the wall. And your cut would be £600 million. That's rather a lot of dosh!"

"Yes, but I could throw in free golf lessons at my Trumpty International Golf Links & Hotel at Doonbuggy, County Clare. Its only 200 miles from the border, so you could keep an eye on the construction every day," offered Trumpty, jumping into his 'Art of the Deal' mode.

"But that's a huge distance!" countered BoJo.

"Not really," said Trumpty. "Mike Penice did that trip every day back and forth when he was meeting with the Irish Prime Minister, the *Tee-shakh, Caddy-shakh or Abendigo*[63], or whatever he is called."

"Whatever for?" queried BoJo incredulously. "There are hotels in Dublin too. Just five minutes' drive from the Irish Parliament buildings."

"Ah yes! But he really wanted to stay at my golf hotel to get a feel for the real Irish countryside. Penice has Irish lineage, you know," proffered Trumpty as though that was reason enough to funnel US Taxpayer's money into his own pockets.

"Hmmmm. It's hard to believe that there is a crazy, drunk Irishman looking for the 'craic', just dying to break out of that cold, unbending albino façade," muttered BoJo to himself so as not to sound like a racist.

Tired of standing in the sun in the big open space in front of the wall, staring up at Trumpty, BoJo decided to sit down in the shade.

---

[63] TEE-SHAKH, CADDY-SHAKH OR ABENDIGO: Another Trumptyism. It was actually Shadrach, Meshach, and Abednego who were three Hebrew men thrown into a fiery furnace by Nebuchadnezzar, King of Babylon. Trumpty probably remembers the story because it's about Jewish men being thrown into a fire. He has probably forgotten the bit where they walked out of it alive. The Irish PM is called the Taoiseach, by the way. But its pronounced - in typical Irish fashion - TEE-shəkh. Go figure.

As he did so he realised that there actually was no shade. Which was odd. And, as he leant back on the wall, he fell backwards, on the ground, because there actually was no wall to lean on. Which was even odder.

"Curiouser and curiouser," came to BoJo's mind for some reason.

BoJo waved his hand in the air where the wall was supposed to be and, instead of bricks, there was a sort of shimmering as his hand went back and forth.

Using his massive powers of deduction and putting two and two together, but getting zero, BoJo slowly (very, very slowly) came to the realization that there was no wall. No way, Jose! No wall, Jose, either!

BoJo jumped up and shouted at Trumpty who was still perched on top of the 'wall'.

"Hey, Trumpty! What the hell is going on here? You seem to be sitting on a wall, but there is no wall. I have just fallen through it. So, it does not exist. What gives? Duuuh!"

"Er, well. Of course, there is a wall! We are busy building a wall. I have written my name on it with a Sharpie," lied Trumpty blatantly.

"Look my dear chap, I know a wall when I see one and this is definitely not one, by any stretch of your obviously vivid imagination," responded BoJo, with emphasis on the vivid imagination bit.

"Aaaahhh! OK. You got me. It's a fair cop! I guess – as they say – you can't bullpucky a bullpuckyer. The whole wall is actually a hologram and I am sitting on top of a ladder behind it," admitted Trumpty, somewhat surprisingly.

"Ha! Gotcha!" splurted BoJo. "I knew there was something fishy about this whole 'wall' thing. So why did you do it with a hologram?"

"Huh! It was the funding – or lack of it. I need about $25 billion and the meanies in the Congress only gave me $2.5 billion. So, I had to 'acquire' or, as I put it officially, 'redirect' another $3.6 billion from military projects that we don't need," explained Trumpty.

"Oh yes! We heard about that," laughed BoJo. "You grabbed some cash that was earmarked for rebuilding overseas army bases and schools for children of military personnel. That made enemies in the Pentagon."

"Well that was just too bad," countered Trumpty. "I got my own back on Jimbo Mattress for criticizing me by firing his ass in December 2018, just before he was due to retire. So that screwed his pension. Hah!"

"Hmmm . . . So, who is the meanie now?" asked BoJo. "And the bottom line is that this whole 'Beautiful Wall' thing is a con-trick. It's just a hologram that anyone could walk through at any time!"

"Awwww! Don't say it like that. I had no choice. That was all the money I could steal, er, I mean 'redirect', at the time. Just enough to pay for a whole bunch of hologram machines to make it look like there was a wall and keep all the low lives in their place," whined Trumpty.

"It looks to me like you were trying to copy *The Hunger Games* [64] and fool all the people with holograms, CGI, digitally engineered environments and huge social media mis-information campaigns. I bet you do that to cover up all the climate change issues too!" sneered BoJo.

THE HUNGER GAMES – JENNIFER LAWRENCE
https://www.youtube.com/watch?v=EAzGXqJSDJ8

"I would never admit to that, of course. Whether it's true or not – and for sure it wouldn't be Russia that had anything to do with it. Plus, climate change is another Dimocratic hoax. But I do think that *Jennifer Lawrence* [65] is really nasty person. Just nasty! And an 'over-rated' actress too, just like Meryl Streep," grumbled Trumpty.

"Remember what Abraham Lincoln said, 'You can fool all the people some of the time, and some of the people all the time, but you cannot fool all the people all the time'," warned BoJo.

---

[64] THE HUNGER GAMES: The dystopian, post-apocalyptic nation of Panem is run by a despotic leader, President Snow, where the rich live in the Capitol – and are very rich and way OTT – and they keep the poor very poor and locked up in 12 different districts with no communication allowed between them. They monitor everything and create digitally enhanced environments and info to suppress the masses. Does this sound at all familiar?

[65] JENNIFER LAWRENCE: Outspoken and very talented movie star - despite the Trumper's comments. Wanted to meet the Trumper face-to-face and given him the short and simple message: "Hey, Trump. F**k you!". Over-rated? I think not.

"Ha! Listen who is talking! Your new deal BREXIT terms are just the same as the ones dreamed up by your predecessor, Mother Theresa. And that Lincoln guy, he let himself get shot. I can't respect people who let themselves get shot. Like those Kennedy's too. And Senator McCain who let himself get captured," spat back Trumpty.

"I assume you mean Theresa May-B'lieve, not Mother Theresa and my terms are waaaay different to hers. Just look at my plan for the Irish backstop. Its brilliant, simple and very cost-effective," countered BoJo.

22.	BoJo's Cunning Plan for the Irish Back-Stop

"Really? That's it? I don't think that would work on any of my borders. The Mexicans would push their packets of drugs under the bar of the gate and then do a Mariachi Limbo to get under themselves. And the Canadians would steal their Mountie's horses so they could get them to jump over the barrier," was Trumpty's off-the-cuff reply.

"It will work for the Irish," said BoJo confidently. "They'll just stand behind the crossbar like they're waiting outside a pub for opening time. Then as soon as someone on the other side lifts it up, they'll all rush through and head to the nearest bar. In both directions, to be sure, to be sure."

"Well, maybe. Let's see," said Trumpty sounding really rather unconvinced. "But look, I am all for your BoJo BREXIT Exit. Whatever the deal you make with crazy French President Macaroon, his 'hot' wife and Frau Right-Angle Meerkat and the rest of them. I am dying to get in there and build lots of Trumpty Towers in England, Scotland, Wales, Northern Ireland and Ireland. And maybe I will buy Scotland instead of Greenland – I heard that they want another referendum to split with you guys, so they can have their own country back again like Mel Gibson was shouting about in Braveheart. If they did that, I have a contractor friend called Hadrian who could build a great border wall between Scotland and England. Plus, I have lots of buddies in medical insurance and 'Big Pharma" who would buy your National Health Service. What was it you said on that bus? The NHS makes £350 million pounds a day or something. The US *HMO* [66] boys would love some of that action!"

"Slow down a bit," said BoJo. "It was actually £350 million per week, but that's still a lot of dosh. And we haven't even had final negotiations with the EU on the exit terms yet. But I did manage to con people to vote for me in the General Election with 'Get BREXIT Done'!"

23. Another Self Preservation Society. Maybe £350m Goes Towards Italian Jobs

---

[66] HMO: They are Health Maintenance Organizations which are medical insurance groups that provide health services for a fixed annual fee. Some people would more accurately call them Health Moneymaking Organizations. What you need to remember when enrolling is never, ever admit to a pre-existing condition. Even just being alive . . .

"I'm with you there," rejoined Trumpty. "I have to get through an election myself – assuming there aren't any more disasters! But a good slogan always helps to pull in the dumb and undecided ones," he continued rather derogatorily about his much-needed 'base' voters.

"Last time I had MAGA – Make America Great Again. And they fell for it, hook, line and sinker. Maybe I will have MAGAA for 2020."

"MAGAA?" queried BoJo.

"Yeah! Make America Great Again – Again," responded Trumpty, apparently not fully appreciating the irony of that statement.

"Er, umm, well, harrumph . . ." mumbled BoJo, "I, er, guess that might work."

"Of course it will!" exclaimed Trumpty, "I will give everyone in the mid-west, all the evangelicals, the coal miners, farmers and the factory workers a free MAGAA hat and they will vote for me – whatever I do!"

"Hey!" BoJo suddenly exclaimed, wanting to change the subject away from what he perceived - rightly - as a rather stupid slogan idea.

"What about helping each other win our respective campaigns? You say I am brilliant with BREXIT and I say you're, er, brilliant. Well, maybe let's not go too far with the accolades. We can call it our '*Self Preservation Society*'[67], like in the Italian Job, you know."

"Italian jobs? What? More favors for immigrants?" complained Trumpty, who obviously wasn't up to speed on his classic British movie history and did not get the subtle linkage of ideas – as was often the case with him.

"No. Nothing to do with immigrants. Duuuuh! The Italian Job was just one of the all-time great movies and the gang got away with the gold bullion – well, almost," explained BoJo, trying to avoid both a Spoiler Alert and putting a jinx on the cunning plan they were beginning to hatch.

"OK. I like it! So, I will tell everyone that BREXIT is a great idea and the UK and US can do a 'special' trade deal. Yeah!" Trumpty burbled.

---

[67] SELF PRESERVATION SOCIETY: Theme song of the 1969 movie starring Michael Caine and three hot Mini Coopers. Very funny and tense at the same time. A great movie and way, way better than the 2003 remake. Classic ending. We can only hope BoJo and Trumpty end up the same way.

THE ITALIAN JOB (1969) – MICHAEL CAINE
https://www.youtube.com/watch?v=bPpgg5rwxpA

"Yes! And I can say FU to the EU. So, they can keep their butter mountain, powdered milk surplus, smelly camembert cheese, Libyan Boat People and Greek insolvency etc, etc, etc," chortled BoJo excitedly.

"Let's do it!" shouted Trumpty, waving his little arms in the air, wobbling and almost falling off the top of the 'wall' in his excitement.

"Yeah baby!!" shouted BoJo with a huge smile on his face, showing way too many teeth but with a slight question in his mind as to why he suddenly came out with that famous Austin Powers catch-phrase.

"OK! Now we have that sorted out, what was your fourth question?" Trumpty asked, surprising BoJo, who had thought that the wall conversation was long gone. But he had underestimated Trumpty's singular – some might say obsessive – focus on his 'Beautiful Wall'.

"Ah, er, er, yes. Ummm . . . Oh, I've got it," BoJo eventually remembered. "Yes. Why is there this big open, empty space in front of your so-called 'wall'?

"That's another easy-peasy one," answered Trumpty. "It's my DMZ, of course!"

"DMZ?" queried BoJo. "Like a De-Militarized Zone in a war? Or the space between East and West Germany before the Berlin Wall came down? Or the area between North and South Korea?"

"Nope! None of those," responded Trumpty with some significant disdain. "And – mer, mer, ma, mer, mer – I have been walking in the North – South Korea De-Militarized Zone with my BFF Kim Jung-Ones. He writes me beautiful letters you know! I have one here in my pocket."

"So! What is the bloody big space for then?" shot back BoJo, getting frustrated with the whole thing.

"Can't you guess?" taunted Trumpty. "It's my De-Mexicanized Zone, dimbo!"

"What the jolly 'fcuk' is a De-Mexicanized Zone for?" asked BoJo.

"It's so I can see the Mexicans when they are coming, of course," smirked back Trumpty. "Also, so that they don't get too near the wall and see that it's actually a digital mirage. I've told the border guards that they can shoot people to stop them getting close if they need to."

"Shoot people!" exclaimed BoJo. "Surely, you can't be serious!"

"I am serious! And don't call me Shirley," responded Trumpty. "I've told the border guards that I will pardon them if there is a problem."

AIRPLANE – DON'T CALL ME SHIRLEY
https://www.youtube.com/watch?v=ixljWVyPby0

"Oh . . .! My . . . ! God . . . ! You really said that? Really? Really?" asked BoJo incredulously. "That must be totally OTT. A President telling his employees to shoot people! I have often felt like doing that in the Houses of Parliament, especially the former Speaker, John Berrrccoww. But if I had stood up with a gun in my hand he would have just shouted 'ORDER! ORDER! The Right Honourable Member is NOT recognised!' and I would have had to sit down, immediately. Those are the rules."

"You know, I have had the same feeling myself over Speaker 'Nervous' Nancy Palooka. Maybe, I should just wait till I can catch her on Fifth Avenue, in New York, and shoot her there, as I can't be investigated or prosecuted, even if I did that in front of the NYPD," chortled Trumpty, obviously relishing the idea greatly.

"Hmmmmm," said BoJo, thinking to himself that he wasn't very comfortable about the direction the conversation was taking. "Well, er. It's really been interesting talking to you, but I must be getting along now . . . So, er, goodbye . . . "

"Oh, really?" said Trumpty sounding almost a little bit sad as he really had virtually no-one who he could call a 'friend' and who he could talk to. BoJo was the first person that he had met in a long time who seemed to have some affinities and similarities to himself.

Of course, Trumpty was so absorbed in himself that he did not realize that this was the very reason that BoJo was leaving. BoJo had also spotted those similarities and it was more than a little bit worrying.

"Where are you going, then?" Trumpty asked, choking back some crocodile tears.

"Er. Well. Er. I think I will follow one of these two roads along the base of your 'Beautiful Wall'," said BoJo a little uncertainly. "There are some signs on the wall. One says EGOISM to the right and the other says ENLIGHTENMENT to the left. Which way should I go?"

"Ah! For me I don't even need to think about. I am always going to go to the right. Often to the far-right. And sometimes even all the way to the alt-right, if the truth were known, Though, hopefully, it never will be . . . at least not all of it!" said Trumpty, breathing in with one of his snorty-hissy breaths and looking to each side and behind, in his usual pompous and supercilious manner, for some positive accession from an audience that did not exist.

"I think I will just toss a coin for it," surmised BoJo. "Then I can't be blamed for whatever happens next in this crazy, crazy place."

"That never works," opined Trumpty, "because you toss the coin once and if you don't get the result that you want, you say 'Best of three'. And then, if that does not work, you start all over again till the toss decides the thing you wanted in the first place."

So BoJo tossed his coin and said, "Heads for ENLIGHTENMENT and tails for EGOISM." It came up tails and, as Trumpty had predicted, said, "Er, best of three."

Luckily for him the next two throws came up with two heads!

"There you go!" chirped BoJo. "That was a fair choice. ENLIGHTEMENT it is, and I am really looking forward to that after all the odd things that have happened to me since I've been here."

But Humpty Trumpty only shut his eyes, and said, "Wait till you've tried."

BoJo waited a minute to see if he would speak again, but, as Trumpty never opened his eyes or took any further notice of him, BoJo, being British, said "Good-bye!" once more, and, getting no answer to that, he quietly walked away along the Yellow-Brick Road towards ENLIGHTENMENT - whatever that was going to be.

But, BoJo couldn't help saying to himself as he went, "Of all the unsatisfactory . . . . . ." (he repeated this aloud, as it was a great comfort to have such a long word to say) "Of all the unsatisfactory people I ever met . . ."

He never finished the sentence, for at that moment, the Russians, who had been listening (as they always did) to Trumpty's conversations, hacked into Battersea Power Station's control panel (as we always knew they could) and switched over the circuit for all his hologram lamps to power something else. Suddenly, the 'Beautiful Wall' disappeared and Trumpty was left exposed, sitting on top of his ladder, in complete shock. He wobbled a little to the left, then to the right, then to the back, each time picking up a bit of momentum as he was waving his tiny arms and hands around like KFC chicken wings. Suddenly, it was one wobble too many, and he fell off the top of his ladder and crashed to the ground, shattering into a thousand and one tiny pieces. So much so, that all the Queen's horses and all the Queen's men, couldn't put Trumpty together again.

"Oooer!" thought BoJo. "I had better leg it out of here before someone mistakes me for a Ukrainian and blames me for this. Good thing I am still wearing my joggers and my 'BREXIT Forever!' sweat-shirt!"

And so off he trotted along the Yellow-Brick Road towards what he assumed would be ENLIGHTENMENT. Little did he know . . .

As he jogged along, he could hear some music in the distance. At first, he could not tell what it was and then he rounded a bend in the road, and he could hear that the music was coming from the Battersea Power Station.

And in the air above it was a large, pink, flying pig.

"Wait a minute!" thought BoJo. "Everyone in the real world knows that pigs can't fly."

But then, this wasn't the real world. It was Trumperland.

However, as he got closer, he realised it wasn't actually a flying pig. It was a very large Baby Trumper. Like the one he had seen at the anti-Trumper demonstrations in the centre of London.

Although those people would all tell you that the Baby Trumper was a flying pig . . .

| 24. | If Pigs or Presidents Could Fly . . . |

The music suddenly became loud. Very loud. VERY LOUD INDEED. And the words of the chorus of the song blasted in BoJo's ears.

All in all, you're just another brick in the wall

PINK FLOYD – ANOTHER BRICK IN THE WALL (PART 2)
https://www.youtube.com/watch?v=YR5ApYxkU-U

"How come," mused BoJo idly, but strangely prophetically, "whenever there is something linked to the Russians, like hacking into a power station, or a DNC server, or some form of anarchy, even just the words in most of Pink Floyd's music, there is always some connection – however tenuous – to the Trumper?"

Perhaps this was the road to ENLIGHTENMENT after all . . .

And, as BoJo jogged by the Battersea Power Station, he almost tripped over 'Moe' Davis, a US Vet on his way to the Trump demonstrations with a signboard that pointedly commented on the fact that Trumpty's wall never was and will be never more . . .

25.	Not a Sucker! Nuff Said!

POSTSCRIPT

Jonathan Pie – in between his 'live' news broadcast – gives a personal opinion on the Trumper's 'Beautiful Wall'.

SHUTDOWN AND BORDER WALL – JONATHAN PIE
https://www.youtube.com/watch?v=XSt3F9XGw9w&list=PLYY7N_
c-qfb5Xkp5ksI1a59BiZTDpgh2Y&index=1&app=desktop

POST POSTSCRIPT

This is NOT 'mansplaining'. But in case you are not aware – or you are a Ripofflican with no sense of humor (like the Trumper) – Jonathan Pie is NOT a real news reporter. He is a British comedian with a very fine-tuned appreciation of satirical sarcasm & irony coupled with a strong sense of outrage at BS in general & politics in particular. Great guy! OK?

POST POST POSTSCRIPT

Trevor Noah, host of the Daily Show, has compiled the Trumper's Best Words for 2018. See the shhtart of the sloppery schhlope of Trump into De-men-shuh-ville. But remember – he hash the Unclear Lunch Codez!

TRUMPER'S BEST WORDS – TREVOR NOAH, DAILY SHOW
https://www.youtube.com/watch?v=MfOQBY5BrUA

POST POST POST POSTSCRIPT

Way back in 1980, the British comedy series, Yes, Minister accurately portrayed how governments run and, particularly, why the UK needed to be in the EU. BoJo seems to have missed this episode. Unfortunately.

WHY UK IS IN THE EU + QUID PRO QUO – YES MINISTER
https://www.youtube.com/watch?v=ZVYqB0uTKlE

9

MEANWHILE PART 4 – AUSTIN POWERS UP

Meanwhile . . .

Meanwhile, back at the Colored House, the Queen was continuing with her tirade. "Andt whots zis abouts you 'Falling in love' with some weirdoh Kooreean guy? I thoughtz you didnundt like za Asians andt hated za gayz?" glowered the Queen of Queens.

"But Millennium, Kim Yung-Ones is really my kinda guy."

"Yours kinda gay? Votcher mean? He hass got ze crazy hairs style andt vears zose Mau See Tongue suitz all ze times. Vot iss he? Som kinda Dr. Evil und Mini Me?"

26.   The Trumper, Mini Me Dicktator & Dr. Evil

"No, Melimania, he is not a Doctor. He is a Dictator! And I want to be one just like him."

"You vont to be za dick or za dicktator? I sink zat most peeples sink you ares already za dick!"

"Millimamamia! Ouch. That's not nice . . ."

"Butts look at zat funnies little mans. You vant to be like hims? He looks kinda vacky-backy. And he iss buildink rockets tzo fire at uss. Ya? Andt zat guy viss him in za pics. I haff met hims before."

"Oh really?"

"Ya! He iss za guy tryink to rule za Vayne's Vorldt."

"Wayne's World?"

"Ya, he iss a real head-banger! Andt he luvvfs za Qveen andt Bohemian Raspberry."

"The Queen? Bohemian Raspberry? Which Queen?"

"Boths of thems. Za Ferdie Mercury Qveen andt za reals British Elizabeth Qveen."

WAYNE'S WORLD - BOHEMIAN RHAPSODY - MIKE MYERS
https://www.youtube.com/watch?v=thyJOnasHVE

"Both of them?"

"Ya. Besides za headt bankink Vayne, alsos he iss an under za covers naughty British agent, vizz za Union Jack on hiss car. He is 'Austin Powers – International Man of Mystery' and 'The Spy Who Shagged Me' viss hiss 'Goldmember'."

"What!!! What do you mean? Shagged you?"

AUSTIN POWERS - MIKE MYERS
https://www.youtube.com/watch?v=5vsANcS4Ml8

"Yeah, babies! Oh, behaayvfe!"

"What!!!!!!"

"Ya. You sink you are ze onlies ones haffink za fun aroundt here under za covers? Do youse thinkz zat I vass sittings at home knitting vooly mittenz ven youse vos out viz your prawn starz? Vots goot for ze ganders isz goot for za gooses."

"That's not fair!" whimpered the Trumper.

"Youse mays thinks zat yous am ze big shot, Mr. Smoothie, like za James Bonds, viz your creepy littles Goldfingers andt all your Pussies Galore. But youse nots any mores. Tzo back offv, yeah baby!"

GOLDFINGER - JAMES BOND
https://www.youtube.com/watch?v=MA65V-oLKa8

"Getz used tzo ze ideas zat I'm za one who iss rulink zis bit off za Trumperland. I'm za Queen off Queens! You izz justs za Queen's Consort like zat Prinz Philip, za originals *Duke of Hazzard* [68]! And zose dumbo boys off yourz, McDon Junior andt Erik, vill not bee inn za line off sucessionz. My boy, Barron, vill be number von, like za Charlez, za guy youse called za *Prince of Whales* [69]! Ha! Stupitdo! LOL!!!"

"But Mollitof . . .!"

"No mores 'buts' or it vill be 'Off viz your headt, babies!'"

Fade to black . . .

---

[68] DUKE OF HAZZARD: Formerly known as the Duke of Edinburgh, the Queen re-knighted him due to his numerous car crashes. As a result, she bought significant blocks of shares in Land Rover and Spec Savers. He is also well-known as being the father of Charles, the *Prince of Whales.*

[69] PRINCE OF WHALES: One of the many Trumper Twatter misspellings was the title for Charles, Prince of Wales, the first in line heir to the British throne. Trumper is a twat!

10

THE MAD HATER'S COVFEFE PARTY

BoJo kept jogging along the Yellow-Brick Road till he figured that he must be far enough away from either Trumpty or the Battersea Power Station to not be mistaken for a Ukrainian or a Russian and therefore relatively safe from being apprehended and blamed for either the 'Beautiful Wall' falling down or for power systems being hacked.

He did not really know where he was going, which wasn't unusual for BoJo, so he wasn't worried at all. But by now his intravenous inocculatte had completely worn off and there was no sign of a Starbucks, or any coffee shop that could charge taxpayers exorbitant prices for cups of coffee while never actually paying any income tax themselves.

Then, from behind a door, he heard the rattle of cups and saucers and his brain started racing with visions of Crapochinos, Flappochinos, Zippochinos, Alpachinos and even just plain old black coffee.

But it wasn't to be . . .

WHATEVER HAPPENED TO COFFEE? – DENNIS LEARY
https://www.youtube.com/watch?v=-f_dxLiuXuw

73

BoJo slowly opened the door and was surprised to see a very strange combination of things that included a massive table with lots of empty chairs, a crazy looking guy with a huge top hat (and crazy looking hair), a Mad March Hare, a dozy Dormouse and a huge coffee pot.

"Er, hello, chaps?" said BoJo tremulously.

The guy with the big hat (and the crazy hair) and the Mad March Hare completely ignored BoJo and continued to try and stuff the Dormouse into the coffee pot, grunting and puffing as they proceeded with the obviously impossible task. Whether it was appropriate or even absolutely necessary to put the unresisting Dormouse into the coffee pot was an obvious issue. But, the main problem, as far as BoJo could see, was that they were trying to squeeze the Dormouse into the spout of the coffee pot rather than taking off the lid and simply dropping it in. From this obvious stupidity, BoJo quickly deduced that he definitely was not in the presence of a stable genius. More likely, the guy was some sort of unstable lunatic . . .

27.	Mad As A Stable Genius

"Er, is this some kind of birthday party or Boston Tea Party?" asked BoJo. "Do you have any Starbucks coffee, by any chance?"

"Of course not, pudgy!" spat back the guy with the hat. "We only have *Turkish Kurds Ethnically Blended Covfefe* [70] or *Constant Negative Press Covfefe* [71] or *Americano Ukraine Favor-Flavored Covfefe* [72]. Take a look at the menu and choose. But quickly, before *Private Eye* [73] spots that we stole some of their dishes!"

MAD HATER PARTY MENU

STARTERS

The Tiny Finger Food Buffet
Grilled Gropefruit
Dressed Grab and Octopussy
Klan Chowder
Presidential Sweet Russian Ritz-Carlton Salad

MAIN COURSE

Tweet and Sour Porky Bars
Red Tie Curry
Donald Duck à l'orange

DESSERT

Impeach Melba with Mexican Walls Ice-Cream
A Selection of Tarts

BEVERAGES

Fake Booze
Choice of Alt-White or Red Neck Bordelleaux
Russian 100% Election Proof Vladka
Stormy Jack Daniels
Moscow Mitch Kentucky Bourbon
Schleppsteiner Jungfrau Lager

AFTER DINNER

59-Year Old Randy Dandy Shooting Party Brandy
With Choice Of:
17-Year Old Kennedy Cuban Missile Crisis Cigars (White House Edition)
Turkish Kurds Ethnically Blended Covfefe
or
Kim Yung-Ones Korean Missile Crisis Cigars (Long-Range Edition)
Constant Negative Press Covfefe
or
Zabaglione Crimea Crisis Presidential Cigars (Javelin Anti-Tank Edition)
Americano-Ukraine Favour-Flavoured Covfefe

---

[70] TURKISH KURDS ETHNICALLY BLENDED COVFEFE: Strong alliance flavor at first sip. Quickly changes to a Russian-backed infusion with a nasty Syrian aftertaste.
[71] CONSTANT NEGATIVE PRESS COVFEFE: A blend of misinformation with white nationalist propaganda in a frothy concoction that only Ever-Trumper's believe.
[72] AMERICAN UKRAINE FAVOUR-FLAVOURED COVFEFE: Typical Americano taste but sadly corrupted with undeniable & impeachable personal and political aromas.
[73] PRIVATE EYE: The funniest and most satirical, political magazine in the world.

"And who are you anyway, chubby chops?" said the hat-man rudely.

"Er, my name is BoJo. I'm the British PM."

"Ah, a riddle! I love riddles! You mean you are the British Afternoon? And if you are the British Afternoon, who is the British Morning? Ha! What's the answer?"

"There is no answer. PM stands for Prime Minister not Post Meridiem. And who are you? I just met a Cheshire Pussy that looked like the Trumper and now your orange face looks like him too!"

"Ah! I'm glad you asked that question. Though you will have to guess my name by figuring out a riddle!" And with that, he burst into song.

"Please allow me to introduce myself, I'm a man of wealth and taste. I've been around for a long, long year. Stole many a man's soul to waste."

"You look more like a Mad Hater to me," thought BoJo. But his Eton upbringing managed to silence his desire for *sarchasm* [74].

"And I was 'round when Jesus Christ had his moment of doubt and pain. Made damn sure that Pilate washed his hands and sealed his fate!"

"WTF!" thought BoJo. "How old is this guy and just how far along the road to senile dementia is he?"

"Pleased to meet you. Hope you guess my name. But what's puzzling you, is the nature of my game."

"Game?" BoJo wondered. "Is this for real, or is it just a mind game?"

"I stuck around St. Petersburg when I saw it was a time for a change. Killed the czar and his ministers. Anastasia screamed in vain."

"Ah got it," ejaculated BoJo. "Are you related to Vladimir Putitin?" But the crazy hat-man just smirked a condescending smirk, waved his tiny little hands negatively and repeated his riddle.

"Pleased to meet you. Hope you guessed my name. But what's confusing you is just the nature of my game."

"You just said that before? And, you are right. I am confused!" BoJo scratched his head and re-tussled his hair as it had somehow miraculously developed a parting.

---

[74] SARCHASM: The gulf between the intelligent author of a sarcastic comment and the bozo who just doesn't get it.

"Just as every cop is a criminal. And all the sinners saints. As heads is tails. Just call me Blank Strap. 'Cause I'm in need of some restraint."

"Blank Strap? Do you mean Jock Strap? It sounds like you have some sympathy with the Devil! With all this crazy stuff going on around here, I wouldn't be surprised," BoJo exclaimed. But the hat-man continued.

"So, if you meet me, have some courtesy. Have some sympathy, and some taste. Use all your well-learned politesse. Or I'll lay your soul to waste."

"What do you mean? Lay my soul to waste? I thought this was just a riddle guessing-game? Like the one about 'Why is a raven like a writing-desk?'" spluttered BoJo with deepening concern and in an attempt to distract the crazy hat-man from his song by throwing a riddle with no answer into the mix.

"Tell me BoJo, what's my name? Tell me honey, can ya guess my name? Tell me BoJo, what's my name? I tell you one time, you're to blame."

BoJo was suddenly scared. The crazy hat-man was metamorphosising into something much darker and more and more evil by the minute.

"I'm out of here! But, if I have to guess your name, I would have to say it's the Mad Hater!" exclaimed BoJo.

28.	The Mad Hater

"Is that one 't' or two? Oh, sorry. I mean one spoon or two - of sugar in your hot covfefe? You know what they say, 'A spoonful of sugar helps the Clorox to go down, in the most delightful way'" he said 'sarcastically'.

"Aaaaaaarrrghhhhh! I don't want any covfefe! Nor do I want any Clorox, even with a spoonful of sugar – whatever that is all about. Just get me out of here! Beam me up Scotty!" screamed BoJo, thinking for a moment that he was on some sci-fi planet full of crazy *Ripofflican Klingons* [75] intent on destroying Earth in a 1970's episode of Star Trek.

Although he didn't know it at the time, BoJo wasn't far wrong about the planet being destroyed. It was just an unlucky Freudian slip. And likewise, he had no idea what was rolling around in the Mad Hater's brain for him to make the weird reference about Clorox. He would only find that out much, much later – along with the rest of the world.

"I don't care about your name!! You are just some kind of anti-war-mongering Devil in politician's clothing, with a stupid hat and a big tie made in China! Please, let me out of this crazy party!" shouted BoJo.

SYMPATHY FOR THE DEVIL – ROLLING STONES
https://www.youtube.com/watch?v=lvlM3-kbBIg

"You mean you want to leave the Conservatories and join the Labial Party and vote against BREXIT like you did in the beginning?" the Mad Hater – living up to his new name - gleefully barbed BoJo.

"Yes! I mean no! I mean get me out of this crazy covfefe party. You are all completely and utterly, stark-staring, raving lunatic party, bonkers here!"

There was a maniacal, demonic cackle from the Mad Hater. "We're all mad here. I'm mad, you're mad. You must be or you wouldn't have come here!"

BoJo spun on his heels and bolted for the door and out into the relative sanity of the forest. And, as he ran down the Yellow-Brick Road, he could hear the Mad March Hare singing a little nursery rhyme.

---

[75] RIPOFFLICAN KLINGONS: A bunch of rich politicians who are desperately trying to cling on to their money and lifestyle by pretending that Climate Change does not exist.

Twinkle, twinkle little bat!
How I wonder what you're at. . . !
Up above the world you fly
like an ICBM in the sky

When he finally got the courage to look back over his shoulder, he could see the Mad Hater having an *Iranoleptic Fit* [76]. But BoJo just kept on running, like Forrest Gump, in the hope that he could make it out of the blast zone before the missiles hit.

Run BoJo, run!

---

[76] IRANOLEPTIC FIT: The frantic dance performed just after you realize that there are a bunch of ICBMs heading your way, and that maybe, just maybe, your foreign policy sucks because pulling out of that Iran Nuclear Arms Treaty might not have been a good idea after all.

11

MEANWHILE PART 5 – KUNG FU FIGHTING.

Meanwhile...

Meanwhile, the Queen of Queens wasn't letting up on the Trumper.

"McDOOONNNAAALLLDDDT! McDOOONNNNAAALLLDDDT!"

"Yyess dear?"

"Nowz I'm hearing zat you ars also coozying ups tzu zat chinky chops Predisent Zi Jumpink off Chinas."

"Not so, Megalamania, dear. He has just made himself 'President for Life' and I just want to get some tips from him how to go about it."

"'Predisent for Laif!' Wotchu wants zat for? Yuse alreadies anointed yourselfd za 'Chosen One' andt za 'Man Viss za Best Vords' andt, ha, 'A Very Stables Genius'. Vhy yuse needt anozzer titles?"

"Oh, it just has a nice ring about it. Like . . . forever."

"Hhmmmm! Andt hows does yuse plannink on makink frendz viss him?'

"Oh. I am going to start a war!"

"VOTTT!!! A VORE?"

"Ah, no! Not a war-war with people up to their necks in mud and bullets. You know how my bone spurs will start playing up if they think I might get dragged into a real war! No, this is going to be a 'Trade War'."

"Ach, reallies! Howz youse thinks zat youse vill beat za Chinese at zat? Ze are tzso unscrutibles zat youse can't tell vat zey are sinking."

"I have a *cunning plan* [77] that I have thought up with my Great and Infinite Wisdom. I will do one of my 'Art of the Deal', deals with him but I'm going to call it a 'Trade War' instead so that the American people won't understand it."

"Ha! Vot do you know aboutz international trade dealz andt so-calledt 'Trade Wars'? Alls you knows abouts fightink za Chinese iss vat youse learnt fromz zat song, Kingk Kongk Fighting!"

"You mean Kung Fu Fighting! And it's a great song!"

KUNG FU FIGHTING – CEE LO GREEN & JACK BLACK
https://www.youtube.com/watch?v=5I2MHj1iDIU

"Ya. Vell yous certainlies looks like zat fat Kungk Fu Panda! Youse haff no problemz losingk monies viz American dealz neffer minds ven you gets ups against sum smart-ass Chinese business typhoon."

"That's not fair . . ."

"McDoonaldt! Youse are ze only personz I know zat had a casino zat lost millionz off dollarz! Ze Natives Indianz can makez monies on casinos evon ven yours friendz at ze Rippofflican Party don'tz allows zem to votes just cos zey don'tz have propers addressez on za reversationz."

"It's OK Mellymamia. I have this guy called Peter Navarro as my Trade Advisor. He is there to provide me with the underlying data that can confirm my intuition on trade. And my intuition is always right in these matters - because Navarro always tells me so."

"Ach! He tsounds like a 'Yes Man' tzo me. Vot color iss hiz nose?"

---

[77] CUNNING PLAN: A catchphrase often used in the Blackadder TV series. Usually refers to a really dumb idea thought up by a less than bright assistant or advisor. It's taken up by the Trumper because he is actually dumber than the assistant and hadn't got any better ideas. Then, bragged about by the Trumper as his own idea, till it goes horribly wrong – as it always does. So, the Trumper then blames it completely on the assistant who gets fired and vilified on Twatter. Replay for the next cunning plan, ad-infinitum.

"But Mollymalonia! Not many people know this, but he has written lots of books about Tschina and he has an economic guru helping him called Ron Vara, who is a professor at Harvard."

"McDonaldtt! Youse ares tzo dumbt sometimes! If youse didt za New Yorkz Timez crossvord pizzle intstead off just looking at all za scandal pictures in za Nationalz Enquiries youse maybe cattch on tooze ze fact zat Ron Vara iss justs an anagram off Navarro."

"You mean that Ron Vara doesn't exist? It's just Peter Navarro's imaginary friend?"

"Off courses he doesn'ts exist. He iss just za fig-leaf off Navarro's imaginationz. And all zose poor farmerz zat voted for you vill be suffering fromz *cashtration* [78] venn zey can'tz sell zere soya beanz to za Chinese andt you haff choppedt offz zere income streamz."

"But it will work, I'm certain. My intuition is always right!"

"Doonaldt! Vy doos you neffer listenz to anies advices? Andt haff youse neffer heard za fairy ztory abouts 'Jack Off andtz za *Soyuz Beanstalkz*[79]'?"

"No, what's that about? My mother never read me fairy stories at bedtime. She just read the latest entries in my bankbook for the money Dad had deposited in my trust fund account. They always made me go to sleep with a smug, self-satisfied smile on my face."

---

[78] CASHTRATION: The end result of starting a trade war and putting tariffs on the importation of household products made in a country run by an autocratic ruler-for-life who is at least 10 times smarter than you are, which renders your own countrymen – particularly soya bean farmers - financially impotent for an indefinite period.

[79] SOYUZ BEANSTALK: The back story, or rather back fairy story, is that Russians found some soya bean plants in the fields surrounding the former Chernobyl Nuclear Power Plant (the one that exploded!). The beans seemed to have some unusual characteristics so they sent them to their Space Station in one of their Soyuz Spacecraft to see what would happen. When they brought them back to earth, they realised that the beans had genetically mutated and exhibited some strange democratic growth tendencies. Naturally, the Russians wanted nothing to do with anything remotely democratic, so they used a drone to drop the 'Soyuz Beans', as they became called, over the border in China. When the Chinese found out, they, realised that they could have a major resurgence of 'Tiananmen Square Fever' if their huge population ever started eating them. Even worse if someone took any to Hong Kong, as there were already a 'few' problems the Party was pretending didn't exist. The solution was to do a 'Trade Deal' with a dumb American and let him worry about democracy and its side effects. Ha so!

"Ach! Dinner und Blotzen! Didt yous neffer read bookz venn yous ver a kidt? Do yous aktualliez know howz too read? Sumtimez I see yous making stuff upps venn yous shuldt be readink za teleprompterz! Ze cablez-carz newz channelz keeps making jokes abouts yous not beingk ables tzo readt."

"Of course, I know how to read! I know my ABC – my Dad taught it to me and all the rhymes to remember it."

A is for Asshole – You meet lots of those,
B is for Buttocks – Wrapped in Pantyhose,
C is for C...

"STOP!!! Enoughs! I chust don'ts vant to knowz za rest!"

"OK, OK! So, tell me the 'Jack Off and the Soyuz Beanstalk' story."

"Okayz! Vell, zere vas ziss poor vidowdt farms lady calldt Mrs. Off andt she hadt onlies von cow. Von day she iss really broke and needs za monies, zo she tellz her son Jack tzoo takez za cow tzoo za market andt sells itz. Zo Jack Off setz off mitt za cow."

"I'm beginning to enjoy this story already!" said McDonald.

"Anyvays. Alongz za roadt he meetz za Chinaman whose smilz a lots, giffs Jack Off a piecez off vunderful chocolates cake, andt offerz himz sumz Magic Soyuz Beanz as a 'Trade Dealz' fors za cow. Jack Off sinkz zat he iss a vizz-kid, vheeler-dealers and zat doingk 'Trade Dealz' iss eazy-peazy – particularlies viz za simple Chinaman. Tzo he tradez za cow for za Magic Soyuz Beanz."

"Yeah! I'm all with Jack. I would have done that too!" said the Trumper excitedly.

"Vait! Holdt yourz crazies horses! Letz me carries on viz za stories."

"Okay, okay."

"Venn Jack getz homes vizz za Magic Soyuz Beanz, hiz muzzer goes interballiztic. 'Yous stupidoz idiotz!! Jack Off bys name Jack Off bys naturez! All zat jacking hazz puddltz yous tinys brainz!' Jack triez tzo cunvintz her, tellink her, 'Itz OK, Mum. Za Chinaman iss paying nows coz he hass tzo buy za foodz for za cow.' Buts Mrs Off iss tzoo pizzed off. 'Youse dunderkopf!' Andt she throwz za beanz outs offs za vindow."

"Oh dear! Why did she do that? What happened next?" McDonald asked, now completely caught up in the story.

"Vell, nexts mornink ven Jack vakes up andt looks outsidez za vindow zere is ziss HUGE Soyuz Beanstalks. Jack Off hass neffer seenz anysink tzo talls. Itz eeffen taller zan za fairies stories zat peoplez tells about za mythicalz *Mexicanz Borders Vall*[80]!"

"Mullyberria! You are really upsetting me now. I think you are making this story up. The Mexican Border Wall is real. I have seen it. I have written my name on it with a Sharpie . . ."

"Shutz ups McDoonaldt! Lets mees finishes!"

"Oh, okay dear."

"Nowz. Vere vass I? Ach, yesz. So, Jack Off decidez zat he vill climbp ups za Soyuz Beanstalk tzo sees vat iss at za tops. Hiz muzzer iss franticks buts he keeps on climbink. Venn he getz to zat tops off za beanstalkz he iss in za cloudz and seez za bigk castles mit za signz zat says."

Keep Out – Especially Conservative Ripofflicans
By Order of Brendan Aiden Roan Arlen Conan Kieran O'Bama

"Jack iss chust about tzo ignorez za signz and ziss elft popz out froms behind a cloudz andt sayz, 'Heyz! I vuldn't goes inn zere iffs I vos youse'. 'Vy notz?' sez Jack, 'Whos iss ziss guys Brendan Aiden Roan Arlen Conan Kieran O'Bama?' Ze elft lookz ats himz laik he iss crazies. 'Youse don'ts knowz? He iss za biiggkestz, baaddarsed, black, Irish giantz zat youse haff effer seenz. Weez shortenz hiss name byz ussink hiss innitialz, B.A.R.A.C.K O'Bama! Sometimez we chust callz hims 44'."

"But what's Jack going to do?" chimed in McDonald.

"Vell, Jacks Offz by names, Jacks Offz by naturez! He'z goink toos ignork za signz and goes intoz za castle. Andt in zere hez seez three boxez viz za inscriptionz on zem. Von sed 'DEMOCRACY'. Von sed 'TRUTH'. Andt za sird von sed 'INTEGRITY'."

---

[80] MEXICAN BORDER WALL: A mythical structure. A beautiful wall. Allegedly, 2500 miles long – from shining sea to shining sea. Supposedly, bigger than the Great Wall of China (just to annoy the Chinese). Reputedly, better at keeping out the Scottish than Hadrian's Wall (mainly because there aren't any Scottish in Mexico). Purportedly, less likely to fall than the Berlin Wall (because all the East Germans are on the inside this time). Apparently, capable of crossing rivers, plains, mountains, swamps ravines and any geophysical formation with no crack or break in its unrivalled continuity. Supposedly impossible to scale - unless someone brings ropes or ladders or, maybe, just a shovel. The thing that makes it truly mythical, though, is that Mexico is going to pay for it.

"Za Jacks Offz had nose ideas vot anies off zose vords meant but za boxez lookedt nice andt ferry expensivz. Soze, he decidedt to steals zem. Butz ass soonz az Jacks Offz picks ups za boxez zere iss a bigg roarz fromz za Giantz O'Bama. 'FEE FI FO FUM, I SMELL THE BLOOD OF A RIPPOFLICAN'. Jacks Offz iss reallies a scaredy catz, tzo he hots feets it backs tzo za Soyuz Beanstalks. Butz za Giant O'Bama cumz runnink outs off za castle, wavink hiss huge chopper arounds hiss headz."

"O'Bama had a huge chopper?" asked McDonald tremulously.

"Off courses he didt. He iss a giant andt he iss black. Soze, eats your heartz out mister!"

"That's not fair!"

"Noze. Itz yours problems. Letz me finishes za story. So, Jacks Offz triez to climbz back downz ass fazt ass he canz but he iss carrying za boxes toos andt – like yous – he only hass tiny handts. Za Giantz O'Bama iss cummink downz za beanstalks too, stills shoutingk 'FEE FI FO FUM, I SMELL THE BLOOD OF A RIPPOFLICAN' andt screamingk 'I WANT DEMOCRACY, TRUTH AND INTEGRITY BACK!'"

"WOW!" said McDonald, "So, what happens next?"

"Vell Jacks Offz makes its back tzo za ground butz za Giant O'Bama catches him andt chops offz hizz tiny handts soze zat he can't stealz anythinks anymores. Za Giant O'Bama grabz za boxes off DEMOCRACY, TRUTH andt INTEGRITY and take zem backs up za beanstalk to restore zem to zere propers place."

"But what about the Soyuz Beanstalk?" asked McDonald.

"Ach. Venn za Giant O'Bama gott back up tzo za castle he choppez downs za beanstalks viz hiss big chopper soze zat no onez canz effer bothers him agains!"

"So, why are you telling me this story?"

"McDONALDT! You haff to learns sumsthink, sometimez. Don'ts yu getz za cleffer underlyingk moral of za story about za Giant O'Bama restoring DEMOCRACY, TRUTH andt INTEGRITY zat voss stolen by za Jacks Off character?"

"Really is that what it's all about? I'm not interested in any of them."

"Zat iss part off it. But za mainz thingk is zat yous said zat Predisent Zi Jumpink off Chinas iss alvayz smilink. Ya?"

"Yes. And he gave me wonderful chocolate cake!"

"Vell. Remembers za Chinaman zat tradez za Soyuz Beanz for za cow? He vas alvays smiling a lots, ya? Oldt Chinese proverbs is 'Neffer trusts a mans who iss alvays smilink. He iss eithers trying to sells yous sumthingk or he iss stupid'. Soze don'ts sink zat zey are stupids andt don't trusts vat zey say abouts za trade dealz."

"But Melonomia, I am not worried about the Trade War. Or what it might do to the price of washing machines in Walmart. Who cares? I wouldn't know what a washing machine looked like if it jumped up and hit me in the face. If I accidentally-on-purpose 'lose' the Trade War, then President Schxzii will be so pleased that he will tell me the secret of how to become a President for Life. That's what I really want! And maybe he can also dig up some dirt on 'Sleepy' Joe Bidet too. I will remind him about that next time I have a chopper-talk."

"Ohs . . . Mein . . . Gott . . .! Iss zat your plan? Screws up za American peeples tzo much zat ze can'tz afford to even shop in za Wallzsmart andt Thrifty Storez? McDonaldt yous are suches an asseshole! Iz ziss anozzer ones off youse friend Putitin's ideaz?"

"No, it's Peter Navarro's . . ."

"Ach! Neffer mindt abouts not trusstingk a man who iss alvays smillingk. My Muzzer vas rights. She tolds me to neffer trusts a man viss a penis. Evens a small, teensy-weensy onse likes yourz!"

"But Millipedia . . . !"

"Shutz ups! One more 'buts' from yous andt itz 'Off vis yours headt!'"

Fade to black . . .

POSTSCRIPT

Hmmm! I wrote this chapter in February 2020. Now it's coming true!

MYSTERIOUS SEEDS FROM CHINA – CBS NEWS 29 JULY
https://www.youtube.com/watch?v=oea-8FFqyes

12

TWEEDLEDUMB & TWEEDLEDUMBER

Eventually BoJo slowed down when he figured that he had put enough distance between himself and the Mad Hater, not to mention the Mad March Hare and its ICBMs. "Poor Dormouse," he thought idly. "I hope he likes covfefe . . ."

"Curiouser and curiouser," he said once again to himself as there was no-one else to talk to. Or at least that is what he thought.

"Hey, you there! You with the funny blonde hair!" suddenly rang out in a way that seemed to be stereophonic. Like it was coming from a pair of Bose speakers on opposite sides of the room.

BoJo spun around and was startled to be confronted with what appeared to be two identical people. Identical in every way! Anyway, almost identical. Except . . .

Well, BoJo was not surprised to see that one of the 'identical' twins looked significantly like the Trumper. In fact, everyone he had met so far in this place seemed to look like the Trumper.

But the other 'identical' twin somehow, some way, seemed to bear more than a passing resemblance to someone he knew. Actually, it reminded him of someone he knew very well, but he could not quite put a finger on it. Who was it? Where had he seen that face before?

Then it hit him. "Aaaaarrgghh!" It was himself! "Oh noooooooo . . ."

Maybe, he thought, if you stay here too long, the people and characters you met started to morph so that they looked like you. That was a terrible realisation for BoJo. Simply terrible!

29.	Tweedledumb and Tweedledumber

"Wwwwho are you?" said BoJo *uffishly*[81] and not really wanting to know the answer.

"I'm Tweedledumb and he's Tweedledumber," they said in unison and stereo. So much so that BoJo had no idea which was which. But he just hoped that the one that looked sort of like himself was Tweedledumb . . .

"Er, which one of you said that?" queried BoJo.

"He did," they answered in unison and pointing fingers at each other.

"But you can't both be both of you," said BoJo.

"Yes, we can!" they responded. "It's not possible to be each other."

---

[81] UFFISH: A state of mind when the voice is gruffish, the manner roughish, and the temper huffish. BoJo was feeling all of those things. And more.

"Contrariwise," continued both of them, "if it was so, it might be; and if it were so, it would be; but as it isn't, it ain't. That's logic."

"Look," said BoJo, "one of you is pretending to be the Trumper and the other is pretending to be, er, me. So, which is it?"

"It's him," they both retorted, "and contrariwise it's me."

"OK! That's enough! I am going to give you a test to see who is who."

"That will be a good time for me and a good time for him," they said.

"First!" asked BoJo. "*Which of you has managed to shut down your government for your own political reasons* [82]?"

"Meeee!" they both gleefully chimed with amazingly accurate alacrity.

"Ah! Right. One each. That doesn't help," said BoJo. "*So, who, allegedly, has had affairs with American blondes and other women* [83]?"

"Me and me!" they said, clapping their tiny hands with bold bravado.

"Er, that's no good! Two each," grumbled BoJo. "*Well, who made campaign promises related to acronyms that were utterly fraudulent* [84]?"

"Me, me and me!" they both shouted as they jumped up and down giggling and laughing like a pair of crazy, adolescent schoolboys.

"Damn! Three each," muttered BoJo in exasperation. "OK! *Who thinks he is the best dealmaker in the world and thinks he can outsmart people in other countries when all others have failed* [85]?"

"Me, me and me and him!" they both shouted almost wetting themselves in excitement and dancing like demented dervishes.

"Right! Four each and still a tie," said BoJo shaking his head. "Oh dash! *Which one of you grew up in a privileged environment, went to fancy schools and never had to worry about money* [86]?"

"Me, me and me and him and me again!" they screamed back crazily.

"Aaargh! Five apiece!" grimaced BoJo, thinking furiously. "Right! *Which of you regularly mis-represents what happened in any given situation even though it was recorded and can be fact-checked, has an alternative truth and never admits that they are wrong* [87]?"

---

[82] ANSWER 1: Border Wall funding = Brexit prorogation
[83] ANSWER 2: Stormy Jack-Daniels = Jennifer Accuracy
[84] ANSWER 3: MAGA – Make America Great Again = NHS – National Health Service
[85] ANSWER 4: China Trade Deal = European Union Brexit Deal
[86] ANSWER 5: Wharton School = Eton/Oxford
[87] ANSWER 6: 20,000++ by July 2020 = A Very Large Number and Growing

"Wooo! Me, me, me and me and him and me again!" they babbled almost incoherent in their exuberance.

"Shhhhhugarlumps!!" hissed BoJo. "Okey dokey. *Who has been accused of illegal campaign spending* [88]?"

"Yeehaah! Me, me, me and me and him and me and him again!" they howled and hooted like a couple of horny hyenas.

"Shiztenhausen!!" spat BoJo. "Ha! This one's got to do it. *Which one has covered up a report on Russia meddling in elections* [89]?"

"Wheeeeeee! Me, me, me, me and me and him and me and both of us again!" they crowed again and again.

"Good-golly-gumdrops. I just don't jolly well believe this!" bemoaned BoJo. "Right! Now you are for it! *Which one of you has had a Campaign Manager with strong links to Russia* [90]?"

"NaaaNaNaNaaaNaa! Me, me, me, me, me and me and him and me and both of us double again!" they hooted and hooted in derision.

"Oh . . . my . . . God. Nnoooo! That's nine all! We need a tie-breaker!" said BoJo exasperatedly.

"OK. OK. OK! Right! Think about this one. This is the $64,000 question. Winner takes all. No holds barred. Deal, or no deal. Let's see who is the weakest link? I know the truth is out there. Give me your final answer . . . *Which of you is an ignoranus* [91]?"

"Are you talkin' to me?" they both chorused in unison, putting on their best Robert De Niro *Taxi Driver* accents.

ARE YOU TALKIN' TO ME? – ROBERT DE NIRO
https://www.youtube.com/watch?v=LpJOxbaC8YU

---

[88] ANSWER 7: Paying Stormy Jack-Daniels for silence = Brexit overspending on promos
[89] ANSWER 8: Miller-Lite Report = Intelligence and Security Committee (ISC) Report
[90] ANSWER 9: Paul Man O'War = Dominic Cummandgo
[91] IGNORANUS: A politician who is both stupid and an assh*le

"Well, of course, that's him!" said Tweedledumb emphatically.

"Woah there, buddy! It's obviously you!" said Tweedledumber, pointing angrily. Well, as angrily as tiny little fingers can point.

"No, it's you. It's not me!"

"No, it's not me! It's you!"

"No, it's not!"

"Yes, it is!"

"Contrariwise it's you!"

"No! Contrariwise it's you!"

BoJo stood back and watched. It looked like his last question had made them each throw their rattles out of their respective baby buggies.

> *Tweedledumb and Tweedledumber*
> *Agreed to have a battle*
> *For Tweedledumb said Tweedledumber*
> *Had spoiled his nice new rattle.*

"Well, I'm getting the British Army to fight you," said Tweedledumb.

"Then I'm going to get the American Marines," said Tweedledumber.

"OK. I'm getting the ANZACs like in WWII," said Tweedledumb

"Ha! I'll get my friend Rocket Man on my side," said Tweedledumber.

"So! I'll get the Canadians. They're half-Brits," said Tweedledumb.

"Well! I'm picking the Chinese on my team," said Tweedledumber.

"Oooh! Then I'm choosing NATO!" said Tweedledumb.

"So, what! I'm gonna ask my Russian buddies to help. They are experts at invading countries!" said Tweedledumber in what was probably one of the truest things he had said in a long, long time.

But, suddenly, a shadow fell across the argumentative double-dimbos. They looked up and there was a Death Star hovering somewhat significantly and ominously above them in the sky.

Then a giant hologram of Darth Vader appeared, and swooped silently down from the Death Star with his billowing black cape looking like the wings of a big black crow.

> *Just then flew down a monstrous crow,*
> *As black as a tar-barrel*
> *Which frightened both the dimbos so,*
> *They quite forgot their quarrel*

"Hey, you two dumb-ass's!" resonated that deep, dark, mellifluous yet frightening voice. "Shut the f*ck up. If anyone is going to destroy this planet and life as you know it, it's going to be me! So, stop this p*ssy play-fighting and get on with the rest of the story!!!!"

"We are not play-fighting. This is real," the Tweedle Twins argued.

"Just do as I say! I haven't got time to hang around here. It's almost lunch time and it's penne all'arrabbiata on the menu at the canteen today."

And with that undisputedly Imperial command, the hologram vanished, and the Death Star disappeared from view at warp speed.

DEATH STAR CANTEEN – EDDIE IZZARD
https://www.youtube.com/watch?v=7p5KpjR93SE

"Ooooer!" said Tweedledumb.

"Oooops!" said Tweedledumber.

"How did that happen?" they said in unison, "That Death Star is supposed to be in a galaxy far, far away, and in a completely different story, even if it was inexplicably in this time zone, contrariwise"

"I think we had better be Best Friends Forever again. OK?" they chimed to each other.

At this point they both tried to give each other a hug but their rotund overweight bodies, short arms and tiny little hands made it impossible and they just looked like a couple of Sumo wrestlers bumping up against each other, testing each other's lard factor.

BoJo, who had been quietly watching the whole proceedings since he asked his last and most important question, slowly backed away and decided to leave the Tweedles alone for now and move on before an intergalactic World War III broke out across numerous time zones.

But it had been a somewhat sobering experience for BoJo as he realised there were some horribly similar parallels between himself and the Trumper.

Of course, BoJo being BoJo, he was more concerned with political survival than what other people thought about him . . .

So engrossed was BoJo in himself – a not unusual state of being for him - that he almost bumped into the White Rabbi again as it crossed the road in front of him. But, like before, the White Rabbi ignored him completely and just stared at his watch.

"Oyvey! I'm late. I'm late. For a very important date! I'm late. I'm late. They're going to close the gate! I'm late. I'm late. I'm late. I'm late. I'm late. I'm late. I'm late!"

And then quickly ran off into the bushes muttering to himself.

Pondering once again on his own self-preservation – a topic on which he had spent many, many hours of his life doing – BoJo meandered along the Yellow-Brick Road.

"What was that conversation I had with Humpty Trumpty about a Self-Preservation Society?" thought BoJo. But then he remembered that Trumpty had fallen off his beloved wall and smashed into a thousand and one pieces – though he did not hang around to count them - so he could not be exactly sure. But there really did not seem much point in forming a Self-Preservation Society with someone who obviously was not very good at it.

He also idly wondered what the White Rabbi was talking about – being late for closing the gate – but was too busy focusing on his own problems to give it much thought.

This was something he would come to regret later . . .

13

MEANWHILE PART 6 – CRIMES IN CRIMEA

Meanwhile...

Meanwhile, someone named McDonald was still in trouble.

"McDOOOONNNAALLLDT!! McDOOOONNNAALLLDT!!"

"Yes, dear?"

"Vots all ziss viz za Wolf Blizzard andt Jake Trapper on za CNN abouts Ukraine? Zey are saayingk zat Putitin hass stolen sum bitz of za countries called Crimea or Urea or somesingk. Is ziss anozzer von of youse dirty trickz tzo sneaks offs viz sum mores Pee-Peeing Russian hookerz?" grilled the Queen of Queens.

"No, no Minniemousia! It's all about smearing 'Sleepy' Joe and 'Crooked' Hillarious and proving Russia didn't help win the election."

"Butz McDonaldt!" she replied. "All zat stuffs iss true! Putitin dids everrysink to make sure zat you von, coz he vanted a new puppetz."

"Mellynoname! That's not fair!"

"Vell vot haff youse been doingk in za Ukraine? Youse betterz not haff been nearz za Russian hookerz - or I vill chops offs youse balls"

"Nooo dear! Roody-Doody has been doing it all. He set up some shady things for me in Ukraine with his buddies Levee and Ignor – the Ukranian/Russian Heavy Mob. They have this great company called 'Fraud Guarantee Inc.' that has been helping me denounce my political opposition for being corrupt, take over their gas supply company, slow down their defense aid money, take out the US Embassy staff who tried to stop me and altogether made my BFF Putitin very happy".

"Ah! Szo, zats vy you are szo busy on za cell phone all za times!"

30. 3 Stooges a.k.a. Tweedledumbski, Tweedleroodyski & Tweedledumberski

"Yes, dear! And I have involved Mike 'Silverback' Penice, Bill 'No Collusion' Barf and Mike 'Koch Addict' Pompayo. Plus, those dumbos - *'The Three Amigos'* [92] - Rick 'The Crotch' Perrier, Kurt 'The Hair' Volkswagen and Gordon 'Egghead' Sunderland are the front-men. So, I can blame it all on them and throw them under the bus if I need to."

"Andt exactlies how yuse going to explainz all of ziss if it leakz out?"

"I am just saying there was no *Quid Pro Quo* [93] and if I say it often enough people will think I actually know what it means."

"Vot kindt off 'Quid' are yuse trying to say zat zere isn't?"

"Well, I have been telling everyone that the $400 million military aid was not connected to the Ukrainians digging up dirt on 'Sleepy' Joe Bidet and them saying that they were helping 'Crooked Hillarious' and the Dimocrats, rather than it was the Russians who were helping me."

---

[92] THE THREE AMIGOS: A movie with a dumb plot about three dumb movie stars who are mistaken for real heroes by some Mexican villagers who want them to bring down the bad guy, El Guapo. They are called Lucky Day, Dusty Bottoms, and Ned Nederlander. The parallels with Perrier, Volkswagen and Sunderland are unique – even to the fact that they gave themselves the name 'The Three Amigos' and being so dumb that they did not see that their actions would bring down El Guapo Trumper. Is it Mexican revenge?

[93] QUID PRO QUO: A Latin phrase that uses the slang term for a British £1 roughly translated to mean that 'I won't give you a quid unless you do me a favor, though'

"Ach! You sink all za Slavic's are tzo stupid to fall for zat? Blamink zemsefls for doink sumsink illegal instead of wot everyvon knowz zat it voss your buddy Putitin? It'z like ze are punching zemselfs in za feces."

"It's OK! When things were getting too hot I just sent out Mick 'Chipmunk Cheeks' Malarkey to have a press conference where he told everyone that of course we did a Quid Pro Quo, that we do that all the time and tell them to 'Get over it!'. OK . . .? So now I can fire him later."

"Butt McDonaldt, zat iss very naughty andt underhandt and yuse vill endt up viss no friendts at all."

"That's really no problem. I can just go and buy some more!"

"Ya sure! Zats vot youse alvayss doos. Everyvonn iss vunderful and really gut at zere job until yuse screw up - but don't admitz it. Zen you blame zem and say 'You're firedt!' like vot yuse uset tzo do on zat fake Reality TV show

31.   Simon Chipmunk or Mick Malarkey?

'Za Apprenticed'. Andt vot happenz if zey try to peach yuse?"

"You mean impeach me? Huh! Well – the more I think about it, Old Billy was right. Let's kill all the lawyers and kill 'em tonight!"

"Buts McDonaldt. Ifs yous go tzoo far, zat Nantzy Pelota might chust do somesink really cleffer to outwittz youse!"

"No way! I can beat her every time. Just look at how I handled her in the Oval Office when she and Jerry Noodler came to talk to me and Mike Penice about infrastructure. And then I beat her by walking out on her when she and Chuck Sherbert came to talk about Syria. I called her a 'Third-rate politician' when they questioned my decision on pulling out the troops. Plus, I have wily Mitch 'The Grim Reaper' McConman as the Capo dei Capi in the Senate and he will do whatever I tell him to do."

"McDoonaldt! Don'tcha underestimated zat Nantzy Pulitzer. She's may be oldt and a bits crinkly round ze edges, buts she iss a real shmart cookie-cutter. She's tolds everybodies zat yous hads za 'meltdown' in za Syria meetingk," warned the Queen of Queens ominously.

"But, Millemiglia, she is no match for the Trumper!"

"Ha! Zen vhy vere youse tzo stupid to tweet zat pictures off Nantzy Pantz waggingk her fingker ats alls of youse oldt men in za Cabinet Room? Youse sed zat she voss havink an 'unhinged meltdown'. Ya right! Tzoo za rests off za world its looked likes she voss za toughs Headmiztressz tellink offs a lots off naughties littles schools boyz!"

"Aaw! Molybdenum! That's not fair . . ."

32.   Now, Tell the Truth. Which One of You is a Very Naughty Boy?

"McDonaldt, I amz varnink yous fors yours own goodt. Don'ts tries tzo playz za smart-asses and telling alls yours versionz off altered realitiez viz me. Remembers, I haff been vatchingk alls yours dumbp 'Trumper-Towers-alls-ovfer-za-worldt' real-estate dealz, za 'How-toos-loose-moniez' Trump Casinoez, plusz za 'Mikey-Mices' Trumper University andt za 'Letz-giff-all-za-charrity-moniez-tzo-myselff-instedt-off-kidz-viz-cancer' Trumper Foundationz!"

"But Millymartini . . . !"

"Shutz ups! One more 'buts' from yous andt itz 'Off vis yours headt!'"

Fade to black . . .

14

I AM THE WALRUS - GOO GOO G'JOOB

BoJo was so engrossed in thinking about all his problems that he had not
realised at all that he had meandered onto a beach which had
unnervingly appeared, or at least it appeared to have appeared, from
absolutely nowhere. He didn't know it, but it was the Big Pond beach.

While it was somewhat disconcerting to suddenly find oneself on a
beach, so far, it was one of the better places that BoJo had found himself
since he had been in Trumperland. So, he wasn't going to complain
about it. At least not for a while anyway. He stopped and sat down on a
rock on the edge of the beach and just stared at the water with nothing
whatsoever connecting one neuron to the next in his brain. It was a
lovely feeling – or rather lack thereof – and one which he enjoyed on a
regular basis. In fact, a little too often if the truth were known.

The beach was covered in oysters or at least oyster shells. It looked to
BoJo that someone or something had been along the beach before he got
there and opened all the oysters and eaten the contents. But inside each
one there was a little slip of paper, like in a fortune cookie, and there
were strange little slogans and phrases written on them.

Some of them were what politicians jokingly call *'oysters'* [94]. But
many of them BoJo didn't understand at all.

---

[94] OYSTERS: Yiddishisms which politicians sprinkle in their speeches in order to raise
campaign funds from the Jewish community. Corblimey hasn't caught on to this yet.

The obvious ones were things like 'Oy vay' and 'If life gives you potatoes, make Latke' and 'You had me at Shalom and *'Never mind the quality, feel the width'*[95] and 'Curb your enthusiasm'. But, many of them were phrases that he had heard on the news, though he wasn't really sure that they were very good for raising campaign funds. Well, at least they weren't unless you had a devoted, cult-like following that thrived on slogans, believed all conspiracy theories and everything Foxy News or Murdork Press and other right-wing media splurted out. Hmmmm!

BoJo couldn't figure out how 'There were good people on both sides' and 'I would give myself an A+' could possibly help raising money unless your party followers were primarily unquestioning sheep. Oh, how he could wish for more of those in the Conservatory Party!

And then there were slogans like 'Quid Pro Quo', 'Get over it', 'Digging up dirt' and 'Everyone was in on it' along with 'Lock Her Up', 'No Collusion', 'We're going to win bigly' and 'No Smocking Gun'. Which were odd in themselves irrespective of the misspelling or use of previously unknown words.

But there were others that were even stranger, such as 'A hand grenade waiting to explode' and 'I don't want to be involved in any drug deal'.

"Who on earth would ever say that in politics?" he wondered out loud.

Actually, he had not realised that he had said it out loud. It seemed that talking to himself had become virtually the norm since he had been in Trumperland, although he mistakenly considered that he was the most intelligent person that he could possibly talk to in this place.

BoJo was suddenly very startled when there was a sound like a large lump of fish tail being slapped in someone's face. And that, somewhat bizarrely, was coupled with a snort that seemed to have emanated from the depths of a cavernous stomach and then had been finally filtered through an oversized white-wash brush.

---

[95] NEVER MIND THE QUALITY, FEEL THE WIDTH: The tongue-in-cheek title of a 70's British TV sitcom about two tailors in London. One was Jewish and the other Irish Catholic creating many opportunities for amusing inter-religious bickering. The title is an obvious Yiddish humorous reference to the piece of cloth being proffered as suit material. Would probably be very un-PC in today's religiously divided communities.

BoJo turned to see what had made the noises and was surprised to see a very, very large walrus with a significantly oversized moustache – even by walrus standards – though exactly who sets the standards and specifications for walrus moustaches has been in dispute for many years.

"Er. Who are you?" queried BoJo, at the same time reeling back a few paces from the extremely fishy breath emanating from the Walrus.

"The name is Bolt-On." said the Walrus in a manner that belied the bizarre fact that a walrus could not only speak, but also knew its name.

"Oh, you mean like Bolton in Lancashire, where it rains all the time, or Bolton, as in Michael Bolton, the singer who used to have all the curly hair?" queried BoJo.

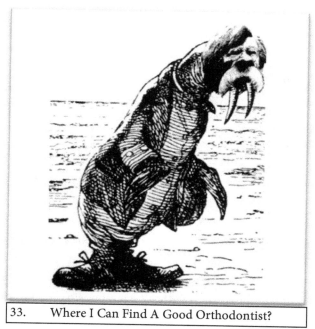

33.	Where I Can Find A Good Orthodontist?

"Neither! Do I look like either of those things?" riposted the Walrus, very huffily. "In the next breath you will be calling me the egg-man."

"Well, man you've been a naughty boy. You let your face grow long." pointed out BoJo, rather obviously, if not a little rudely at the same time. It seemed like he had suddenly lost all the good manners they had taught him at Eton since he had been in Trumperland.

"Maybe that is because I am the Walrus, goo goo g'joob." responded Bolt-On the Walrus, perhaps a little obviously, though the second part of his comment seemed to ring a dormant bell in BoJo's overtaxed brain.

"I've heard that phrase before," he thought to himself, "but it beats me where exactly." Not realising he was only two letters away from the answer, he absentmindedly ran his hands through his mop-head of hair.

"But you seem to be one of the first people I have met in this place that does not look like the Trumper. How did you manage that?" asked BoJo while wondering where he had seen the moustachioed face before.

"It's not easy, I can tell you." said Bolt-On the Walrus. "You have to work very hard at maintaining your own opinions and beliefs and not just agreeing with everything the Trumper says or does or wants to do. You only have just one lifetime and it's really hard sticking to it."

JUST ONE LIFETIME – STING AND SHAGGY
https://www.youtube.com/watch?v=DNobqcfLb2Y

"Why is that so difficult?" asked BoJo.

"Because the Trumper is surrounded by so many sycophants, servile flatterers, fawning parasites, bootlickers, groveling groupies and 'yes-men' with brown noses that he actually believes in the alternate reality that he self-generates because they all agree with him completely," responded Bolt-On the Walrus without even pausing for breath.

"I say! That's a bit harsh isn't it?" said BoJo, while silently wondering what the Walrus' opinion might be of him, but not daring to ask.

"Look, in another lifetime and in another reality, what I would call a real-world reality, the alternative one to the alternative reality that spins around the Trumper, I used to be what was called a National Security Advisor. That meant I advised the Colored House about who we should bomb the shit out of, who we should sell arms to, who we should not sell arms to, who we should fight wars against and who we should have as our allies. And it was lots of fun!" bragged Bolt-On the Walrus.

"Oh, I see. You mean it was a bit like playing Risk but with real bullets, bombs and nuclear weapons? Sort of like Eddie Izzard on steroids!" said BoJo, which went completely over the Walrus' head as he had no idea what *Risk* [96] was, nor *Eddie Izzard* [97].

RISK – EDDIE IZZARD
https://www.dailymotion.com/video/x2vq9a4

"Risk? Of course, there were risks! Being a 'hawk' and starting wars in other people countries is always a risk. But it's mainly risky for them as we are usually more than ten thousand miles away," chortled the Walrus.

"But," responded BoJo, "their planes and missiles can fly from there to here and do rather a lot of damage. What about Pearl Harbour? And, for 9/11, their bad guys flew in your planes to get to New York!"

"Herrumpf!" coughed the Walrus. "Well, I had it all under control and then all sorts of other people started getting in on the act."

"Yes, I noticed." said BoJo. "The Trumper pissed off everyone in NATO, withdrew from the Iran Nuclear Treaty, cuddled up to Kim 'Billy the Korean Kid' Yung-One, got a call from Recep 'The Turkish Tyrant' Ne'erdoowell and dumped the Kurds, pulled out of Syria and opened the door for Vlad 'The Invader' Putitin and the Russians to become top dog in the Middle East. A pretty impressive track-record all round."

"And that is not all." said Bolt-On the Walrus in a melancholy tone. "I also had to deal with Jarhead Kushynumber trying to buy a 'Peace Deal' with the Palestinians for $50bn and mess around in Saudi selling American planes, weapons and bone saws. Believe it or not, I was trying to control the Trumper, but there were always too many side interests."

---

[96] RISK: A board game in the 60's where players tried to have world domination by throwing a dice and taking over countries. Apparently, it was Putitin's favourite . . .
[97] EDDIE IZZARD: A cross-dressing, transgender, personage who has called himself 'a lesbian trapped in a man's body'. Hence, would be considered part of the LGBTQ community that Ripofflicans, allegedly, don't actually believe exist.

"So, what happened in the Ukraine mess with Roody-Doody, Levee, Ignor and The Three Amigos?" queried BoJo.

"Ha! That was just the straw that broke the camel's back!" barked the Walrus, belching clouds of rotting fish-flavored vapor as he did so. "Those bozos were hatching some kind of crazy 'drug deal' which was so 'wacky-backy' that it was a like a hand-grenade with no pin. It was going to explode in someone's hand at any second. Typical Roody stuff!"

"Ah! Now I understand some of those oyster 'fortune cookie' remarks." said BoJo. "But what is the story with all these oysters?"

"Oh well, it was Thanksgiving, so the Carpenter and I went to Alice's Wonderland Restaurant. But she didn't have any turkey because the Trumper had pardoned them all so he could get in practice for pardoning all his crooked henchmen. The only thing Alice had available was Oysters a' la Fortune Cookie. So, we had those," replied the Walrus. "And the Carpenter and I ate the entire stock in the restaurant, much to Alice's annoyance. I have to admit that I ate the most, though think that Alice reckons that we were both very unpleasant characters."

ALICE'S RESTAURANT – ARLO GUTHRIE
https://www.youtube.com/watch?v=-yLg_bzwvxg

"So where is the Carpenter now?" asked BoJo.

"Oh, he has gone off to find seven maids with seven mops to clean up all the oyster shells and all this messy sand, though it's likely to take them half a year and even then I doubt it would be clear," he mused. "I just hope he doesn't bring seven brides for seven brothers by mistake!"

"And the other fortune cookie slogans?"

"Oh, they were from 'The Three Amigos' I think that Kurt 'Mr. Smoothie' Volkswagen came up with 'Quid Pro Quo' to try and throw the American public off the scent of what was essentially bribery and shaking down the new President of Ukraine by leveraging foreign aid," said Bolt-On the Walrus.

"That is the sort of activity that Mick 'Chipmunk Cheeks' Malarkey was telling everyone that they should 'Get over it'," he continued.

"Rick 'The Crotch' Perrier was involved in, allegedly, trying to get his buddies and donors into the Ukraine national gas company – which was just like the alleged 'dirt' they were trying to 'dig up' on Hunter Bidet. And, of course there was the classic 'Everyone was in on it' by Ambassador 'Egghead' Sunderland, confirming that everyone, from the Trumper down, knew what was going on and why," explained Bolt-On the Walrus, quite simply.

"It sounds like a mess," said BoJo.

"It was! And I told the Trumper that it was going to blow up in his face and create lots of problems, long before the Dimocrats started even thinking about the impeachment process. But he wouldn't listen to me. The man has the intelligence of a rotting cabbage!" said Bolt-On the Walrus shaking his head, tusks and moustache ruefully.

"Is that the reason the Trumper fired you?" queried BoJo.

"He didn't fire me! I quit!" shouted Bolt-On the Walrus angrily.

"Ok, OK, OK! I believe you!" said BoJo quickly, trying calm down the Walrus, who was significantly agitated by the contention that he was fired. "So, it seems that the Trumper upset your sense of institutional correctness ('Even those of a certified, war-mongering hawk', BoJo said quietly under his breath) by ignoring all the usual steps of government procedures and protocols. It sounds like he just wants to be an autocratic ruler."

Suddenly the melancholy Walrus launched into reciting a poem.

"The time has come," the Walrus said,
"To talk of many things:
Of shoes—and ships—and sealing-wax—
Of cabbages—and kings—
And why the sea is boiling hot—
And whether pigs have wings."

"Oh . . . My . . . God!" exclaimed BoJo. "Do you think the Trumper wants to be the King of America?"

"Well!" said the Walrus. "The Trumper can't seem to get his tiny hands around the basic fundamentals of our democracy, government and constitution. Plus, he certainly has the IQ of a testosterone-driven cabbage, which seems to be one of the fundamental qualifications of royalty, judging by your Randy Dandy's lack of judgement in having one of the Trumper's party pals, Jeffrey Schleppstein, as a best buddy."

"I say old chap, easy on the boy!" defended BoJo, possibly thinking of some of his own extra-curricular peccadillos and mis-deeds – though hotly denied in public. "He is, or at least was, the Queen's favourite son, but I am not sure how long that will last this time."

"I know there are occasional rumblings in the UK about whether we actually need royalty in the 21st century, but a least we have had a monarchy since time immemorial – even if the lineage may be a bit screwy. However, I admit that there has been a lot of interbreeding for reasons of national alliances – though probably no more than in the Georgia backwoods a' la *Deliverance* [98]," pointed out BoJo.

"Yes, that may be true," Bolt-On said, "but our backwoods boys don't get as much in their social security checks as your royals do!"

DUELLING BANJOS – DELIVERANCE
https://www.youtube.com/watch?v=gsC4kf6x_Q0

"Touché!" smiled BoJo testily while pointing out the obvious 'duuuuuh factor' to the Walrus. "But at least we don't need to have U.S. District Judge Ketanji Brown Jackson to rule who can and cannot be king and to be so specific– for the benefit of the Trumper – that the primary takeaway from the past 250 years of recorded American history is that Presidents are not kings."

---

[98] DELIVERANCE: A subliminally very frightening movie. Definitely enough to put you off hunting trips in the backwoods and make you think twice about having your kids join the Boy Scout's annual camp.

"Well, the whole thing is a mess and our so-called Cummerbund-in-Chief is meddling in many things he does not comprehend and some he cannot even spell correctly!" grumbled Bolt-On the Walrus

"Yes, I noticed the significant grammar and spelling errors in the Trumper Oyster Fortune Cookies with quotes like 'We're going to win bigly' and 'No Smocking Gun'," opined BoJo, who despite his many, many faults – too numerous to mention – actually can spell. And, while he often appears to make up *porky pies* [99], he doesn't invent new words.

"But what can I do to set it right?" asked Bolt-On the Walrus abjectly.

"You said a while ago that 'The time has come to talk of many things'," pointed out BoJo, "You must know all the inside stories and all the dirty linen. Why didn't you testify at the House Judiciary impeachment hearings?"

"Well, yes I could have. But then I would have to tell the truth – and that may have been very difficult," said Bolt-On the Walrus shaking his head slowly. "Particularly as I was a diplomat and civil servant!"

"Oooooh, yes!" responded BoJo. "And even harder for elected politicians. This concept of 'The truth, the whole truth and nothing but the truth' is really alien. Especially that last bit about 'And nothing but the truth'. There is just no wiggle room in that one!"

"Yes, I know!" said Bolt-On the Walrus, "And my many, many bits of truth are worth a lot of money. So, I don't just want to give them away!"

"Aaaahh, right on! I had heard that you are getting a $2 million 'tell-all' book deal . . ." said BoJo while wishing it were his.

YOU LIED – YES, PRIME MINISTER
https://www.youtube.com/watch?v=8keZbZL2ero

"Yep! And that one really has to be the truth, the whole truth and, maybe even, nothing but the truth," mused Bolt-On the Walrus.

---

[99] PORKY PIES: English Cockney rhyming slang. Porky Pies = Lies

"I guess it will be good to get your own back for the Trumper sacking you," said BoJo having had the unusual experience of sacking several MPs from the Conservatory Party for not agreeing with his 'party line' edict about BREXIT.

"Aaaargh!! I told you before, he didn't sack me. I resigned!!" shouted Bolt-On the Walrus.

"Yes, yes, yes! Sorry!" responded BoJo, also suddenly remembering how sensitive he had been to questions about his own brother, MP Jo Jockstrap, resigning from BoJo's government over disagreements about BREXIT, shortly after he had taken over from Theresa May-B'lieve.

"And you know what?" grumbled Bolt-On the Walrus through his moustache, "He actually had the gall and temerity to say that I screwed up regarding things I did with Gaddafly and his lover-buddy, Kim Yung-Ones. This is a guy whose grasp of geopolitics and geography is so bad that he thinks *Wakanda* [100] is a real country and that he is going to build his precious wall in Colorado. What a dummy! And he says I'm the one who is not smart . . ."

TRUMPER IS BUILDING A WALL IN COLORADO – CNN
https://www.youtube.com/watch?v=rn6mzlhx31c

Bolt-On the Walrus was gathering mental momentum and just kept rolling. "As everyone knows – well everyone except the Trumper - Colorado has a border with the US state of New Mexico, not the country of Mexico. Who is going to pay for that wall? Maybe the residents of El Paso to stop any more lunatic Trumper followers from coming and shooting up their Walmart again!"

---

[100] WAKANDA: The Trumper has been known to mention Wakanda, a fictional country created by Marvel Comics and home to the superhero Black Panther, as though it really exists and trades with the US. Possibly he wants to get some Wakandan Vibranium as he thinks it's either a very rare metal that will give him superpowers or a sex toy for one of his (alleged/denied) centerfold girlfriends. Of course, it's actually just comic currency.

And Bolton the Walrus just kept going, "I know I might sound angry now, but I'm not really worried. For sure, even though McConman won't allow me or any other witnesses to testify at the Senate trial, I will have my say in due course," he concluded very ominously.

"Hmmmmm! Er, yes! I had heard that last phrase on the US news, specifically on Lawrence O'Donnell's Last Word show. He knew it was super-dumb for the Trumper to say you weren't smart!" BoJo responded.

"Well, changing subjects! I would offer you one of these very tasty oysters, but The Carpenter and I seem to have eaten them all. And we have nothing else left in the larder. No cornflakes, no eggs, no yellow matter custard, no eggs, no crabalocker, no eggs, no semolina pilchards, and, definitely no eggs. It must have been that lazy Carpenter who ate them all and I bet he has sneaked off for a snoozy-woozy instead of sweeping up all the oyster shells and the sand on the beach," opined Bolt-On the Walrus.

"In that case, I think it's about time I moved on," said BoJo. "The tide is coming in and you are much more suited to the water than I am. I actually don't like getting my hair wet as it just goes straight, and I look like one of those Beatles from the 60's."

"I think you are right. I should get back to my roots and have a nice swim. After all, I am the egg man, I am the Walrus, goo goo g'joob."

And with that he turned and waddled into the sea.

I AM THE WALRUS – THE BEATLES
https://www.youtube.com/watch?v=D1jVie2fzog

BoJo slowly walked off the beach and set foot on the Yellow-Brick Road which had once again appeared, as if on command.

"Well, I know what I wish I could do, and that's get back to my roots, get out of this crazy place and back to reality," said BoJo out loud to himself – or at least that is what he thought.

There was a splash in the water behind him. So, he turned around to see the head of Bolt-On the Walrus sticking out of the sea and looking at him intently.

34.   Be Careful What You Wish For!

"Be careful what you wish for! Do you remember what John Lennon said?" asked Bolt-On the Walrus.

"No, what was it?" responded BoJo.

"Reality leaves a lot to the imagination!"

With that, he disappeared under the water, leaving BoJo pondering on the remark. As he did so, BoJo slowly – very, very slowly – came to the realisation as to where he had heard that 'Goo goo g'joob' phrase before. Yes! It was in the Beatles 'Magical Mystery Tour' TV film and the 'I Am The Walrus' vinyl *EP* [101] that his immigrant *Mum and Dad* [102], Stanley and Charlotte, had played incessantly in 1967 when BoJo was about three years old, growing up in New York City. He could never get to sleep because of John Lennon and the Beatles continuously singing that damn song!

"But . . . growing up in New York City!" As he thought about it, BoJo realised that it was yet another subliminal connection between himself and the *Trumper* [103], who had also been born and grew up in New York City with a European immigrant bloodline. "Oh Nooooooo!"

---

[101] EP: Does not stand for Extended Penis - shorter than everyone else's but technically improved. It's an Extended Play disc. Shorter than an Album, but longer than a Single.

[102] MUM AND DAD: Between them they have Russian-Jewish, Turkish and Germanic ancestry. BoJo is also a US Citizen, so, why does he want to be out of Europe so strongly?

[103] TRUMPER: Grandfather (not Father) was born in Germany. Mother was Scottish.

So internalised was he in thinking about growing up in New York that he almost bumped into the White Rabbi, yet again, as he crossed the Yellow-Brick Road in front of BoJo. But, like each time before, the White Rabbi ignored him completely and just stared at his watch.

"Oyvey! I'm late. I'm late. For a very important date! I'm late. I'm late. They're going to close the gate! I'm late. I'm late. I'm late. I'm late. I'm late. I'm late. I'm late!"

And then quickly ran off into the bushes muttering to himself.

Now BoJo had two things to worry about; New York and something about the gate. Shuddering, more than ever so slightly and trying to dismiss both of those thoughts from his head, BoJo wondered exactly what to do next.

But, as was often the case, nothing at all came into his mind . . .

15

MEANWHILE PART 7 – DO ME A FAVOUR, THOUGH

Meanwhile . . .

Meanwhile, back at the Colored House, McDonald was just about to get into trouble again, again.

"McDOOOONNNAAAALLDDT!! McDOOOONNNAAAALLDDT!!!"

"Er, yes, dear?"

"I toldt youse nott tzo mess viz zat Nantzy Pepsicola. Now she hass peached youse!!

"Er, well. Peached me? I think you mean the 'I-word'. You know I think that the I-word is a dirty, filthy, disgusting word!"

"Vot youse means, ze I-vord? Do youse means I-ncumpetant or maybe I-mpootent or I-lltampered or I-gnooriant or I-mmooral or perhaps even I-ndiscreedt or I-napproopriate or I-nsufferablez?"

"Er, well. No. I really can't say it. I will have to just spell it out. I mean I-m-p-e-a-c-h-m-e-n-t."

"Ach, yesz. Peachment! I toldt youse soz. Andt vots all ziss abouts za 'Perfects Calls' tzu za Ukrainze? Were youse trying to get za date viz za goot lookingk Russian calls girls againz? Youse vants one zat iss looking 'perfect'?"

"Melonmelonia, it had nothing to do with any call girls!"

"Ha! Pull ze ozzer leggsz, it haz ze jingle bells on."

"You know I don't do that, er, anymore. It wasn't me. And I never did it before anyway, either way. Well, not since I got caught," saying the last sentence almost under his breath.

"Vott vass zat youse saidt!?!"

"Er. Oh. I said, 'Don't give it a thought!'" said the Trumper trying desperately to think of some *ex-culpatory* [104] evidence or alibi that could explain it all away and get him off the Meellymania hook.

"Tzo, iff it voss nots about za calls girls, vot vass it's all abouts? Andt vy voss its tzo perfects zat Nantzy Polisi can peach youse for it?"

"Well, I told you before that Roody-Doody was setting things up for me. So, when everything was in place and the timing was right – meaning that Ukraine was desperate for the $400 million aid. Oh, and we had got rid of all the messy busy-bodies in the Kyiv Embassy - like that Marie Sonovabitch. Then, I called that joker, President Zabaglione."

"Andt ziss voss za 'Perfect Call'?"

"Yes, dear. We were talking about the usual 'men's stuff', and Zabaglione wanted to buy some more Javelin anti-tank missiles. So, I asked him to 'do me a favor, though'. And that was the time when I suggested he looked into 'Sleepy' Joe Bidet, his kid Hunter, 'Crooked' Hillarious and the D&C server. Nothing at all wrong with that. It was a 'perfect' deal."

"Vell vy didn'tch youse chust sell him za Javelins zen za Pentagoons vud be happies and its vud creates lottsa jobs at za Javelin factory?"

"I couldn't do that. Zabaglione would have fired them at Russian tanks and Putitin would have been very angry with me and possibly done something I wouldn't like in revenge."

"Ach! Like maybeez release zose sose-calledt pee-pee tapes?"

"Yes! I mean no!! It wasn't me! They don't exist!"

"Tzo vot didt yose do?"

---

[104] EX-CULPATORY: Some kind of excuse or defense, made by the Trumper to his current and ex-wives to try and explain away whatever it was he did with some other female that he should not have been doing, and which, while unlikely to be the truth, it still had to sound defensible, explainable, forgivable, justifiable, pardonable, passable, permissible, plausible, reasonable and above all, ever so slightly believable.

"I had this Whistleblower on my back who was telling all these stories about my 'Perfect Call'. So, I decided to release the cleaned-up memo of the call and call it a 'word-for-word transcript'. And I had the actual original transcript locked away in a very, very, very secure server."

"Butts, vy yous tzso stupids? Didn'tcha sink zat allz za peoples whose voss listening to za call knews zat vot youse say in za 'transcriptz' iss different from vot youse actuallies saidt?"

"I thought it would be fine. I never let people take notes anyway – especially when I'm talking to other world leaders - so I assumed that they would soon forget what was actually said. I know I do – so I just make up a new reality that suits the situation at that moment and then keep repeating it till I believe it myself – and everyone else does too."

"McDonald, ven youse ares doingk somesink zat iss not kosher, somebodies maybes hass a conscience abouts it and vants to tells everyone."

"Conscience? What's a conscience? I don't understand what that is."

CONSCIENCE & MEETING NOTES – YES, MINISTER
https://www.youtube.com/watch?v=jNKjShmHw7s

"Ach! Somesink vass missing in yours childhut! Maybees youse voss neffer actuallies a childt. Youse chust vent straights fromm beingk a baby to beingk an assholes!"

"But Mellymania, that's not fair."

"McDooonaldt, a conscience is zat little voices insides yours head zat sayz 'Maybe I shudent be doingk ziss?' or, 'Maybe zat person shudent be doingk zat'. Becoz its wrongk or illegal or badt for ze country or for za ozzer persons."

"I never ever, ever, ever have any thoughts like that. Why should I? I am always right, and I am always doing something for my own benefit. And if it's good for McDonald Trumper it must be good for the country. So, what could possibly be wrong with that?"

"Zat doos nots surprisingk me von littles bits. Butt youse might be surprisedt zat ozzer peoples zat vork in za govermment - evens some zat vork in zis Colored House – doose haff za conscience!"

"You mean that all those people who testified in the I-i-i-m-p-p-e-e-a-ch-ch-ch . . . thingy, are just doing it because they have a 'conscience'? As far as I'm concerned, they are rats or stoolpigeons or traitors or insubordinate to their Commander-in-Chief! How could they do that to me?"

"McDoonnaldtt! Venn ares youse goingk to understand zat ze U.S off A iss notts yours own private country? Its vass notts given tzo youse by yours Dad viss a $1 million gift card? Youse don'ts own it like za Trumper Organizationz. It belongks tzo za 330 million citizenz of ziss country! Youse can't chust do vot effer youse vants viz it."

"Why not? I am the President! I can do whatever I want!"

"Nots tzo fast mister! Youse haff tzo follow za rules off za government andt za laws andt za Consztitutionz."

"Well, the Constitution and the rules say that I can do whatever I want, and I can't be prosecuted for it. I could shoot someone on 5th Avenue, New York in front of the police and they can't arrest me. I have super-powers under Article II of the Constitution. I am above the law!"

"Ha! Yeah right! Haff youse effer actualies read za Constitutions? Maybe even read chust yours beloved Articles II?"

"Well, er, no, actually. It's a lot of words and it includes some really long ones, so I heard. But Bill Barf told me all about it one time."

"Youse chust don't gets it do youse? Zat iss exacterlies vy Nantzy Pensacola iss peaching youse. Vatch her on za TV. She's allvays says 'No von iss above za law'. Evferry times!"

"So, all those government employees or former employees who testified at the I-i-i-m-p-p-e-e-a-ch-ch-ch . . . thingy hearing, really have this 'conscience' saying things in their heads and telling them what is right and what is wrong?"

"Ya. Efferybodies does! Well, excepts maybees Ted Bundy andt a few ozzer serial killerz. Oh, andt maybe mosts of za 'fixers' and 'lawyers' and peoplez zat youse surround youselfs vis."

"But it makes me really bigly angry when all those people who work for me are not loyal when I am in trouble."

"Zat iss youse problems, right zere. Zey don't vorks for youse. Zey vorks for za govermment off za U.S off A!"

"So Vindalooman, Sonovabitch, Sunderland, Volkswagen and all the others have this 'conscious' thing talking to them in their heads? How weird!"

"Looks McDoonaldt. Iffs youse vants to survives za peachment youse need tzo haff all za Ripofflican committee memberz on yours sides. Like zat Senator Rabbit-Warren alvays says, 'Youse better haff a plan for zat'."

"I know! I have a great idea. I am going to invite them to the Colored House for a Movie Night! And I have some really good movies to choose from. Just check out this list of great titles."

"Okayz, mister. Tellz me vot moviez!"

"Right! *Deep Throat – Mark Felt.* I'm sure that's the one with that woman called Linda Lovelust or something and how her boyfriend Mark felt when she almost swallowed him whole."

"Achh! Zats nichten abouts anyvons swallowing anyvons! Mark Felt isz za FBI guy whose told za newspapers alls aboutz vot Tricky Dicky didt. Itz abouts a vistleblowerz, notz za blowjobz. You really vant zat??"

"Ahh. Errr. Umm. No. Better not. OK. What about *Vice?* That sounds a fun title. It's got Batman and Lois Lane, Superman's girlfriend in it. My kinda movie!"

"McDonaldt! Zat iss notzz za porno movie! Itz about zat dumb-ass Georges Dubbya Bushes viz yourz Batman, Cristian Bale, playingk fat Dick Cheyngang, za Vice-Prezidents. Andt Amy Adams iss notsz Lois Lane, she iss Lynne Cheyngang, za VPs toughs cookiez vife. Cheyngang voss tzo crooked hees almost making yous looks likes a cviorboy. Za bigk different vass zat he voss a reallies schmart operatorz – not za numpbty likes youse!"

VICE – CRISTIAN BALE & AMY ADAMS
https://www.youtube.com/watch?v=jO3GsRQO0dM

116

"Aaaww! Manilia. That's not nice! I'm not a numpty. You know I have told everyone that I have 'a very good brain' and that I have 'great and unmatched wisdom'. Why don't you believe what I tell them?"

35. Trumper Engaging in his Favourite Pastime(s)

"Zat iss super simple, McDonaldt! I am married tzo youse, so I know za real stories. Youse canntz foolz mee! I haff seenz youse sittingk on za toiletz off za Colored House residence atz 4:00am (notz za pretties sightz) andt tvattingk avay likes crazies. Vy doos youse doo zat?"

"I just get these great ideas for nasty things to say to people and I just can't wait until the morning."

"Ha! I sink zat you are chust a pathageological, invertebrate, lyingk *twat* [105] andt – ass zat cleffer Rachel Mad-Dog likez tzo say – vot youse writez abouts uzzer peoples ist usuallies *e-gregious* [106] tzoo!"

"But I don't really sit on the toilet tweeting at 4:00am!"

"Yesz youse dooz. Andt zey even haff a porcelain replica off youse doingk itz. It's availables fromz yours buddies, Jeff Bozo, on Amazon.com fors onlies $13.97! So cute (NOT)."

---

[105] TWAT: A person that spends way too much time tapping out way too much nasty stuff on Twatter and other social media phone apps.

[106] E-GREGIOUS: The extraordinarily bad digital sh*t tapped out on social media by the Trumper and his bunch of sycophantic, parasitic Twatter followers.

"Hhhhffff! Jeff Bozo is no friend of mine. I hate him! He has more money than me and that's not fair. And he never pays his taxes! He is just like that 'Mini' Mike Billionberg who has $60 billion or so and change and wants to spend it on getting me out of office."

"Ha! I vud be ferry carefuls abouts talking about taxes as youse and yourz families haff spent za lifetimes avoidink paying taxes. Hass anyvone actuallies effer seen yours tax returnz? Andt vot happened tzo zat sister off yourz, who voss a judge, but coincidentallies decided tzo retire chust before zey started tzo checks on hers business dealinks viz yourz Trumper Orgoonozation?"

"It's a beautiful tax return. It's perfect. I just don't want anyone to copy my ideas on how to fill it in. That's all!"

"Vell, Jeff Bozo must haff some evenz betters ideaz as he chust divorced hiss vife MacKenzie andt za settlement vos $38 billion. He gaveff avay manies times more zan you even haff got!"

"Bah, the little, shiny-headed, sh*t! What a terrible settlement. I could have done much better! He has obviously never read my book – The Art of the Deal."

"Chust vatch it McDoonaldt! I haff beens chattingk tzo MacKenzie on za socials media and she hass givent me lotz off ideaz. Tzo don'ts eeffen startz tzo sink abouts trading me in forz za newer, younger model. Try its andt I vill hangk youse outs to dry bys yours littles testicularz tea bagz!"

"OK, OK! Let's change the subject. Please, Millionia, please! I have another film suggestion. There is this film that is all about the people around the President. It's called 'All the President's Men' starring Robert "Sundance Kid" Redsocks and Dustin "Tootsie" Hoffwoman. They are really good actors – not like that nasty Robert "F.U." de Nimo. He is just a grumpy old Irishman. The movie sounds like it's all about the President having lots of people who love and worship him unconditionally whatever he does. Just like all my staff and cabinet."

"McDONALDT! Don'dt youse know anythings? It's za movie abouts two reporterz from za Vashington Post zat write ze story abouts vot Naughty Nixon didt at Vatergates. Za titles comez from za fact zat one by ones all za President's men turn on himz andt tell za truth about vat zey did andt vat Nixon knew. Pluss, zey had za 'smokingk gunnz' tapes!"

"Aaaw! And I thought it was going to be a beautiful movie. What a pity! Maybe we scrap the movie idea for the Senators, and I will invite them for lunch instead. I can give them something top of the line, like a real bigly McDonald's Gourmet Burger, while I persuade them to vote to acquit me in the final vote at the I-i-i-m-p-p-e-e-a-ch-ch-ch . . . thingy trail in the Senate."

The most devastating detective story of this century.

REDFORD/HOFFMAN "ALL THE PRESIDENT'S MEN"

36.   Tricky Dicky's Demise

"Zat is it?? A McDo burger tzo keeps for youse za presidency? Youse really arz zat ultimates cheepskates, McDonaldt!"

"I would have preferred to give them the movie and popcorn – it's a much better deal. It's all the Washington Post's fault! I hate that newspaper. Jeff Bozo owns it and he is always stirring up trouble for me. Their reporters are always making up flake news. I bet it was the same back in Nixon's day too. I wouldn't be surprised if there was no 'smocking gun' and one of the reporters planted the evidence or the FBI were the ones who faked the break-in. Poor Richard!"

"Zats all youse ever say. Fake newz! Fake newz! Fake newz!"

"Well, I never used to have any problems with the National Enquirer when my good friend David Pickapeckov-Pickledpecker was running it."

"Ya. Vell zats because you voss payingk him a $130,000 a go tzo bury za bad stories abouts Stormy Jack-Daniels andt Karen McDoughnuts, zen lock zem ups in hiss safe. Jeff Bozo doeszn't need zat sort off pocket monies. Bye za vays, who hass za combinations tzo zat safe?"

"Er, I don't know what you are talking about. I never met those girls. I don't know them. Well, er, maybe I met them at some event and had my picture taken with them – like thousands of other people."

"Ya. Zat iss vot yous alvays says. 'It vasn't me. It voss somebodies else.' I chust knows vot youse are likes ven youse are trying tzo imprezz somes jung chikkas. Youse triez all zat *foreploy* [107] viz zem in za hopez zat youse can getz laid! And za stories zat I heardt vas zat youse vass vastingk zere timez becoz youze vass *lymph* [108]. Ha! I canz vouches fvor zat."

"But, but, er, but. That's a 'nasty' remark. Even if it were true – which it isn't. And, anyway it can't be true because it must have been someone else . . ."

"Ya off courses! Maybe, it voss zat friend off yourz - Jeffrey Einstein, Echstein, Sexstein or vot effer. Ze one zat somehow cummitted suicide on himselfs andt diedt 'alone' in za New York chjail. Ifs youse can belief zat."

"I keep telling everyone. I never really met Jeffrey. I don't really know him. I think he hung out with a 'younger crowd' and I heard he liked to hob-nob with royalty too. He was very buddy-buddy with that Prince Randy Dandy. But I wasn't a fan of Schleppstein."

"Ya right! Sure! I haff see za videoz on za newz viz youse at a Mar-a-Lago party gawpingk andt drooling andt sniggeringk at za youngk girls."

"What!"

"Andt anozzer von showingk youse cavortingk andt grabbing zose cherryleaderz for za Buffalo Wingks andt Miami Doldrumz on za dantz-floor."

---

[107] FOREPLOY: Any misrepresentation about yourself for the purpose of getting laid. A tactic frequently employed by the Trumper. Like telling young innocent Playboy centerfolds & porn stars that he is a self-made, multi-billionaire and that they should not pre-judge the size of any other appendages just because he has ridiculously small hands.
[108] LYMPH: How one porn star with a lisp described the Trumper's attempts at intercourse

MAR-A-LAGO PARTY - TRUMPER & SCHLEPPSTEIN
https://www.youtube.com/watch?v=DMS234rzYTQ

"Please, Melbania. It wasn't me. I wasn't there. It's not my scene."

"Ha! Vot vas zat youse saidt? 'I'm not za fan'. 'Neffer reallies met him.' Right! Youse looked pretties buddy-buddies on zat video tzoo mee. Pull ze ozzer pudding. I chust don'dt belief youse!"

"But Moldovia . . . !"

"Shutz ups! Anymore 'buts' from yous andt itz 'Off vis yours headt!'"

Fade to black . . .

POSTSCRIPT

The Prince, known as 'Randy Dandy' to his friends, acquaintances and the general public at large, has always had a significant reputation for being a party animal. He has also been known throughout the years for a number of lapses in judgement – even before the latest Schleppstein scandal.

Another pal is the controversial British financier David 'Spotty' Rowlocks, criticised for previously being a tax exile. Fancy being rich and not paying one's taxes! Where have I heard that one before?

There were also family birthday party dramas. *The Sun on Sunday* recently published pictures of his daughter, Princess Beetroot's 18th birthday, in the grounds of Windsock Castle in 2006. It was apparently attended by several unsavoury characters including Jeffrey Schleppstein, his girlfriend and alleged agent-procurateur, Caffeine Maxwell-House, along with film mogul Harvey 'The Groper' Whinestein, recently convicted and jailed for sexual harassment.

More recently, Randy Dandy was accused of 'meetings' with a then 17-year-old American girl but his alibi was that he had been in Pizza Express, Woking for a birthday pizza with Beatrice at the time. If true, it seems like a somewhat economy style birthday celebration for a princess.

Randy Dandy gave a taped interview denying all of the allegations on the grounds that he did not sweat. All together now, say, "Duuuuuh!"

HELP FROM NEXT DOOR – RANDY DANDY INTERVIEW
https://www.youtube.com/watch?v=ylF53eJZniw

POST POSTSCRIPT

The back story with Schleppstein is that he was investigated by the Palm Beach Florida police and then the FBI over several years culminating in an arrest in 2008/9 on charges of soliciting and procuring a person under age 18 for prostitution. After much heavy lobbying by a band of expensive lawyers, headed by, no less than, a certain Attorney Alander Showbiz (more on him later), a 'secret' plea deal was reached with the then Miami U.S. Attorney, Alexander Acostacovfefe. And Schleppstein avoided a possible life sentence and served 13 months in 'jail'.

37. Too Much Time, Money & Testosterone = Filthy Rich

The plea deal also covered all his alleged accomplices, named and un-named, including Caffeine Maxwell-House, daughter of much unloved, British media mogul, Robert Maxwell-House. It also meant that all his victims of abuse, rape and manipulation were not able to prosecute him. They were not happy with that as you can well imagine.

Although he was supposed to be in the Palm Beach County Jail, he was actually allowed out on 'work release' for up to 16 hours a day, 7 days a week. And when he was out, he was supposed to stay in his home, but, was often in violation of this basic demand. Eventually, he finished his 'incarceration' and allegedly went back to his predatorial, pedophilic activities. Anecdotally, Alexander Acostacovfefe was 'rewarded' by the Trumper with the post of Labour Secretary and Alander Showbiz was a defense lawyer at the Trumper's (Mock) Impeachment Trail. Things often come full circle in Trumperland. Remember the old Ripofflican motto: 'You scratch my back and I won't squeeze your balls'.

Things also went full circle for Schleppstein, but not quite in the way he probably expected. In July 2019, he was arrested in New York on multiple charges, including sex trafficking, and locked up in the Metropolitan Correctional Centre without the option for bail. At 6:30 am on the morning of 10 August 2019, he was found dead in his cell, allegedly having committed suicide. But there were a number of unusual circumstances and pieces of evidence (or lack thereof) that have given rise to many other, as yet, unproven conspiracy theories.

So, it's possible to imagine that a lot of senior people in the current and previous governments, plus many famous people and others from legal circles and high society breathed a collective sigh of relief when Schleppstein's death was reported in the news. "Phew, that was close!" must have echoed around many breakfast tables.

In May 2020, Netflix released a docu-series about Jeffrey Schleppstein, called Filthy Rich, which details his apparent horrific, relentless pursuit of young, malleable girls that he could manipulate to match his tireless perversions. In early July 2020, the FBI arrested Caffeine Maxwell-House. When asked about it at a news conference, the Trumper commented that he had met her many times and, very inappropriately, said, "I just wish her well." You can't make this stuff up!

POST POST POSTSCRIPT

It's now 46 years since the first publishing of *All The President's Men*, a book about the June 1972 break-in at the Watergate Office Building and the resultant terminal political scandal for President 'Tricky Dicky' Nixon. A 'sequel' has been written by Bob Woodward called *Rage*, this time about the Trumper administration and its many scandals and failures. Published on 15 September 2020, just in time to expose even more lies by McDonald before the election. Thanks Bob!

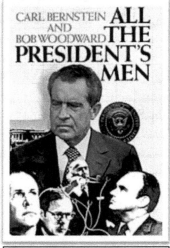

| 38. Nixon's Version | 39. Trumper's Version |

16

MOSCOW MITCH THE MOCK TURTLE
& THE MOCK IMPEACHMENT TRIAL

Still shuddering more than slightly from his encounter with Bolt-On the Walrus, BoJo wandered absent-mindedly along the Yellow-Brick Road. Having an absent mind seemed to be becoming a somewhat common occurrence since he had been in Trumperland, but BoJo had not particularly noticed as it also happened often to him in the Houses of Parliament. The only thing that used to break him out of his twilight reverie was the oft-heard shout of "Ordeeeeeerrrr!" from the Speaker of the House, John Berrrccoww. But, sadly, he was now gone, so what would keep BoJo awake in the future? Perhaps the infinite continuum of debate about how he could make BREXIT work. And he really needed some help with that as other MPs seemed to delight in mounting a non-stop barrage of trick questions that he often did not have the answers for.

HELP FROM NEXT DOOR – BOJO ON BREXIT
https://www.youtube.com/watch?v=ddHHPWL5cOA

He was so wrapped up in his internal BREXIT deliberations that he almost tripped over the sleeping Gryphon. If you have no idea what a Gryphon looks like, imagine an animal with the head of an *American Eagle* [109], but with lots of scales, the front half of a dragon from *Game of Thrones* [110], complete with wings, plus the body and rear haunches of a lion from *The Lion King* [111]. Have you got it?

BoJo did not like the look of the creature, but decided it would be reasonably safe to stay with it as, despite their bizarre looks, most of the people/creatures he had met so far in Trumperland seemed more likely to confuse you to death rather than physically attack you. So, he waited.

The Gryphon sat up and rubbed its eyes: then, much to BoJo's relief, it chuckled "What fun!" half to itself, half to BoJo.

"What is your name and exactly what is the fun?" said BoJo.

"My name Spicy Sean is, the dancing Secretary of the Press I am and you, the fun are," said the Gryphon. "A personage of this place not before seen but heard of."

BoJo didn't like sci-fi movies and had therefore never seen any of the Star Wars series, nor one its famous characters, *Yoda the Jedi Master* [112].

40.   Yoda or BoJo's Grandad?

---

[109] AMERICAN EAGLE: The de-facto symbol of America. But also known as the name of a bar - otherwise called 'The Bird Who Cannot Be Named' - in the 1980s folklore of the Manila Hash House Harriers. You had to be there to appreciate it. But let's just say that Monica Lewinski's internship resume would have been welcomed.

[110] GAME OF THRONES: Does anyone not really know what a GoT dragon looks like? If not, you must have been living under a rock for the past few years. Or in't shoebox in't middle 't road. (See 'You Were Lucky' in my *TSB – Confessions of an Ex-Hooker* book).

[111] THE LION KING: An animated movie, famous for its *Circle of Life* song by Elton John. The movie was recently rehashed in super-digital-animated-photo-synthesised-computer-generated-images, thereby sapping out all the character of the original.

[112] YODA: A small but powerful person with large eyes, mouth and ears. Although he has less hair than BoJo, there is a certain familial resemblance. In *Return of the Jedi* he reveals his age to be 900, making him the oldest living character in the *Star Wars* franchise and, technically, older that the Victorian-era Gryphon.

As a result, BoJo was totally confused by the anastrophic style of speech as he found the object–subject–verb word order difficult to understand. BoJo thought, "And this guy was the Press Secretary?"

"Powerful you have become, the dark side I sense in you," said the Gryphon with amazing prescient accuracy. What did he know . . . ?

"Wwwhat?!?" stuttered BoJo.

"You heard. And my meaning know you full well," responded the Gryphon. "To meet someone, you need to do. Come on!"

"Everybody says 'Come on!' here," thought BoJo, as he went slowly after it: "I never was so ordered about in all my life, never! Not even when I was a fag at Eton. And now by a dancing Gryphon?"

They had not gone far before they saw Moscow Mitch the Mock Turtle, sitting sad and lonely on a little ledge of rock, and, as they came nearer, BoJo could hear him sighing as if his heart would break.

"What is his sorrow?" BoJo asked, and the Gryphon answered, very convolutedly as before, "It's all his fancy, that: he hasn't got no sorrow, you know. Come on!"

So, they went up to Moscow Mitch the Mock Turtle, who looked at them with large eyes full of tears, but he said nothing.

"This here, er, young gentleman," said the Gryphon, "he wants for to know your history, he do."

"I'll tell it him," said the Mock Turtle in a deep, hollow tone. "Sit down, and don't speak a word till I've finished."

So, they sat down, and nobody spoke for some minutes.

BoJo thought to himself, "I don't see how he can even finish, if he doesn't begin." But he waited patiently.

"Once," said Moscow Mitch the Mock Turtle at last, with a deep sigh, "I was a Real Turtle."

41. Moscow Mitch the Mock Turtle

These words were followed by a very long silence, broken only by an occasional exclamation of "Hjckrrh!" from the Gryphon, and the constant heavy sobbing of the Mock Turtle.

BoJo was very nearly getting up and saying, 'Thank you, sir, for your interesting story," but he could not help thinking there must be more to come, so he sat still and said nothing.

"When I was little," the Mock Turtle went on at last, more calmly, though still sobbing a little now and then, "I went to school in Sheffield."

"What?" BoJo's cavernous ears pricked up, "You mean in Sheffield, Yorkshire, UK? Up North in 'Ee By Gumm' land?"

"No!" said the Mock Turtle, "I mean Sheffield, Alabama, USA. And then I went to university in Lexington and Louisville, Kentucky."

"So, well to the south of the Mason-Dixon Line then!" said BoJo, trying to show off some of his previous skills as *Foreign Secretary* [113]. But, equally, forgetting some of his diplomatic ones in bringing up the historic divide between the Union and Confederate parts of the country.

"Hherrrumpff! Well, er, yes. Alabama and Kentucky are good solid Ripofflican States and that's why I got into politics and eventually became Senate Majority Leader in January 2015." said the Mock Turtle. "And that is a real job for a Real Turtle, no doubt about it!"

"Sounds good so far!" opined BoJo and the Gryphon nodded sagely.

"It is! And I had lots of fun in the last couple of years of the O'Bama administration blocking this, that and absolutely everything."

42.   McConman's Idea of Having Fun in Congress

[113] FOREIGN SECRETARY: Geography 101 skills. At least as long as we overlook his gaffe about Africa being a country rather than a continent. Nuff said!

128

"In fact, I had so much fun killing those Dimocrat's bills that they called me the 'Grim Reaper'. And I loved that name. Yeeehaaah!" said the Mock Turtle in a voice which was often described, using morbid metaphors, as two slabs of Kentucky granite headstones being rubbed together, or the slamming of Lexington coffin lids.

| 43. Moscow Mitch McConman in His Work Uniform |

"I can imagine that," said BoJo. "The Dimocrats must have hated it. I know I did when every time I tried to get my fantastic BREXIT deal through the House, it kept getting voted down."

"Yes, I heard about that. Didn't you have a really long string of losses?" said the Mock Turtle. "Followed by a *mass walk-out* [114] of Conservatory Party MPs?"

"But, but, but, er, er well, er, herummmpff!" stuttered BoJo, "It wasn't my fault. They just didn't agree with what I was trying to do and how I was trying to do it. They were like those folks on the London Assembly when I was Mayor – great, supine, protoplasmic, invertebrate jellies."

"Hmmm!" said the Mock Turtle, "I see that you have no problem criticizing your political opponents. Somewhat like my boss, The Trumper. Though perhaps with a slightly more *extensive vocabulary* [115]."

---

[114] MASS WALK-OUT: In September 2019, BoJo had a defection to the Lib Dems by Philip 'Bruce' Lee over BREXIT, which left him without a majority. The same day, he threw 21 MPs out of the Conservative Party for voting with the opposition. A couple of days later his own brother Jo resigned from the Party too. In July 2020, BoJo named his brother for a peerage. What a nice 'kiss and make up pressie' Sir Jo, bro!

[115] EXTENSIVE VOCABULARY: Nick Clogg, former Deputy PM under David Macaroon, described BoJo as "Like McDonald Trumper with a thesaurus".

"I should jolly well hope so! Or all that expensive Ashdown House, Eton and Oxford education, studying the Classics – Latin and Greek - would have been wasted," boasted BoJo unreservedly.

"Well, I heard you were only awarded an upper second-class degree and not a first at Oxford. Maybe it was all that messing about trying to be Union President and pretending to be a Social Democrat and a Liberal just to get their votes," jibed the Mock Turtle.

"Er, mmmm, er, well, er . . ." BoJo mumbled, as it had long been a very sensitive issue with him. "Anyway, at least I went to proper schools!"

"Oh, lah de dah!" riposted the Mock Turtle. "You think we don't have proper schools in Trumperland? I will have you know I was taught in one of the best Schools of Fish on the eastern seaboard."

"Yes!" said the Gryphon. "And I to the Dancing Master and the Classics Master went. Though he an old crab, really was."

"I never went to him," the Mock Turtle said with a sigh: "he taught Laughing and Grief, they used to say."

"So he did, so he did," said the Gryphon, sighing in his turn; and both creatures hid their faces in their paws.

"What on earth are you two talking about?" queried BoJo. "That's not what I would call a proper curriculum. What about real subjects?"

"Well, I couldn't afford to learn the Classics," said the Mock Turtle with another sigh. "So, I only took the regular course. What you would call 'real subjects', I suppose."

"What were those?" inquired BoJo.

"Reading and Writing, of course, to begin with," the Mock Turtle replied, "and then the four different branches of Arithmetic — Ambition, Distraction, Uglyfication and Derision. In fact, I was lucky enough to study Reading, Writing and Arithmetic in the same class as the Trumper. Though I must say, he was a real dunce at Reading and Writing. But, please, please don't ever tell him I said that."

"Well that explains a lot!" said BoJo. "He does seem to have problems with reading any book, *The Bible* [116], teleprompters and Constitutions."

---

[116] THE BIBLE: He says it's his favorite book, but he is unable to quote any passages.

"But he was **really, really** good at Arithmetic. He just loved all that stuff they force-fed us about Ambition, Distraction, Uglyfication and Derision," said the Mock Turtle emphatically.

"I can absolutely see that," said BoJo. "He is really ambitious. He is always trying to distract the press and public from what he is really doing. He has made an ugly mess of the USA's reputation. And heaps sh*t and derision on anyone who he believes opposes him in any way."

"Whoah, whoah there, boy! That's the head of the Ripofflican Party, the President of the United States of America and the Leader of the Free World that you are talking about there!" jumped in the Mock Turtle.

"Exactly!" rejoined BoJo.

"But he is really good at lots of things," pleaded the Mock Turtle; "and he is always telling us that nobody knows things or does things better than him. He's always on Foxy News saying it. So, it must be true."

---

24 THINGS NOBODY DOES BETTER – McDONALD TRUMPER
https://www.youtube.com/watch?v=YA631bMT9g8

"Balderdash! Wiff-waff! Gobbledegook!" shouted BoJo. "He is just mouthing nonsense and blatantly exaggerating his capabilities to the nth degree and probably to infinity and beyond."

"It's true I tell you. He has told me lots of times that he is a stable genius. And, as Majority Leader of the Ripofflican-held Senate, it's my duty to believe him, come what may!" the Mock Turtle shouted back.

"TURTLE! More you should tell of your story to us," interjected the Gryphon in an attempt to stop the p*ssing contest between the two of them.

"OK. OK," said the Mock Turtle. "One of my finest achievements during the O'Bama administration was that I blocked him from appointing any judges to the Supreme Court, even though there were vacancies. And I loved being able to tell him that to his face!"

"Hmmm. I thought the judiciary was supposed to be independent. Isn't that the point?" posed BoJo.

"Mah boy! There are bigger issues than independence! There is abortion. There is tax reform. There is the amplification of corporate powers while weakening individual rights - particularly of the poor - so that big business keeps funding the GOP. There is protecting the Trumper from all kinds of attacks," blustered the Mock Turtle.

"I wish I had a system like that in the UK," said BoJo wistfully.

"Right. And then in July 2018 I got a new judge appointed to that vacant Supreme Court position despite very strong opposition. That was a great coup for me and for the Trumper," preened the Mock Turtle.

"Yes, I heard. It was that famous Brett 'I Like Beer' Cavernous nomination speech," said BoJo. "It seemed that he liked beer so much it apparently affected his *hippocampus* [117] functionality, which was very convenient for him when denying that he raped someone."

"Aaah well, let's not go into that anymore! Let's just say we managed to get Brett on the Supreme Court - despite himself - and his love of beer," said the Mock Turtle somewhat ruefully.

"So, you were rocking and rolling along really well in mid-2018. What happened to turn things against you and your Ripofflicans?" asked BoJo innocently – even though he knew the answer.

"The Mid-Terms happened. That's what happened," grunted the Mock Turtle. "And the suburban White women and the Black voters and the Latino voters and the multi-racial college kids all clubbed together and voted for a whole bunch of new Dimocratic Congressmen and a few State Governors and top officials. Bah humbug!"

"So, you lost control of the House of Representatives to a phalanx of newbies of all colours, shapes, sizes, ethnicities and religions. What a blow, especially considering that the Ripofflican Party is primarily older white Christian males . . ." said BoJo to the very significant dismay of the Mock Turtle.

---

[117] HIPPOCAMPUS: The hippocampus is associated with declarative and episodic memory as well as recognition memory. Another job of the hippocampus is to project information to cortical regions that give memories meaning and connect them with other connected memories. Alcohol can impair that function. It's why we can't remember what happened the night before when we were drunk. Lucky Judge!

Then, he rather tactlessly rubbed it in by saying. "And a whole lot of them were women too, including that New York, Latino former waitress, Alexandria Occasional-Vortex."

"Isn't she the youngest woman ever elected to the US House at 29 years old. She is a real, unpredictable and unstoppable socialist tornado force!" said BoJo, pushing home his point rather dramatically.

"Well, er . . ." the Mock Turtle tried to interject.

But BoJo blundered on in his usual inimitable fashion, not listening to what the Mock Turtle was saying nor seeing his increasingly dismayed expression and the tears starting to well up in his eyes again.

"Yes. I heard that a couple of them are also Muslim, coloured, immigrant and female. A quadruple hit by those two!" BoJo prattled.

"Er, yes but . . ."

"Plus, plus, you had the first Native American woman elected to Congress. That must have made the Trumper's 'Pocahontas' dig at Elizabeth Rabbit-Warren a bit old hat, old chap!" chortled BoJo insensitively as he tapped his hand over his mouth, mimicking the Hollywood movie-style Indian battle cry. "Ow! Ow! Ow! Ow! Ow!"

The Mock Turtle was not amused. He was almost in tears again as this was very far from his favourite subject. But worse was to come.

"So, a few setbacks. But you were still a Real Turtle at this point, right?" asked BoJo cheerfully.

"Well yes, actually. But then the Dimocrat majority in the House were able to choose and appoint a new Speaker. And they chose Nancy Palooka, a real American political pugilist if ever there was one," the Mock Turtle sighed. "Don't tell him this, but she is way too smart for the Trumper. He will never outwit her on a one-to-one basis."

"Yes, I have seen her in action. She is a bit like *Maggie Thrasher* [118], but with an American drawl. The Trumper called her 'Nervous Nancy', but she is very far from nervous. I think a better name would be 'Nuclear Nancy' as one day she is going to totally annihilate the Trumper and all that will be left of him will be his scalp of bleached blonde hair floating on top of the mushroom cloud," chortled BoJo.

---

[118] MAGGIE THRASHER: The British Prime Minister from 1979 – 1990. Often referred to as 'The Iron Ladle' due to her uncompromising politics & extraordinary love of soup.

"I fear that you may be correct. That's why I spend all my time focused on protecting the Trumper's back," said the Mock Turtle shaking his head from side to side.

"OK. So, she was appointed Speaker in January 2019. What happened next?" asked BoJo. "I assume you were still a Real Turtle after that?"

"Ah, well yes. But things were starting to change. Around that same time the Senate voted to lift the sanctions on Russian companies, originally imposed by O'Bama when they invaded the Ukraine, much to the annoyance of the Dimocrats and Nancy," the Mock Turtle said.

"I'm sure that created a lot of disapprobation, vexation, umbrage and chagrin between the parties," opined BoJo in one of his usual verbose vilifications.

"Er, yes. Whatever. And Nancy threw a hissy fit too," responded the Mock Turtle, not being quite sure what BoJo had actually said, many of the words not being in general usage in the American version of the English Dictionary. "But it was what happened next that really started to make things turn on me."

"Yes, yes! I heard there was something about an aluminium plant, or, as you trans-Atlantic cousins would say, an aluminum plant." chuckled BoJo, always happy to throw a bit of additional Anglo-American language imperfection into the mix.

"Hmmm. Er, well. Totally unconnected with any partisan dealings, the alleged Russian interference in the elections, the Miller-Lite Report, the lifting of sanctions or any other political considerations, a Russian company did decide to invest $200 million in a US-based aluminum plant," mumbled the Mock Turtle into one of his many chins.

"Ah yes. But wasn't that plant to be built in Kentucky? And wasn't one of the so-called 'former' shareholders in that Russian company a guy called Derrypasta? And wasn't Derrypasta an Irish-Italian-Russian oligarch with almost direct connections to Putitin?" shot BoJo in a tirade of quick-fire questions - a handy skill he had learned on the *Front Benches* [119] of the British Parliament. "And, and, and! Correct me if I'm wrong. But don't you just happen to be the Senator for the Great State of Kentucky?" spat BoJo, saving his pièce de résistance till last.

---

[119] FRONT BENCHES: Ministers sit on the front row of seats in the House of Commons.

"Look, er, yes but no. Not really. I told reporters in May 2019 that my position on the lifting of the sanctions and the investments of that Russian company was completely unrelated to anything that might happen in my home state." said the Mock Turtle sheepishly.

"Ah, but that was the moment the press started calling you Moscow Mitch, if I recall correctly," said BoJo, metaphorically twisting the knife in the back of the Mock Turtle.

"Ummmmm, er, well, er, yes. And I HATED IT. AND STILL DO!!! Bah! Me called MOSCOW MITCH???" shouted the Mock Turtle so loudly that the name echoed and reverberated around in his shell for several seconds like a reminder that just would not go away.

"MOSCOW MITCH, MITCh, MITch, MItch, Mitch . . ."

"I can see you are upset about that one. Just a teensy-weensy bit," offered BoJo in his usual non-reconciliatory fashion. "And then, later in the year, the Dimocrats started the Impeachment Hearings about the Ukraine 'perfect phone call' fiasco. That must have hurt!"

"Well, it wasn't so bad when it started as we mounted a campaign to discredit the process and I knew that, if it ever got to the Senate, I would have full control of the outcome," responded the Mock Turtle, brightening slightly.

"Hmmm. In my experience, discrediting the process usually means that you have not got any strong legal or factual grounds on which to base your defence or opposition," poked BoJo.

"I am not admitting to that, but I heard that you regularly used that same tactic with your BREXIT promotions and your general election promises," jibed back the Mock Turtle.

"But, but, but aaahh, er, but!" babbled BoJo. "I always tried to answer any questions I was asked."

"Ah, but from what I saw, you often answered a question that hadn't been asked or simply bumbled and blustered with lots of long words and fancy phrases and similes about Greek mythology, Shakespeare, crazy science theorems and political gobbledegook," said the Mock Turtle, pushing back strongly on BoJo.

"I say, I say, old chap. That's a mite on the strong side, especially coming from a Ripofflican who has managed to sit on hundreds of bills passed by Congress without even blinking a gymnophthalmidic eyelid."

ROOM NEXT DOOR-ELECTION SPECIAL – BORIS JOCKSTRAP
https://www.youtube.com/watch?v=TpyglTJWm6Q

"Having listened to your answers on the Election Special, I rest my case. Though, pray tell me please, what on earth is a *gymnophthalmidic eyelid* [120]?" asked the Mock Turtle in exasperation.

"See! This is what comes of going to the School of Fish instead of having a proper education. You need to know these things," smirked BoJo. "You will be telling me next that you learnt everything you know about social media from an iPod of Whales! LOL!"

"I resent that absolutely!" responded the Mock Turtle. "We learnt many sophisticated and important things such as poetry and dance. Just listen to the 'Lobster Quadrille' by *Charles Lutwidge Dodgson* [121]."

"Will you walk a little faster?" said a whiting to a snail,
"There's a porpoise close behind us, and he's treading on my tail.
See how eagerly the lobsters and the turtles all advance!
They are waiting on the shingle—will you come and join the dance?
Will you, won't you, will you, won't you, will you join the dance?
Will you, won't you, will you, won't you, won't you join the dance?

"Herrruummpfff! coughed BoJo. "That is not really classic poetry. It's a plagiarised version of 'The Spider and the Fly'. But enough of this piffle-paffle. What is the inside story on the Impeachment and what about all those testimonies by former and current government staff?"

---

[120] GYMNOPHTHALMIDIC EYELIDS: The transparent eyelids on some lizards and snakes that allows them to protect their eyes and still see things without ever appearing to blink. Very useful for politicians when trying to convince others of something that is patently false. The fact that they occur on many snakes and lizards does give them a certain commonality with politicians. I'm just saying!

[121] CHARLES LUTWIDGE DODGSON: The real name of the writer of the poem and the book it's in. Lewis Carroll was his pen name.

THE QUADRILLE/MOCK TURTLE SONG – STEELY DAN
https://www.youtube.com/watch?v=1XATkBETOjE

"Well, I fully agree with my Cummerbund-in-Chief that those people – like Alex Vindalooman, Marie Sonovabitch, Gordon Sunderland, Fiona Hillbilly and the rest - were committing treason by telling all those 'nasty' stories. And we definitely did not want them to do it all again in the Senate," grumbled the Mock Turtle. "So, we decided on an Impeachment Trial without witnesses."

"Isn't that an oxymoron?" said BoJo. "A trial without witnesses? It's like *Bangers without Mash* [122]. Or Strawberries without Cream. Or Roast Beef without *Yorkshire Pudding* [123]. Or Fish without Chips. Or *Toad without Hole* [124]. Or, or, or . . ." BoJo was getting quite carried away with his food-related similes as he suddenly realised that he hadn't eaten for some considerable time and his little stomach (another oxymoron) was starting to rumble.

"Er, aahh, not really – whatever those things are," the Mock Turtle tried to answer, despite his obvious confusion.

"But in a real trial – like, say, if someone shot somebody on 5th Avenue, in plain sight – there would be a trail with witnesses for the prosecution and for the defence. Right?" pushed BoJo slyly.

"Weeell, that would kinda depend on who was doing the shooting," responded the Mock Turtle, realizing that BoJo was trying to trap him with an allegory linked to a somewhat dumb, bravado comment the Trumper had made about his Article II powers under the Constitution.

---

[122] BANGERS & MASH: Sausages & mashed potatoes. Like me muvver used ter make!
[123] YORKSHIRE PUDDING: It's called a pudding – which is usually a dessert – but is always served as a main course with Roast Beef for a traditional British Sunday Lunch. A weird but wonderful-tasting sort of savoury batter full of air and smothered in gravy.
[124] TOAD IN THE HOLE: A combination of the two dishes above. It's the bangers laid in an oven dish covered in Yorkshire Pudding. Very Brit!

"But the Senate is not a Court of Law and impeachment is not about real 'crimes'. And many of the people that the Dimocrats wanted to call as witnesses – like Mick Malarkey, John Bolt-On and Don McGannet - didn't want to testify. Plus, it's my Senate so I get to make the rules. End of story!" the Mock Turtle bounced back.

"It seemed to me that all the people who believed he was guilty were willing to testify and all the ones who said he was innocent didn't want to. Hmmm! That gives some food for thought," pointed out BoJo, though that last phrase started his stomach to rumble again.

"Oh, so now you think you are some kind of expert on impeachment! Tell me, whatever happened that time back in 2004 when you tried to impeach Tony Bland, the British Prime Minister, for 'high crimes and misdemeanors'?" asked the Mock Turtle.

"Well, er, umm, er, aaah. He had been a very, very naughty boy and had told all sorts of porky pies about the reasons for getting involved in the war and about his secret agreements with Bush and telling people that the world was in danger because Iraq had lots of *WMDs* [125]."

"Oh, and those were the only reasons to impeach him? We have had a quite a few presidents who have done a lot, lot more than that and never even come close to impeachment for it – Bush included. And just remind me what political party Tony Bland was from?" asked the Mock Turtle, as innocently as he could.

"He's er, well, er. It, of course, wasn't about partisan politics. It was not about the Labial party. It was about the principle of politics. He shouldn't have blatantly lied to the British Public," said BoJo pompously.

"Admit it. You just hate Tony Bland and would have done anything to get him out of office, even host HIGNFY," pushed the Mock Turtle.

HIGNFY: TONY BLAND – BORIS JOCKSTRAP
https://www.youtube.com/watch?v=gSIPiYdhAhs

---

[125] WMDs: So-called, non-existent Weapons of Mass Destruction. The reason for the war

"Erm, er, harrumph, hmmmm, er, well. That's not strictly true –
although I did once host *Have I Got News For You* [126] and they did sort
of 'set me up' by having a 'Bash Tony Bland' segment. Which was lots of
fun, by the way – even if the panellists did sometimes get a bit strong
with the ripostes and comments directed at yours truly," burbled BoJo.

"Yes. I saw the clip. They really took the p*ss out of you!" chortled
the Mock Turtle.

"Look, er, look. Ahh. Let's get back to this Impeachment Trial. I am
really interested in how you came to the conclusion that it was the best
option to have no witnesses even though the Dimocrats were going to
slag you off forever about it," queried BoJo, again masterfully changing
the subject when it got too close to home for him.

"Oh, that was easy. We had this big pow-wow down at Mar-a-Lago
one weekend because the Trumper insisted that he did not want to miss
his golf game, even for an important strategy meeting about the
impeachment. We gathered the Ripofflican Party senior caucus from our
House of Cards and all the potential witnesses that the Dimocrats were
saying they wanted to call. And those that couldn't be there in person, we
hooked them in by video conferencing," said the Mock Turtle.

"Wooo! Video conferencing. I bet that was a major technology
explosion for some of your party seniors . . .!" jibed BoJo. "Your good 'ol
boys were probably more used to, shall we say, *'Havin' lunch at The
Petroleum Club. Smokin' fine cigars and swappin' lies'*. And saying to the
illegal immigrant waiters *'Give me another slice of that barbecued
brisket. Give me another piece of that pecan pie'*. Mind you, I have heard
it's pretty much like that at Mar-a-Lago too."

The digs about the Petroleum Club were lines from the Eagles song,
Long Road Out of Eden [127], but BoJo knew that the Mock Turtle would
never catch on as it was way over his head and way below his age group.

---

[126] HAVE I GOT NEWS FOR YOU: A very topical and satirical quiz programme where
guests comment and answer questions about events in the news the preceding week.
Guests & hosts are usually politicians, media and showbiz personalities. A different
person hosts the show every week and they are usually mocked or ridiculed by the panel.
[127] LONG ROAD OUT OF EDEN: A political commentary about the US fighting wars in
the Middle East to protect the oil industry. Soldiers in the desert while the fat cats were in
the Club. It had become a favourite of BoJo's when he was trying to impeach Tony Bland.

"I er, say. Take it easy about Mar-a-Lago and don't let the Trumper hear you talking about illegal immigrant workers there. It sends him into an apoplectic fizzy fit," warned the Mock Turtle.

"OK," said BoJo, thinking to himself that he would save that ammunition for a future time when he might need it as a distraction. "So, what was the video conference all about? Who said what?"

"Well here. You can read this *'perfect' transcript*[128] . . ."

So BoJo started to read, with some difficulty due to the redactions.

Ref 271395/GOP/15 January 2020

DISCUSSION OF WITNESSES @ MAR-A-LAGO

TOP SECRET – FOR YOUR EYES ONLY

RIPOFFLICANS: Right. You all got it straight?
ALL THE WITNESSES: OK. We all agree. This is what happened.
RIPOFFLICANS: None of you were in the room!
BOLT-ON THE WALRUS: Well, I was in the ███████
RIPOFFLICANS: Shut up! Who asked you? You are a liberal & got fired.
BOLT-ON THE WALRUS: I'm a lifelong Ripofflican & National Secu…
RIPOFFLICANS: Shut it moustache! Where's the first Security Advisor?
MICKEY FINN: Sorry guys I'm going to jail (unless Bill Barf intercedes).
RIPOFFLICANS: What! Why?
MICKEY FINN: For lying to the FBI about the Russia investigation.
RIPOFFLICANS: What idiot told you to do that?!
MICKEY FINN: The ████████
RIPOFFLICANS: Shut up! No one believes you or the Walrus!
JOHN F JELLY: I believe them. And I was the Trumper's Chief of Sta . . .
RIPOFFLICANS: Shut up! Who is the current Chief of Staff?
MICK MALARKEY: It's me. Sort of. Well, I'm the Acting Chief of . . .

---

[128] PERFECT TRANSCRIPT: Transcripts have a way of not being exactly what was said. Ask Alex Vindalooman about that. James Tabeek wrote the original of this one and there were some minor changes to protect the innocent – of which there are very, very few.

RIPOFFLICANS: Shit! Never mind. No point in asking him! He's out.
LEVEE & IGNOR: We were in the ████ And here is a cellphone video.
RIPOFFLICANS: What! How did you sneak a cellphone in that meeting?
LEVEE & IGNOR: It was easy. We just walked right in and ██████████
RIPOFFLICANS: Shut up! Anyway, you're criminals.
LEVEE & IGNOR: So? That's what the ██████ wanted.
THE ██████████ : I don't know him. I have never met him before.
LEVEE & IGNOR: We are besties. Here's 500 pics of me with Trumper.
THE ██████ : I have no idea who he is or how he got here.
RIPOFFLICANS: Wait! Which idiot introduced you to the ██████████?
LEVEE & IGNOR: His personal lawyer.
RIPOFFLICANS: Michael Cohort??
MIKE COHORT: (in orange jumpsuit) Hey! Sorry guys, I am in jail.
RIPOFFLICANS: You as well? Why?
MIKE COHORT: Campaign finance violations, hushing up sex scandals.
RIPOFFLICANS: Whose sex scandals? Whose campaign?
MIKE COHORT: The ██████████
RIPOFFLICANS: Shut up! Who was the Campaign Chairman?
MAN O'WAR: (in orange jumpsuit) Yeah! Me! I'm also in jail. Heyyyy
RIPOFFLICANS: IS EVERYONE IN JAIL???
ROGER ROLLING-STONE: I'm not! And I'm expecting a pardon soon.
RIPOFFLICANS: What did you do?
ROGER ROLLING-STONE: Wikileaks - Seven counts plus overdressing.
RIPOFFLICANS: Who told you to do that – not the overdressing?
ROGER ROLLING-STONE: The ██████████
RIPOFFLICANS: Shut up!
LEVEE & IGNOR: Hey! We are still here and not in jail. Yet . . .
RIPOFFLICANS: OK! Which dumb██ introduced you to ██████████?
LEVEE & IGNOR: It was Roody-Doody of course!
SONOVABITCH: Roody-Doody! He had me fired from my job!
RIPOFFLICANS: Whoah! Who are you? A witness?
SONOVABITCH: I was the Ambassador to Ukraine
RIPOFFLICANS: Roody – you fired her? You work for the Government?
ROODY-DOODY: Yes, I did & no I don't. But who follows rules, so...?
RIPOFFLICANS: So, if she was fired, who did the Ambassador's job?

ROODY-DOODY: The Three Amigos, of course!
RIPOFFLICANS: Who the ████ are the Three Amigos??!!??
SUNDERLAND: It's me and my buddies Volkswagen and Perrier.
RIPOFFLICANS: So, you and your 'Amigos' were involved?
SUNDERLAND: Yes! We ran the whole thing. And I was in the room!
THE ████████: And we spoke by cell phone in Ukraine every day.
RIPOFFLICANS: F@$&!!!! DEFINITELY NO WITNESSES!!!

BURN AFTER READING

BoJo finished reading the 'perfect transcript' and seeing the stamp at the bottom of the page it reminded him of the movie *Burn After Reading*[129] with Brad Pitt.

BURN AFTER READING – BRAD PITT
https://www.youtube.com/watch?v=SVCHSiRWjJM

He decided to have a little fun with the Mock Turtle, knowing full well that the old beast would never have been to the movies to see it.

So, he started. "Wow! And I mean WOW!!! Is that what really happened? You could make a crazy *Spy vs Spy vs Spy*[130] movie by the Coen Brothers about this," BoJo rattled on faux-excitedly.

---

[129] BURN AFTER READING: It's a comedy spy thriller about a disgruntled former senior Intelligence Officer who writes a 'tell all' memoir and then loses the CD with the manuscript on it. A dumb fitness trainer (Brad Pitt) finds it and tries to sell it back to the author or highest bidder. The CIA, FBI and Russians are all involved. Storyline familiar?
[130] SPY vs SPY vs SPY: A *MAD* magazine cartoon strip. Was a parody of the political ideologies of the 60's Cold War. The Black Spy and the White Spy were always trying to outwit each other but often failed by trying to be too clever. The Grey Spy was a female who always won by using the infatuations of Black Spy and White Spy to her advantage.

"It would be 'perfect' with Sam Elliott as the Walrus, J.K Simmons playing Sunderland, George Clooney could be Dumbitry Flirtish, the oligarch holed up in Austria, allegedly paying Levee, Ignor and Roody's bills. John Malkovich could play John Malkovich; a Russian secret agent and Brad Pitt could play somebody dumb like Eric Trumper and . . ."

"Wait! Eric wasn't allowed to be anywhere near all that stuff," said the Mock Turtle. "We were always worried he would screw it up!"

"Oh, er, well. Never let the truth get in the way of a good story! He could be written into the script for comedy effect. Maybe as goofy, young real estate tycoon who always lost money – like his dad. Movie plots do that all the time. And I do it in Parliament. But don't tell the rest! And I have great idea for a title," said BoJo. "It's *'I Was in The Room'.*"

| 44. The Walrus | 45. Sam Elliott | 46. Ambassador | 47. J.K. Simmons |
| 48. The Oligarch | 49. The Clooney | 50. The Idiot | 51. Brad Pitt |

| 52.   The Russian Secret Agent | 53.   Being John Malkovich |

"Woah there boy!" said the Mock Turtle suddenly waking up to what BoJo was inferring. "We had a lot of trouble with 'that book' by the Walrus during the trial. He wanted to release it and we had to suddenly pretend that there might be disclosure of some national secrets in the book. So, we had to block it while our people allegedly read it."

"Did the Trumper read it?" BoJo asked, faking a combination of innocence and stupidity – which he was well-practiced at doing.

"Er, ahh, er. I don't think so. Someone else will have read it for him," said the Mock Turtle sheepishly. "Perhaps, Jarhead Kushynumber."

"Ah yes. I wondered what his actual qualifications were for working in the Coloured House – apart, of course, from being the Trumper's son-in-law. I guess being able to read was a bonus," chortled BoJo.

"I think that is a little tough on the boy!" responded the Mock Turtle. "He is a smart businessman, after all, and he negotiated a *Middle East Peace Plan* [131]."

"Hmm. Smart businessman? How come he bought that albatross tower, 666 Fifth Avenue, for way more that it was worth and then couldn't afford the mortgage? But then, in 2018, he did miraculously manage to get Brookfield Asset Management, which, allegedly, has links to the *Qatar Investment Authority* [132], to bail him out! Maybe his trips to the Middle East weren't just about peace . . ."

"Hhherrrummmphhh! I thought you were interested in the Impeachment Trial?" said the Mock Turtle, using BoJo's favourite 'changing subjects' tactic. It seemed that even the impeachment was better than opening the can of worms linked to Jarhead.

"Well, er, yes. OK," replied BoJo. "Where were we? Ah, yes, the witnesses – or rather lack thereof!"

"Exactly. We decided that it would likely be a really bad idea for the Trumper if we had witnesses – even though he wanted them initially," said the Mock Turtle.

---

[131] MIDDLE EAST PEACE PLAN: Negotiated by Jarhead and the Israelis for a peace deal with the Palestinians. Unfortunately, Jarhead forgot to ask the Palestinians to join at the negotiation table, so they rejected the terms unilaterally. Funny that! How unexpected.

[132] QATARI INVESMENT AUTHORITY: QIA said they were not aware. As a result of the negative press, QIA has decided that, in future, it will avoid putting money in funds & investment vehicles it does not have full control over. Especially Jarhead Inc. vehicles.

"So, despite all the protestations of the Dimocrats, you made up your own rules for the trial and sort of, sort of, didn't say that there would not be witnesses. Instead, you said that it would be decided along the way – blah, blah, blah - depending on the cases presented by the Dimocrat 'Prosecution' and the Ripofflican 'Defense'," said BoJo, more as a statement than a question.

"Yes. Exactly!" agreed the Mock Turtle.

"But, come on! You knew that you would never allow witnesses – whatever the case that was presented sounded like. It was just your plan to distract the Dimocrats and make them think you were being fair – even though you have a zero track-record of fairness. Its either the McConman way or no way!" poked BoJo.

"Weeeell. I would never like to admit to that in a court of law – or even in an Impeachment Trial that I was in control of. But I guess that is what happened," the Mock Turtle hesitantly replied.

"Aha! So, you let the Dimocrats lay out all those irrefutable, undeniable, undisputable, previously testified to facts which showed that the Trumper was undoubtedly guilty. Then you 'refuted' them with nothing at all substantive, carried on the persistent red herring of false process claims, and said there was no need for witnesses," accused BoJo.

"Not me. It was the Counsels for the Defense who made the case," objected the Mock Turtle. "I and the rest of the Senators merely listened as we were the jurors in the trial."

"The 'jurors' right!" said BoJo, leading the Mock Turtle in the direction of the trap that he was setting. "You all swore an oath of impartiality, but then you said that you were in full 'lock-step' with the position of the President and the Coloured House. Those two positions seem to be opposite to each other. Wouldn't you agree?"

"Not really. We all voted our conscience and whether we agreed with the cases made by the two sets of counsel," refuted the Mock Turtle.

"Oh yes, conscience and absolute partisan fealty to King Trumper!" shot back BoJo. "I can imagine that the McDonald's lunch at the Coloured House really swayed those votes. The power of a Gourmet Big Mac is truly amazing."

"It wasn't partisan. Two Ripofflicans voted for witnesses!" said the Mock Turtle very defensively.

"Hmmm. My guess is that you let those two Ripofflican Senators vote for witnesses to make it look like it wasn't 100% partisan. It was a set up!" challenged BoJo.

"I wouldn't do that, would I?" the Mock Turtle tried to weasel. "Even if it does make the optics better."

"Ok, whatever!" BoJo responded. "So, then the leading Dimocrat Prosecution Counsel, Adam Stick-Schift, and his team all went through the whole case showing how undeniably guilty the Trumper was and your Defense boys still hadn't got any sort of case to plead."

"Weeell, I wouldn't say that." countered the Mock Turtle weakly. "And we had some really tip-top counsel on our team. What about *Alander Showbiz* [133] and *Ken 'Ziggy' Stardust* [134]?"

"Ha . . .what can I say? For starters, Alander Showbiz came up with the super-scary concept that left the Dimocrats and many legal scholars absolutely gobsmacked. He had the fallacious argument that, in a Senate impeachment trial, a President cannot be removed from office for an action he believes could help get him re-elected." said BoJo shaking his head in abject disbelief.

"And what's wrong with that? It seems perfectly reasonable to me," muttered the Mock Turtle.

"Oh, I guess it is," said BoJo and then paused for emphasis. "As long as it's a Ripofflican President who is moving heaven and earth to be re-elected. What would you do if it were a Dimocrat trying that stunt?"

"Er, ummm. Well, that would be different, of course," responded the Mock Turtle.

"You bet your sweet bippy it would! Even I wouldn't try something as brazen as that!!!" exhaled BoJo in exasperation. "And then you had the famous Bl*w J*b counsel himself, Ken 'Ziggy' Stardust. He is so old now that I am sure he can't even remember what a Bl*w J*b was, never mind prosecute one. Ha!"

---

[133] ALANDER SHOWBIZ: Loves defending stars and high-profile clients. Examples are O.J. Juice and Jeffery Schleppstein. Often uses lofty arguments that have so many legal twists and turns that even the judge cannot follow the thread. It's OK for a President to do absolutely anything – legal or illegal – to get re-elected, is one of his more far-fetched.
[134] KEN 'ZIGGY' STARDUST: Prosecuting Counsel in the Impeachment Trial of President Bill Clingfilm for having the Divine Miss M perform under the Resolute Desk!

"That's a bit cruel! Ken is just a young whippersnapper who is five years younger than I am," defended the Mock Turtle.

"Exactly what I meant. You are 78, right? So, he is a real spring chicken at only 73!" BoJo shot back, somewhat insensitively. "And I have to laugh that he was arguing to impeach Bill Clingfilm just for having a bit of hankey-w*nkey-pankey. Now he is trying to convince the world that the Trumper is a 'perfectly' innocent man and that it's a complete 'witch hunt'."

"But Ken is a man of principles and is very well-respected in legal circles," argued the Mock Turtle.

"Principles he may have," said BoJo, "but he changes them depending on which side of the fence he is sitting. Or rather, being paid to sit on by his client. And talking about principles – or perhaps the lack of them – what about the mid-trial revelations that Pat Cannelloni, one of your Defense counsel, was, as we say, 'in the room' during a discussion of the Trumper's allegedly corrupt Ukraine dealings? So, he was defending the man while himself being part of the cover up! Surely, just a teensy-weensy bit of conflict of interest? As your man Sunderland was wont to say when he was testifying – 'He was in the loop'."

"I think you are just trying to hang all these salacious facts together to make it look like the Trumper was guilty of something!!" protested the Mock Turtle.

"I don't need to hang them together to make him look guilty. Its plainly obvious that he is guilty as charged, plus a whole lot more and then some. But, of course, your right-wing hack media, 'Friends on Foxy', owned by Rupert 'The Dirty Digger' Murdork, made him sound like he was the oppressed one." stirred BoJo.

"Not true. Foxy has very balanced coverage," the Mock Turtle argued with about as much conviction as he could muster – which wasn't much.

TRUMPER, MURDORK & FOXY NEWS – JONATHAN PIE
https://www.youtube.com/watch?v=XSt3F9XGw9w

"Yes, right! Really balanced," retorted BoJo. "That Foxy anchor, Sean Insanity, has his head so far up the Trumper's rectal orifice that he must be able to tell what he had for breakfast. And I daren't mention Judge Jammin' Pyro. She is so inflammatory that she could have played one of the dragons in Game of Thrones."

"Oh, oh, oh – and your Conservatory Party is so innocent, of course!" charged the Mock Turtle. "I read that in the lead up to the election, the Party set up a fake website, called '*Labialmanifesto.co.uk*', which purported to contain the opposition Labial Party manifesto, but which actually was full of Tory attack lines."

"Pppphhhhhhhh." spluttered BoJo. "I say, that's a bit unfair, old boy!"

"Then you paid Google to push the website to the top of the search results." reamed the Mock Turtle. "And that was on top of the fake fact-checking service '*factcheckUK*' which the Party set up on social media. It was totally bogus and was actually controlled by your press office and used to pump out Tory messaging and endorsements of a certain Boris Jockstrap."

"Look, er, look, er, that was a totally innocent mistake," burbled BoJo. "The tecchie IT people completely misunderstood the terms of reference for the job. Well, er, that's what Dominic Cummandgo told me to say at the press briefing."

"Yeah, sure, of course. A totally innocent cock-up that just managed to be incredibly favorable to you and your Party. It happens to us all the time too . . . ," smirked the Mock Turtle.

"Er. Llets, er, gget bback tto ththat Ssenate Ttrial," stuttered BoJo, desperate to change the subject again. "You were going to tell me about the final vote by all the Senators."

"Well, my boy, I am dee-lighted to tell you that on February 5, Trump was acquitted on both counts by the Senate as neither count received the necessary 67 votes to convict him. On Article I, the Abuse of Power, 47 Dimocrat senators and one renegade Ripofflican, Mitt Romney-Marsh, voted for conviction, while 52 Ripofflican senators voted for acquittal. On Article II, Obstruction of Congress, it was a party line vote with 47 Dimocrats voting for conviction and 53 Ripofflicans voting to acquit," explained the Mock Turtle.

"Ahaa! So, Romney-Marsh was the only one with the guts to break party lines and became the first U.S senator to vote to convict a president of his own party in an impeachment trial," said BoJo. "Good on him!"

"You weren't saying that when your party members crossed party lines with your ill-fated BREXIT deal vote!" chided the Mock Turtle.

"Ah but, ah but, ah but, that was different," BoJo tried to argue "My vote was on a matter of policy. Yours was about guilt for trying to twist the Ukraine President Zabaglione's arm with a bribe. If he did the Joe and Hunter Bidet investigation, he got his $400 million."

"As far as we Ripofflicans are concerned, we agree with Alander Showbiz that a President can do anything he wants if it is for the benefit of his re-election," said the Mock Turtle pompously.

"Now I understand it all. (1) You were the judge and the jury. (2) You were working on behalf of the defendant. (3) You wouldn't allow any witnesses. (4) You wouldn't allow the submission of any new evidence. And (5), you pressured all the Ripofflican Senators to vote along party lines as opposed to on the basis of their oath, their conscience and the evidence presented," BoJo ran down the list. "Right??"

"Well, I think that's a bit strong and I wouldn't like to be quoted on it. But 'off the record', I am really pleased that the Grim Reaper managed to kill that impeachment stone dead!" chortled the Mock Turtle.

"Yes, yes, yes! It's all very clear now. It was a Mock Trial and 5 February 2020 was the day that democracy died. So, you got transformed from being a Real Turtle to a MOCK TURTLE!" said BoJo triumphantly.

"Aaaawwww . . . Aaaaaaawwwwww . . ." the Mock Turtle started sobbing, gathered all his multiple chins together and pulled his head into his shell so that all you could hear were the words "Real Turtle. Mock Turtle. Democracy died. Real Turtle. Mock Turtle. Democracy died. Real Turtle. Mock Turtle. Democracy died", echoing around inside the shell.

The Gryphon shook his head and said, "That I am thinking for the day is IT." Which, although grammatically confusing, seemed to be absolutely correct.

The Mock Turtle had retired into his shell for the day. And nothing was going to get him to come out again.

"Yes, I think you are probably right," agreed BoJo. "So, I think it's time for me to thank you for the introduction and bid you farewell."

BoJo turned away from the headless shell of the Mock Turtle and stepped onto the Yellow-Brick Road that had once again re-appeared, unbidden, at exactly the right moment.

"Curiouser and curiouser," he thought to himself, though he had no idea why, as he wandered along the Yellow-Brick Road away from the Mock Turtle without looking back. If he had done so he would have seen Spicy Sean the Gryphon doing pirouettes and tango steps in front of the Mock Turtle's shell in a vain attempt to get him to come out again.

BoJo stared down at the yellow bricks as he walked, thinking about what the Mock Turtle had said and, in particular, about the Trumper being impeached by the opposition for various indiscretions and abuses of power. He realised that he needed to be careful himself in case anyone in the Labial Party got the same idea.

He knew that he had been safe in the past with Jeremy Corblimey as Party Leader. But now he was gone and Sir Keir Starman, Knight Commando of the Order of the Bucket (KBC) and Queen's Cross-examiner (QC) was the new head honcho. Starman was obviously in a different social class and a different intelligence league to Corblimey.

"Ouch! What was the Labial Party coming to? Peers of the realm and legal beagles! Where were all the *cloth caps* [135], *Lancashire accents* [136], *braces* [137] and *clogs* [138] when you needed them most? My God. I might have some intelligent and very vocal opposition in the House of Commons," he thought to himself.

And, as he thought that disconcerting thought, he almost bumped into the White Rabbi, yet again, as it crossed the Yellow-Brick Road in front of him. But, like each time before, the White Rabbi ignored him completely and just stared at its watch.

"Oyvey! I'm late. I'm late. For a very important date! I'm late. I'm late. They're going to close the gate! I'm late. I'm late. I'm late. I'm late. I'm late. I'm late. I'm late!"

And then quickly ran off into the bushes muttering to himself.

---

[135] CLOTH CAPS: Flat hats with a small peak as worn by mill workers in the 1930's, sports car drivers in the 1960's and off-duty jockeys even today.

[136] LANCASHIRE ACCENTS: Broad, working-class dialect & flat vowels. 'Ee by gumm!'

[137] BRACES: Elasticated straps over shoulders to hold trousers up. American suspenders.

[138] CLOGS: Wooden soles and leather uppers. Sometimes with metal irons – like hooves.

"What on earth is that White Rabbi talking about?" said BoJo to the empty space around himself, half expecting an answer from some new animal or character that he had not seen before. But none came – much to BoJo's disappointment – little realising that it was somewhat important that he found out.

So, he wandered along the Yellow-Brick Road humming the words 'The Day Democracy Died' which somehow fitted to the tune of 'American Pie', a song by Don McLean that, if the truth were known, he abso-bloody-lutely hated. He had no idea what brought the tune into his head, but he just could not shake it off however hard he tried . . .

THE DAY DEMOCRACY DIED – THE FOUNDING FATHERS
https://youtu.be/-Ue5F57dZMU

POSTSCRIPT

Two days after his acquittal, the Trumper flipped into 'The Apprentice' mode and fired two of the witnesses from the Impeachment Hearing in the Congress. His $1 million ambassador buddy, Gordon 'Egghead' Sunderland (so that was an expensive testimony) and the much-decorated, purple hearted, no bone spurred soldier, Lt. Colonel Alexander Vindalooman. Both of whom testified about his conduct and all the things that the Trumper denied/lied about doing.

Never one to miss a chance to be truly vindictive, the Trumper also fired Vindalooman's twin brother, probably just because he couldn't tell the two apart and wanted to make sure he got the right man.

POST POSTSCRIPT

The reason that BoJo abso-bloody-lutely hated the song 'American Pie' was that he had abso-bloody-lutely no idea what all the words meant. This was probably because Don McLean's verses were all about things related to the origins of rock music, sub-culture, anti-government politics and the American Way of Life. Maybe, also, like 'I Am the Walrus', he hated the song because his parents played it over and over again when he was a kid as it came out in 1971 when he was seven.

There were a lot of very significant meanings and allegories in the lines of the song, many of which are explained in the following video.

AMERICAN PIE – DON McLEAN
https://www.youtube.com/watch?v=bLEUlvRi8m8

POST POST POSTSCRIPT

Netflix have a wonderful two-part series called *'Dirty Money'*. In the first series there is an episode about the Trumper and in the second series, released in March 2020, there is one about Jarhead Kushynumber. I am not sure which is more nauseating.

The one about the Trumper shows him doing real estate deals, going bankrupt many times, being a flashy, obnoxious, con-man and losing millions of his Dad's dollars running casinos. And it makes you wonder how anyone would be stupid enough to vote for him.

The one about Jarhead is called 'Slumlord Millionaire', a nod to the movie 'Slumdog Millionaire' about a poor Indian kid who got lucky. Just like Jarhead 'got lucky'. It's a mind-blowing expose of Kushynumber!

Spoiler Alert: The start of the episode sets the scene by showing how Jarhead's father went to prison after a scandal nicknamed *Sex, Lies and Video Tapes* [139]. It shows graphically how Jarhead and the Kushynumber Company brought bogus lawsuits against tenants for allegedly not paying their rent after a carefully orchestrated campaign of adding late fees to the rent so that it spiralled ever upwards. The other trick was to force tenants out of rent-controlled buildings by having continuous construction going on inside the building so that tenants were so disturbed they wanted to leave. Jarhead's company then refurbished the building and got new tenants at rents several times higher than before.

Jarhead looks like a choirboy but has the heart of a Devil – if he has a heart at all. He was also very fortunate to be able to marry into the Trumper family. I am sure that the Trumper was very happy to let his favourite daughter, Iwanka, marry Jarhead as he could undoubtedly see his potential for underhand deals, cruelty and total disregard of the law. It gives rise to some serious concerns about the gene pool when their kids grow up with a combination of attributes from the two families.

During the episode we also see the world-famous illustrator, Drew Friedman, slowly working on a project, as he had done many covers for Jarhead's New York Observer magazine. It's finally revealed to be Jarhead as Dorian Gray, the ageless, amoral, hedonist who'se sold his soul to Satan to ensure that his portrait, rather than he, will age and fade and record every sin. This is my version. Judge it for yourself.

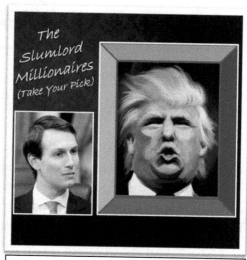

The Slumlord Millionaires (Take Your Pick)

54.   The Sorcerer And His Apprentice

---

[139] SEX, LIES AND VIDEOTAPES: 1989 movie by Steven Soderbergh. About a disturbed man who videotapes women discussing their lives and sexuality. Jarhead's father paid a prostitute to videotape a tryst with his brother-in-law to blackmail him. Nice one Dad!

POST POST POST POSTSCRIPT

Jordan Klepper does regular outside interviews, for the Trevor Noah Daily Show, with people on the street and attending Trumper rallies. Most of the people he interviews are Ripofflicans who, en masse, are incredibly ill-informed, have bizarre beliefs about the Trumper and what he has done or is doing and are totally impossible to convince of any other opinion than their own, even when confronted with the facts. The incredible level of stupidity is difficult to comprehend and Klepper often uses the interviewee's own arguments against themselves and yet they just can't grasp it. It goes straight over their heads. Watch the video with Klepper's questions about impeachment. It's unbelievable!

TRUMPER IMPEACHMENT INTERVIEW – JORDAN KLEPPER
https://www.youtube.com/watch?v=NzDhm808oU4

POST POST POST POST POSTSCRIPT

On 01 April 2020 there was media reporting of a Trumper coronavirus press briefing given the day before. It was a very serious briefing where the medical experts were predicting Covid-19 deaths could be as high as 2 million if nothing was done, but that this could be reduced to a high of 240,000 deaths if everyone followed the US Government's recommendations about social distancing, working at home and constantly sanitizing. This was a very somber event given the increased numbers of deaths being predicted.

After the medical and immunology experts had spoken the Trumper did his usual long, rambling version of the story.

But, in the middle of it all, he veered back into history and started talking about all the 'hoaxes' that he had lived through and beaten during his presidency. In the first place, this shows the linkages – tenuous though they may be – in his mind. Talking about coronavirus reminded him of other hoaxes. He also denied calling the coronavirus a hoax, even though there is video footage of him saying that.

He eventually started talking about the FBI reports, along with James Coney-Island and Andrew McCrab, who he fired because they were investigating the Russian interventions in the 2016 elections. But the classic Trumper moment came when he said that he believed that he had handled the whole impeachment beautifully and that 'he would give himself a rating of A+ for it'.

Yes, in the middle of a coronavirus briefing where they told America that deaths could be in the millions, the Trumper gave himself an A+ for his handling of the impeachment! Hard to believe, yes?

Of course, the point is that, at school, if you have the teacher 'in your pocket' and telling you the answers to the test, it's really easy to get an A+. In the case of the Impeachment Trail, he had Mitch McConman 'in his pocket' as McConman announced the acquittal verdict even before the trail started.

On the day before, the Trumper tweeted, bragging about how his ratings had improved a lot since he was doing the daily press briefings. Yes, he focused on his own ratings as a result of briefing the public about the national disaster – then 180,000 cases, nearly 4,000 dead – highest numbers in the world. Everyone thought that was a new low.

But, again and again, the Trumper totally exceeds our expectations of how low he can go. He is like the limbo dancer who can get under the bar when it's only inches above the ground. Sadly, I don't think we have reached that point yet with the Trumper.

The Impeachment A+ story was reported on April Fool's Day, right? Are we sure he really said that? Or was it just a very bad April Fool's joke? I wish it were . . .
By 21 September it was 7,005,686 cases and 204,122 dead! Is that A++?
USA has 4% of the world's population and 25% of the cases. Is that A++?
On that day, at a rally in Ohio, Trump said, "It affects virtually nobody."

17

MEANWHILE PART 8 – CORONAVIRUS HOAX

Meanwhile . . .

Meanwhile, back at the Colored House, the Queen of Queens had not finished with the McDonald and he was about to get into more trouble yet again and again.

"McDOOOONOLDDT! McDOOOONOLDDT!"

"Er, yes, dear?"

"Haff youse reallies finishedt viz zat Peachment Trial yet? I am reallies fedt ups viz its!"

"Er, yes dear!"

"Youse ares surez?? Chust how didt youse manage zat venn youse voss so definitlies von hundert andt ten percendt guilties?"

"Well, my old chum, Mitch McConman fixed it for me. And that McDonald's Gourmet Big Mac lunch really sealed the deal!"

"Vow!!! Zoes Ripofflicans ares reallies cheepskaterz."

"It was a total party line vote, too."

"Vott! Vozzent zere somesink on za newz about za Senatorz Mutt Roman-March votink against za panties line?"

"Er, I think you mean 'party line'. But yes, he did vote to convict me on the Abuse of Power article!"

"Vy didt he dooz zat?"

"Well, I don't know. Maybe Mitt Romney-Marsh has some throwback ancestors from *Kent*[140] in England. He seems to be fixated on rebelling against the party instead of being part of the Washington Swamp culture and following what the party tells him to do like all the other political sheep."

"Zags realliez amazink! Vonce agains youse haff managed tzo slips through za dragnet vizzout gettingk caught. I chust don'ts knowz howz youse do its."

"I have had many, many years of practice and I can usually talk my way out of a situation. And if I can't see a way out, I can always make up an alternative truth and then blame the Flake News. It always works!!"

"Ach McDonaldt! Von days youse vill meet your matches. Somesink vill comes alongk zat youse can'tz covers up, payz off or chust pretends itz didn'kt happenz. Von dayz all zat - 'I vasn'tz zere. Itz vasn't meez. I don'tch knowz ziss persons. I neffers metz hims beforez' – McDonaldt Trumper storylinez chust von't vork. Beliefs meez, I can feels it in mys Slavic bonez."

"What can possibly be worse than everything I have got away with so far?"

"Vell, zere is ziss Toyotacorollaviruz zat started in China andt zay sayz zat its cans spreadt fassterz zan a prawn starz leegz!"

"Naaah. I don't believe it. It's just a Dimocrat hoax. They are trying to find something else to kill my presidency and stop me being re-elected. Have you seen the numbers? Fantastic numbers! The economy is the best it's ever been. There are more jobs than ever before. Everybody loves me. Just look at the people at my rallies. Check out my ratings on Foxy News. And the stock market is booming, absolutely booming. Nobody does it better!"

"I ams telling youse McDonaldt, zat Toyotacorollaviruz iss coming andt youse better be readies tzo acts likes za real president intsteadz off all za vishy-vashy, flim-flams stuffs zat youse usuallies do."

---

[140] KENT: A county in the south-east of England and home to the Romney Marshes wetlands. A paradise for many smugglers in 17th to 19th centuries and now for lots and lots of sheep. The smugglers kept a low profile in the backwaters of the swamp and rebelled against the rule and the Lord of the Manor. This sounds like a lot like Mitt, who always goes his own way.

"Look, I will just do what I always do. Play it down so people don't panic. I always like to play it down. Tell everybody 'happy talk' stories and they will all believe me because it's what they want to hear."

"Iz don'td sink zo. Nots ziss times!"

"Yeah. There are only 15 cases and pretty soon those will be down to zero. And then, when it gets a bit warmer, it will all magically disappear and we can get on with Making America Great Again, again."

ROOM NEXT DOOR: CORONAVIRUS – McDONALD TRUMPER
https://www.youtube.com/watch?v=NAgydBbF5mQ

"McDoonaldt! Zat iss cumpleat *balderdash*[141] andt chusst abouts ass fake ass yours combed-froms-herez-tzo-over-zere-andt-backwardz-forwardz hairstylez."

"Huh! I'm not worried. The Dimocrats have tried to throw everything at me. One - Crooked Hillarious Clingfilm; two - the Russian election interference scandal; three – the Inauguration budget; four - the Mexican border wall; five - the kids in cages; six - the Miller-Lite Report; seven - the Emoluments clause; eight - being buddies with dictators; nine - killing Qassem O'Solomio in Iran; ten - pulling out of Turkey and dumping the Kurds. Er, what comes after ten?"

"Eleffen, stupidt McDonaldt!"

"Oh, yes, er, eleven - the Ukraine 'perfect' call; twelve – is that right? Er, twelve - abuse of power and blah, blah, blah. And yet they couldn't make any of them stick!! It's just too beautiful!"

---

[141] BALDERDASH: Being unable to admit that you have a rapidly receding hairline, getting transplants from either your armpits or your asshole, or both, then combing your hair in a huge sweeping loop across your forehead and fixing it in place with so much hairspray that you create a hole in the Bozone layer.

158

"Sirteenz? Vot abouts sirteenz? Youse missed von!"

"What do mean? Sirteen? Sirteen? What?"

"McDoonaldt! Vot comez afterz tvelf? Sirteenz, rights?"

"Oh, you mean thirteen! What about thirteen?"

"Youse forgotz yourz favorites prawn star, Stormy Jack-Daniels!"

"Oh no, er, no . . .! That wasn't me. I wasn't there. I don't know that person. I - did - not - have – sexual - relations – with – that - woman!"

"Ach, tzo now youse are becoming a Dimocrat!"

"What do you mean? I was never a Dimocrat. Not many people know this, but, well, er maybe I did give Bill Clingfilm some campaign funds many years ago to help oil the wheels . . ."

"Ya. Maybeez you dids. Andt maybees youse chust tooks za leafs out ov za silvfer liningk playbookz ov Bill 'Slick Willie' Clingfilm. He used zose exzactly vords venn dennyingk vot he said zat he neffer didt viz Monicle za Intern in yourse Oral Officez. On zat sames seat zat youse sit on and at zat same Yousalute Desks."

"But, er, but, er. I didn't do anything in the Oral Office so why do you keep bringing up all this stuff that I didn't do?"

"Ha! Maybees zere isz somekinda magicz spellz on zat desk! I haff been reading zat so manyz off za presidentz haff been doing za naughties around zere. Zere voss W.G. Hardink, FDR, LBJ, JFK, William J. Clingfilm andt now McDoonald J. Trumper. Funniez zat youse guys alls haff 3-letterz namez. Vott a co-insidingks!"

"Oooooooooh! That's not fair! Why can't you ever forget anything bad that you think I did, even though I didn't do it and wasn't there?"

"McDoonaldt, itz because I amz a voman! My brainz iss programmed tzo remembers in absolutes detailz eerythingk zat youse effer said. Especiallies venn youse ver lyingk – vitch iss mosts of za timesz. I canz replays za videos perfectlies andt freezez framez at anyz moments in timez venn youse voss doingk somesink naughties!"

"Aaaaw, that's cheating . . ."

"Zat iss notz a gut choice off vords for youse in particulars. Cheetingk seems tzo be yours favouritez hobbyz alongk viz zat so-calledt 'England Trump' buddies off yours, Boriz Jockstraps."

"Boris? BoJo? What has he done?"

"Vell for starters he has more namez zan anyz reasonables personz shud haff. Hiss fulls namez iss Alexunder Boriz de Piffle Jockstrap. Andt he hass soze many kidz zat he vont effen admits on za TV hows maniez zere are."

"Really! Not many people know that."

"Vot I knowz iss zat he has four kidz viss hiss firsts vife, von vizz a mistsrezz andt anuzzer on za vay. Tzso zat iss six in alls. A bussies boy!"

"What! BoJo doesn't look like he has one in him, never mind six!"

"Ya, andt zey haff za crayziestz names in za vorldt. Lotta Lettuce, Cansof Peaches, Milo Milkyway andt Apollo Thirteen, alls viz hiss ex-vife, pluss a girl called chust Stephersnie viss a formers bit-on-za-side."

"I thought you said he had six? That's only five so far."

"Ach, vell he hass anuzzer von up za spoutz of hiss so-called fiaancee, who iss livingk in sin viss him in za Numbers 10 Downingk Street. Zat iss za firsts times for an unmarriedt, illicits relationships viz za reigning Primez Time Ministerz livingk ins za PMs residenz."

"Wow, and what crazy names he gave the kids!"

"Ya, buts I betz he rememberz za namez off hiss kidz. Cans youse?"

"Er, of course I can! Well, there is Iwanka, McDonald Jr and er, Iwanka and what's that other guy? Something beginning with E. Oh, yes Edsel (he really loves me). Plus, Iwanka. And there is that one who I named after a jewelry store I bought so I could build Trumper Tower. What was it, Cartier? No. Bulgari? No. Paiget? Er no. Ah, I know it. It's Tuppenny, just like that movie about having breakfast. There! Got it!"

"McDOOONALDT! Vot abouts ours ownz son? Rememberz hims? I certainlies dooz. Ve hadt tzo do za baby makingk nuptualzes tzo many timez tzo makez its haaappenz. (Yukz!) Iz cans neffer forgetz zat in za months off a millionz Sundayz!"

"Yes, yes dear of course, I hadn't forgotten that one. Yes, he is a beautiful boy, doing an amazing job, getting 10 out of 10 for everything, just like his dad. And he knows so many words. All the best words. Nobody knows more than him about getting good grades – he got that from me you know. And when he grows up, he will know more about the military than anyone – I just hope he hasn't got those hereditary bone spurs. Yes, lovely boy, amazing boy," babbled the Trumper, stalling for time while he tried to rack his feeble memory for the kid's name.

"McDOOOOOONAAALDT! Vat iss hiss names? Cantz youse remembers????!!"

"Erm yes. Of course, I do. It begins with, er, don't tell me. Oh yes. With 'B'. And it has some 'Rs' in the middle. I think. Yes, got it. Borring? Borrow? Barrow? Burrow? Borron? Barren? Barring? Am I close?"

"Itz BARRON youse dunderdickzheadt! Youse forgotz zat namez alreadiez. He hass been vizz uss for za 14 yearz andt youse cantz remember? Even zo youse choses zat namez so zat he soundeds likez za Britisher royalty families. Likez Lordz ziss andt Dukez zat or Prinz ze ozzer. Troubles iss, youse don'tz even knows hows tzo spell za name. Itz should be chusst B-A-R-O-N viss one 'R' notz two. Vot a dodo youse iss!"

"But Milomania . . . "

"Andt 1 know zat youse neffer forgetz za names off zat favorites daughter Iwanka, from your firsts wifes!!! And zat 'sharkz inz sheeps clothzing' huzbandt of hers, Jarhead. You iss alvays praising him!"

"But Milomummia . . ."

"Von more 'But Milomummia' andt it vill be 'Off vizz yours headt!!'"

Fade to black . . .

18

CATCH THAT SUMBITCH – SMOKEY & THE BOJO

BoJo was thankful to get away from Moscow Mitch the Mock Turtle and his grammatically dysfunctional friend, the Gryphon. If truth be known, BoJo was significantly aware that the Made-in-Hell combination of the Trumper and the Grim Reaper was likely to leave scars on the US democracy that would take many years to heal. If at all.

"Maybe Dominic Cummandgo and I could do the same thing to the British political system," BoJo thought to himself.

But as he thought that thought he also thought that he was somewhat surprised at himself for thinking thoughts like that. And then he thought, "What sort of a thought was that?" Thinking thoughts like that were bordering on sedition for an active politician such as himself.

"Was he going soft? Or was he just having soft thoughts? How thought-provoking was that?" thought BoJo.

Even just having any sort of thoughts about anything at all since he had been in this non-stop crazy Trumperland was proving to be extremely difficult and rapidly approaching nigh on impossible.

And then he remembered something! He was looking for the Coloured House. "Yes! At least that was a 'proper' thought," he thought.

"Why not ask a policeman?" he thought. "Gosh, two real thoughts in a row. Amazing! But where was a real policeman when you needed one? Eating doughnuts and drinking coffee in Dunkin' Doughnuts no doubt!"

BoJo's *morphically resonant* [142] prayers were soon to be answered.

"'Hello, hello, hello . . . now what do we have here, bhoy?" said a very Texan voice with an underlying assumption of an authoritarian note.

BoJo turned around to see the rotund and familiar, but completely unexpected, figure of *Sheriff Buford T. 'Smokey Bear' Justiss* [143] tapping his nightstick menacingly on the palm of his hand.

55. 'The' Sheriff Buford T. Justiss

"Hey, bhoy, jus' where do you think you're a'goin'," said the Sheriff.

"Er. Aaah. I wasn't going anywhere. And, actually, I was looking for you. Well, not necessarily 'you', but someone like you. Any real officer of the law, in fact," said BoJo.

"Woah there a darn tootin' minute, boy! I am not just 'any' officer of the law," said the Sheriff, sounding very affronted. "I'm 'the' Sheriff Buford T. Justiss of Portague County, Texas."

"Yes, yes, yes, I am aware of that! 'Smokey and the Bandit' was 'sort of' my favourite when I was a teenager. But you're not a real policeman you're just a movie one, and not a very good one at that," replied BoJo.

"Jus' you be careful what you're asayin', bhoy! Nobody, and I mean NOBODY makes Sheriff Buford T. Justiss look like a possum's pecker. You can't just go walkin' around makin' 'nasty' and dis-para-gin' remarks about every sumbitch. It's very un-American!" said the Sheriff.

---

[142] MORPHIC RESONANCE: It's the theory that everyone's brain emits millions of brainwaves and they all encircle the world like radio waves. That's why, when you think you should phone your wife, your cell phone rings and it's her and you say, "Yes, dear!"

[143] BUFORD T. JUSTISS: The chubby, cigarette smoking and somewhat inept Texas Sheriff in the movie 'Smokey and the Bandit'. The 'Bandit' is played by Burt Reynolds as a smooth-talking, fast driving, likeable redneck rogue. He is trying to race across several states with a truck load of bootleg Coors beer from Texarkana to Georgia in 28 hours. Spoiler Alert: The Sheriff is in hot pursuit but never quite catches the Bandit.

"Ha! Try telling that to the Trumper," said BoJo rather imperiously.

"Bhoy, you're askin' for a 'real' officer of the law. But how many 'real' sumbitches have you met since you've been in Trumperland? About zero to none I would wager!" smirked the Sheriff

BUFORD T. JUSTISS QUOTES – SMOKEY & THE BANDIT
https://www.youtube.com/watch?v=uN3c64j2DPE

"Hmmm, I guess you are right. The Cheshire Pussy, Humpty Trumpty, the Mad Hater, Tweedledumb and Tweedledumber, Bolt-On the Walrus, the Mock Turtle and the Gryphon could hardly be called 'real' by any stretch of the imagination. However vivid or stretched an imagination anyone had," agreed BoJo.

"So, bhoy, how can this officer of the law be of a-ssistance to you? Can I chase some bandits? Lock up a few sumbitches? Solve a crime for you?" asked the Sheriff in his most obsequious Texan drawl.

"Not really," said BoJo. "I just needed some directions to get to a place I have been looking for ever since I arrived here."

"Oooohhh, god-damnit!" said the Sheriff very disconsolately. "I was really ahopin' for a crime to solve. Ever since I lost that sumbitch Smokey, I got trans-ferred here and the Captain took me off crime patrol and put me on god-damn traffic duty. I'm just standin' at this inter-section and wavin' my arms around in the air all day. It's more borin' than watchin' cars rust in a Tallahassee junk yard! Dontcha need any help appre-hendin' a criminal? Investi-gatin' a crime? Having a trial? Sendin' someone to jail? Isa jess LOVES that real Sheriffin' stuff."

"Well actually, you could probably do all of those things for me as I have never been in a place where so many basic governing principles, laws, rules, Constitutional powers, duties and rights have been ignored, flouted, disobeyed and - let's call a spade a spade – BROKEN, by the PEOPLE who are supposed to be THE GUARDIANS OF THOSE VERY THINGS!!" chanted BoJo.

It was a crescendo he usually reserved for dealing with any quivering, neophyte Labial Party *Back-bencher* [144] who may have had the extremely foolish temerity to ask him an embarrassing question in the House of Commons.

"Easy theah, bhoy! What we're dealin' with here is a complete lack of respec' for the law," said the Sheriff. "You're gonna bust a blood vessel if you don't calm down."

"OK. OK. I'm taking deep breaths," BoJo replied.

"You gotta slow down, slow down," said the Sheriff. "I sure wasn't able to get all of that down in my Texas State po-lice officer's notebook. And my pencil-lead broke in the middle of what you were sayin' there!"

"Oh, you don't need to write it all down," said BoJo. "We make inflammatory accusations like that all the time in the British Parliament and, luckily, the Sergeant at Arms doesn't arrest anyone."

"So, does the Desk Sarge' put those folks down on the Po-lice Blotter for mis-be-havior and other crimes?" asked the Sheriff innocently.

"Absolutely not!" replied BoJo. "He is not a 'Desk Sarge', he is a Sergeant at Arms and he would be way too busy if he did!"

"But, but, but, bhoy" said the pedantic Sheriff. "What the hell is the world comin' to? Surely, you can't be serious! If there has been a <u>crime</u> there has to be a <u>punishment</u>!"

"I am serious and don't call me Shirley!" reposted BoJo before he even had time stop himself as he realised that Humpty Trumpty had replied the exact same thing when he had asked him the same question.

"Uugh!" BoJo shuddered as he awakened to the fact that Humpty Trumpty had planted something bizarre in his brain. "And, by the way, there's an excellent book called 'Crime and Punishment'. It was written by Fyodor Dostoevsky in 1886 in St. Petersburg, Russia, translated by Constance Garnett and published by Random House in 1956!" BoJo very pompously intoned.

---

[144] BACK BENCHERS: Usually newly elected Members of Parliament, but ones not yet chosen to be Ministers in the Cabinet. The Ministers sit on the front benches, the others sit on the back benches – and can often be seen sleeping - or looking shocked and aghast at the antics of the other MPs who have been in the House for longer. The shouting, cheering, booing, jeering, cat-calls and general mayhem are an amazing sight. Ordeeeeer!

And then added, "I do, naturally, have a First Edition, collector's copy in my personal library at Number 10."

Typically, BoJo was, as usual, unable to resist showing off his Eton/Harrow/Oxford knowledge of the classics to the poor Sheriff, who had been unable to even graduate from High School with any sort of diploma. But somehow despite that, or maybe because of it, he managed to get into the police force. He was, of course, required to attend the *Police Academy*[145].

56. Desk Sergeant's Blotter (1886)

"Oooooh, that sounds my kinda story, bhoy!" said the Sheriff. "And has it got lots of pictures? I like books with lots of pictures! Can I borrow your copy? It sounds like it's an old one anyways, so you probably won't be bothered about getting it back in good con-dition. I usually highlight stuff and write in the margins. That's OK isn't it?"

"Hhhhhrrruumphhhh. Absolutely NOT!" replied the aghast BoJo.

"Ooooo! Well, excuuuse me for askin' . . ." said the Sheriff, totally oblivious of the internal pain that BoJo was feeling even just thinking about his precious First Edition of 'Crime and Punishment' being scribbled in.

"Look here my good man, if you want to get involved in some real crimes you can help me find the Trumper in this place they call the Coloured House. Though why they call it that name I have absolutely no idea," said BoJo trying to change the subject and dismiss the mental images of his precious 'Crime & Punishment' with lots of highlights and margin notes.

---

[145] POLICE ACADEMY: If you have ever seen any of the Police Academy movies you will appreciate that it wasn't difficult for Buford T. Justiss to get in just by quoting his name. And having that probably meant he was over-qualified. For sure he would have made Captain in today's cop shop show, Brooklyn Nine-Nine. It's that dumb. I'm just sayin'.

"OOOOOooooooooOooooooo!" exclaimed the Sheriff. "Now that sounds like real po-lice work. And you know the name of the 'perp' and where he lives. That's great de-tective work, my new-found BFF."

"Er, umm, er. Not so much of the BFF, whatever that means, and pray what is a 'perp'?" asked BoJo, who was good on the 'classics' but woefully behind the times on current lingua-franca.

"Well now, bhoy. When you are an im-portant officer of the law like myself you have to keep up-to-date with the latest catch phrases and words so that you seam-lessly blend in with the rest of the people on the streets," Buford T. Justiss pretentiously pontificated, despite the fact that it was blatantly obvious that the Sheriff – wearing his uniform and Stetson – stuck out like a sore thumb in any street crowd.

"For your in-for-mation, 'BFF' means 'Best Friend Forever' and 'perp' is a po-lice technical term for 'perpetrator' – the person who co-mmitted the crime," he added condescendingly as though he was divulging state secrets.

"Whatever . . ." intoned BoJo. "I really just need to find the Coloured House. Do you know where it is?"

"Of course, I do bhoy," huffed the Sheriff. "It's at the top of Trumpsylvania Avenue. Number 1600 to be pre-cise. You jes' can't miss it. Jes' look out for the big gold letters on the roof!"

"Righto then. Let's get going. Yes, as fast as we can. I'm eager to meet the Trumper after all I have heard about him from various people here," BoJo said as he rubbed his hands together in anticipation.

"Whoah there bhoy. Jess a darn tootin' minute. I've been on duty here all mornin' and I am feeling just a mite like I need some vittals. Let's jess pop into a diner and grab somethin' be-fore we go." said the Sheriff with a fixed smile that meant he was going nowhere till he ate.

"OK. OK." agreed BoJo, remembering that he also had not eaten for what felt like an eternity – whatever an eternity actually did feel like.

They walked round the corner to what was obviously the Sheriff's favourite local diner and went in through the screen door and up to the counter. There was a gap between the folks sitting on stools, eating. Strangely, no-one moved, and conversation stopped. It was like the scene in Dirty Harry IV when the waitress put way too much sugar in Harry's coffee to alert him that there were some bad guys in the diner. Hmmm!

"Give me a *Diablo Sandwich* [146] and a *Dr. Pepper* [147] and make it quick, I'm in a god-damn hurry," said the Sheriff. "And the same for my BFF here. He's payin'."

BoJo spluttered as he had absolutely no idea what a 'Diablo Sandwich' was, much less a 'Dr. Pepper' but decided that discretion was the better part of valor and it wasn't an appropriate moment to argue with the Sheriff. A wise move in most circumstances.

A good-looking Redneck guy with a moustache and a Stetson, sitting at the counter turned to the Sheriff and said, "You must be in a helluva hurry, huh, Sheriff?"

"You can bet your ass on that bhoy!" he replied.

"You gotta little mess here on your tie. Let me help you wipe that off," said the guy as he wiped his tie – much to the disdain of the Sheriff.

"I'm much obliged," he responded, his Southern good manners over-riding his dislike of having a stranger touch his Texas Police issue tie.

"Who are you chasin'? Or is somebody chasin' you?" asked the over-friendly Redneck.

The Sheriff turned to the Redneck, half eaten sandwich in hand and said menacingly, "No-body's a-chasin' me bhoy!! I was a-chasin' a god-damned maniac all the way from Texar-kana, Texas!!!"

"Really! You're a longways from home! What happened?" asked the Redneck cheekily.

"I'll tell you what happened! That bhoy Junior is what happened. That bhoy is so dumb that he dis-tracted me and caused me to lose that Bandit! There is no way, NO way that he came from my loins. The first thing I'm gonna do when I get home is punch his momma in the mouth!" exploded the Sheriff with a mouth full of Diablo Sandwich.

---

[146] DIABLO SANDWICH: A weird concoction, but no-one is quite sure what really was in it. One version is a sloppy-joe style recipe with seasoned ground beef, corn and sour cream. Another idea, based on images from the film, is pulled pork and hot sauce on a hamburger bun. Others reckon it's of any of the various Louisiana-style hot sauces on Texas Toast bread. Either way, BoJo, more used to cucumber sandwiches, hated it.

[147] DR. PEPPER: Allegedly, apparently, a drink. Invented in the 1880's by a pharmacist in Waco, Texas - the same place they had the Waco Siege of the David Koresh, Branch Davidian Cult. Allegedly aids digestion and sort of tastes of prune juice. The drink that is, not the cult. Now sold in cans, like Coke, but similarly, has no original ingredients.

The Sheriff didn't seem to realise that it was no longer 1977 in Texarkana, or anywhere else for that matter, and the 'Me Too' movement had taken a strong leap forward for women's rights.

"I see . . . So, what are you doing now that's got you in so much of a hurry? Chasin' a bank robber?" the Redneck kept probing.

"Bank robber? Hah! Bank robbin' is babysh*t alongside what this dude is doin'." shot back the Sheriff. "What we are dealin' with here is a com-plete lack of re-spec' for the law. That guy don' even know how to spell the word Cons-tit-ution never mind abide by and uphold one."

"Wow Sheriff, who is that?" asked the Redneck.

"That perpetrator is President McDonald J. Trumper. That's who that is! And Sheriff Buford T. Justiss of Texas is gonna get him." he bragged.

"Holy steer! You mean you are 'the' Sheriff Buford T. Justiss?? I've heard of you. You're 'effin' FAMOUS with a capital F." said the Redneck, both mocking and massaging the Sheriff's ego at the same time.

BoJo had been watching what was going on and realised that the Redneck was actually the Sheriff's arch foe – The Bandit. So, he started to tap the Sheriff on the shoulder.

"Sheriff, Sheriff. I need to tell you something," interrupted BoJo.

"Jus' a darn minute there bhoy. I am havin' a good con-versation with this nice young man." said the Sheriff ignoring BoJo's insistent tapping.

The Redneck continued, "But Sheriff, if you are from Texarkana, as sure as a buckin' bronco bucks, yo gonna be a Ripoffican, right?"

"Bhoy! As sure as there is black gold in them thar Texas hills, I am a LIFETIME member of the Ripofflican Party. But no-one is above the LAW! Remember that bhoy!"

"Oh er, sure Sheriff. I will take good care to remember that. But where did you hear that phrase?" asked the Redneck, full-well knowing the answer while thinking of his own exploits, way, way above the Law.

"I'm not sure. I think it was some woman here in the Government. Nancy something . . ."

"You mean, er, Nancy Palooka, the Speaker of the House?" asked the Redneck.

"Yeah, bhoy, that is her. She is a real Texas Ranger. Always gets her man. One Riot, One Ranger!" said the Sheriff.

This was great praise, if totally misplaced, in that she comes from California and is a Dimocrat. Not just 'a' Dimocrat, but 'the' Dimocrat. The Speaker of the House rules the House. What Nancy says, goes.

BoJo was still tapping the Sheriff on the shoulder.

"Sheriff, Sheriff. There is something you need to know." said BoJo.

"Bhoy, just a mo' there!" said the Sheriff again.

Realising what was going on and that BoJo had recognized him, the Redneck knew he had to make a hasty retreat.

"Well, Sheriff, it's been nice talkin' to you, but I gotta go," he said and headed for the door. Just as he put his hand on the screen door, the Sheriff paused eating his Diablo Sandwich and turned around.

"Hold on there a boon-doggling minute, bhoy. Your voice sounds very fam-iliar to me. You sure ain't from around these parts. Jus' where yo' from?" asked the Sheriff with a tight-lipped but menacing smile.

"Ah, er, from down Texas way, Sheriff. From around, er, Texarkana, actually…" said the Redneck ever so slowly.

"Really, bhoy. Hmmm. Texar-kana, you say. And just what did you say your name was, again?" asked the Sheriff.

"Bo B. Daredeville, Sheriff," said the Redneck as he opened the door.

"Really!" said the Sheriff staring at the back of the Redneck's head in slow recognition. "And what does the 'B' stand for, bhoy?"

"Er, it stands for, er," the Redneck said. And, just as the screen door slammed shut, he said the word. "Bandit".

"Woah there BHOY!!" shouted the Sheriff and rushed to the door just in time to see a black 1977 Pontiac Trans Am with the license plate BAN–ONE sliding out of the car park in a wheel-spinning, 4-wheel drift.

57.	Smokin' … !

GOD-DAMNIT!!! shouted the Sheriff and threw his hat on the floor in anger and disgust and stamped on it in fury. "That SUMBITCH BANDIT jes' made a fool out of me AGAIN! I told you before that no-body, and I mean NO-BODY makes Sheriff Buford T. Justiss look like a possum's pecker."

"I'm sorry to be the bearer of bad tidings," said BoJo, "but it seems like he just did. I recognised him when you were talking."

"Well, why in tarnation didn't you tell me bhoy!" growled the Sheriff.

"I was trying to, Sheriff, but you kept ignoring me and then the Bandit realised that I knew who he was. It was the Stetson, the moustache and the amiable smile. Everyone remembers that from 'Smokey and the Bandit'," BoJo explained. "But why didn't you recognise him, Sheriff?"

"Be-cause, bhoy, I could never catch that sumbitch! All I ever saw was the back of his god-damned head plus listening to his tauntin' me all day long on the *CB Radio* [148]. It was somethin' about his voice that suddenly made a light go on in mah head." said the Sheriff very disconsolately.

"Don't worry, Sheriff," BoJo said cheerily. "We have much bigger catfish to fry. And all his chuckleheads too!"

"Yeah bhoy, right on! But tell me. If you are goin' after a big catfish, why don' you get help from the FBI or the A-ttorney General of the Depart-ment of Jus-tice himself? Why pick me? I'm jes' a simple County Sheriff from the State of Texas an' I can't even catch that god-damned sumbitch Bandit!" said the Sheriff in a rare moment of humility - which was unlikely to last very long.

Like any predatory politician would, BoJo sensed that this was his moment to strike and get the Sheriff hooked on his plan.

"Tell me Sheriff," what does the 'T' stand for in your name?" asked BoJo as innocently as any politician can when he knows the answer.

---

[148] CB RADIO: Citizen Band Radio is used by long-haul truck drivers for everything from relaying info on road conditions, the location of police speed traps and other travel information, to basic socializing and friendly chatter. It started in 1976 but was popularized in 1977 by the movie. The Sheriff was 'Smokey Bear' – a name still generally used on CB to denote the police. Bo Daredeville was 'Bandit', Carrie, the runaway bride, was 'Frog' and the truck driver with the bootleg beer was 'Snowman'.

"Well, I don't usually tell many folks this 'cause my daddy, was Buford R. Justiss, and his middle name was 'Rough'. He had a bit of a cruel sense of humor. And he came from a long line of po-licemen – with equally cruel senses of humor – his daddy was Buford M. Justiss where the M was for 'Mob'. My daddy always wanted me to join the force, right from the moment I was born. So, my middle name is 'Tough' yesiree!!" admitted the Sheriff finally.

What the Sheriff did not realise was that BoJo was 13 years old when 'Smokey and the Bandit' was released and he had a HUGE crush, not to mention an even HUGER hard-on for *Carrie* [149], the runaway bride. As a result, he had spent many nights having pubescent fantasies about bonking her while fervently trying to relieve the tumescent pressure in his teenage loins. This also meant that he had researched everything he could about the characters in the movie. So, he knew what the Sheriff's middle name was and had stored the information for over 42 years, somehow anticipating it would be useful someday. BoJo was that calculating - even so far back in time - and even when his mind was significantly distracted by incessant teenage masturbation.

"So, Sheriff, your full name is Buford Tough Justiss! That's wonderful and just what I need!!!" clapped BoJo, ingratiating himself indelibly with the Sheriff.

"Oh, REALLY!!" exclaimed the Sheriff with a huge leery smile.

"Yes, Sheriff, I would have liked to enlist the help of James Coney-Island or Andrew McCrab, but they got sacked by the Trumper for doing their job. And Bill 'No Collusion' Barf simply cannot be trusted to do the job of being the Attorney General of the Department of Justice. And, by the way that's J.U.S.T.I.C.E not J.U.S.T.I.S.S."

"OK, bhoy, let's go and get that sumbitch!!" said the Sheriff gleefully.

"Right, Sheriff, how far is it to the Coloured House?" asked BoJo.

"Aww. It's way across town. But we can drive in my po-lice car."

---

[149] CARRIE: In the movie, Carrie was played by Sally Field and was auspicious for often pointing her derrière at the camera in her tight white jeans. This obviously stimulated BoJo's erectile tissues ad-infinitum. He has taken his obsession so far as to have multiple relationships and marriages until he finally found a woman called Carrie that fell for him. Carrie On-Regardless and BoJo were engaged on 29 Feb. 2020 and she already fell pregnant with his 5th child. (or 6th, depending whose counting). Yes, he's a fast worker.

"Wonderful. Where is it?" asked BoJo.

"It's jes' parked a-round the back of the diner. Follow me," said the Sheriff.

They went to the back lot and there was the Sheriff's police car – he still had the same car - without the roof - ever since he had the incident when the car went under a concrete beam on a semi-trailer.

58. Pontiac LeMans Police Car – Convertible (and then some)

"OH – MY – GOD!" exclaimed BoJo. "You still have that car!"

"Yo' sure god-damned right I do bhoy! Why would I give up my State of Texas, po-lice issue, ve-hicle? I will have you know that as a senior officer of the law I am accountable for my po-lice car and, on top of that, this ve-hicle is evidence of the heinous crimes co-mitted by that desperado, the Bandit." said the Sheriff as if it needed explanation.

"OK, whatever! I guess that there's not much choice right now," said BoJo. "At least it's better than a USSR Moskvitch Moscow Mitch Mk3."

"Well, let's get agoin'. We have bandits to catch," said the Sheriff as he jumped in the police car, which was easy as there was no driver's door. "Make sure you wear your seatbelt – clunk, click every trip - and jes' hold my hat on so she don' blow away, if you don' mind bhoy."

Fortunately, the Pontiac LeMans had seen significantly better days, so it just chugged, rattled and squeaked along the road at a slow grovel. They could have actually walked faster. But BoJo said nothing.

They were trundling, bumping and grinding their way along the road, the Sheriff was smiling blissfully and, as usual smoking a cigarette, when all of a sudden, he slammed on the brakes. Nothing much happened, 'slamming' being a relative term in a 1977 Pontiac LeMans, but the vehicle just about decelerated from a slothful crawl to a quivering halt.

"What happened?" asked BoJo. He had just fallen into a fitful doze and had not been watching the road ahead.

"Take a look for your-self, bhoy," said the Sheriff. He had almost bumped into the White Rabbi as he crossed the road in front of the police car. But, just like each time BoJo had seen it before, the White Rabbi ignored them completely and just stared at his watch.

"Oyvey! I'm late. I'm late. For a very important date! I'm late. I'm late. They're going to close the gate! I'm late. I'm late. I'm late. I'm late. I'm late. I'm late. I'm late!"

And then quickly ran off into the bushes muttering to himself.

"What on earth is that White Rabbi talking about?" said BoJo to the Sheriff.

"Well, bhoy, the Trumper really likes to con-trol the borders of this place. So, he has big fences all around it and the gates only open at a certain time to let people in or out. Mostly out, by the way. And if you miss the time slot you are to-tally screwed. I can tell you there are some sorts of people that he jes' doan' wanna' let in here. And if you sneak in when he is not alookin' he will jes' put you in a cage whether you are young or old. He is like that crazy, god-damned *Tiger King* [150] guy. He is not a racist of course – in fact, he will tell you that he is the least racist person on the planet (without actually sayin' which planet). But it's mighty inter-estin' that he jes' seems to prefer white cau-casian Christian folks. So, those with even a tiny dash of color or a diff-erent religion jes' seem to be, shall we say, 'less fav-ored'," explained the Sheriff.

"That's interesting. Especially as he seems to be trying to turn himself from a white-skinned person to an orange one. Sort of like Michael Jackson in reverse! And also, that while he says he is very religious and that The Bible is his favourite book, he can't actually quote any single thing from it," chortled BoJo, somewhat mercilessly.

---

[150] TIGER KING: Anyone without Netflix needs a subscription to believe that crazy story.

"Yesiree!" said the Sheriff. "That's why the White Rabbi is tryin' to get outta here be-fore some gun-totin' Ripofflican with a Facebook full of Trumper-butt lickin' statements, a van covered in syco-phantic bumper stickers and an arsenal full of a-ssault weapons bursts into his par-ticular synagogue and blows everyone to pieces."

"For a home-grown Texas boy, you seem to be very anti those 2nd Amendment-quoting, gun-toting, free radicals!" said BoJo with a smirk.

"I tell you bhoy, those folks are a causin' so much trouble for law enforce-ment officers, like yours truly, that I believe that guns should be jes' for the po-lice. That way, if anyone is firin' a gun, it's the bhoys with the badges not the bad guys!" pronounced the Sheriff emphatically.

"Hah!!! I couldn't have morphically resonated for anyone better!" said BoJo. "My sincere and unfettered felicitations along with my abject and unremitting, unadulterated and earnest expressions of one's regret, remorse and sorrow for having insulted, verbally injured and willfully wronged you when I made some significantly disparaging, condescending and condemnational remarks regarding your capabilities as an officer of the law."

"What???" asked the Sheriff, having no idea what BoJo was talking about and definitely not realising that he was simply apologizing for earlier being his usual boorish self.

"Er, ah, er. I am just saying that I need someone just like you," said BoJo trying to simplify it down to the Sheriff's comprehension level.

"Right on, bhoy. Let's get back on the job," said the Sheriff as he started the LeMans again and slowly wound it up to its torpid gait.

Time was passing slowly, almost slower than the police car was passing the buildings on the streets, as they inched their way across town towards Trumpsylvania Avenue and the Colored House.

BoJo had been snoozing again, as he often did at No. 10 and in the Houses of Parliament. He would never admit to snoozing, of course, and, if woken unexpectedly, would bluster and try and bluff it off that he was having a Japanese-style 'Power Nap'. It was nothing of the sort – he was usually just bored with the debate going on around him – and the nearest thing to Japan about it was that he would often snore like a dragon and his breath would be steaming from too much wasabi on his sushi lunch.

The LeMans hit another bone-shaking, massive pothole, causing yet another piece of bodywork to fall off. And the Sheriff cursed again. "That god-damned Trumper and all his B.S. about being a fan-tastic builder and 'Better than anyone at infra-structure'. He can't tell a hole in the road from a hole in his ass!"

"What? What? What?" said BoJo, woken by a combination of the shuddering of what was left of the LeMans and the cussing of the Sheriff.

"Where are we? Are we there yet Dad?" BoJo asked soporifically as he had been dreaming about going on long drives in the back of his father's car when he was young.

"I'm not your dad, bhoy! I have more than en-uff stu-pid-ity for one family in that so-called son of mine, Junior." shot back the Sheriff, but wishing he could have shot his Deputy. "But yes, we are almost there. Jes' take a look up the road. There's your Colored House."

59.	The Colored House – 1600 Trumpsylvania Avenue

And yes, there it was, gleaming in the late afternoon sun. Well, at least the big gold T.R.U.M.P letters on the roof and the golden charging gladiators on the front lawn were gleaming. The words "I am Maximus Decimus Meridius" were echoing from the speaker in one and "No, I am Maximus Decimus Meridius" was blaring from the other, ad-infinitum.

"I guess I should have expected the T.R.U.M.P. letters on the roof! The Trumper's ego is so fragile that he always has to have his name in big letters on anything that is his. I'm surprised he doesn't have it emblazoned on the First Lady. But I see that at least the CHAVs were right about the four big pillars still being there. Though there was a bit of confusion as to whether he was talking about pillars or pillocks," chortled BoJo. "I guess we will have to see what the inhabitants are like before we make that judgement."

"Sure thing bhoy, let's get rootin' tootin' on with the job," exclaimed the Sheriff.

"By the way Sheriff," asked BoJo, "why is it now called The Coloured House? It used to be called the White House and it still looks white to me."

"Well, the Trumper was always bein' called a racist and shot at in the media for not liking people of co-lor. He was always asayin' that he 'was the least ra-cist person that anyone knew!' I don' know about that 'ceptin' that he musta' known some REALLY ra-cist people if he was the least of them. So, anyways, one day he a-nnounced he would change the name to the Colored House to prove he wasn't racist. That was all fine and dandy till one day one of the re-porters heard him sayin' to one of his golfin' buddies that "People are so stupid and easy to outsmart. Don't they know that white is a color – and it's my favourite one!"

"He just never ceases to amaze." said BoJo, thinking to himself how his own hang-ups, indiscretions and political tricks just paled into insignificance against those of the Trumper

So up Trumpsylvania Avenue they trundled, not really noticing that the road surface was made of yellow bricks. And even if they had, they probably still wouldn't have grasped the significance . . .

Till at last they got to the gate of the Colored House.

19

MEANWHILE PART 9 – THE CHURLISH MONARCH

Meanwhile . . .

Meanwhile, inside the Colored House, the Queen of Queens was still lambasting The McDonald due to his poor performance on all counts, including in the bedroom, and he was about to get into more trouble yet again and again and again.

"McDOOOONOLDDT! McDOOOONOLDDT!"

"Er, er, yyes, ddear?" The McDonald stuttered in fear.

"I ams hearingk all za times abouts how youse are screwingk up za wholez country viz vot youse are doingk – or mores preciciselies vot youse are notz doingk – tzo solvfs za Toyotacorollaviruz problem, za economy, za out off work peoplez, za financials aids tzo folkz andt efferysink elze tzo!"

"Bbut Melleemalarkey, that's not fair . . ."

"Notz fair? Notz fair? Vot iss fair abouts za USA haffingk more casez of za virus andt more peoplez dyingk zan anyvere elses in za vorldt?"

"We have it under control. Trust me. It will soon be all over and I've told everyone to forget all about it once it is, so that they won't hold it against me when they vote in November. My beautiful ratings are up too, ever since I've been doing the daily campaign, I mean virus, briefings"

"Cuntrolz! Cuntrolz! Youse can'ts evens keeps yourz penitz inz yours pantz unders za cuntrolz – evens zo its izz onlies a teensie weensie von – neffer mindz za Toyotacorollavirus andt za rest off za country!"

"But why are you saying all those 'nasty' things?"

"Becozes zat youse ares allvays sayingk za dumbezt sings. Likes ven Doktor Flatoucchie sedz zat efferyvon shouldt coffer zere facez viz somez sorts off maskz, youse straightavayz says zat youse vont do zat. Tzo STUPIDT! I hadt tzo qvickly tellz efferyvon zat zey shouldt vear a mazk venn zey are outsides."

"I don't want to wear a mask. I would look too much like a bandit if I did."

"McDonaldt! Youse ares za biggest bandit zat zis country hass effer seens. So, iff za mask fitz, vear its! Here, try ziss black face mask on."

"Me? A bandit? I am just a New York businessman – who also happens to be President - struggling to make a buck or two to make ends meet. Do I have to wear this mask?"

"Ya, putz za damn sing on. NOW! Zat iss yourse profflem – youse vant to be BOTH za President and za Buzzinezzman. Youse vant tzo haff yours cookiez andt eats zem!"

The Trumper reluctantly put the mask on and was just about to respond when, out of nowhere, the doorbell rang.

TRRRRIIINNNNGGG! TRRRRIIINNNNGGG!

The Trumper and the Queen of Queens looked at each other in surprise. No-one ever rang the doorbell these days. The McDo delivery boy used to ring the bell when he brought The McDonald his breakfast, lunch, dinner, supper and midnight snacks. But everyone got fed up with answering the door, so they gave him his own key so he could let himself in. He didn't have an official security clearance, but neither did most people who worked in the Colored House these days.

"Vhoo za hells iss zat?"

"I have no idea. I have not ordered anything from McDo's for at least 30 minutes and I already ate that delivery."

TRRRRIIINNNNGGG! TRRRRIIINNNNGGG!

"Youse are surez zat itz nots von off yours prawn starz or centercreasez commingk tzo picks up herz $130,000 pay-offz checkz?"

"Er, er, I hope, I mean I am sure, er, that it's nothing like that and even if it is, it was not me and I wasn't there. Why do you keep saying that? It's like replaying the same video tape all the time."

"Zat iss simplies because youse keepz doingk za same sh*tz times and timez agains and agains and agains. Youse neffer learnz. For surez yours brainz ares inn yours dickz. And itz a ferry smallz dickz, soze zere cantz be spacez for manies brainz cellz in zere!"

"Aahh . . ."

TRRRIIINNNNGGG! TRRRIIINNNNGGG! TRRRIIINNNNGGG!

"McDoonaldt! Do somesink! Getz von off yourz Secretz Surface guyz or McDon Jr or Erik offz zere fat buttz tzo checkz za securitiez cameras at za door beforez vhoeffer it iss breakz za bladdy doorbellz!"

TRRRIIINNNNGGG! TRRRIIINNNNGGG! TRRRIIINNNNGGG!

"Boys! Check who the hell is at the door."

"Sure, Mowgli!" said Erik

"Erik, I have told you before, don't call me 'Mowgli'. That's my code name used only by the Secret Service guys. You can call me 'Sir'."

"But if you don't want me to call you Mowgli, can't I call you 'Dad'? Please!"

"Certainly not! That is not allowed. I don't want you kids to get too familiar – except Iwanka, of course. She's my favourite. Beautiful!"

TRRRIIINNNNGGG! TRRRIIINNNNGGG! TRRRIIINNNNGGG!

"McDOOONAALLDDTT! Za door!!!!

"Oh, er, yes dear!" he replied and then hissed, "Erik – get your finger out and get on with it!"

"Sorry. Yes, Mowgli, er, sorry, er, Dad, er, sorry, er, sir!"

"ERIK!"

TRRRIIINNNNGGG! TRRRIIINNNNGGG! TRRRIIINNNNGGG!

"I'm coming. Hold on to your horses," said Erik, which was actually useless as the people were outside and could not hear him until he got to the security desk, looked at the screen and pressed the speaker button.

"Who is it Erik?" asked the Trumper before Erik could even ask.

"Dad, er sorry, sir. It's a big, fat guy with a moustache, wearing a Sheriff's uniform and a smallish, chubby guy with blonde hair that looks like he just got out of bed and he's wearing running shorts, sneakers and an old sweat-shirt that says something about 'BREXIT Forever!' on it."

"What???"

"Yeah! And Dad, sorry, sir, they are driving what looks like what is left of a 1977 Pontiac LeMans police car with no roof!"

"That sounds weird. Pontiac didn't make a convertible LeMans in 1977."

"No, sir Dad. I don't mean a convertible. I mean a LeMans with no roof. Oh, and no doors either."

"I don't get it. Ask them who they are and what they want."

"Sure, er, Dad, sir Dad."

Erik pressed the speaker button and said in his best imitation of a security guard voice. "Halt, who goes there? Friend or foe?" He had seen it in an old black and white movie, and it was that only thing that came into his head – a not unusual experience for Erik.

"Bhoy! Is that Erik Trumper who is askin'?" said the Sheriff. And then turned to BoJo and said quietly, "Cause it sure as tar-nation couldn't be dumb e-nuff to be anyone else."

"I heard that! Who are you people and what do you want?" said Erik, trying, but failing, to sound important.

"Bhoy, tell yo' Daddy that Sheriff Buford T. Justiss of Portague County in the Great State of Texas and the Right Honorable Alexander Boris de Piffle Jockstrap, Prime Minis-ter of the U-nited King-dom are here to see him forth-with and toot-sweet. And be god-damned quick about it, bhoy!!" the Sheriff responded in no uncertain terms.

"Er, OK. OK," blathered Erik unconvincingly.

"Who the hell is it Erik?" asked the Trumper.

"Er, Dad, sorry, sir, it's a Justice Burger from Texas and someone called Boris something or other that says he is the Minister of Prime Time in England. They want to see you," said Erik getting about half the message right and most of it wrong.

"Ach, Erik! Youse are evens stupiderer zan yourse Dadt andt zat iss sayingk somesinks. Don'dt youse know zat dat iss Boriz Jockstrapz, ze Primez Minizter off za Uniteds Kinkdom? I haff no ideaz who zee ozzer guy zizz. Muzt, maybeez, be hiss bodyguardz."

"Er, Erik. She is right. Let them in," ordered the Trumper though he was a bit miffed about both he and Erik being called stupid, yet again, by the Queen of Queens.

Erik clicked the button to unlock the door and the Sheriff and BoJo blustered their way into the Colored House.

"About time there, bhoy," said the Sheriff. "You sure took yo' sweet time to let your es-teemed guests in here!"

"Exactly!" agreed BoJo. "I have been trying to find this place ever since I arrived in Trumperland and then I'm kept waiting at the door. It's not what one is used to as the senior political figure of a major western nation and – I might point out - an ally of the USA. We are not one of those 'sh*t-h*le' countries your father often disparagingly refers to. At least we had better not be!"

BoJo was significantly peeved at the treatment so far and, after all the strange, disturbing and often unfathomable things he had encountered on his way there, he was not his usual jolly, feckless self. Far from it, in fact.

"Er, ah, er, ah, er, I, er, I'm sorry. I wasn't aware till the Queen of Queens explained it to me," quivered Erik.

"The Queen of Queens? I thought this was a republic not a monarchy?" queried BoJo, who, being an Eton/Harrow/Oxford alumni, and, as some would say, an upper-class snob, was very, very, very particular about hierarchical royal protocols.

As far as BoJo was concerned, there is a pecking order, and as long as you were at the top of it, that was the way it should stay. Just check out *Burke's Peerage* [151] if you have any doubts on the matter.

"I er, have no idea and definitely I am not allowed to have any opinion on the matter," said Erik, somewhat morosely. He obviously knew his place in the pecking order – and it was pretty near the bottom.

"Ah! Is the Queen of Queens your mother then, bhoy?" asked the Sheriff, who was obviously not fully aware of all the intricacies of the Trumper's multiple marriages and liaisons.

"Er, my mother? No. She is just Barron's mother," answered Erik.

"Oh, so you have a Queen and a Baron, then?" asked the singularly innocent Sheriff. "This is star-ting to look like a mo-narchy to me."

---

[151] BURKE'S PEERAGE: A very British genealogical publication, founded in 1826, devoted to the ancestry and heraldry of the peerage, baronetage, knightage and landed gentry of UK. Don't you just love that term 'landed gentry'? Classic upper-class snobby.

"Hmmm, Sheriff. I think I am starting to get a handle on this," said BoJo. "The Queen is so named because she is the undisputed ruler of the household. Being the Queen of Queens is a double entendre. On the one hand, the Trumper family had lowly beginnings in the Borough of Queens, New York. On the other, this particular Queen is going to make sure she is very much the 'top dog' in the lengthy list of Trumper women. So, Queen of Queens is a perfect title and constant reminder of her status to the Trumper."

"Aaah I see! I think," said the Sheriff with a puzzled look in his face. "But what about this here Baron and the Trumper? How the be-jesus do they fit in to this so-called re-publican mo-narchy?"

"Well, Sheriff, they only fit in an aspirational way. The Trumper has lofty aspirations of being a monarch, or at least a dictator, so he named his son Barron to give him some kind of pseudo-heraldic, non-hereditary, peerage. Actually, its spelt with two Rs in the middle – B.A.R.R.O.N – so he didn't even get that bit right as it should only have one R for a real Baron," explained BoJo to the Sheriff, as they walked through the corridors of the Colored House, out of earshot of Erik so as not to upset him.

"From what I have seen of this President on TV he is way too darn grumpy, vin-dictive, mean and gen-erally 'nasty' to be a mo-narch. But he sure would make a god-damned, good dic-tator and would cer-tainly enjoy that if he got half a chance," said the Sheriff.

"Yes, at least one very learned, U.S. constitutional historian dubbed him a *churlish monarch* [152] which I think is a perfect simile for the Trumper. In fact, if we said, 'He wants to rule like a churlish monarch' it's almost a mixed metaphor or even an oxymoron," said BoJo just as they reached the residential quarters in the Colored House.

Erik let them into the main living room, but then scuttled off quickly before he got blamed for anything that someone else had done wrong – which happened on a regular basis in the Trumper household.

---

[152] CHURLISH MONARCH: A phrase beautifully coined by Jon Meacham on Stephen Colbert's A Late Show, in Easter 2020. He also said that the US needs an Avengers Team of Presidents: FDR, LBJ & Obama to solve its pandemic & economic crises. Both true!

"Who is a moron!??!" asked the Trumper somewhat churlishly, though with an underlying taint of expectation that the barb was aimed at him – even though he had mis-heard it – and forgetting that he was in the presence of the Queen of Queens.

"McDOOONNAALLDTTT!! SHUTS ZA FACKZ UPZ! Showz your guestz somes respec'. Youse knowz vat I means. R – E – S – P – E – C'."

"Er, yes dear! Sorry, dear! I forgot myself for a moment," grovelled the Trumper.

BoJo and the Sheriff were looking at each other, wide-eyed while this was going on. This was a different Trumper than most of the outside world knew.

"Er, er. My apologies, er, your, er, Royal Highness," said BoJo, not quite sure, for once, of the appropriate 'royal' protocol for this situation. "We did not call anyone a moron. I was actually talking about an *oxymoron* [153], which is a figure of speech containing a few words which produces an incongruous, seemingly self-contradictory effect. For example, 'She was pretty ugly'."

"Ach, I getz its," said the Queen. "You meanz like 'A stabledt geniuz' or 'A Trumper Universityz' or 'A McDonald Trumper Charity'?"

"Aaahh, er. Well *Ma'am*,[154] er not quite. But it's close enough," said BoJo, who, having heard her tirade at the Trumper, did not want to upset her needlessly. Also, having had a moment to think about it, he also decided to use the British protocol, as used when addressing the current Queen, Elizabeth II. He did note also, though, that she was using three of the Trumper's biggest cons as examples.

"Er, Ma'am we weren't in any way, shape or form casting defamatory, calumniated aspersions about your, er, husband," BoJo tried to faintly apologise.

"Hmmm! Itz OK. He iss za totalz moronz anyvays!" said the Queen.

---

[153] OXYMORON: Two words or ideas put together in a phrase which, at first glance, seem to be contradictory to one another. Such as 'A little pregnant', 'American culture', 'Act naturally', 'A German sense of humor', 'British cuisine', 'Happily married' or the mother of all oxymorons 'Scientific American', formerly a magazine, but now . . . ?

[154] MA'AM: It's protocol to call the Queen 'Your Royal Highness' the first time you address her. After that it should be Ma'am pronounced 'Mam' as in Spam not 'Maaam' as in Marmalade. So, if ever you get a 'gong' or knighted you now know the drill. OK?

BoJo coughed to cover his surprise and looked over at the Sheriff who had a sort of drop-jaw expression on his face at the Queen's comment.

"Er, whatever you say Ma'am!" BoJo rejoined, almost automatically.

"Vell, youse voss rinngink za bell likes crazies. Vot does youse vant tzo tsee uss aboutz?"

"Er, well, Ma'am I am Boris Jockstrap the Prime Minister of the United Kingdom and ever since I have been er, here – wherever exactly 'here' is – I have been meeting lots of very weird characters. Well, er sort of creatures actually, and they have been telling me all kinds of very strange, almost unbelievable stories, about things that have happened or are happening. And most of them are either illegal or unconstitutional or crooked in some way. And some of them are just plain dumb."

"Ach, reallies. Realliez! Tellz me mores."

"Actually, Ma'am they all really revolve around your husband, the, er, 'King'," BoJo started to explain but was interrupted before he could go any further, and was way under-prepared for the response . . .

"ZAT MAN ISS NOTZ ZA KINGK!! I AM ZA QUEEN OFF QUEENZ, BUT HE ISS NOTZ ZA KINGK!!!! He iss justz za KONSORT!!"

"Oooh. Aaaaah. Yesss! Absolutely. Got it. Er, sorry. For sure Ma'am," mumbled BoJo in as a reconciliatory tone as he could muster.

"He iss alvays tryingk tzo throws his veight around. And, beliefs me, he hass plenties tzo throw – ziss Misters Chuppy Choppz heres. He iss likez za schoolyardt bullies whose alvays ansvers a qvestion viz a threadt because hes tzoo dumbp tzo knowz za real ansver."

The Sheriff had been silent ever since entering the room, but, apart from the occasional glance at BoJo, had hardly taken his eyes off the Trumper, undoubtedly because he was still wearing the black face mask that the Queen had told him to wear.

Suddenly, the Sheriff nudged BoJo, nodded towards the Trumper and whispered, "I think I found my bandit!"

And before BoJo could stop him, the Sheriff walked over to the Trumper and – much to his surprise - kicked him in the butt and saying,

"That's an a-ttention-getter."

"Wwwhatttt?" said the Trumper indignantly.

"You, bhoy, look to me like some sorta' serious bandit, awearin' that mask, and all!" chided the Sheriff, wagging his finger in the so-called suspect's face. "I want you to put your little hands on this here table and spread them legs wide. And don' go any-wheres, and don' go to eat, and don' play with yourself. It wouldn't be nice to stain this pretty carpet."

60.　　The Bandit Trumper

The Queen had been watching this with keen interest, but with apparently no intent to interfere.

"Ach, Sheriffs. Youse knowz zat ze mosts difficult von off zose instructionz for him tzo obey vill be za von abouts 'don'ts go tzo eatz'. Ha! LOL!" said the Queen with some significant amusement. "Andt I don'tz sink zat youse vill need tzo stopz hims playingk viz himself. Hiss handts and hiss vinkie ares tso tinies zat zey vud bee off nose uses tzo eachs ozzer, effen iffs he vanted tzo!"

The Queen was obviously enjoying the moment, whereas the Trumper definitely was not.

"Bhoy, you seem to be more than guilty of some very se-rious crimes against your Queen, the A-merican people, the Gov-ernment, the United States Con-sti-tution, the world we live in, hu-manity as a whole and the very fabric of the LAW itself! And, as an officer of the law, I jes' can-not abide by that. So, I am arresting you for violatin' Corpus Christi, Habeaus Corpus and bein' found In Flagrante Delicto without an approved safety device," said the Sheriff, who was on the roll of his life.

BoJo was too shocked, for once in his life, even to utter a single word. And, for BoJo, that is truly, truly shocked!

And the Trumper was even more than shocked. He had gone the whole 73 years of his life abusing everyone around him, bending and battering the law to the point of breaking, but had never been arrested. He had led a charmed life, managing to slip and slide through the cracks in the system.

And yet here was a hick, redneck Sheriff from the boondocks of Portague County, Texas, actually arresting him. The Trumper was also stunned to silence! Where was Bill Barf when you needed him most?

But the Sheriff hadn't finished yet and read the Trumper his *Mirinda Rights*[155]. "Bhoy, you have the right to remain orange. Anything you say, bhoy, can and will be god-damned used against you in a court of law. You have the right to an attorney, bhoy. If you cannot afford an attorney bhoy, one will be provided for you (but don' expec' a good un)."

"Tzo, vot happenz nows Sheriffs?" asked the Queen.

"Well Ma'am, there will have to be a trial of course. Anyone who co-mmits crimes has to go to court and be judged by a jury of his peers."

"Woooooowoooo! Zat iss greatz! Ize chust luvff trialz," said the Queen gleefully clapping her hands. "Andt zat meanz whoeffer iss guilties, I getz tzo say 'Off viz yours headt!!'. Zat iss tzo much funz."

"Bbbut why? This is not fair! I have just been through an Impeachment Trial and been acquitted. Why do I have to go through another trial?" argued the Trumper.

"Ha! McDoonaldt, zat vos notz a trials. Youse saids zo yourselfs. I toldt youse beforez zat alls zeze 'nasty' singks zat youse are doingk vill cums back andt bitez youse in yours fatt buttz!"

"It **was** a trial. There was a judge and jury and everything," wheedled the Trumper in his whiniest, spoilt-brat voice.

"Lookz. Youse hadt Moscow Mittdch McConnmans ins yours pocketz befores itz effen startedt. Andt za tso-calledt 'jury' voss all yours buddies who hadt cottonz vull in zere earz ven effer za Dimocrat persecutionerz voss telling za factz."

"Bbbbbuuutt, bbbuutt, Malaria!"

"McDDOOONNAALLLDDTTT!"

"Er, yes dear. Sorry dear!"

The Sheriff and BoJo had been watching this exchange without comment, not daring to interrupt the Queen in any way and hoping that she would not turn on either of them. But then she did just that.

---

[155] MIRINDA RIGHTS: Basically, it means you have the right to drink this PepsiCo orange beverage/concoction but don't expect any lawyer will defend you if you complain that it affects your skin color and turns it orange like an orangutan.

"SHERIFFS! Youze take za McDonaldt downz to za Rozy Gartenz!"

"Yes siree, er Ma'am," responded the Sheriff, confused with the protocols which no one from Portague County, Texas had ever needed to know before. "Er, Ma'am, but why the Rosy Garten? We need a court of law for the trial."

"Sheriffz! Za Rozy Garten iss perfects forz za trial. Zere iss a podiumz vere za McDoonaldt likez tzo standt andt tell hiss liess and more liess. And zere is lotz off spacez forz za juries off za peoples. Pluss zere ares plenties off seatz forz za Flakes Prezz, whos can alsoz askz za McDoonaldt lottza qvestionz. He vill hates zat! Butz whose carez?"

"OK Ma'am," said the Sheriff and then turned to the Trumper and said, "Bhoy, let's go. I'm gonna barbecue your ass in hot mo-lasses."

"Andt youse, Mr. BoJoz Prime Timez Ministers, youse haff to go viz him andt be svorn inz hass a vitness forz za persecutzion."

"But, but, but, me – a witness? I'm not a witness!" objected BoJo.

"MR. BOJOS! YOUSE HEARDT ME. Youse are a VITNESS iff I say soze - alongk viz allz za ozzer characterz arounds heres. Gott itz?!?"

"Er, yes Ma'am. Of course! Er, absolutely," agreed BoJo hurriedly.

"I sink I amz begginingk to likes takingk onn za job off beingk a churlisht monarch!" said the Queen of Queens with relish.

"Really?" said BoJo.

"Ya! Iff everysink goes tzo planz, it vill be 'Off viz hiss headt'!"

Fade to black . . .

POSTSCRIPT

The following clip was from 'A Late Show with Stephen Colbert' aired over the Easter Weekend 2020. His guest was Jon Meacham.

A CHURLISH MONARCH – JOHN MEACHAM
https://www.youtube.com/watch?v=Lp9I8wS3GqA&t=5s

20

TO KILL A MOCKINGBIRD

As with most things in Trumperland, the time-space continuum was very convoluted, resembling a *Möbius strip* [156] and it often seemed that things due to happen in the future had already happened and things from the past were still sitting around on the side-lines waiting to happen. And, likewise, things happening in the present could quite possibly not be bothered to happen at all.

As a result, by the time that BoJo, the Sheriff and the Trumper got to the Rosy Garten, the Queen was already there, sitting on a very, very large throne, the jury members were in the Jury Box and the gallery – where the press corps usually sat – was, of course, full of the Flake Press. An expectant buzz was going around the court – but that was just the bees getting on with collecting honey in the Rosy Garten.

There was a huge crowd in the Rosy Garten as word had spread very quickly due to all the different social media platforms that everyone in Trumperland subscribed to. The most important one was Twatter, as that one was beloved by the Trumper and his followers, the Twats.

---

[156] MöBIUS STRIP: Has the shape of an infinity sign (like a number 8 on its side) but has one continuous surface with no beginning or end, achieved by making it from a strip of paper and twisting the ends before you stick them together. So, the outside becomes the inside and vice-versa. To infinity and beyond . . .

But the other social medialites had been busy spreading the word too on Slap Chat, Tok Tik, Face-Off, Instanoodle and WhatsUpDoc!

There were all sorts of birds and beasts, from the Flake Press, each with their different approaches to any news, including CNN - Charlie the Naughty Nightingale, (sings like a bird on any story), TRMS - The Rachel Mad-Dog Show, (gnaws right down to the bone of the matter), ABC - American Buzzard Company, (always there for the kill), NYT - New York Tyrannosaurus, (likely to rip your head off for a byline), WAPO - the Washington Porcupine, (prickly and grumpy), MSNBC - Minnesota South & North Bison Co., (bred to stampede over other reporters), FOXY - Foxy the Fox News, (sly, cunning and unlikely to tell the truth), BBC - British Baboon Corporation, (primates who always think they are better than the other reporters because they are the only ones with opposable thumbs enabling them to hold a pencil).

On the front row of seats were all the characters that BoJo had met along the way like the CHAVs and the Trumper's avatar alter-egos like the Cheshire Pussy, Humpty Trumpty (or rather a pile of the pieces of him), the Mad Hater, Tweedledumb and Tweedledumber, along with Bolt-On the Walrus, the Gryphon and Moscow Mitch the Mock Turtle (who'd finally stuck his head out of the shell again). Plus, there was every member of the House of Cards from the Ripofflican Party.

The Sheriff handed the Trumper over to two very grumpy-looking *Navy Seals* [157] to guard him. He was handcuffed to them both and they were not going to let him get away – under any circumstances.

In the very middle of the court was a table, with a large plates of Hamberders and Fries upon it: they looked so good, that it made BoJo quite hungry to look at them—"I wish they'd get the trial done," he thought, "and hand round the refreshments!" Then he realised that they must have been put there to torture the Trumper to tell the truth. If they offered them to everyone else, he would not be able to stand that for long and he would soon break down. But that was likely to take a while, so BoJo began looking at everything around him, to pass away the time.

---

[157] NAVY SEAL: The Seals were very unhappy about the Trumper messing with the chain of command and reversing the demotion of one of their own after he committed allegedly 'freaking evil' acts in Iraq. Seals have a Code of Honor. The Trumper doesn't!

BoJo had been in court [158] a few times before, but he was usually the defendant rather than on the prosecution side. So, while he knew the name of everything there, this was a new experience. Little did he know!

"That's the Judge," he said to himself, "because of his black gown and grey wig. But I don't know him, and he looks old, even for a judge"

Everyone else in the court knew exactly who the judge was and Boris, having been born in the USA, should have known also. But lack of attention during American History classes at Eton meant that he did not recognise James Madison the 'Father of the Constitution'. And the reason he looked 'a bit old' was that he had been born in 1751, so he was 269 years old, but still going strong!

61.   James Madison 1751 - 2020

And, near the Judge, was the White Rabbi, who was the Herald of the Court, with a vuvuzela in one hand, and what looked like dead sea scroll of parchment in the other. BoJo assumed that he was going to read the charges from them. Or some old Hebrew scriptures to chastise the Trumper for his many anti-Jewish comments. Or quite possibly both.

"And that's the jury-box," thought BoJo; "and those twelve, unfortunate people, I suppose, are the jurors." He had been so busy with getting rid of Theresa May-B'lieve, taking over the leadership of the Conservatory Party, all his 'BREXIT or Bust' activities, followed by having a General Election – not to mention keeping his end up with his slightly pregnant fiancée - that he had not been following all the details of the impeachment hearings in the Congress. If he had, he would have known that the jurors were actually the government employees who had testified against the Trumper in the televised hearings.

---

[158] BOJO IN COURT: He had been a couple of times to get divorced, recently for his alleged misconduct while in office regarding the £350 million BREXIT Bus and when the Supreme Court had to rule as to the legality of his attempt at prorogation of Parliament. They decided it wasn't legal. Nuff said!

Looking round for a familiar face to help him understand what was going on, BoJo spotted Spicy Sean the Gryphon, so he signalled him to come over so they could sit together. The Gryphon sashayed, flounced and strutted across the Rosy Garten towards BoJo, doing a few fandango and flamenco steps, for good measure, finally twirling into a seat next to BoJo with a breathless if confusing, "Hello buddy there, how you are?"

"Er, er, fine thank you," BoJo replied, having unfortunately forgotten how complex the sentence structure of the Gryphon was and now wishing he had asked someone else to sit with him. But who?

The jurors were all writing very busily on iPads and Android tablets, except for the Dormouse, who was still using a slate and chalk. "What are they doing?" BoJo whispered to the Gryphon. "They can't have anything to put down yet, before the trial's begun."

"They're down their names putting" the Gryphon whispered in reply, "'for fear they may forget them they do, if they 'somehow' erased shall be, from the National Records, the end of the trial before."

"Stupid things!" BoJo began in a loud, indignant voice, but he stopped hastily, when the White Rabbi cried out, "Silence in the court!" and the Judge put on his pince-nez spectacles and looked ominously around, to make out who was talking. The Judge was suffering from a bit of age-related, macular degeneration (AMD), as you might imagine in someone who was 269 years old. BoJo was hard to miss in any crowd, but in this one - having that stupid tousled blonde hair and even stupider 'BREXIT Forever' sweatshirt in a Rosy Garten full of all sorts of very bizarre people and anthropomorphic animal characters – he stuck out like a very proverbial sore thumb.

"THEE THERE!" shouted the Judge. "The sore thumb with the very strange clothing apparel. What is thy name? Mr. Forever?"

BoJo suddenly realised that Judge James Madison was from the 18th Century, so casual, sloppy old jogging gear must look very weird to him.

"Er, my apologies your Honour. My name is BoJo, sir."

The Judge's eyes were not really very good, even with the pince-nez, so to him, in the distance, the word BREXIT could very well have been BoJo. Both began with a 'B'. And, as far as he was concerned, if you were stupid enough to walk around with words printed in large letters on your shirt, it was most likely to be your name. Why not?

"Well, Mr. BoJo Forever, this Bench doth appreciate your silence unless an officer of the court addresses thee. Is that clear, young man?"

BoJo thought that he rather liked the sound of 'Mr. BoJo Forever' as it had an air of permanence about it, so decided, for once, not to argue.

"Yes, your Honour. My apologies your Honour," grovelled BoJo. But that was only for a moment. As soon as the Judge looked away, he turned back to the Gryphon and whispered, "Who are the jurors?"

"All they are from the Hearing Impeachment and big television stars became they," said the Gryphon. "Telling you who they are I shall one by one, do."

"Juror One Fiona 'Hawaay the Lads' Hillbilly is. Colored House Russia Advisor. A tough cookie she for sure is. And County Durham is from in the Kingdom of United."

"Juror Two, Colonel Alex Vindalooman is. A real soldier with a Heart of Purple and many chests on his medals. NSC Director for things Ukraine to do with. Too was born there with an identical clone brother."

"Juror Three, Gordon 'Egghead' Sunderland is. Rich guy at an Ambassador he is playing. Likes on cell-phones very much talking."

"Juror Four, Laura Mini-Cooper is. Assistant Defense Secretary Deputy or some such. Fast talker and with sporty chassis."

"Juror Five, Marie Sonovabitch is. Ambassador to Ukraine was. But in the way got of Doody-Roody and of his buddies. Not liked is by the Trumper."

"Juror Six, Kurt 'The Hair' Volkswagen. Envoy of Speciality to Ukraine was. Famous is a member of the Three Amigos and a hair stylist."

"Juror Seven, Bill 'And Ben' Tailormayed is. In chargé of d'affaires the Ukraine staff of the Embassy was. A 'very naughty boy' he was."

"The rest, less slightly probably important are, but contributed all to testimony of the Trumper against. Eight, Jennifer 'Formula One' Will.i.ams is. She a high-tech rapper is and lover of black-eyed pea soup Nine, George 'Kent' Uckyderby is. Horse and bourbon fan. Ten, Tim 'Morris' Minor is. A good guy, old-fashioned who loves British old cars. Eleven, David 'Hale' Nhearty is. Health food lover. Twelve, David 'Homesweet' Home is. Family guy all through. And thirteen, the Dormouse is," finally rounded up the Gryphon.

"Wait a minute!" complained BoJo. "There can't be thirteen jurors. It's always 'Twelve good men and true'. What is the Dormouse doing there? The last time I saw him he was being stuffed into a covfefe pot by a crazy guy with a big hat."

"He, wherever the Mad Hater goes, also goes he. See over there, the big crazy hat sitting is." pointed out the Gryphon.

"Wooooooo. He scares me a LOT!" replied BoJo with a shudder.

"Once before, the Dormouse to be a juror, called he was. And now thinks he, that he shall do the job each time a trial there is. Telling him otherwise that he is required no more falls deaf on ears. Methinks that full of covfefe they must be," the Gryphon explained.

"Well, that makes sense in a way that would only be possible in Trumperland I suppose," said BoJo. "I recognise that guy at the front table. That's Roody-Doody Joolianose. What's he doing?"

"Ah. He the Counsel the Defense for is of the Trumper."

"But wasn't he involved in all that Ukraine 'shenanigans'? And wouldn't that be a conflict of interest?" opined BoJo.

"True it is that he was and for sure some conflict there may be. But expect I that more than that conflict will be between the Trumper and the Roody-Doody. The Roody-Doody has a blabbing too much tendency – even worse than the Trumper – if that believed can be."

"But what about the prosecution? All I can see is a young, fresh-faced kid in a dark blue, dress US Navy uniform. He doesn't look like he is old enough to drink beer never mind handle this case. He looks very 'wet behind the ears' as you Americans say. Is he straight out of Law School?" asked BoJo with a somewhat snide tone.

"Oh, him. He the 'Second Seat' is to the Counsel for the Prosecution, who very late, will be to arrive from the DC of Washington. His name, Cruz, something like is. The Second Seat, probably, will never to speak get the chance. Just he takes the notes and all the papers carries. The Prosecuting Counsel Leading, all the talking will do."

"So, who is the Lead Counsel for the Prosecution?" asked BoJo.

"Know I do not," said the Gryphon. "He some retired attorney black guy is from DC, or some said Kenya. He went allegedly to the Dukes of Harvard Law School, whatever is that, I do not know."

BoJo was just about to ask another question when the White Rabbi stood up and blew an almost ear-piercing blast on the vuvuzela which immediately stopped the buzzing and the whispering in the Rosy Garten. But a group of South Africans on a guided tour of the Colored House heard it and popped out of the bushes and started singing Waka Waka.

WAKA WAKA (THIS TIME FOR AFRICA) – SHAKIRA
https://www.youtube.com/watch?v=pRpeEdMmmQ0

One of the Flake News reporters found the video on YouTube and the Courtroom, sorry, Rosy Garten, erupted in song and dance. All the South Africans started doing the Zulu 'stomp' dance and waving their arms in the air. All the black folks in the gallery leapt to their feet and started the rhythmic gospel-style clapping and shimmying to the left and to the right. Then the Latinos joined in when they realized it was Shakira from Colombia who was singing.

Even the Queen of Queens was on her feet and doing the Ellen Degenerates 'Twerk' to the music.

The Trumper just glowered at her from between his Navy Seals, both of whom were doing a perceptible sway to the beat. They were perfectly in time with each other, as all good soldiers would be, which meant that on each sway they bumped the Trumper from opposite sides – just hard enough to really annoy him.

Everybody was having such a good time that they couldn't hear the Judge banging his gavel non-stop. But no one was taking any notice.

The White Rabbi was shouting, "Silence in court! Silence in court!"

It looked like nothing at all was going to stop the dance party. Nobody was taking any notice till suddenly there was a shout from the back of the crowd. It was a familiar voice, at least to BoJo anyway.

"OOOOORRRRDDDDEEERRRR!! OOOOORRRRDDDEEERRR!"

It was John Berrrccoww, former Speaker of the House of Commons, and a very well-known character to BoJo. Why exactly he had appeared at this very opportune moment in the bizarre Trumperland was a mystery, but one which BoJo didn't even question. He was just glad to see a familiar face – even if it meant hearing those dulcet tones and the words OOOORRRDDEERRR!! OOOORRRDDEERRR!! yet again.

SPEAKER TO HOUSE OF COMMONS – JOHN BERRRCCOWW
https://www.youtube.com/watch?v=EY7EIZl4raY

Amazingly, if not surprisingly, everyone in the Rosy Garten had fallen immediately silent, as if by magic. Such was the power of that voice with its 10 years of practice in the British Parliament. No-one has come close, neither before nor since.

The White Rabbi said, very quietly, "Order in the court. Please . . ." and everyone sat down with a smile on their faces, nodding to all their neighbors and doing 'high fives'.

Even the South African tour group went quiet as they realised that something interesting was about to happen. It was probably even more interesting than a Colored House tour of the Lincoln Bedroom with the Trumper as a tour guide - which he often did when he wasn't busy 'ruining' the country - which was most days. The South Africans were pretty savvy, they knew about having *political figures in incarceration* [159] and could see the Trumper sandwiched between the Navy Seals. They could tell that he wasn't going anywhere! They correctly figured that the guided tour was probably off and so they prepared to watch the show and chew on their favourite *Biltong* [160] snacks.

---

[159] POLITICAL FIGURES IN INCARCERATION: Nelson Mandela spent 27 years in South African prisons for political activism. He was released in 1990 and became the first black president of the country. The Trumper probably liked him even less than O'Bama.
[160] BILTONG: Dutch *bil* (buttock) & *tong* (strip or tongue). Chewy dried ass meat. OK?

While that was happening, BoJo signalled to Berrrccoww to join himself and the Gryphon and watch the proceedings. BoJo figured that possibly going deaf in one ear from Berrrccoww's loud voice was at least a small price to pay for not having to unscramble every sentence that the Gryphon uttered. He may regret that decision by the end of the trial.

"Glad to see you, Berrrccoww," said BoJo in that so-called friendly Eton/Harrow/Oxford style where you call your friends that you have known for many years by their last name rather that their first. "What in heavens name are you doing here, old chap?"

"Well, I was just passing, you know. Now that I'm retired, I have plenty of free time on my hands, so to speak." replied Berrrccoww nonchalantly. "And that was a bit of fun! I haven't had cause to say 'ORDER!' for several months now and I do miss it."

"Yes. Jolly lucky you arrived just at that moment!" BoJo responded.

"Let's just hope that the Trumper doesn't say anything about Sh*t H*le countries in earshot of the Saffas or there will be a riot!" Berrrccoww whispered (which was actually several decibels above most people's normal speaking volume).

"SSssshhhhh!" the Gryphon said. "Something about to happen is!!"

"What is he saying????????" asked Berrrccoww.

"Oh, it takes a while, but you'll get used to it," said BoJo, smirking.

"Order in the Court," said the Clerk of the Court who, it turned out, was the Carpenter, the missing friend of Bolt-On the Walrus and co-consumer of all the Oysters. He had been given the job because he was the only person, beside the Judge, who had anything resembling a gavel. He used his carpenter's hammer to bang on the desk to get attention.

BANG! BANG! BANG! went the hammer. "This Court is in session for the case of McDonald J. Trumper versus the Crown. ALL RISE! Presiding shall be the Honorable Judge James Madison, 4th President of the United States, 'Father of the Constitution', promoter of the US Bill of Rights, co-writer of The Federalist Papers, co-founder of the Democratic-Republican Party and all-round good guy," was the Carpenter's introduction.

"Yes, yes, yes!" said the Judge. "That's way too long. I hath not got all day to wasteth on introductions. Let thee get on with it! Introduceth the Defendant and the Defense and Prosecution Attorneys."

"Er, yes your Worship, er, I mean Mr. President, er, sorry, er, your Honor!" bumbled the Carpenter, now scared of the Judge.

"Get on!" hissed the Judge, "Or I'll pronounce him GUILTY now!!"

"I OBJECT!" said the Trumper. "You can't have a former President judging a current President. It's a conflict of interest!"

"Objection overruled! Young man, thou can't object as thou hast not been properly introduced yet. So, officially, thou doth not exist. And it's not thy job to object. SIT DOWN and SHUT UP!" said the Judge.

"Er, yes dear! I mean yes, your Honor!" the Trumper mumbled.

The Carpenter started again. "Er, sorry. Er, the Defendant is McDonald Jockstrap Trumper, current President of the United Shtaysh of Trumperland, Cummerbund-in-Chief of the Army, the Navy, the Air Force and, er, ('Is this right?' he whispered to the White Rabbi who nodded, shook his head then nodded again) and, er, the Space Force(?), Defender of the Faith, Land of the Free, Home of the Brave . . ." prattled on the Carpenter, getting completely carried away in his new-found role.

BoJo was listening to the Carpenter and, at first, he didn't quite believe what he heard. "What was it?" he thought. "McDonald *Jockstrap* Trumper? That couldn't be, surely? He had never heard the middle name before as it was always just 'McDonald J. Trumper'. But he was Alexander Boris de Piffle *Jockstrap*. Was he related to the Trumper???"

Both had been born in New York. Both had blonde hair. Both on the chubby side. Both had a predilection for beautiful women – marrying them and having affairs with them. "Maybe, there was some distant relative that had somehow got the crossover factor?" BoJo agonized. "This was really terrible. Really, really terrible news! *OMG*[161]!!!!"

OH MY GOD! – FRIENDS
https://www.youtube.com/watch?v=iMs9feeSknk

---

[161] OMG: Is the abbreviated version of 'Oh my God!'. Came into popular vernacular usage as a result of it being said many times in the 'Friends' sitcom by Chandler's girlfriend, Janice, & then it spread to the others. Now used regularly in SMS's and Twats.

But, meanwhile, as BoJo had his personal apocalyptic panic meltdown, the trial opening continued. The Carpenter was doing his next introduction and getting bolder by the minute.

"My Lords, Ladies and Gentlemen, non-Ladies and non-Gentlemen, LGBTQs and any Hybrid, Embryonic, Genetically-Modified Creatures and Organisms," spouted the Carpenter, trying to encapsulate the physical, human and animal range in the audience. "Oh, and not forgetting the members of the Press Corp a.k.a. The Flake News. I am pleased to announce that the Counsel for the Defense is Roody-Doody Julianose, one time Americas Mayor, part-time Associate US Atty General, some-time US Attorney for SDNY and, most of the time, lawyer to the rich, the famous, crooked politicians, presidents, dictators and would-be monarchs."

"I OBJECT!" said the Trumper. "I don't want Roody-Doody as my lawyer. He knows too many of my secrets. It's a conflict of my interests! And besides, he is terrible lawyer as he usually says way too much, contradicts himself, and then agrees that he said it in the first place. I want a better lawyer!"

BANG! BANG! BANG! went the gavel. "Objection overruled! The defendant cannot object to the court-provided lawyer unless thou are willing to payeth for one of thy own. Dost thee have the money to pay?" asked the Judge.

"Of course I do!" said the Trumper. "I'm worth US$2.1 billion. It says so in Wikipedia, so it must be true!"

"Can thou prove it?" asked the Judge. "Show us thy Tax Returns!"

"Er, er, well they are very beautiful, powerful Tax Returns. I would show them, but they are being audited and they are very complicated. So complicated that you wouldn't understand." weaseled the Trumper.

"If thou are not willing to show us thy Tax Returns, then thou are stucketh with Attorney Joolianose." *BANG! BANG! BANG!* Went the gavel. "OBJECTION OVERRULED!"

Then the Judge glowered at the Carpenter and said, "Clerk of the Court, RESUME!"

"Ah, er, yes your Honor," said the Carpenter and looked over at the Prosecutor's table. But only the young, fresh-faced kid from the Navy was sitting there looking at Tok Tik on his cell phone.

The Lead Prosecutor's chair was empty! *"WHERE THE HELL IS HE???"* the Carpenter mouthed silently to the Navy kid, who just held up his hands, shrugged and shook his head from side to side negatively. And then went back to Tok Tik.

"OH, SHIT!!!" mouthed the Carpenter to himself and everyone else.

Just then, the doors of the Colored House burst open and out into the Rosy Garten rushed a tall, distinguished-looking, black guy with slightly greying hair, a big, wide smile and even bigger, wider ears . . .

"My . . . apologies . . . your Honor! My name is . . . Brendan Aiden Roan Arlen Conan Kieran O'Bama. But sir, . . . you can call me B.A.R.A.C.K O'Bama for short. I am . . . the Lead Counsel for the Prosecution!" he said in his usual slow, measured, verbal delivery style.

"WE OBJECT!!!!" bellowed across the Rosy Garten in unison from the Trumper and Roody-Doody.

"SHUT UP thou two! Thou cannst not object as he hast not yet been formally introduced as the Lead Counsel for the Prosecution." countered the Judge somewhat testily. It was obvious that the Trumper and Roody-Doody were already getting on his nerves. Not a good thing to do when you are the Defendant.

"Attorney O'Bama, thou art late! What happeneth to thee? Why art thou so late?" asked the Judge.

"Ah, . . . your Honor . . . my very sincere . . . . apologies. I got held up . . . by some *Beltway Bandits* [162] . . . on the way here," he answered.

"Beltway Bandits? Thou meanst like bandits on horseback held you up at gunpoint? Were thou riding alone or were thee on a stagecoach?" asked the Judge assuming that they were still in the 18th century.

"Sorry, your Honor . . . I don't understand . . . Held up at gunpoint? . . . On horseback? . . . On a stagecoach?" queried O'Bama.

This initially confused him until he realised that, as the Judge was James Madison, he thought that there were still people riding on horses and in stagecoaches. "Ah, your Honor, no, not robbers on horseback!"

---

[162] BELTWAY BANDITS: The 'Beltway' is the I-495 circumferential road around Washington DC. There are many consulting firms situated around the Beltway, all trying every way possible to get lucrative contracts from the Government offices in the Capitol. And then do as little as possible for the money. They were generally referred to – very appropriately - as the 'Beltway Bandits'. That's life in the Swamp!

"But the 21ˢᵗ century version. . . Just a litigation . . . for a global pandemic consultant . . . a B&C malpractice case that ran over time."

"Global pandemic? Consultant? B&C? Malpractice? I just do not understandeth any of those terms," said the Judge.

"Welcome to the Washington Swamp, your Honor!" said O'Bama.

"Washington Swamp? And thy other terms?" asked the Judge.

"Well, your Honor . . . I think that you will find that . . . many things have changed . . . since, er, your time in office! . . . A global pandemic is a virus or disease . . . that spreads all over the world . . . while the Administration pretends that it's not serious . . . till it's too late for anyone to stop it! . . . The consultant in a global pandemic . . . is someone who is called in at the last moment . . . and paid enormous amounts of money . . . to assign the blame! . . . B&C is easy to explain . . . it's Bribery and Corruption! . . . Malpractice is doing something you know you really are not supposed to do . . . and then, stupidly, getting caught! . . . And the Washington Swamp, is all the above combined . . . but with politicians involved!" summarized O'Bama, wonderfully.

"Thanking thee Attorney O'Bama. That hath helped to make things a little clearer going into this case. Now, I believe that the Clerk of the Court needs to introduce thee so we can get on with the proceedings," said the Judge. "Clerk, thou may continue."

"Thank you, your Honor! Ladies and Gentlemen of the Jury, the Flake Press Corp., and the gallery in general. *It's wonderful to be here, It's certainly a thrill, you're such a lovely audience, we'd like to take you home with us, we'd love to take you home. So, may I introduce to you, the act you've known for all these years, B.A.R.A.C.K. O'Bama's Lonely Hearts Club Band!!!"* the Carpenter even singing the last few lines. He had, again, got totally carried away in the excitement of the moment, mainly, as we had forgotten to mention, because he was a person of color, that color being predominantly black, he was originally from Liverpool and the BFF of Bolt-On the Walrus (Goo Goo G'Joob). So, he was a HUGE fan of O'Bama and, of course, an even bigger fan of The Beatles.

"CLERK OF THE COURT!!!" shouted the Judge. "What are thou doing, my good man?? I told thee before. Do not messeth about. GETTETH ON WITH IT!"

"Er, sorry, your Honor. I will. I will. Hear yea! Hear yea! Hear yea! *We love you. Yeah! Yeah! Yeah!* . . . (Sorry!) Er. Ahem. The Lead Counsel for the Prosecution is none other than 'The' Brendan Aiden Roan Arlen Conan Kieran O'Bama, often known as B.A.R.A.C.K. O'Bama, 44th President of the USA, US Senator for Illinois, Member of the Illinois Senate, teacher of constitutional law at the University of Chicago School of Law, graduate of the Harvard Law School and really super-duper-duper guy!" said the Carpenter, exuding pride in the telling.

"WE OBJECT!!!!!" yet again bellowed across the Rosy Garten in unison from the Trumper and Roody-Doody as soon as the Carpenter had finished his introduction!

"SHUTTETH UP you two! Mr. Trumper, it is not thy role nor thy right to object. That is the job of thy Attorney," chided the Judge, once again showing some disdain for the Defendant's behavior.

"THEN, I OBJECT!!" shouted Roody-Doody. "He cannot prosecute and cross-examine my client because the Trumper is a Ripofflican President and Attorney O'Bama is a former Dimocrat President. There is a partisan conflict of interest!"

"Atty. Joolianose, THIS is a court of LAW, not a court of POLITICS. The LAW is not partisan. And NO-ONE IS ABOVE THE LAW!" Those last words rang out loud and clear and struck significant fear in Roody-Doody as he had heard them many times from the lips of Nancy Palooka, the Speaker of the House. And she was not kidding.

"But your Honor. A President can't prosecute a President!" argued Roody-Doody.

"Where doth it sayeth so in the Constitution - which, by the way, I wrote - or in the United States Code, or in any Federal, State or Local Laws?" responded the Judge.

"But, er, but, er, but, er. That's not fair, your Honor," complained Roody-Doody.

"Not 'fair', or not 'the law', Counsel? Thou can pleadeth something is not 'the law' but not being 'fair' doth not cut it. The Lead Counsel is perfectly entitled to cross-examine the witnesses. But I will take 'under consideration' thy plea regarding cross-examination of one President by another. However, I shall withholdeth my decision till a future point in the proceedings. No further discussion on this matter!"

"OBJECTION OVERRULED!!" *BANG! BANG! BANG!* went the gavel. "Herald of the Court, let us proceed with hearing the accusiations against the Defendant."

The White Rabbi started to slowly unroll the scroll and it went on and on until it reached the floor and started rolling up again. It looked like there were going to be a LOT of charges. And that turned out to be the case.

When he got to the beginning of the list, the White Rabbi, without thinking – which he rarely did anyway – automatically raised the vuvuzela to his lips and blew a piercing blast . . .

The court erupted once again to cries of "Waka! Waka!" and all the Saffas jumped up and started stomping and singing. It was crazy, until!

"OOOORRRRDDDEEERRRR!! OOOORRRDDDEEEEERRRR!!!" shouted John Berrrccoww, almost automatically.

And, once again, everyone smiled at each other. Gave 'high fives' and just sat down in unison.

"Silence in court," said the White Rabbi, rather redundantly; "while I read the charges against the Defendant. This may take a while . . .!"

"Guiltiez ass chargedt!!!" said the Queen loudly.

"But, oyvey, I haven't read the charges yet," said the White Rabbi almost in a whisper as he was very, very scared of the Queen. And quite rightly so.

"Guiltiez ass chargedt, I saidt. Andt if I say itz, itz must haff been saidt correctedly!!" bristled the Queen. "Za Senates decidedt zey vere goingk tzo acqvit him on za peachment charches effen before tza trial startedt. Tzo, vy can't I say he iss guilties befores za charches are readt here? At za leastd ve got za trials startedt befores I decided zat. Ja? No? Ja?" she said turning purple and looking around for someone who might dare to disagree.

Fortunately, the Judge being a former President, was not scared of the Queen, so he responded, "Respectfully, your Royal Very Highness, it is usual court proceedings to allow the accusiations to be read as the Defendant has the opportunity to admit his guilt immediately. And, if he does so, then we can all go home for tea."

"Ha!! Poppycooks!! Proceed then if you insist!!!" she sort of agreed without actually agreeing.

"Er, umm, er, ah," dithered the White Rabbi. "Er, the, er, accusiations er, charges against the defendant are as follows . . .

1. Coming down the escalator in Trump Tower and deciding to run for President. (This was the start of all the problems!)
2. Covering up collusion with Russia to fix the election (All lies!)
3. Saying he could 'Fix the Swamp' (So it worked better for him!)
4. Talking about 'Grabbing p*ssy' (It's OK because he's a star!)
5. Being ultra-creepy behind Hillarious in their debate (Yuk!)
6. Inciting fans to chant 'Lock her up!' (His favourite phrase!)
7. Letting his 'fixer' do jail time for paying off his women ($130k!)
8. Bragging about size of inauguration crowd and doctoring the photos to try and prove it (First big lie on Day 2 of presidency!)
9. Having biggest budget but cheapest show (C-grade stars!)
10. Scamming a cute school-girl dance troupe to perform at one of his rallies and not paying them. (Shame on him!)
11. Pulling out of the Paris Agreement on Climate Change because he doesn't believe it's real. (Because it still snows!)
12. Firing James Coney-Island, FBI Director due to Russia investigation and saying so on TV (One of his first mistakes!)
13. Pulling out of the Iran Nuclear Arms Treaty (They cheat!)
14. Having too many dictators as BFFs (He wants to be one!)
15. Paranoia about **anything** President O'Bama did (A wimp!)
16. Proposing to build a 'Great big, beautiful wall' on the Mexican border (Not realising its 2,000 miles long!)
17. Believing that Mexico was going to pay for it. (Duuuh!)
18. Pretending it was being built when it wasn't (Just repairs!)
19. Calling all Mexicans rapists and drug dealers (Nasty racist!)
20. Locking up Mexican kids in cages (Inhuman!)
21. Trying to cut millions of poor off food stamps (Cruel!)
22. Having racist immigration policies and being xenophobic (!)
23. Pretending to 'divest' himself of all his businesses, but not really doing that (His kids still run them for him!)."

"Haff youse finishedt YET??" asked the Queen.

"Er, sorry, er, not yet your Royal Very Highness," dithered the White Rabbi even more.

"Vell, getz on viz itz ZEN!"

"Er, umm, oyvey, yes Ma'am. Er, continuing with charge No. 24 . . .

24. Nepotism in the Administration (Those damn kids again!)

25. Having the highest turnover of staff and appointees in US govt. history (Thinks it's still The Apprentice – 'You're fired!')

26. Deregulating so many industries to the benefit of his buddies and donors (More emissions and chemical dumping!)

27. Pulling out of Syria just because his BFF, the Turkish President, asked him to (And Trump Tower in Budapest?)

28. Dumping Kurd US allies, without a 2nd thought (Or even a 1st!)

29. Skipping War Veterans in Paris due to rain (And his hair!)

30. Truly believing that everything which is not positive about him is 'Flake News' (And being 'nasty' to all their reporters)

31. Making USA the laughingstock of the world (It's no joke!)

32. Lifting sanctions on Russian companies (Aluminum anyone?)

33. Being super paranoid about his tax returns (What's in them?)

34. Falling 'in love' with Kim Yung-Ones (Weird on weird!)

35. Making Germans laugh at him in NATO speech (Ja, really!)

36. Wanting to get Russia back into the Group of 7 (Why?)

37. Pretending he is being tough on Russia but having secret one-on-one talks with Putitin ('I don't believe it's Russia')

38. Cancelling NAFTA trade agreement and making one called USMCA with basically same terms (Except he signed it!)

39. Launching the 'Space Force' (Yep. It's not a joke. Honest!)

40. Promoting business at Trumper properties contravening the Emoluments Clause (Has too many syllables for him!)

41. Letting Jarhead do a Middle East Peace Deal that didn't include the Palestinians (And then puzzling why they said no!)

42. Routing USAF transports via his Scottish resort (Pockle!)

43. Visited his own resorts almost 280 times while President, at a cost of $141M, charging very high rates to his staff (Grifter!)

44. Telling 20,000+ lies as President (Whenever his lips move!)

45. Operating Trumper University as a fraud. (Dumb Dean!)."

"Haff youse still notz finishedt YETZ??" asked the Queen, grumpily.

"Er, sorry, er, still not yet your Royal Very Highness," mumbled the White Rabbi while quivering from head to toe.

"Vell, getz on viz itz AGAIN ZEN!"

"Er, umm, oyvey, yes Ma'am. Er, continuing with charge No. 46 . . .

46. Closing down Government like a spoilt brat when he did not get the money he wanted for his wall (Nancy 1- McDonald 0!)
47. Running his Foundation as a fraud (Cheating cancer kids!)
48. Sharing classified info with Russian diplomats (Glupyy!)
49. Sexually assaulting multiple women (Me Too will get you!)
50. Engaging in international corrupt business dealings ($$s!)
51. Personally, instructing the US Postmaster General to double the shipping rates for Amazon to hurt Jeff Bozo (Jealousy!)
52. Referring to African countries as 'sh*t-h*les' (Diplomacy 101!)
53. Faking a 'National Emergency' to get $s for Wall (Cry wolf!)
54. Calling neo-Nazis 'very fine people' (Dad's German ancestry?)
55. Indulging in bigotry, racism, and white nationalism which are impeachable offenses (Divisive, dividing, disgusting!)
56. Trying to block a merger between AT&T and Time Warner in order to try and punish CNN (Petulant back-stabbing!)
57. Wanting to jail reporters publishing leaks (1st Amendment!)
58. Threatening to revoke media licenses (1st Amendment 2!)
59. Wanting to have lots of Republican Judges (Fix the courts!)
60. Pushing Brett Cavernous onto Supreme Court (He likes beer!)
61. Firing Jeff Jam-Sessions, recused Atty. General (You're Fired!)
62. Appointing Bill Barf a compliant Atty. General (No Collusion!)
63. Trying to fire Miller-Lite from Russia investigation (Not Out!)
64. Obstruction of justice - ten times (Stop that!)
65. Trying to kill O'Bama-Care (To help Big Pharma & HMOs?)
66. Fueling racism and Islamophobia (WASPs are OK!)
67. Pretending 'Pee Pee' tapes don't exist (Ask Putitin!)
68. Perjury for denying he knew about Wikileaks deal (Ask Roger!)
69. Making over 400 visits to his properties & clubs (McDon $$s!)
70. Having Bill Barf hold Miller-Lite Report & redact it (BFF Bill!)
71. Tax evasion with his Dad on his real estate deals (Ask Sister!)
72. Inciting violence in his supporters (Punch him in the face!)."

"Haff youse sill notz finishedt EVENZ YET??" grumbled the Queen

"Er, sorry, er, still some more to go your Royal Very Highness," mumbled the White Rabbi.

"Vell, getz on viz itz AGAIN AND AGAIN ZEN!"

"Er, aahh, oyvey, yes Ma'am. Er, now I am on charge No. 73 . . .

73. Negligence and incompetence causing deaths of nearly 3,000 in Puerto Rico, after Hurricane Maria (Need any paper towels?)
74. Demanding Jarhead got a security clearance (McDon'll fix it!)
75. Blocking DC FBI HQ land sale (Location, location, location!)
76. Dropping bombs on Syria without Congress OK (For BFF??)
77. Attacking Congresswomen of color in 'The Squad' (What?)
78. Pitching his Doral resort for next G-7 summit (McDon $$s)
79. Starting unnecessary trade war with China (China pays, OK?)
80. Soleimani drone attack in Iraq without Congress OK (Fire!)
81. Adding Sharpie path to Alabama for Hurricane Dorian (Oops!)
82. Coercing EU Ambassador Gordon 'Egghead' Sunderland to help with 'a political campaign' (Everyone was in the loop!)
83. Withholding military aid from Ukraine (Good for Putitin!)
84. Having Roody-Doody fire Marie Sonovabitch, Ambassador to Ukraine (Get her out of my way!)
85. Having the 'Three Amigos' try to get President Zabaglione investigate Joe and Hunter Biden (Make an announcement!)
86. Have Levee Painarse involve Russian oligarchs (Rubles=$)
87. Making a 'perfect' call to 'ask a favor, though' (Perfect!)
88. Denying any 'Quid pro quo' related to call (What's that?)
89. Withholding Oral Office visit for Ukraine President (No!)
90. Hiding the 'transcript' in a very secret server (Deep State!)
91. Getting everyone to participate in the cover up (Red Alert!)
92. Abusing the power of Office of the President (Dictatorship?)
93. Refusal to testify or produce papers (Obstruction 101!)
94. Blocking other witnesses from testifying (Obstruction 102!)
95. Discrediting closed-door hearings (In the basement?)
96. Witness intimidation 'live' during hearings (What a Twatter!)
97. Making sure that Moscow Mitch guarantees that Red Senators vote to acquit the Trumper (Grim Reaper strikes again!)
98. Being vindictive by firing Vindalooman after trial (How petty!)
99. Total incompetence in dealing with coronavirus. (Duuh!)."

"And, finally," said the White Rabbi, almost out of breath . . .

"No. 100. For thinking he is the Messiah and being a very naughty boy."

"Arez youse FINALLIEZ finishedt??" asked the Queen. "Zat's a ferry, ferry longk lizt! Von hundredt chargez. Vow, zat iss zome goingk, evens vor McDoonaldt!"

"Er, er, yes, your Majesty," said the White Rabbi. "Just the one hundred charges. Actually, there were more, but I ran out of scroll . . ."

"Cunsiderz yours verdictd," the Queen said to the jury.

"Not yet, not yet!" the White Rabbi hastily interrupted. "There's a great deal to come before that!"

"Whoze doos youse sink youse arez talking tzo!??" said the Queen angrily. "I don'ts needz tzo hear any mores. I haff heards enuff!"

"Er, er, I'm sorry your Very High Royalness," mumbled the White Rabbi, getting the Queen's title mixed up in the process; "We have to, er, hear the testimony of the, er, witnesses first, Your Royal High Veriness."

"Ach! Ferry vell, iff ve must!"

"Call the first witness, and let's GET ON WITH IT!" said the Judge.

Again, without thinking – he had not learned from the last time – the White Rabbi blew a piercing blast on the vuvuzela . . .

Once again all the Saffas shouted "Waka! Waka!" and jumped up and started stomping and singing. But not for long!

"OOOORRRRDDDEEERRRR!! OOOORRRDDDEEEEERRRR!!!" shouted John Berrrccoww.

And everyone just smiled at each other, gave 'high fives' and sat down laughing and giggling.

"Silence in court," said the White Rabbi, because he thought it was a duty rather than because it was a necessity. Not with John Berrrccoww in the court, anyway. "Call to the stand, the Mad er, Hater!!"

Roody-Doody stood up to start the cross-examination for the defense. The Mad Hater went into the Witness Box with a covfefe in one hand and a piece of bread-and-butter in the other.

"I beg pardon, your Mr. Counsel Doody-Roody," he began, "for bringing these in, but I hadn't quite finished my covfefe when I was sent for."

"The name is Counsel Joolianose! And you ought to have finished," said Roody-Doody. "When did you begin?"

The Hater looked at the March Hare, who had followed him into the court and was busy waving at the Dormouse over in the Jury Box.

"Fourteenth of March, I think it was," the Mad Hater said.

"Fifteenth," said the March Hare.

"Sixteenth," added the Dormouse from the Jury Box.

"Write that down," Roody-Doody said to the jury. They eagerly wrote down all three dates on their on their iPads and Tablets and then added them up and reduced the answer to shillings and pence.

"Three and ninepence!" said the Dormouse first, who, although he only had a slate rather than an iPad, was good at mental math. At least he was if he didn't fall asleep in the middle of the calculation – which he often did.

"Take off your hat," Roody-Doody said to the Hater.

"It isn't mine," said the Hater.

"Stolen!" Roody-Doody exclaimed, turning to the jury, who instantly made a memorandum of the fact.

"I make them to sell," the Mad Hater added as an explanation; "I've none of my own. I'm a hatter."

"What do you mean 'I'm a hatter'? I thought you were a hater?" asked Roody-Doody.

"I make hats. Look at these new models. Lovely red color and a beautiful logo," said the Mad Hater and took off his big crazy top hat to reveal a small red baseball cap, pulled way too far down onto his head, making him look really, really dumb – though it seemed that no one had ever dared tell him that - as he always wore it that way.

Roody noticed that there was something not quite right about the logo on the hat, but he was somewhat dyslexic, not to mention significantly scatter-brained, so it didn't really seem to be very important at the time.

"Hhhhhreerruuumph!" said Roody-Doody, as he was rather frustrated by the way the cross-examination was going, or rather, not going, "No more questions, your Honor! Your witness, Mr. Lead Counsel for the Prosecution."

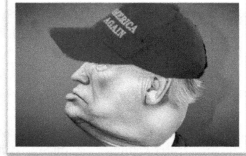

62.   MAGA – Make America What Again?

Just at that moment BoJo felt a very curious sensation, which puzzled him a good deal until he made out what it was. He was beginning to grow larger and he thought at first that he would get up and leave the court; but on second thoughts he decided to remain where he was as long as there was room for him.

"I squeezing wish you wouldn't do so much," said the Gryphon, who was still sitting next to him. "Breathing I hardly can manage."

"I can't help it," said BoJo very apologetically; "I'm growing."

"You're growing, having no right here to do," said the Gryphon.

"Don't talk nonsense," said BoJo pointedly; "you know that you're growing too."

"Yes, but growing at only a pace of reasonableness," said the Gryphon; "not ridiculously that fashion in." And he got up very sulkily and crossed over to the other side of the Rosy Garten. Fortunately, this left more space for BoJo's expanded size.

Berrrccoww had been behind the bushes for a call of nature while BoJo had been growing but appeared not to notice any change in him.

"Hi, old chap! I feel a lot better now. Nothing like a good tinkle on the tulips, I always say," Berrrccoww, as usual, offered way too much information.

"I say, Berrrccoww, what was that charge almost at the end of the list? Something about coronavirus. What's that? I've never heard of it before." asked BoJo.

"No idea old man! I learnt a long time ago in the House of Commons, never to actually listen to any of the long speeches. I just nodded, smiled, grimaced or shook my head every now and then as though I was understanding everything they said. Usually, as you well know – being really, really good at it yourself – politicians usually talk a lot of old tosh most, if not all, of the time."

All this time the Queen had never left off staring at the Hater, and, just as the Gryphon crossed the Rosy Garten, she said to one of the officers of the court, "YOU! Bring me the list of the performers at the Inauguration!"

On hearing that, the Trumper looked very unhappy and the wretched Hater trembled so much that his MAGA hat fell off his head and onto the ground in front of the Witness Box.

Smiling broadly – which was always a good technique to disarm a witness – B.A.R.AC.K. O'Bama stood up to start the cross-examination for the prosecution. As he walked over to the Witness Box he bent down and picked the MAGA hat up, but he did not return it to the Mad Hater. Instead, he just held it in his hands as he started to question him.

"Tell me . . . about yourself, Mr. Hater," asked O'Bama softly. "Tell me about . . . your business dealings. About making . . . hats for instance."

"*I'm just a poor boy, I need some sympathy,* your Honor," the Hater began, singing as he had done when he met BoJo. But in a trembling voice, " - and I hadn't begun my tea - not above a month or so ago - and what with the bread-and-butter getting so thin - and the Quid Pro Quo - which there wasn't - and the twinkling of the tea . . ."

"The twinkling of the what?" asked the Judge.

"It began with tea," the Hater replied. "And the telephone call began with a line – not a phone line – and not a voting line. It became a famous line. A very beautiful and famous line!"

"Of course, telephone and twinkling begin with a 'T', not a line!" said the Judge sharply. "Do you take me for a dunce? Go on!"

"*I'm just a poor boy, nobody loves me,*" the Hater went on. "And most things twinkled after that - only then the Zabaglione said – 'We are almost ready to buy more Javelins'."

And, immediately, O'Bama interjected, "And you said – 'I would like you to do us a favor, though' . . ."

"I didn't!" said the Hater.

"Do you deny it!" said the Judge.

"You just have to read the transcript. And there was no Quid Pro or even any Quo," the Hater dodged.

"I did read it – but it's not a 'transcript' as some of the depositions said that things were missing or altered." said the Judge matter-of-factly.

"Well, at any rate, the Walrus said . . ." the Hater went on, looking anxiously round to see if he would deny it too: but the Walrus denied nothing, being fast asleep. Which was really lucky for the Mad Hater.

"*Is this the real life? Is this just fantasy?*" O'Bama responded in song. "It seems very difficult to tell the difference with you Mr. Hater."

"*I'm caught in a landslide. To escape from reality,*" he sang, sadly.

"But what about the hats – like this one I'm holding?" asked O'Bama.

"Well, those were a special order for the Trumper. He wanted millions of them so that all his redneck, 'conservative' Ripofflican supporters could buy one to wear at his beloved rallies," the Hater said.

"And show . . . fealty to his leadership? Is that why . . . they had the words MAKE AMERICA GREAT AGAIN on them?" poked O'Bama.

"Well, maybe. But it was mainly to raise money for his campaign – or himself – who knows. The hats were dirt cheap to have made and were sold with a huge mark up. You know that everything is transactional with the Trumper," explained the Hater.

"And you made them personally," asked O'Bama, 'innocently'.

"Why no, of course not. I was just the middleman. They were made in a huge sweat-shop, er, sorry, factory," bumbled the Hater.

"And where . . . is that sweat-shop, sorry factory?" he asked.

"Er, aaah, er, I think I would like to *plead the 5th* [163] on that," the Hater wriggled.

"OK. If the hats were made . . . in a sweat-shop, (er, sorry your Honor), . . . in a factory, then you would be . . . responsible for quality control, right?" said O'Bama, but again, in an apparently oblique comment-style question.

"Er, yes. That's right. And I had to drink many, many cups of tea and covfefe to keep me awake while doing it. And the Dormouse was no help. He was always sleeping on the job," grumbled the Hater.

The Dormouse might have objected to this disparagement, but he was actually asleep in the Jury Box at the time. So, at least that part of the Hater's story was corroborated. And the rest of the jury nodded, sagely.

"So, it's possible that sometimes a below-standard product might have slipped through the quality control," opined O'Bama, smiling.

"Yes, that's possible, I suppose," responded the Hater, warily.

"So, it's possible this hat - Exhibit A - slipped through un-noticed?"

---

[163] PLEAD THE 5TH: For non-Americans reading this, the 5th Amendment to the US Constitution allows citizens to refuse to answer a question, in a criminal trial, on the grounds that you might incriminate yourself. A very useful tool for anyone who is guilty! It's also useful for the prosecution as anyone who uses it must be guilty of something.

And, as he said those words, O'Bama held up the MAGA hat which he had picked up off the floor after it had fallen off the Hater's head. He turned around to show the jury, along with everyone else in the Rosy Garten, and the phrase 'MAKE AMERICA GRETA AGAIN' could clearly be seen embroidered on the front of the hat.

| 63. | To MAGA or not to MAGA? That is the Question. |

There was a huge gasp from everyone in the Rosy Garten (GASP!) and a much smaller, slightly delayed one from the Dormouse (Gasp!), who was woken up by the first gasp. That was followed, after what seemed like an almost interminable delay, by a shout from Roody-Doody, as he had also fallen asleep, like the Dormouse.

"OBJECTION, YOUR HONOR! That is a flagrant case of plagiarism and infringement of copyright of a product totally associated with my client, the President of the United States of America!" pontificated Roody-Doody, fully expecting a rebuttal from O'Bama.

"I agree, your Honor. Absolutely, one hundred percent!" responded O'Bama, much to the surprise of Roody-Doody.

"You, er, agree?" asked Roody-Doody incredulously, but with a gnawing suspicion that he was walking into a trap. And he was right about that, at least.

"Yes, your Honor, I agree . . . with the 'learned' Counsel for the Defense," said O'Bama. "That there . . . is a flagrant case of plagiarism and infringement of copyright . . . of a product totally associated with a President of the United States of America. . . But, not McDonald J. Trumper. For your information, President Ronald Reagan . . . used the slogan "Let's MAKE AMERICA GREAT AGAIN" . . . in his successful 1980 presidential campaign. As you can clearly see . . . on this button – Exhibit B – from that time."

He walked around the court and showed the button to the members of the jury and everyone said "Aaahhh, I see", then looked at the Trumper.

He was rapidly changing color from his usual 'Glow-Stick Orange' to a very significant 'Deep Purple' and white vapor was starting to pour out of his ears. Talk about 'Smoke on the Water'. This was something else!

64.   MAGA - First Edition

SMOKE ON THE WATER – DEEP PURPLE
https://www.youtube.com/watch?v=MQA0m2M14Fg

For sure, if the Trumper had been 'some stupid with a flare gun', he would definitely have 'burned the place to the ground'. He was absolutely livid with the Mad Hater for talking too much and Roody-Doody for falling into O'Bama's trap.

"So, Mr. Hater, was this just a quality control slip or something else?" asked O'Bama. "I have seen a lot of these available on-line. Maybe, you were also the middle-man for Ms. Greta Thunderbird's hats?"

"Er, er, well, er, yes, actually I was," the Hater almost whispered.

"WHAT! YOU DOUBLE DEALING, NO GOOD SON OF A BITCH!" shouted the Trumper. "You're using my factory in Tschina and Iwanka's patent to make hats for that know-nothing grumpy schoolgirl, Greta Thunderbird!! The Climate Change Kid!!! She's just a spoiled, petulant and immature brat who knows nothing about climate change!"

BANG! BANG! BANG! "The Defendant shall refraineth from such verbal expositions in this court. It is not thy place or privilege to hath discourse with the witnesses. It is the task of thy Counsel. Any more such *poutbursts* [164] and I shall hath no option but to holdeth thee in contempt of court." said the Judge in no uncertain terms. Unfortunately, the threat of being in contempt of court was somewhat pointless as it was well-known that the Trumper held all courts in contempt. The only exception to this was, perhaps, the Supreme Court as Moscow Mitch had taken great trouble to load that one with partisan Ripofflican judges.

"But, your Honor, the Hater cheated on me and Roody-Doody is an absolute idiot!" responded the Trumper and, in once sentence, both got upset for the Hater doing just what he would have done himself and threw his long-time attorney under the bus. Some chickens were starting to come home to roost.

"SILENCE!!! The Defendant shall siteth down and waiteth until he is addressed to giveth testimony," shouted the Judge.

"But, your Honor . . .!!!"

"McDOOOONNAAALLLDDDTT!!!!!! SHUTZ ZA FACKZ UPZ!!" shouted the Queen across the Rosy Garten. The birds stopped chirping and many flowers wilted, so powerful was the acid blast from her throat.

"Er, yes, dear. Sorry dear . . ." the Trumper whimpered.

"Mizter Chudge, youse mayz proceed!"

"Thank you, your Royal Very Highness," said the Judge. "Attorney O'Bama, please continue."

"So, Mr. Hater, it seems . . . . we have established, beyond a reasonable doubt, that you supplied . . different versions of MAGA hats, made in China, to both the Trumper . . . and Ms. Greta. Is that correct?"

---

[164] POUTBURSTS: Angry outbursts, complete with pouty lips, when the person is just not getting his own way. Often accompanied by stamping of the feet and throwing of toys out of the pram/buggy/stroller/crib. The Trumper is very, very famous for these.

"Er, well, er, I, er, aaahh, umm, suppose so . . . But, it's not my fault. I'm just an avatar of his alter-ego. So, I just do whatever he would do - but in another body. *I'm easy come, easy go. Nothing really matters.*" sang the Hater, wringing his little hands. *"Any way the wind blows!"*

"Good. Thank you, Mr. Hater," said O'Bama, along with one of his widest of wide smiles. "And I would like to introduce into evidence – Exhibit C – these photographs."

He walked over to the Jury Box with the photos and showed them to the twelve jurors – and the Dormouse.

"Please take a good look at these pictures of the two people who have been the subject of previous testimony about different MAGA hats. Just to be clear, and for the avoidance of doubt. One is a spoiled, petulant and immature brat who knows nothing about climate change . . ."

| 65. Guess Who? | 66. No Need to Guess |

". . . and the other is Greta Thunderbird."

He turned back to the Judge and said, "No further questions for this witness, your Honor."

"Herald. Call the next witness," ordered the Judge.

"Yes. Certainly, your Majestic Honor," responded the White Rabbi. He put the vuvuzela to his lips and was about to blow when all the Saffas stood up and looked at him expectantly. He took the vuvuzela away from his lips and all the Saffas sat down. He lifted it back to his mouth and they all stood up again! He was a slow learner but even he was catching on. So, instead of blowing the horn, he just shouted "Waka! Waka!" and all the Saffas clapped hands and sat down, laughing.

"CALL MICK MALARKEY TO THE WITNESS STAND."

"Phew! That was close!" said Berrrccoww. "I thought I was going to have to do crowd control again."

"Stay close," said BoJo who was starting to swell again and get taller.

"I say, old boy, are you OK?" asked Berrrccoww.

"I have absolutely no idea," replied BoJo, growing a bit more as he spoke. His trusty 'BREXIT Forever' sweatshirt was starting to get tight.

Just then, Mick Malarkey walked across the court to the Witness Box. As he passed by the Defending Counsel's table, the Trumper whispered to him, "Deny everything, Malarkey. Everything!"

Malarkey nodded, very quietly said, "Yes, boss," and entered the Witness Box.

"Counsel for the Defense, would you liketh to cross-examine the witness?" asked the Judge.

"Yes. Thank you, your Honor," said Roody-Doody and stood up. But the Trumper coughed loudly, glared at him with a testicle-piercing look and stroked the side of his hand across his throat. Roody-Doody got the message that the Trumper did not want him to do any questioning of Malarkey. And no more screw ups. He said, "Er, no further questions, your Honor." And sat down again, very quickly indeed.

"Er, but . . . ," the Judge started to ask a question, then decided that it was pointless in the circumstances. This trial was turning out to be significantly strange. Possibly the strangest in his last 269 years on the Bench. "Attorney O'Bama, Counsel for the Prosecution, you may cross-examine the witness."

"Thank you, your Honor," said O'Bama and turning to the witness asked, "Your name is Mick Malarkey, correct?"

"No!" responded Malarkey, denying everything, as instructed.

"I see," said O'Bama. "What is your name?"

"John Michael Malarkey."

"Ah, OK. You were the Colored House . . . Chief of Staff for President Trumper?"

"No!" responded Malarkey, again making a denial.

"I see. What position did you hold . . . in the Trumper Administration?"

"Director of OBM and Acting Colored House Chief of Staff."

"Were you party to the discussions . . . when President Trumper made the call to the President of Ukraine?"

"No!"

O'Bama quickly grasped what was going on – and that he was going to get denials on everything – so he decided to change his questioning tactics and to test Malarkey's adherence to making denials.

"You were not out of the room . . . when the President made the Ukraine call?" asked O'Bama, negatively.

"No!" responded Malarkey

"You did not mis-hear what the Trumper was saying?"

"No, I did not!"

"There was no misunderstanding by you . . . as to what the Trumper was asking President Zabaglione to do?"

"No, there was not."

"There was no likelihood at all . . . that President Zabaglione misunderstood what favor the Trumper was asking him to do?"

"No, there was not!"

The Trumper had started to realise – at last – what O'Bama was trying to do by posing all negative questions, knowing that Malarkey would make a denial. Hence, that would be a double negative, resulting in a positive affirmation to the question. So, he started gesticulating to Malarkey across the court. He dared not speak for fear of the dire consequences that might result from getting the Queen angry again. He was shaking his head, waving his tiny hands and doing the 'cut-throat' gesture to try and get Malarkey to stop saying "no" to everything.

Unfortunately, a combination of Malarkey, not being the brightest crayon in the box and the Trumper never having played *Charades* [165] when he was a child - because he was too busy poring over his bank book - meant that Malarkey totally misinterpreted the mimed message.

He thought that he was being told – very strongly – to carry on and keep denying everything, not to stop doing it, as the Trumper wanted.

---

[165] CHARADES: A fun family party game where two teams compete against each other by silently miming the names of films, books, TV shows etc. and the opposing team has to guess what it was. The words 'fun', 'party', 'family' and 'game' were unlikely to have ever appeared in the same sentence in the Trumper household when the McDonald was growing up. It would have been a quadruple oxymoron if they ever had.

So, Malarkey just carried on denying everything.

"President Trumper was not vague . . . about who he wanted investigating?" asked O'Bama.

"No, he was not."

"President Trumper did not fail . . . to omit mentioning the names of former Vice President Joe Bidet and his son Hunter Bidet?"

"No, he did not."

"And after the call you did not fail . . . to advise President Trumper that he had just requested a 'Quid Pro Quo' in return for military aid?"

"No, I did not"

"Further, for the avoidance of doubt, . . . you would not have been deleterious in your duties . . . as 'Acting' Colored House Chief of Staff by advising President Trumper . . . exactly what 'Quid Pro Quo' really meant?"

"Certainly not!"

And, finally, at the subsequent Colored House press briefing, you had no desire to avoid telling the press that 'Quid Pro Quos' were a regular feature of 'diplomacy' with foreign governments and that they should – and I quote here – 'Get over it!'."

"No, I did not."

By this time, the Trumper was sitting with his head, face down, on the table in front of him and his tiny hand over his ears so that he could not hear Malarkey's answers.

"So, to summarize. There was no doubt in your mind . . . that President Trumper was basically leaning . . . on the President of Ukraine, . . . shall I say by leverage or extortion, . . . to do him the favor (though) . . . of turning up some 'nasty' information . . . on the Bidet's that he could use for political gain . . . in the November 2020 elections?"

"I have no doubt in my mind at all!" Malarkey said, smiling, looking over at the Trumper and, stupidly, giving him the 'thumbs up'.

"Thank you, Mr. Malarkey. No more questions, your Honor," said O'Bama and sat down with a very, very satisfied smile on his face indeed.

But, as you can imagine, the Trumper was far, far from happy and he leaned over to his Counsel and said, "Roody, *I could just kill a man. Put a gun against his head, pull my trigger, then he's dead. Roody, my life had just begun. But now he's gone and thrown it all away."*

"Boss! Don't do anything! We have an airtight case. I am sure I can get you off. Just leave it to your old pal Roody-Doody. You are in my hands now," he said with that famous, positive, all-teeth, goofy smile.

"Yes, that's what I am afraid of . . ." said the Trumper, gloomily. It would have been better with a sarcastic tone but, as we have already established, the Trumper doesn't do sarcasm very well at all.

Roody-Doody stood up and turned to the Judge. "Your Honor, it's been a long day. May I suggest we have tea and snacks and then recess till tomorrow?"

"Excellent proposal Attorney Joolianose! I am feeling a little peckish myself. I haven't eaten since perhaps 1836," said the Judge.

"Aahh, you mean yesterday at 18:36 in the evening. That's a long time," responded Roody-Doody, thinking that he was starting to develop a positive rapport with the Judge. He was significantly wrong about that.

"NO, Attorney Joolianose! I mean in the year of the Lord, 1836, back when I was a mere whippersnapper of 85 years," shot back the Judge, who did do sarcasm, very well indeed.

"Clerk of the Court. Hand round the, er, victuals," ordered the Judge. "By the way – pray tell me what those strange items of provender, viands and nourishment are called and what is in them?"

"Er, your Honor, they are Hamberders and Fries and you really don't want to know what is in them," answered the Carpenter.

"Oh great! At last, something to eat," said the Trumper. "I've been staring at those Hamberders and Fries ever since I got here!"

Suddenly there was a disturbance at the back of the Rosy Garten and a huge, muscular figure stood up and glowered at the Trumper through red-pupilled eyes. The Trumper looked down at his body and there were red laser-beam dots dancing around on his chest and they were coming from the eyes of guy who had just stood up.

"NO FOODT FOR THE PRISONER!" the new guy said in a slightly Austro-American accent.

"Who are thee?" asked the Judge, who had no idea at all what a laser beam was, much less a cyborg from the future.

"Apologies, your Honor. I am 'The Terminator', andt I am appointed to be za executioner off the prisoner when, sorry if, he iss foundt guilty," he answered in a deep, but slightly metallic, monotone.

"I OBJECT!" said Roody-Doody. "You are a cyborg who was sent back in time to 1984 to kill Sarah Connor, whose son will one day become the savior to lead the people in a fight against the machines taking over the world in a post-apocalyptic future."

"Ja, thatd iss true," said the Terminator. "But it happendt to be tha Queen's favourite movie franchise because, by tha sixth movie, Terminator: Dark Fate, I haff changed sides and I am protecting the planet by keeping young Dani Ramos alive so she can become za leader off za Resistance. And anyvay, the Queen hass a soft spot for a happy endink!"

"So why you?" asked Roody-Doody.

"Ach! Because I am perfect for za role off someone who kills za bad guy zat wants to ruin za planet by letingk za machines take over and haff lots off 'nasty' CO_2 emissions and causing za apocalypse off climate change meltd down. Gottit?" snarled the Terminator. "So, she appointed me for za job off za executioner. Ass I said, za Queen hass a soft spot for a happy endink and especially ven it hass a guy vizz a funny Euro-American accent zat she can understandt perfectly!"

TERMINATOR: DARK FATE – ARNIE GOVERNATOR
https://www.youtube.com/watch?v=oxy8udgWRmo

"But, in another life, you are a Ripofflican and a former Governor of California," asked the Trumper. "Why would you want to execute me, a fellow Ripofflican President?"

"Zat iss easy. One - remember you vass calling me 'Crazy Arnold'? Hah! And two - if it vasn't for your stupid Constitution rule zat only people who are born in Trumperland can run for President, I might be za President now, instead off you! You haff my dream job, baby!"

The fact that 'Governator' Arnie wanted his job was a worry for the Trumper but, subconsciously, not half as much as being called 'baby'

The Trumper turned to Roody-Doody and gave his deep and well-considered opinion of the situation, "Roody, we are in deep doo-doo!"

"Who is the 'we', *Kemosabe* [166]?" asked Roody-Doody, right on point.

"What do you mean?"

"Boss, he is gunning for your job, not mine!" replied Roody, remembering that the Trumper had earlier thrown him under the bus, and it was time to return the favor.

"Whatever happened to 'loyalty'?" asked the Trumper poutily.

"I think you mean 'loyalty' to you, don't you?" chirped Roody.

"Well, er, of course. Is there any other kind?"

"Many of your former Administration staff and West Wing employees, that you fired on a whim, might just say so," replied Roody facetiously.

"Hmmm. I don't understand. But let's get back to something more important than my loyalty to employees. What about those Hamberders?" he grumbled as his stomach rumbled.

"Aahh, Mr. Terminator, why is my client not allowed food when everyone else is eating?" asked Roody-Doody.

"Ach! That iss simple. In a hospital you are not allowed to eat 24 hours before an operation, right? Vell, it's the same for an execution. If the prisoner hass too much food inside andt you chop off hiss head, lots of nasty stuff comes pouringk up out off za throat. Andt, usually, zey poo in zeir pants too. Very messy! I like my executionz to be clean andt tidy!"

"But, but, but, er, you are presuming my client to be guilty and therefore denying him his 1st Amendment rights."

"Vell, from what I hear, everyvone knows he is guilty, just like in the Impeachment Trial. The difference here is that the jury is not rigged. Andt anyway, your client does not seem to care much about the Constitution and only seems to apply bits that <u>he</u> wants in ways that <u>he</u> wants. So, I am prepared to forget the 1st Amendment in his case."

[166] KEMOSABE: The Lone Ranger was a 1950's US TV series western, reprised in the 2013 movie with Jonny Depp playing Tonto, the Indian sidekick. Kemosabe is the Indian word for friend and what Tonto always called the Lone Ranger. One day, they are surrounded by a tribe of angry Indians about to attack them. The Lone Ranger says, "We have a problem." And Tonto, being an Indian himself, says, "Who's the 'we' Kemosabe?".

BANG! BANG! BANG! The Judge intervened. "Counsel for the Defense shalleth not question the instructions of the court-appointed executioner, whose decisions on rules and procedures shalleth be final. As will his executionary actions on the guilty prisoner! Ahem, should he be judged so, of course, by the jury of his peers."

"But, but, but, your Honor!!" riposted Roody-Doody.

"SILENCE! After the distribution – excluding any to the Defendant - and consumption of the court victuals, the, er, Hamberders(?) and, the, er Fries(?) – whatever they mayeth be – this court shall recess till 12 of the noon tomorrow. The Defendant shall be remanded in custody overnight," said the Judge with significant force and severity in his voice.

"I OBJECT!"

"Whateth for this time???" asked the Judge testily.

"I object to the fact that you want to keep my client in custody overnight. He is a well-respected businessman, not to mention President of Trumperland. I request bail for my client and an unfettered release," pleaded Roody-Doody.

"Well, if I alloweth overnight release, thy client will have to posteth bail of $1 million with the court," said the Judge expecting the sum to be a deterrent.

"Yes, that's fine your Honor," said Roody-Doody unexpectedly.

The response was so fast and so unprecedented that Attorney O'Bama smelled something fishy about it. Most bail bonds only cost a small percentage of the actual amount posted. O'Bama started to see a plot hatching in the Trumper's febrile, but feral, mind. So, he decided to request that the bail requirement go up a notch.

"I OBJECT!!" said O'Bama. "That sum is too low. I recommend. . . a bond of $1 billion. And, of course . . . in order to verify such funding capability . . . the Defendant shall be required . . . to submit his tax returns . . . for the court to review," he said with just the twinkling of a smile on his face.

"I OBJECT!!!" was the expected answer from Roody-Doody.

"But Attorney Joolianose," responded O'Bama smoothly, "your client has said himself, . . . under oath, . . . that he is worth over $2 billion. . . So, verification of that fact is all I am proposing. . . Show the court the tax returns."

"But, but, but, Attorney O'Bama, why do you want my client to post such a large bail amount?"

"Well, I consider that he may be a flight risk. He could easily leave this court . . . go out onto the front lawn . . . give one of his usual unintelligible and unhearable press briefings in front of that noisy Marine One helicopter and then take off for the airport. . . There he could climb the stairs of Air Force One, either with his umbrella . . . that he cannot close . . . or a piece of toilet tissue stuck to his foot . . . that no one told him about."

A ripple of laughter rang around the Rosy Garten much to the pain of the Trumper. His mouth was in a tight grimace and he looked even more stone-faced than usual.

O'Bama smiled around the court and continued. "He could fly to Florida . . . at tax-payer's expense . . . adding to the almost $200 million it has cost the American people . . . for his golfing trips over the last 3 years. . . Then he might hunker down in his Mar-y-Lago golf resort . . . declare it a new sovereign state . . . and crown himself 'King for Life'. . . And if that happened, this court . . . and any other in Trumperland . . . would have no jurisdiction over him. . . Hence, I am recommending to your Honor . . . to set bail at $1 billion . . . and have his tax returns submitted for review . . . in order to let the Trumper leave this court."

That was all said in rapid fire delivery – well as rapid as any speech ever can be by O'Bama - much to the amazement of the Trumper, Roody-Doody and everyone else in the Rosy Garten.

At the end of it there was a brief, slightly pregnant, silence, then . . .

Clap! . . . . Clap! . . . . Clap! A slow hand clap was started by the Queen, which gradually spread around the gallery, the Saffas, the Press Corp, the Jurors and the assembled multitude. It got louder and louder and faster and faster as more people joined in, just like the Icelandic Football team supporters clap in the World Cup.

The only people not clapping were the Trumper himself, Roody-Doody, the witnesses, the Trumper's avatar alter-egos and the Ripofflican members of the House of Cards. I wonder why not?

"Aaaahhh, eeeehhh, bhbuhbut, bhhuttt! OMG!" was about all that Roody-Doody could manage at first. Then the Trumper slapped him hard on both cheeks and he was shaken out of his stupor.

"Listen to me Roody!" whispered the Trumper between clenched teeth. "Agree to that and you are DOA!"

Roody-Doody didn't need to be told twice that the Trumper would NEVER willingly show his tax returns.

"I OBJECT! Er, your most estimable, veritable Honor. Er, is there an alternative to that? Please?"

"Well, Attorney Joolianose I have three options for your client to consider," said the Judge. "First, the Guantanamera Bay Military Detention Camp. Second, the Trumperland State Correctional Facility. And third, is house arrest in the Defendant's bedroom in the Colored House. You choose!"

"Aahh, er, thank you your Honor," said Roody-Doody. "Well, first, I understand that at Guantanamera Bay they torture prisoners by continuously playing a loop tape of the 'Guantanamera' song in Spanish. Plus, they force feed them with El Chapo Bell burritos till they either burst or have such a bad case of the Mexicali Belly that they cannot step away from a toilet for several days. Given my client's less than favorable ratings among the Mexican and Latino communities, I feel that he is likely to suffer some form of Montezuma's Revenge and may not get a fair treatment at that facility. So, my client will not choose that option."

GUANTANMERA – CELIA CRUZ
https://www.youtube.com/watch?v=9jaoXKpi7N4

"Second, your Honor," Roody-Doody continued, "we feel that the Trumperland State Correctional Facility may not be an appropriate incarceration for my client. Because of his blonde hair, the inmates may see him as an attractive, if slightly chubby, object of desire and he may suffer from some sexual harassment to the point of being forced into undesirable, non-consensual relations. Plus, it is becoming common knowledge, that prisons are major hot spots for the coronavirus, and he may be exposed to infection. So, my client will not choose that option."

"Therefore, my client is more than happy to accept the third option of house arrest at the Colored House. Thank you, your Honor. We are very grateful for your kind consideration," said Roody-Doody obsequiously.

"Certainly, Attorney Joolianose," responded the Judge. "I can appreciate the reasons for thy choices. Thy client's interactions with the Mexican and Latino communities hath been somewhat less than pleasant and hath bordered on racial profiling. So, I can understand why he would not wanteth to be in Guantanamera. I am also, well advised that thy client is more than usually well-acquainted with sexual harassment. Therefore, I can see why he would not wanteth to be on the receiving end of it, especially given the unrepresentatively high proportions of black and people of color in our jails. They may want to taketh some retribution for his alleged and perceived bias against them. Hence, thy choice of house arrest was not unexpected."

"Er, well, thank you again your Honor," said Roody-Doody.

"Aahh! There are just a couple more things I forgot to mention Attorney Joolianose," said the Judge. "First, the Defendant, at all times, shalleth be manacled to a Navy Seal by each arm. Second, he will not be allowed to partake of any victuals or viands at any time. Third, he will not be allowed to goeth to the bathroom in case he trieth to escape, and so, he will be required to wear an adult diaper to deal with his bodily functions. Fourth, he shalleth not be allowed to watch any Foxy News or other right-wing media on the television or internet. And fifth, he shall be prohibited access to any cell phone, iPhone, android, iPad, tablet or other communication device so that he cannot access Twatter and all the Twats that follow him. Do I maketh myself clear, Attorney Joolianose?"

"But, but, but, but your Honor . . ."

BANG! BANG! BANG! "This court is now in recess till 12 of the noon tomorrow!"

Roody-Doody could not believe it. "I've been out-maneuvered by B.A.R.A.C.K. O'Bama and Judge James Madison, one of whom has sticky-out ears and the other is 269 years old. Where is the justice in that? Bah, humbug!" he thought to himself.

What Roody-Doody did not realise, as he metaphorically kicked himself in the butt, was that the Trumper was just about to strangle him.

The Trumper would probably have succeeded too, if it were not for the strong grip of the Navy Seals holding him back by his manacled wrists. He was absolutely livid. And that was a British understatement!

"ROODY! This is bullsh*t. I am going to be locked in my own bedroom all night with these two goons!!! And no food, no TV and NO TWATTER!!!! What sort of a deal is that?? Grrrrrrrrrrrr!"

"Well Boss, it's better than $1 billion bail and your tax returns . . !"

Just then O'Bama passed by the Defense's table.

He smiled his best O'Bama smile and said, "Attorney Joolianose, I am so looking forward to tomorrow. . . I trust you are too. And sleep well, MISTER President!"

And with a wink of his eye he walked away whistling like a bird.

"He is mocking me! Mocking me just like he did in 2011 at that Correspondent's Dinner. I'M GOING TO KILL THAT MOTHER MOCKER!!!!"

Before he had time to say anything else, the Terminator also passed by the table and gave a jaunty, irreverent salute.

"Goodt eveningk Mr. Cummerbund-in-Chief! See you tomorrow after za trial!"

"You're going to be here tomorrow? Why? What for? And what do you mean 'after the trial'?" asked the Trumper somewhat tremulously.

"Ach, yes! Don'tchu worry. I'LL BE BACK!"

POSTSCRIPT

Would O'Bama mock the Trumper? Really? Really!

O'BAMA MOCKS TRUMPER – CORRESPONDENT'S DINNER
https://www.youtube.com/watch?v=HHckZCxdRkA

The Trumper has not been to the Correspondent's Dinner since 2016.

21

MEANWHILE PART 10 – HOUSE ARREST CAN BE FUN

Meanwhile...

Meanwhile, inside the Colored House, the Queen of Queens was looking for The McDonald as he was supposed to be on lock-down, in his bedroom, for his house arrest.

"McDOOOONOLDDT! McDOOOONOLDDT!"

"Er, er, yyes, ddear?" The McDonald stuttered in fear, as usual.

"Vhere ares youse??"

"I am in my bbedrroom, ddear"

"Vhere iss zat? I haff neffer effer been zere!"

"Er, it's the one at the end of the, er, corridor with the double doors, er, dear . . ."

"Ha! OK! So zat iss it! Zat iss vere I seez all za homez deliffery boyz commingk effery nightz viz McDoz andt KFC andt Pizza Hutz!"

The Queen flung open the double doors to the Trumper's bedroom and she stood in the entrance, with her hands on her hips, glowering at him with a look that would have curdled yogurt.

"WHAT ZA FACKZ!!!!???!!!!"

The sight that greeted the Queen when she opened the door was beyond belief. Way beyond belief! And even beyond that too!"

The Trumper was laid on the bed, naked except for an adult diaper, which looked more like a plastic garbage bag than a diaper. Very suave! His legs were spread-eagled open and each ankle was manacled, with cuffs, to the bottom bedpost. There was a Navy Seal sitting on a chair at each side of the bed, near the head. And each of the Trumper's wrists was manacled to one of the Navy Seal's wrists with a pair of handcuffs.

On his stomach was a Hamberder and every time he reached out to try and grab it, the Navy Seal would let him get almost there and then jerk his hand back.

It was absolute torture for the Trumper. He was like the pizza delivery boy - he could smell it, but he couldn't eat it! Aaaarrrgghhh!

The room was in an absolute shamble. There were Hamberder wrappers, empty French fry packages, empty pizza boxes and loads of old, empty KFC buckets, all over the floor, on the chairs, on top of the drawers and on the shelves. Plus, there were hundreds of empty bronzer tubes, everywhere. In fact, there was some garbage on every flat space.

It was absolutely unbelievable! And even the Queen was shocked into silence for a moment. But only for a moment.

"VHAT A SH*T-H*LES!! In fack it'z mutch, mutch, mutch vorse zan von off zose tso-calledt sh*t-h*les countries zat youse ares alvays talking aboutz. McDoonnldt, ziss iss digsustingk!"

"But Malarkeyania, it's not my fault. The Mexican cleaner stopped coming because I was paying her below the minimum wage. So, she went off to work on the Joe Biden campaign. I have no idea why!"

"Ach! Realliez! Itz neffer yours faultz iss itz?"

"I don't take any responsibility . . ."

"Off courses! Youse coulds notz possiblies be repsponsibles. Zat iss vy youse ares trussed ups like za Sanksgiffink Turkey, readies tzo be roasted ins za offen. Youse ares chusst ans innoscented victimz!"

"Don't worry. Trust me. I will get away with it. I always do!"

"McDoonaldt, youse are likes za cat viss nines lifes zat allvays landts onn itz feetz effen ven youse throws itz off za Trumper Tower. Butts ziss times I sink zat youse alreadies usedt ups ALLs off za nines off yours lifes. No fackingk jokez!"

"Really? Really? Do you think they are really gunning for me this time? They are going to try and get me in some trumped-up charge?"

"McDoonnallddt! Za chargess ares nots trumperedt upps. Zey are reals, juss likez alls za uzzer vons zat youse gott avay viz befores. Youse andt zat BoJos Joockstrapt ares chusst za sames. Zat nicez Davfid Cameroon vonce saids abouts Jokestrop 'Za singk abouts za greazeds piggletz iss zat he managerz tzo shlipz throus ozzer people'z handtz vere merely mortalz failedt'. Andt youse ares chust likez zat toos."

"But I didn't do all of those things. It wasn't me. I wasn't there!"

"Ya! Ya! Ya! Replayz za Betamaxz tapes. It'z vasn't meez. I vasn't zere! Pahhh!!"

Then she turned her attention to the two Navy Seals.

"Boyz youse lookz a bitz Slavic! Vot ares yorz namez?"

"Sergeant Frank Kovacevic, your Royal Very Highness," said one.

"Sergeant Marjan Potocnik, your Royal Very Highness" said the other.

"Ach, I recognizes zose family's names! Youse are boths fromm Solvenia, right? So youse canz calls me Ma'am."

"Yes, er, Ma'am. Well our parents were, Ma'am. We were both born here. The Captain chose us specifically for this duty because he thought that you would be more comfortable knowing that Mr. Trumper was safe in the hands of your fellow countrymen, Ma'am," said Kovacevic.

"Yours Capitan voss rights zere!"

"If there is anything we can do, Ma'am, we are at your service."

"Sangk youse boyz! I amz fines. Butts youse mustz be hungriez by nowz. Doos youse vant somesingk to eatz?"

"Well, if it's not too much trouble, Ma'am." replied Kovacevic happily.

"Ach, boyz. Youse knows vat Slovenian hospitalitiez iss likes. Ve lovff tzo ffeedt ours guestz."

"Well, thank you, Ma'am!"

"Letz goes downs tzo za Residentz kitchenz and tsee iff zey cans rastle ups za couples off pizzas. Vot does youse sayz?"

"Ah, but what about the prisoner, I mean Mr. Trumper, Ma'am? What shall we do with him?"

"Achs! Chusst handt-cuffz himms tzo za beds heads. He vill notz be goingk anyveres in za hurries!"

"Are you sure, Ma'am?"

"Absoluteliez!! Letz goes. Ve cans chatz aboutz za 'Oldt Countriez' vhile youse eats za pizza tzoo."

"But, what about me? Can I have something to eat?" asked the Trumper despondently.

"Noze!"

"But, can you put the TV on? Please, please! I want to watch my favourite newsreader Sean Insanity. He will be on soon," the Trumper pleaded.

"Noze!"

"But, okay, okay! Well then, can I have my cell phone so that I can Twatter to all Twats following me? Please, please and pretty please," begged the Trumper.

"Noze! Youse knowz vat za Chudge said!"

"But, Melovania . . ."

"Andt youse betters didt notz try tzo steal zat Hamberder ons yours stomach vile za guardz ares avay viz me . . ."

"But . . ."

"Not anozzer 'but' or its 'Off viz your headt'. Andt it cann be done tonichten, coz I haff za Terminator ons speedt dials."

Fade to black . . .

22

A FEW GOOD MEN – AND A FEW GOOD WOMEN TOO!

BoJo and Berrrccoww wandered back into the Rosy Garten the next morning, talking earnestly as they walked.

"But I say Berrrccoww, did you hear that comment from Attorney Joolianose about coronavirus in penitentiaries? That's the second time in the trial that they mentioned that virus – whatever it is," said BoJo worriedly.

"I have no idea, old boy. It does not mean anything at all to me," responded Berrrccoww.

"I thought it might be a computer virus or a Russian bot-hack the first time they mentioned it in the list of charges. But then when the Judge gave the options for where the Trumper would stay overnight, Roody-Doody declined the Trumperland State Correctional Facility on the grounds that there was a high infection rate amongst prisoners. So, what the hell is it?" BoJo wondered out loud.

"It's probably something and nothing, old chap. You know what these Yanks are like. They easily get their knickers in a twist!"

"Hmmm. I am not sure. I have a funny feeling in my water about this!" said BoJo with a frown.

"Don't fret, old boy. I am sure it's nothing!" jollied Berrrccoww.

"And what about that business of his middle name being 'Jockstrap'? Please, please don't say that I am related to this guy. That would be the living end!!" BoJo went on.

"I do hope for your sake that it's some kind of mistake. That would really be a major hole in the head, not to mention a political torpedo!" offered Berrrccoww with somewhat less than any real solace for BoJo.

"Maybe I can grab the Clerk of the Court and have a chat with him about the name thing? Hope so!" responded BoJo gloomily.

By then they had got to middle of the Rosy Garten and looked around them, realising that underneath every tree and bush there were bunches of Saffas. They had enjoyed the trial so much that they had decided to camp out, I mean what else would you do if your guided tour of the Colored House was cancelled?

"I say! You chaps have been here all night?" asked BoJo in amazement.

"Yo bro! We wanted to get a good seat for today's show, so we decided to camp out, *sink some tinnies* [167], have a *jol* [168] and get some *lekker boerewors on the braai* [169]. But I think a few of the folks are a bit *babelaas* [170] due to a bit too much jolling," answered one of the Saffas, totally confusing both BoJo and Berrrccoww.

"Well, er, right. Of course. Whatever!" they responded, no wiser for the explanation.

People were starting to congregate in the Rosy Garten again and there was an expectant hum in the air from the crowd and from the many bees.

The young kid in the Navy uniform was back at the Prosecution Counsel table. Sitting with his feet up on the desk-top and, as usual, intently tapping on his cell phone to his friends on ChatSnap, Tok Tik and Instanoodle. What else would he be doing just before the start of a big day in court? I guess he could be playing Fortnite!

---

[167] SINK SOME TINNIES: Drink a whole load of cans of beer. Preferably Castle Lager.

[168] JOL: Party time, big time, Saffa style.

[169] LEKKER BOEREWORS ON THE BRAAI: Tasty sausages on the barbecue.

[170] BABELAAS: Hungover. Usually, as a result of way too many tinnies, too much jolling and lots of lekker boerewors with your bros.

The Clerk of the Court, a.k.a. the Carpenter, was back at his desk and the Herald, a.k.a. the White Rabbi, was standing to attention with his vuvuzela in his hand. Roody-Doody was sitting at the Defense Counsel table twiddling his thumbs and trying desperately to stop from nodding off to sleep.

People were looking round waiting for something to happen and, eventually, something did. The doors leading into the Rosy Garten from the Colored House were thrown open and the Queen entered. Just behind her, the Trumper was marched out between the two Navy Seals.

Well, 'marched' may have been something of an exaggeration. Certainly, the Navy Seals marched, perfectly in step with their outer arms swinging in time. But, in between them, the Trumper, handcuffed on each arm to one of the Seals, just shuffled and ambled along. Gone was the suit. Gone was the immaculately starched shirt and its bright Ripofflican red silk, perfectly Windsor knotted, but ridiculously long tie hanging down below his groin. And most of all, gone was the 'perfect' coiffured sweep-over hair with its gallons of hairspray to keep it in place, replaced by a tousled mass (read: mess) of hair, totally unkempt. Instead of the suit, the Trumper was wearing a baggy old sweatshirt with the words *'MEXIT Forever!'* [171] on the front, some fraying running shorts and old trainers.

Also, the orange bronzer, fake tan was gone and the Trumper looked pale and white, just like he had been injected with bleach – as if anyone would be crazy enough to do that!

In fact, apart from the very slight difference between the words BREXIT and MEXIT, the Trumper could have been mistaken for BoJo. The likeness was incredible.

Actually, to BoJo, the likeness was more than incredible. It was totally, totally scary! And remember, BoJo was still wearing all his jogging gear including the 'BREXIT Forever!' sweatshirt, frayed old tennis shorts and well-worn trainers. Talk about a Doppelgänger!!

The Trumper shuffled to the Defense Counsel table and sat down.

---

[171] MEXIT FOREVER!: Someone had plagiarized the BREXIT portmanteau of Britain and Exit – the acronym for Britain leaving the EU. Instead, it was MEXIT, a portmanteau of Mexico and Exit – the call to become an illegal immigrant in the US. Wall or no wall!

Suddenly, as if by telepathy, the Carpenter leapt into action.

BANG! BANG! BANG! "All rise for Judge James Madison. This court is now in session!"

The Judge entered, sat down at the head of the court and looked around, very quickly spotting the absence of Attorney O'Bama.

"And where, pray, is the Attorney for the Prosecution this day?" he asked witheringly.

"Ah! Sorreee! Here I am your Honor," said O'Bama as he moved quickly across the court to take his seat. But as he did so there was an audible gasp (GASP!) from the Flake Press Corp and the spectators in the gallery. The gasp was not for O'Bama but for the person with him. It was none other than 'Crooked' Hillarious Clingfilm!

"I see thee, Attorney O'Bama. Late again! More bandits on the beltway again today, perchance?" said the Judge with extreme sarcasm.

"Ah, er, no, your Honor. . . I had to wait for my co-counsel. . . She needed a little more time to . . . finish her hair and make-up. . . She wanted to look good . . .for the Bench, your Honor," O'Bama explained.

"Attorney O'Bama! My concern is not about the beautification of thy co-counsel, but rather the proceeding of this trial without further delay. Is that understood?" grumbled the Judge. "And, if you plan to use co-counsel, thou must introduce her accordingly and justify her presence in this court."

"Er, ah, yes, your Honor. . . My co-counsel is Attorney Hillarious Rodthem Clingfilm . . . former First Lady to President Bill Clingfilm . . . former US Senator for New York . . . former Secretary of State in my Administration . . . and Dimocratic Presidential Candidate in 2016. . . She also has the distinction . . . of being one of the attorneys . . . on the team who prosecuted Richard Nixon . . . for the Watergate scandal," he said proudly.

67. Atty. Hillarious Rodthem Clingfilm

"I OBJECT!!!" came the cry from Roody-Doody at the prodding of the Trumper who, it was well-known, hated her. It was he who coined the nickname 'Crooked' Hillarious. Obviously, a case of 'the pot calling the kettle black', but that was the usual thing with the Trumper. He invariably mirrored his own misdemeanors onto others.

68. Atty. Roody-Doody Joolianose – Doubly Shocked About His Opposite Counsel

"And why, pray, do thou object, Attorney Joolianose?" asked the Judge.

"Well, well, er, I object because it's 'Crooked' Hillarious and she is totally partisan in her opinions and therefore will not be able to make an unbiased case against my client. And she has changed her hairstyle," blustered Roody-Doody.

"First, of all, thou must refrain from using the term 'Crooked' to describe an opposing counsel. It doth not befit this court. Second, I assume that thee are a Ripofflican and therefore, also totally partisan in thy opinions and, likewise unable to make an unbiased case for thy client. Naturally, Attorneys for the Prosecution favor the 'State' and Attorneys for the Defense favor their clients – whether they are guilty or innocent. That is the way of the courts. Do thou agree Attorney Joolianose?" queried the Judge.

"Well, er, ah, but, your Honor!" complained Roody-Doody. "Attorney Hillarious just really hates my client and that's not fair. And there is something strange about her hair and her face!"

"I am sure the feeling of hate is more than reciprocated by thy client about her. So that balances out. Agreed?" the Judge poked at Roody.

"Er, but, but, but . . ." burbled Roody pointlessly.

"Well, Attorney Joolianose, you objected to Attorney O'Bama cross-examining your client, so he has delegated to his co-counsel Attorney Clingfilm. Your choice!" jibed the Judge.

"But, your Honor, we thought it would be delegated to the kid in the Navy uniform, not someone like Attorney Clingfilm," whined Roody, frustrated at having been out played by O'Bama, yet again.

Behind him, the Trumper was banging his head on the table-top in despair and anger. His face had gone from bleached white to purple with rage. It seemed like his skin had the capacity to radiate all the colours of the rainbow depending on his mood. It appeared that he had the lizard-like attributes of a chameleon. Quite appropriate really, as he changed his stories just about as often as a chameleon changes color.

BANG! BANG! BANG! "Objection overruled," ordered the Judge. "Let's proceedeth with the case. Herald, calleth the next witness!"

"Yes. Certainly, your Majestic Honor," responded the White Rabbi. He had totally forgotten about the antics of the Saffas the day before, but they had not forgotten at all. In fact, they were waiting for the White Rabbi to put the vuvuzela to his lips and, as soon as he did, all the Saffas stood up and looked at him expectantly. But he just could not stop himself in time and he blew a huge blast on the vuvuzela! All the Saffas shouted "Waka! Waka!", someone hit the play button on his boom-box, and they all jumped up and started stomping and singing. It was crazy, until!

"OOOORRRRDDDEEERRRR!! OOOORRRDDDEEEEERRRR!!!" shouted John Berrrccoww, once again restoring calm in the court.

And, yet again, everyone smiled at each other. Gave 'high fives' and just sat down giggling.

"Silence in court," said the White Rabbi, as redundantly as before, "Call Moscow Mitch the Mock Turtle!"

"You really want me as a witness?" grumbled the Mock Turtle.

"The witness shall taketh the stand and not prevaricate!" said the Judge emphatically. "Attorney Joolianose, your witness."

"Er, ahh, thank you your Honor," replied Roody-Doody thinking desperately as to what line of questioning he could take that would prevent O'Bama from tricking him again.

"Your name is Moscow Mitch McConman the Mock Turtle. Is that correct?" asked Roody-Doody expecting a simple 'yes' answer.

"NO IT IS NOT!! I OBJECT AND WISH THAT THE 'MOSCOW MITCH' BIT TO BE STRUCK FROM THE RECORD, FORTHWITH!" erupted the Mock Turtle. The alliteration and association with Russia really irked him.

"That is not possible, your Honor, as its part of the court records, in perpetuity, ad-infinitum and forever and a day," said the Carpenter in his best official Clerk of the Court voice – which turned out to be just the same as his ordinary Carpenter voice.

"HERRUMPFF!" snorted the Mock Turtle. "Let's just get on with it, I am in a hurry." As if turtles were known for their speed and alacrity.

"Ah, er, OK. You are the Senate Majority Leader and also known in political circles as 'The Grim Reaper'. Correct?" asked Roody.

"Yes, and I am very proud of that," smirked the Mock Turtle.

"That has to be struck from the record," said the Carpenter. "It has satanic, religious connotations and we are not allowed to record things like that in case it, er - unleashes thunderbolts from the sky."

"What! You have to keep the 'Moscow Mitch' that I hate but cannot include 'Grim Reaper' that I love!!! Bah! Humbug!!" grumbled the Mock Turtle. "What do you want to ask me?"

"OK. OK. Er. You presided over the Senate Impeachment Trial of my client, the Defendant?" asked Roody.

"Yes, I did, with all the powers vested in me!" the Mock Turtle bragged.

"And you declared at the outset that you believed that my client was innocent. Correct?" Roody queried.

"I most assuredly did!" responded the Mock Turtle.

"And nothing that was said by the Dimocrat House Managers for the prosecution changed your mind in that belief," clarified Roody.

"Nothing. Nothing whatsoever!" confirmed the Mock Turtle.

"So, my client was not guilty of all charges. Correct?" asked Roody.

"Absolutely. Innocent as the day he was born!" said McConman.

"Thank you. No more questions, your Honor," finished Roody, with one of his too-many-teeth-in-his-mouth smiles.

"Your witness, Attorney O'Bama," said the Judge.

"Ah! Thank you, your Honor," said O'Bama, who stood up and turned to the Mock Turtle and looked him unwaveringly with a hard steely glint in his eyes but, at the same time, had one of his most warm and friendly smiles. It was most un-nerving.

"How are you Senator McConman . . . my friend? . . . We haven't met . . . for some considerable time now. . . Correct?" asked O'Bama, disarmingly.

"Er, Er, ummm. Yes, I guess you could say that," responded the Mock Turtle rather uncertainly. He was not at all sure why O'Bama was calling him a friend and asking about when they last met.

"You are a . . . Ripofflican, right? A party for the people . . . right? A party for democracy . . . for the people, right?" O'Bama asked.

"Er, well, yes, of course!" the Mock Turtle had to answer.

"Would you say . . . that you are a proud man . . . Senator McConman?" asked O'Bama, veering off in an unexpected direction.

"Er, well, er, yes. I suppose so," he answered, non-plussed.

"And what then . . . would you say . . . was your proudest moment?" O'Bama asked.

"Aaww! I er, don't, er, really rre c call . . ." stuttered McConman, as he knew the answer, but did not want to say it.

"Well then . . . let me remind you, Senator," said O'Bama slowly. "You said . . . that it was when you looked me in the eye . . . and said, 'Mr. President, you will NOT fill that Supreme Court vacancy'. Correct?"

"Er, er, well, aaaahh, er, well yes, maybe I did say that . . ." McConman was forced to admit.

"I believe we have some video footage of that. Could we roll it?"

MY PROUDEST MOMENT – MITCH McCONMAN
https://www.youtube.com/watch?v=qxhz8bPxXew

"So, when I was President, you denied me, and the American citizens who had elected me, the democratic right to appoint my chosen judge to the Supreme Court. Is that correct?" pushed O'Bama.

"Er, well, if you put it like that, I suppose so . . ." McConman slowly admitted.

"I do put it like that Senator," said O'Bama emphatically. "And then you went on to push, promote, prod and wrangle to have your man, Brett 'I like beer' Cavernous, on to the Supreme Court so that you would have a conservative, right-wing, Ripofflican majority there. Is that correct?"

"Hhheerrruummpphh! I, er, suppose so." said McConman, studiously looking at his feet.

"Therefore, that Ripofflican majority would protect your man, the Trumper, and try and repeal all the laws, policies and bills that my administration had put in place. And, I would put it to you, that it was very partisan and totally against the principles of democracy which you previously said – under oath – that you stood for! Would you agree, Mr. Senator?" said O'Bama, coming full circle in a pincer movement.

"I er, er, well, er. I plead the 5th," whispered McConman, basically pleading guilty to the crime but constitutionally excusing himself from admitting it.

"Aaah! I will take that as a 'yes' then," pounced O'Bama. "And, Senator McConman, you may find it somewhat interesting to reflect that you are now in the Witness Box, your prized and protected 'Capo Dei Capi' is now on trial, I am the prosecuting Counsel and former President James Madison, who wrote the Constitution and many of our other legal frameworks, is the presiding Judge. Isn't it ironic?!? Who would have thought, it figures . . . ?"

ISN'T IT IRONIC – ALANIS MORISSETTE W/ JAMES CORDEN
https://youtu.be/6GVJpOmaDyU

"Hmmm. I particularly like the line about your best friend . . . being a racist . . . and the one about Twatter. . . . Do they remind you of anyone you know, . . . Senator?" O'Bama queried while smiling all the time.

"Well, I, er, wouldn't like to hazard a guess right at this, er, moment," stumbled McConman, knowing full-well that O'Bama was referring to the Trumper.

"Well, not to . . . worry about that, Senator," said O'Bama, his voice becoming much more forceful with each word. "I think you might be more . . . concerned about your abuse of power, . . . your undermining the principles of democracy . . . and perjury of your oath of office to . . . uphold the constitution . . . and to act on behalf of the citizens of the United States!"

"Aaaaaww! Gosh darn it. That can't be right!!" wailed McConman.

"I assure . . . you it is so," said O'Bama slowly and deliberately. "And then there are your actions . . . relating to the Senate Impeachment 'Trial'. . . I am using the word 'trial'. . . in its most liberal sense here, by the way. . . . You agreed with my 'learned' colleague, Attorney Joolianose . . . to the fact that you had declared at the outset . . . that you believed his client to be innocent. Correct?"

"Yes, I surely did, and why not?" asked McConman.

"Because you then swore an oath of impartiality . . . to the Supreme Court Justice . . . who was the moderator for the Senate Impeachment Trial. . . . But you chose to break that oath . . . when you first of all refused to allow any evidence or witnesses to be included by the prosecution, . . . undoubtedly because you had none for the defense. . . . And second, you ignored all the testimony provided . . . by each of the Prosecution Managers . . . despite its compelling nature and content of obvious truth," O'Bama explained.

"Well, what if I did?" shot back McConman.

"I put it to you that, not only do those actions undermine the fundamental principles of a trial and divert the course of justice, but also you committed perjury by lying to the Chief Justice when you swore your oath in the full knowledge that you were going to ignore it. That would be my second charge against you personally," charged O'Bama.

"But, but . . ." cut in McConman.

"But, but . . . I know exactly what you are going to say," O'Bama interrupted. "It is not you who are on trial today. . . . It is McDonald J. Trumper. . . . And I fully agree with you. . . . Hopefully, your day in court . . . will come soon enough, . . . given how many transgressions of democracy, . . . self-interest over that of the people, . . . diversion of justice and many, many, more . . . . unconstitutional and potentially illegal acts . . . that you have 'allegedly' committed over the years."

"I DISPUTE those allegations!" argued McConman.

"That you may," replied O'Bama calmly but very forcefully. "But, nonetheless, . . . the actions you took personally . . . and in your position as Senate Majority Leader, . . . fundamentally changed the course of justice . . . and resulted in McDonald J. Trumper being acquitted, . . . despite his obvious and blatant guilt."

"Well, I was just doing my job!" McConman tried to wheedle.

"And that may be true, . . . if your job description happens to include . . . perjury, destruction of democracy and perversion of justice!" O'Bama countered perfectly.

"Er, umm, I . . ." was all that McConman could respond.

"Oh, and one last thing, Senator," said O'Bama. "Your contention that the Trumper was as innocent . . . as the day he was born . . . was totally correct!"

"Excuse me? I don't understand. You just argued that he was guilty. Now you are agreeing that he was innocent?" replied a very confused McConman.

"Aah! Not quite, Senator. . . .You were not listening to what I said," rejoined O'Bama with one of his best disarming smiles. It is true that he is . . . as innocent . . . as the day he was born. . . . Very simply because on the day he was born . . . he was gifted with a considerable trust fund . . . in his name. . . . And, it is alleged, . . . that the sources of that fund were probably . . . . the proceeds from a number of very disputable tax evasion 'maneuvers' . . . resulting from some potentially illegal book-keeping practices . . . by the Trumper family businesses. . . . And, irrespective of where the money came from, . . . the trust fund itself was a way of tax avoidance, . . . possibly bordering on evasion."

"And so?" rebuffed McConman, as the hypothesis was rather too convoluted for him to understand.

"He was not innocent . . . on the day he was born . . . as he was the recipient of what were essentially . . . fraudulently acquired or generated funds, . . . thereby being implicitly guilty of a crime. . . .Therefore, if he was guilty of a crime on the day he was born . . . so, following your own logic pattern . . . he must be guilty today. . . .Wouldn't you agree?"

"Aahh, bbba, er, er, bbut, but . . ."

"Thank you, your Honor. No more questions," O'Bama smiled and sat down.

McConman looked helplessly around the court for some support. Roody-Doody pretended to fumble in his briefcase because he knew he had, again, set up a witness, who was supposed to be for the defense, in such a way that he ended up being a bullet in O'Bama's prosecution gun. And the Trumper was trying to stand up and rush across the court but was fortunately being restrained by his Navy Seal guards. He was venting and gnashing his teeth like a man possessed – as he probably was.

"Let me at HIM! I want to punch HIM in the face!!! I HATE HIM!!!" ranted the Trumper while his Navy Seals tried to restrain him.

"Silence in court!" said the White Rabbi, ineffectually.

But the Trumper continued to rant and rave.

"Mr. Trumper! Compose thyself," said the Judge.

But to little avail. The Trumper continued to spit fire and brimstone.

"OOOORRRRDDDEEEERRRR!! OOOORRRDDDEEEEERRRR!!!" shouted John Berrrccoww, but, for once, he was not able to restore calm in the court. The Trumper was throwing a tizzy fit as though someone had messed up his McDo order in the Oral Office. He was that angry!

"McDOOOOONNNAAALLDDTT!! SHUT ZA FACKZ UPS!!!!" the Queen bellowed across the Rosy Garten. And the Trumper stopped immediately.

"Er, yes dear. Er, sorry dear," he whimpered obediently.

"Zat iss betters! Stays shtummz!" the Queen ordered.

While all the noise and commotion were going on, BoJo realised that he was growing again, and starting to tower over the people around him. But, strangely, they either did not seem to notice or did not seem to mind. Or perhaps it was some combination of the two. BoJo was at least a little comforted by the fact that his clothes appeared to be growing too.

"Berrrccoww! Berrrccoww! Look at me! I am growing again!" said BoJo worriedly.

"I say old chap, yes you are. It's getting a teensy-weensy bit squashed on this bench. Can you stop it?" Berrrccoww asked.

"I can't help it," said BoJo very frustratedly: "I'm just growing."

"You've no right to grow here," said one of the Queen's footmen who was sitting on the same bench as BoJo and Berrrccoww.

"Don't talk nonsense," said BoJo more firmly: "I already had that same argument with the Gryphon yesterday. You know you're growing too."

"Yes, but I grow at a reasonable pace," said the footman, "not in that ridiculous fashion."

"Well, who actually defines what pace is 'ridiculous'? There are so many 'ridiculous' things in this place that, if I started, it would take me much longer than the time I've got," replied BoJo testily.

"But who gave you that time? And how do you know how much you have got? It's half past Tuesday on the 35th of Marpril. So, I would say that you have lots of time, indeed. And anyway, don't argue with me as I am always Right!" shot back the footman. "I can't be bothered anymore explaining everything to you. I'm going to join my colleague, the Queen's Left Footman."

"So, who are you?" asked BoJo, innocently and at the same time rather stupidly.

"I just told you! I am always Right - the Queen's Right Footman. And my colleague is always the Left. Don't you know that everyone, even the Queen, has a Right Foot and a Left Foot and they each need a shoe? Paahh!" and with that he got up very grumpily and crossed over to the other side of the court to join the Left Footman.

Just as he did so the Judge said, "Herald, calleth the next witness, please."

"Yes, your Worshipful Honor! Certainly!" responded the White Rabbi, but then realised that it was going to be the Trumper so there was likely to be some disruption in the court. So, he was rapidly scrambling through his brain for ideas as to how to do it. He dared not use his vuvuzela as he knew that the Saffas would erupt into 'Waka Waka' again. So, what could he do?

Then it came to him!

He just turned to the Navy Seals and shouted "ATT-EN-TION!" Instantly, the two Navy Seal Sergeants automatically jumped to their feet and stood bolt upright, dragging the Trumper up with them. They were programmed to react instantly to orders. It was in their Navy Seal DNA.

When the White Rabbi realised his idea was successful, he shouted, "FORWARD MARCH!!" The Seals reacted exactly on cue and, in unison, started marching forward. Of course, the Trumper wasn't ready for it and got dragged along with them, puffing and grunting, as his overweight and unfit body tried to catch up. The Trumper was a graduate of the New York Military Academy, but his alleged 'bone spurs' gave him the 'excuse' not to serve in Vietnam. So, he had never been in an active military unit, where an order – whatever it was – was obeyed instantly and without question.

"Wha, wha, what? Wwwwait!" puffed the Trumper. But the Seals were not programmed to wait. They just kept marching forward dragging the Trumper between them.

The White Rabbi was staring to enjoy himself. "LEFT TURN!" he ordered. "FORWARD MARCH!" He let them go five paces then shouted, "RIGHT TURN!" This was fun. Well, it was for the White Rabbi, but not at all for the Trumper. He was just being dragged around like a wet blanket. And if you looked closely, very, very closely, you could just see the very tiniest hint of a smile – well a smirk, really – on the clenched lips of the Navy Seals.

"ABOUT FACE!" ordered the White Rabbi and the Seals spun around so fast it was almost like they were doing a Scottish Highland Twirl. The Trumper was spun around and sagged at the knees, completely disorientated and out of sync with the Seals.

The Trumper had ended up exactly where the White Rabbi had planned it. In front of the Witness Box.

He gave his final order, "THE DEFENDANT SHALL BE PLACED IN THE WITNESS BOX!" And the Seals lifted him up by his manacled wrists and dropped him in the box.

The court erupted in a huge round of applause lead by the Queen and everyone was cheering the White Rabbi.

And, as he sat down again at his desk, the White Rabbi muttered quietly to himself, "And that's one for your antisemitism over the years and your lack of sympathy and empathy after the Tree of Life congregation massacre in Squirrel Hill, Pittsburgh in 2018. Shalom!"

"Clerk of the Court! Sweareth in the Defendant," ordered the Judge.

"Yes, your Honor," said the Carpenter and turned to the Trumper. "Raise your right hand, put your left hand on the Bible and read the Oath on this card."

"Do I have to do this? I took an oath once before, at my Inauguration. And it was the biggest most beautiful Inauguration crowd ever. Do I really have to do another oath?"

BANG! BANG! BANG! "The Defendant shall taketh the Oath before I loseth my patience!" said the Judge. "NOW!"

"Er, yes dear. I mean no, dear. I mean yes, your Honor!" he grovelled and said to the Carpenter. "Give me the card with the Oath."

"Please?" said the Carpenter.

"What? Please?" said the Trumper, not expecting to be challenged by other people. He was far too used to everyone in the room agreeing with him. Unfortunately.

"Say, PLEASE!" shouted the Judge getting angrier by the minute.

"Er, OK. Apologies your er, Honor. Please can I have the Oath?"

"Certainly," said the Carpenter sarcastically, and knowing that the Trumper had some obvious reading deficiencies he continued. "You start at the top left-hand corner. Read from left to right and finish at the bottom right corner. OK? Got it?"

"Ahh. OK, sure," responded the Trumper naively, proving yet again that sarchasm was alive and well in Trumperland.

He raised his small right hand and put his even smaller left hand on the Bible. Smoke started rising from the Bible around his fingers, there was a sizzling noise, like frying bacon, and a distinct smell of burning. The Trumper seemed not to notice. But everyone else did!

"I, er, swear that, er, . . . the evidence (evidence?) that I shall, er, er, give . . . shall be the (what?), the, er, ttrruu . . .th, the, er, wwwwhollle, er, er, cougghhhruth, and, er, (what's th, that?) nothing but the, the, the, er, er, ttttrrruu . . .th, so, er, er, help, er, mmmmeeeeee Ggggg . . .od. (Phew!)."

"Attorney Joolianose, you may cross-examine the Defendant," said the Judge.

"Thank you, your Honor," replied Roody-Doody and stood up.

"No, he will NOT, thank you all the same, your Honor," responded the Trumper, not wanting his own Defense Attorney to feed the prosecution with any cues and clues, as he had done with Mitch McConman.

"Er, thank you, your Honor. No further questions," said Roody-Doody, even though he had not actually asked any questions, and quickly sat down again.

"Attorney O'Bama, the Counsel for the Prosecution may cross-examine the Defendant," said the Judge.

"Thank you, your Honor. In accordance with the objection raised by the Counsel for the Defense regarding my potential conflict of interest, I will concede the cross-examination to my Co-counsel Attorney Hillarious Rodthem Clingfilm," O'Bama said very sweetly with just the right hint of sarcasm in his tone.

"Proceed," said the Judge with an equal hint of sarcasm in just that one word.

Attorney Clingfilm stood up and walked forward to be close to the Witness Box. "Good afternoon, Mister President," she said, emphasizing the 'Mister' strongly as a subliminal jibe. "Did you sleep well?"

It was very obvious from the Trumper's totally unkempt appearance and scruffy old sports-wear – which, naturally, did not suit him at all – not to mention the huge bags under his eyes and his ashen, white pallor, that he had hardly slept at all. Plus, she knew he had not eaten because of the instructions issued by the Terminator the day before.

"What? Of course not! I was manacled to a bed, stark naked except for a garbage bag pretending to be an adult diaper. I had a Hamberder on my stomach that I could not reach. I had no cell phone, so no Twatting. No TV. And my wife, the Queen, was down in the Residence kitchen feeding these two Slovenian Seal goons with pizza. So, NO, I did not sleep well!" grumbled the Trumper, which was a stupid thing to do as both the Seals yanked his handcuffs simultaneously in reaction to it.

"Oh, I am soooo sorry to hear that," Attorney Clingfilm replied, insincerely, at the same time as she smiled sweetly at the two Seals.

"But, but what have you done to yourself? You look different!" the Trumper asked, peering closely at her for the first time. Up to that point he had been so engrossed in his own misery – as always - he only thought of himself first (and second and third!).

"Ah. I've just had a bit of a makeover. Nice of you to notice, Mr. President. You always were a 'ladies' man'!" she replied, baiting him with unveiled and unnoticed, facetiousness.

"Well, thank you," he replied mistakenly basking in his own shallowness.

"Yes, I got those nice guys from *QUEER Eye* [172] on Netflix. I am sure you know the ones I mean. They decided I should have my hair dyed blonde. Then the stylist recommended a new, shorter style, swept from one side to the front, low across the forehead and then brushed to the back. And a completely different make up. He wanted to give me a sort of orange glow about my face. They made all my clothes different too. A more corporate-style plain, charcoal grey suit with pants and an oversized jacket. And they even pushed me to go as far as having a formal white shirt with collar and cuffs, plus this lovely bright red silk tie. It's a bit long, though – I think it's made in China. What do you think of the whole 'look'?" she asked, as innocently as possible, given that the whole effect was to mimic the Trumper.

Slowly, ever so slowly, it dawned in him that it was intended to make fun of him and to make him angry – which it did wonderfully well.

"You're MOCKING ME!! Just like your buddy O'Bama, last night. With all his smirking and bird-whistling! I could have KILLED him!"

"MOI?!? MOCKING YOU!?" she said, doing an impression of Miss Piggy from the Muppets. "It's a good thing that you didn't kill him. Just think of the NTY headline. 'Trumper Tries to Kill a Mockingbird'."

The whole Rosy Garten erupted with laughter, which only made the Trumper even more angry as he HATED being laughed at. The symbolism was completely lost on the Trumper, of course, as she knew he would never have read the book, or any book, much less one which questioned the automatic assumption of guilt of any black person accused of any crime.

---

[172] QUEER EYE: LGBTQ fashionista & stylist makeovers. Trumper surely would hate it!

"Baaaaaahhhh!!!! I don't want this woman quest-croshtioning me. She has no right to be here!" complained the Trumper.

"Certainly, Mr. Trumper. If thou prefer to have Attorney O'Bama cross-examine thee, that is perfectly within thy rights," offered the Judge, smiling as he did so, as he already knew the answer.

"WHAT!!! O'Bama? No way! Even 'Crooked' Hillarious is preferable to O'Bama," whined the Trumper.

"As you wisheth," agreed the Judge. "Attorney Clingfilm, you may proceed with thy cross-examination."

"Thank you, your Honor."

She turned to face the Trumper.

"For the avoidance of doubt. You are McDonald J. Trumper, 45th President of Trumperland and you were sworn into office on 20 January 2017. Correct?" asked Attorney Clingfilm.

"Yes, yes. Of course, I am!" responded the Trumper, angrily, as though it was a completely pointless question.

He was soon to learn that there was no such thing as a pointless question when it came from the lips of an attorney. Especially one like Attorney Clingfilm.

"And, when you were being sworn in for this appearance in the Witness Box just now, you told the Clerk of the Court that, when you were sworn in as President, it was the biggest Inauguration crowd ever. Is that correct?" she asked.

"Yes, it was the biggest, most beautiful Inauguration crowd ever and it was a beautiful sunny day. God loves me! The sun always shines on the righteous, you know," bragged the Trumper.

Attorney Clingfilm smiled at him, turned away from the Trumper and walked towards the Jury Box. She picked up two photos from the Prosecution Table as she passed.

"Members of the Jury. I would like you to take a look, a good look, at Exhibits D and E - photos of Inaugurations."

She covered the dates on the two photographs so they could not identify the source and said, "I ask the Jury but one question. Which is the bigger crowd? The one on the LEFT or the one on the RIGHT?

Unanimously the members of the Jury said, "The one on the LEFT!"

69. & 70.   Even Without The Dates You Could Guess Which Was O'Bama's Crowd

"Well, I have to tell you that the one on the LEFT is the Inauguration, on 20 January 2009, of my learned colleague, Lead Counsel for the Prosecution, President B.A.R.A.C.K. O'Bama!" she said with a smile and a flourish as she revealed the date on the photo.

"And the one on the RIGHT is the Inauguration of the Defendant, McDonald J. Trumper, on 20 January 2017." she said with an air of questioning finality as she also revealed the date on that one, with its very obviously much smaller crowd.

"So, as per the indictment in Charge No. 8, it would seem that, right from the very first moment of his presidency, the Defendant started lying to the American people. And he stayed absolutely true to form today, even telling a lie about the size of his Inauguration crowd as he was being sworn in on the Holy Bible," said Attorney Clingfilm, 'setting the scene' before the cross-questioning had even got into its stride.

"That's BULLSH*T! FAKE NEWS! My crowd was bigger than O'Bama's. The Flake News photoshopped the pic to make the crowd look bigger!" argued the Trumper.

"Well, Mr. President . . . I do agree with you there. The picture was photoshopped to make the crowd look bigger!" Attorney Clingfilm smilingly agreed.

"There. I told you so!" smirked the Trumper, looking around the court like he had won a major battle.

"Yes, definitely the Inauguration picture was photoshopped. But you had National Park Service fix YOUR picture, not O'Bama's. Please have a look at Exhibit F," rebutted Clingfilm with a condescending smile.

71. & 72.	Crop It A Lot – But The Trumper Crowd is Still Smaller

"You also said earlier – and many times before on TV – that the sun was shining, which must have been 'God's blessing'. Well then, I can only assume that you must think that the Queen, who is sitting on the left of the picture, is a complete idiot, as she had a huge transparent umbrella, plus many people were wearing waterproof ponchos and you were wearing a coat, as can be seen in Exhibit G." said Atty. Clingfilm.

73.	New First Couple: One is an Idiot. Other is Mrs. Trumper

"Tell us. Is that correct, Mr. President? Do you think that the Queen – the same lady that is sitting over there on that throne - is an idiot?"

There was an audible growl from Queen, "McDOONNALLDDT!!"

"No, no, no! The, the, er, QQQueen is nnnott an, er, idiot, of, of, of ccourse. It wwas dddefinitely rrraining," stuttered the Trumper, in abject fear of retribution from the Queen of Queens.

"Members of the Jury," said Attorney Clingfilm, as she stood in front of them once again. "I believe that I have illustrated that this man, this person elected to be our President, lied the moment he was sworn in to take that office, and continued to do so today, as he was being sworn in to give testimony – allegedly in his own defense – regarding the litany of lies he has told to the American people from that day until this. It was 18,000 in October 2019. It's probably 20,000 by now! It will therefore be very difficult to believe anything he says during these proceedings and you must bear that in mind when making your final judgement."

"I OBJECT!" shouted Roody-Doody.

BANG! BANG! BANG! "OBJECTION OVERRULED!" said the Judge emphatically.

"But, your Honor! You haven't heard my objection yet," whined Roody-Doody.

"I do not needeth to. I heard all the ones before, and they were all nonsensical. So, I am sure this one wouldst be too. No further discussion on this matter. Do thou understandeth me, Attorney Joolianose?" the Judge asked.

"Er, yes, your Honor," said Roody, desolately.

"Your Honor, if I may proceed?" Atty. Clingfilm asked politely.

"Certainly!"

"Thank you, your Honor," she replied and again turned to the Jury. "Members of the Jury I would like to bring your attention to charges No. 9 and No. 10. Namely, the budget of the Inauguration and payment of the performers."

And then, approaching the Witness Box, she asked, "Mr. President Trumper, to entertain, what you seem to delusionally call the biggest Inauguration crowd, you also had the biggest budget. Is that correct?"

"Yes. Everybody loves me so much that they all contributed to the Inauguration. We raised $107 million, almost twice as much as O'Bama did for his Inauguration," said the Trumper, bragging himself into a 'honey trap' of his own making. He just could not resist!

"Really!" exclaimed Atty. Clingfilm in mock surprise, as she already knew the answer. "That's excellent, actually, except for one small thing. And that is - how you spent it."

"What do you mean?" queried the Trumper.

"Well it seems that – somehow – you had double the budget but a much smaller crowd. The latter which, *prima facie* [173], we just proved. And, also, the entertainment you provided was really only second tier and not star quality, as it had been for O'Bama."

"It was top quality entertainment and very expensive too!" argued the Trumper. "And the crowd was bigger. You could see all those prime faces on the photos!"

"That's not quite what 'prima facie' means Mr. President, but never mind," she replied, still smiling. "Plus, you have, shall we say, a 'nasty' habit of not paying your entertainers (and likewise your contractors). And, I believe that you were previously sued by the USA Freedom Kids dance troupe. Just a bunch of school kids who performed at one of your rallies. But you didn't pay them. Is that correct?"

"Er, well, er. You would need to ask the organizers about that. I don't sign the checks," the Trumper weaseled, as usual.

"Ah, yes! You only sign the checks for paying off porn stars, I believe . . ." Atty. Clingfilm countered pointedly."

"Wa, wa, wa. I, er, I, er, don't, er . . ."

She continued. "Perhaps, we can ask your daughter, Iwanka, about the Inauguration and her BFF, Stephanie Winstone Walk-off, who got paid $26 million for organizing the entertainment and who you made the 'fall guy'. But Iwanka is one of your advisers, right? Though that does seem a bit strange. And did I say that nepotism in Government is covered by Charge No. 24? I just wonder, if having her work for you at the Colored House, doesn't somehow create another conflict of interest due to the fact that she is part of your family who is running your Trumper Organization businesses that you were supposed to either divest or put in a blind trust. What do you have to say, Mr. President?" asked Atty Clingfilm at the end of a significant set of indirect allegations.

---

[173] PRIMA FACIE: At first sight - based on what appears to be the truth when first seen or heard. It does not mean there were prime faces in the photos. Duuuh!

"Well, I, er, um. My Iwanka is so beautiful. She is my favourite you know. She can do no wrong – even though her hubby, Jarhead, is sort of a bit Jewish. You know I would go out with her myself if she wasn't my daughter," rambled the Trumper, as usual, not actually answering the question.

"Yes, Mr. President, we are all well-aware of your preferences for young, attractive blondes. But I think that having a relationship with your own daughter is probably one step too far – even for you. Yes, even for you," Atty. Clingfilm replied. "But to get back to my point. Only - and I use that word 'without prejudice' – only $26 million was spent on the entertainment. What about the other $81 million?"

"Oh, er, I don't know. I am sure more than that was spent on the entertainment. We had some top acts. Like the Mormon Tabernacle Choir, for instance. They are really 'hot'," the Trumper bamboozled on.

"I see. Well, the Counsel for the Prosecution has just been handed a piece of paper from the equerry of the Queen. It pertains to the list of performers for the Trumper Inauguration, and what they were paid."

Turning to the Queen she said, "Thank you, your Royal Highness."

Using the, now famous, Trumper 'scamming' technique of *waving pieces of paper at the media* [174], Atty. Clingfilm held up in the air a piece of paper that, allegedly, had the details of all the acts at the Inauguration and how much they were paid.

"This is the proof that the acts were cheap, and that less than a quarter of the money raised, was used to pay for them. So, what happened to the rest, **Mister** President?" she drove home the point.

"I, er, er, wouldn't like to say. I, er, plead the 5th!!" said the Trumper finally, knowing that any further disclosure would incriminate him.

"Thank you, Mr. President. Based on your plea, I determine that the indictments in Charges No. 9 and No. 10 are proven to my satisfaction and I trust to the satisfaction of the Jury," Atty Clingfilm concluded.

---

[174] WAVING PIECES OF PAPER AT THE MEDIA: He pulls random pieces of paper out of the inside breast pocket of his jacket and waves them around as though this somehow makes the lies that he subsequently tells more believable. These range from 'love letters' from Kim Yung-Ones to 'trade agreements' with China or Mexico and even include his alleged phone call with 'Egghead' Sunderland with 'Quid Pro Quo' on it a few times.

She walked back to the Prosecution Table to get a drink of water and put down the 'evidentiary' piece of paper.

"Nice one Hillarious!" said O'Bama. "That was a bit of luck, the Queen giving you that list!"

"She didn't," whispered Hillarious. "It's just my phone bill with all my international calls when I was Secretary of State!"

She threw the piece of paper over to the kid in the naval uniform, who was still engrossed in his cell phone, 'talking' to his 'friends' on ChatSnap.

"Here, son. I'd like you to do me a favor, though. Just put this in my briefcase under the desk," she asked.

The kid just grunted and picked up the paper without taking his eyes off the phone and put it in Clingfilm's briefcase.

Attorney Clingfilm stood up once more and walked over to the Jury Box again.

"Members of the Jury, I would like to address Charges No. 5 and No. 6 which are somewhat personal to me. The indictment in Charge No. 5 is for Mr. Trumper, as he was then, being ultra-creepy on the Town Hall debate stage before the 2016 elections. And Charge No. 6 is for then candidate Trumper inciting his crowds to chant 'Lock her up!'. Thank you," she said and turned to address the Trumper.

"Mister President, in all presidential candidate debates, prior to the one between you and I in 2016, the two people on the stage were given their respective spot to stand or sit. And they stayed there. However, during our debate, at one point I was facing the camera and the audience, and you came up behind me like a creepy old pervert . . ."

"I OBJECT," shouted Roody-Doody.

"SHUT UP, Atty. Joolianose! OBJECTION OVERRULED. Let Atty. Clingfilm finish," ordered the Judge. "I want to heareth this juicy bit."

"Thank you, your Honor," said Atty. Clingfilm and continued where she left off but taking care to repeat the thing that Roody-Doody had objected to, just to make a point. "As I was saying. . . You came up behind me like a creepy old pervert and you were peering over my shoulder. Well, I am not quite sure what you were doing behind me as it also looked like you could have been sniffing my hair or something equally weird."

"I WAS NOT SNIFFING YOUR HAIR!" shouted the Trumper. "I don't fancy you and your hair isn't blonde – well it is now but it wasn't back then – and you are way too old for me in any case and not my type at all." said the Trumper trying to extract himself, but only added to the insults – which was often the case - the longer he spoke, the deeper the hole he dug for himself.

"Can we run the tapes please?" she asked.

TOWN HALL DEBATE – TRUMPER vs CLINGFILM
NYT https://www.youtube.com/watch?v=a0bULxydHX0
SNL https://www.youtube.com/watch?v=qVMW_1aZXRk

NYT   SNL

Atty. Clingfilm knew she just needed to let him dig a little more.

"So, I guess you weren't talking about me on that bus in the 'Access Hollywood' tape," she said, prying deeper.

"Hah! No way. I wouldn't be wanting to grab you by the p*ssy."

"I suppose I would just have to be younger and taller and slimmer, then, before you tried that on me?" she poked one more time.

"Absolutely! That would do it for me!" his super ego replied before the slightly more rational part of his psyche realised what he'd said.

"McDOOOONNNNAAAALLLLLLLDDDDTTTT!!!!" came the shout from the Queen. "I WEEELL KEEELLL YOUSE!!"

"Er, sorry dear! Er, I, er, didn't quite mean it the way it sounded. It wasn't me. I wasn't there. I didn't fancy her!" he said, trying all his usual excuses, which rarely worked even in normal circumstances, never mind after he had been tricked into a confession by a smart, female lawyer.

"Actually, you were very lucky that I really did not know you were there and could not see what you were doing. I only saw it afterwards on the news replays," explained Attorney Clingfilm. "If I had known you were doing that, I would have turned round and kneed you in the b*lls!"

And a soon as she had said it there was huge cheer and clapping from all the women in the Rosy Garten, led very vociferously by the Queen.

"BRAVOZ!! BRAVOZ!! Sockz its tzo himm Attorneyz!" cheered the Queen. The rest of the women were up on their feet clapping and all the Saffas were dancing and stomping their feet in true Zulu style. Someone switched on the boom box and 'Waka! Waka! blasted across the Rosy Garten. It was party time!!

Even the Navy Seals were getting in the groove and waving their arms about in the air. So, they were having fun, but it meant that the Trumper's arms were also being forcibly waved around as he was handcuffed to them.

It looked like he was enjoying himself because his arms were waving around but, for sure, the one person who was not in the party spirit was the Trumper. He was fuming. Absolutely fuming and angrily thinking to himself, "That woman, that 'Crooked' Hillarious, tricked me into admitting that I like young, tall, slim, blondes. Damn!! I hate that bitch!!!"

Everyone was having fun, but the poor White Rabbi was trying desperately to get some semblance of quiet and order – but without any success at all. "Order in court, order in court!" he kept saying to no avail.

Eventually, Berrrccoww couldn't resist any longer and just had to shout "OOOOORRRRDDDEEEERRR!! OOOORRRRDDDEEEERRR!!"

As usual, that did it, and everyone settled back in their seats to await the next chance to have dance.

"Silence in court!" said the White Rabbi once everyone had sat down and had stopped singing and laughing. He looked around, saw that everyone was sitting and smiled to himself as though he had done a really excellent job. "Let us proceed!"

"Thank you, your Royal Highness," said Atty. Clingfilm. "I appreciate your support and would like to bring to the Jury's attention the Defendant's direct attacks on me personally."

"Mister President, you remember when you started to make a HUGE issue of the fact that I had sent some non-sensitive emails on a private server?" she asked.

"Yes, of course I do!" replied the Trumper.

"That this was all, allegedly, about endangering our national security?" she questioned further.

"Yes, of course I do!" he responded. "Other hostile governments could have read those emails."

"Well, that's an interesting comment, because in one of your campaign rallies you said 'Russia, if you have those emails, release them all'. Is that correct?" she asked.

"Yes, yes! I wanted the American people to know what you had done!" the Trumper emphasized.

"Yes, of course you did. And Russia obliged by doing that via Wonkileaks a few hours later. But how did you know that Russia had them? And if you knew they were 'allegedly' full of state secrets, why did you ask for them to be released so all the world could read them rather than having them quietly and safely returned to the US Government?" came the cutting questions.

"Er, someone must have told me that Russia had them, probably, possibly. And, er, if, er, we had got them back, er, safely, er, maybe no one would have noticed. And anyway, I wasn't a government employee at that time – you were – so they weren't my state secrets. They were yours."

"Am I also correct in assuming that your son, McDonald Jnr and your son-in-law Jarhead Kushynumber were also not government employees when they met with Russian, shall we say 'businessmen', at your very own Trumper Tower during the campaign and 'coincidentally' just before you asked Russia to release my emails?" Atty Clingfilm asked, changing direction slightly again.

"Er, yes. They worked for me. Not the government."

"So, in fact they were committing acts against the US Government by dealing in our 'state secrets' illegally with the Russians. Wouldn't you agree?" she asked, turning the screw.

"Oh, er, no. They were just talking to the Russians about adoption. Yes, I remember now. It was adoption," the Trumper tried to wheedle.

"Aah. That was a very high-powered meeting just to talk about 'adoption'. Were you thinking of adopting a Russian baby? I thought you were capable of making your own babies? You have five children, don't you?"

"Five or four? Er, McDon Jr, Erik, Iwanka – she's my favourite you know, beautiful girl – and, er, er, wait, it will come to me. Let me go through the alphabet. A . . no. B . . . ." he stalled.

"BARRON!!!!! BARRON!!!!! YOUSE FACKINGK DUMBKOPF!! shouted the Queen in an absolute fury that he could not remember her son's name.

"Er, er, sorry dear, yes dear. Three Barron's full dear! I mean, er Barron was her name. I mean, is his name," rattled the Trumper.

"Oh, but what about the other one - Tuppenny? We never hear much about her. Maybe you are putting her up for adoption by some Russian? Maybe, your BFF Putitin will adopt her?" she poked him again.

"No, no, er, of course not. Tuppenny – adoption – Putitin - I had never thought of that. I just prefer Iwanka that's all. Beautiful girl."

"Hmmm. I see. So, when you were a private citizen, it was OK for McDon Jr and Jarhead, also private citizens, to ask one of our 'enemies' – Russia – to, shall we say, 'adopt' a plan to dump our so-called 'state secrets', that they had stolen from me by hacking a sever, and let them be read by everyone. Is that correct?" she asked, pulling all the pieces together.

"Umm, er, no, er, not really. I didn't think of it like that. No, er! That's a very 'nasty' question!" he said, quoting the 'fallback' line that he used when he did not have an answer for a journalist. He was starting to realise that the line of questioning was getting deeper and deeper.

"OK. Do you remember when you started using that now-famous chant 'LOCK HER UP!'" Atty. Clingfilm appeared to change direction with the questioning.

"Yes, of course!" he responded, smiling and basking in his fond memory of it.

"And it was specifically directed to me over that email matter, correct?" she asked to make it clear.

"Yes, yes, yes. I enjoyed that every time the crowds at my rally's would start it up," he bragged.

"So, in November 2018 it was discovered that your favorite daughter, Iwanka, had been using private emails for official business while she worked in the Colored House as your special advisor. Is that correct?" she asked, creeping towards the Trumper's soft spot.

"Oh, but that that was completely different. They were just to help her personal scheduling and logistics to balance her home and work life," he replied, giving the 'stock' answer - obviously written by one of the West Wing spin doctors – and used hundreds of times when the matter came up in 2018. He could never string a sentence like that together himself.

"I see. But why does the person who is the very 'Special Advisor' to the President of the United States of America need to spend time during her very busy working day in the Colored House 'balancing' her home and work life? Shouldn't she be absolutely 110% committed to the President's every need?" delved Atty. Clingfilm, ever deeper.

"She is a very busy girl - a wife, mother, businesswoman and my 'Special Advisor' – so she needs to be able to access her own emails all the time," he tried to justify it but only made things worse.

"Aaah! Yes, I heard she was a busy businesswoman. She was really 'lucky' to get those manufacturing patents in China – just when you were negotiating a trade deal. And she had her US fashion line too. How did that go? So, if she is doing those multiple tasks all at the same time, maybe she should not be paid a full-time salary by the American people. Especially as she is your daughter too and also running your Trumper Organization for you on the side . . ." she kept digging and digging.

"I, er, well, she can handle it. She is a very clever girl. Not like Erik and McDon. She is really smart. And beautiful. She is my favourite you know!"

"Mister President, I put it to you that you and members of your family were 'allegedly' involved in 'adopting' a scheme to smear my presidential campaign by accepting emails stolen from me by Russian entities and having them released to the public. You then promoted the concept of my guilt via the 'Lock Her Up' chant at your campaign rallies. Further, your daughter is married to Jarhead Kushynumber and hence, as he was, 'prima facie', a central figure in that illegal plan, we must deduce that she was either a co-conspirator or at least aware of the scheme. But, once you were elected, while she was multi-tasking in the West Wing, and being fully paid as your 'Extra Special Presidential Advisor', your daughter, Iwanka, also used private emails to do government business as well as her own – possibly mixing up the two."

"Er, er, er, ummm, er. That's not true. It's all lies. It's another Dimocrat hoax. We are all innocent. Especially Iwanka. She has such beautiful blonde hair. She really is my favourite, you know," bumbled the Trumper.

"Yes, I know about innocence too. All the subsequent investigations by the State Department that I used to head up and by the FBI cleared me of any and all wrongdoing. I was always innocent – it was all just a scheme to help you during the election. I guess it worked in a way as you won the Electoral College. But I am always proud that there were 3 million more of my fellow Americans that voted for me, rather than you. I bet that a lot more of them NOW wished they had voted for me given how much you have screwed up the country," she kept on stirring and stirring.

"Ha! Innocence is for losers. You lost. I won. I'm President! You're not! Ha!!!" goaded the Trumper, not realising the errors he was making and the trap he was falling into.

"Absolutely, Mister President. I lost and I was innocent. Innocence is for losers – you just said it. And you won. So, if I was INNOCENT, you MUST have been GUILTY of all the FALSE smears that made me LOSE!......Wouldn't you agree Mister President?"

"Bu, bu, bu, bu, but. That, that, that, that's er, er, not fair . . . ." he whimpered, not having the mental acuity to be able to respond in any way, shape or form.

"Fair, fair. Oh, really, fair. That's an interesting concept coming from your lips. I'll tell you what is fair," she paused for effect and turned to face the court, the Flake Press Corp, the spectators in the gallery and everyone in the Rosy Garten. "I have already pledged my support for Joe Biden in the coming elections. At every rally and at every press briefing and every interview I will be telling the story of how you cheated me. And of how Iwanka was part of it and then she went and did the self-same thing that you accused me of – using personal emails for government work. So, every chance I get, I will be starting the chant, 'LOCK HER UP! LOCK HER UP!'. And we will see how it affects your re-election campaign and how you like it when everyone is chanting 'LOCK HER UP' at your favourite daughter!" Attorney Clingfilm sunk the 'knife' deep into the soft underbelly of the Trumper with her threat.

"NO, NO, NO, NO!! You can't do that! It's my Iwanka. She's my precious, my precious . . ." rasped the Trumper in a very Gollumesque voice while rubbing his hands together and curling up in the Witness Box.

"Yes, I certainly can do it! You did it to me. I can do it to you. Oh, and by the way. Iwanka isn't a 'real' blonde. She colours and bleaches her hair, just like her Daddy does . . ."

"WHAT!?!"

"No further questions from me, your Honor," said Attorney Clingfilm and went back to the Counsel for Prosecution table and sat down.

O'Bama immediately said "Great line of questioning . . . and fantastic closing. . . You threatened to knee him where it hurts . . . and then destroyed him mentally . . . where it hurts . . . with all that Iwanka stuff!"

The kid in the Navy uniform never even looked up when she sat down. He was still fully consumed by what was happening on the screen of his phone as now he was playing the video game 'Fortnite'.

Then, from across the Rosy Garten, the Queen bellowed out, "LET'Z HEARS ZA SENTENZE!"

"Excuse me Ma'am. It's supposed to be the verdict first – then the sentence," interjected the Judge.

"Sentence? I'm gonna barbecue his ass in hot mo-lasses," said a sleepy voice from the Witness Box. It was the Dormouse, who somehow had overheard the Sheriff saying those words to the Trumper over and over again as he brought him into the Rosy Garten. The Dormouse had no idea really what it meant, but it sounded good and that was enough.

"Collars zat Doortmouzes," the Queen shrieked out. "Beheadt zat Doortmouzes! Turns zat Doortmouzes outs off courtz! Zuppress hims! Pintch himz! Off viz hiss vhiskerz!"

For some minutes the whole court was in confusion, getting the Dormouse turned out, and, by the time they had settled down again, the Trumper had been moved back to the Counsel for the Defense table by the Navy Seals.

"Call the next witness," ordered the Judge.

BoJo watched the White Rabbi as he fumbled over the list, feeling very curious to see what the next witness would be like. "They have a whole lot of jolly good evidence already," he said to himself. Imagine his surprise, when the White Rabbi – not daring to even touch his vuvuzela - read out, at the top of his shrill little voice, "MR. BOJO FOREVER!"

"HERE!" shouted BoJo, quite forgetting in the flurry of the moment how large he had grown in the last few minutes. He jumped up in such a hurry that he knocked over the Jury Box with his knee, upsetting all the jurors on to the lawn. And there they lay, sprawling about, reminding him very much of a bowl full of goldfish he had accidentally upset when he was about seven years old.

"Oh, I do beg your pardon!" he exclaimed in a tone of great dismay and began helping to pick them up again as quickly as he could. The accident of the goldfish kept running in his head, and he had a vague sort of idea that they must be collected at once and put back into the Jury Box, or they would die.

"The trial cannot proceed," said the Judge in a very grave voice, "until all the jurors are back in their proper places - ALL," he repeated with great emphasis, looking hard at BoJo as he said so.

BoJo looked at the Jury Box, and saw that, in his haste, he had put in Kurt 'The Hair' Volkswagen head downwards, and the poor guy was kicking his legs about in the air in a melancholy way, being quite unable to get the proper way up again.

BoJo soon got him out again, and put it right, "Not that it signifies much," he said to himself. "I should think Volkswagen would be almost as much use in the trial one way up as the other. Especially as it's going to take him absolutely ages to fix his hair again."

As soon as the jury had recovered a little from the shock of being upset, and their iPads and Tablets had been found and handed back to them, they set to work very diligently to make copious notes and write a history of the accident. As had been seen in the Congress depositions and hearings, they were all copious note-takers. All except Kurt 'The Hair' Volkswagen, who seemed too much overcome to do anything but sit with his mouth open, gazing into a vanity mirror, looking at his messed-up coiffure and quietly sobbing.

"Atty Joolianose, you may cross-examine the witness," said the Judge.

"Er, ahh, thank you, your Honor," said Roody-Doody and turned to look up at BoJo who, by now had grown extremely, extremely tall.

"What do you know about this business?" Roody said to BoJo.

"Nothing," said BoJo.

"Nothing whatever?" persisted Roody.

"Nothing whatever," said BoJo.

'That's very important," Roody said, turning to the jury. They were just beginning to write this down on their iPads and Tablets, when the White Rabbi interrupted: "Unimportant, is what Attorney Joolianose means, of course," he said in a mock respectful tone, but frowning and making faces at him as he spoke.

"Er, yes, er, unimportant, of course, I meant," Roody hastily said, and went on saying to himself in an undertone, "important – unimportant – unimportant – important . . ." as if he were trying to see which word sounded best.

Some of the jury wrote down 'important,' and some 'unimportant.' BoJo could see this, as he was tall enough and near enough to look over their screens; "But it really doesn't matter much at all," he thought to himself.

At that moment, Roody, who had been busily writing in his notebook, slammed it on the desk with a bang.

"Silence!" he cackled out and read out from the book, "Rule Forty-two. All persons more than a mile high, who are not giving helpful testimony for the defense, shall leave the court."

Everybody looked up at BoJo.

"I'm not a mile high," said BoJo.

"Yes, you are!" said Roody.

"Actually, nearly two miles high," added the Carpenter, who not only was a stickler for facts, being the Clerk of the Court, but was also very good at measuring things because of his day job.

"Well, I shan't go, at any rate," said BoJo: "besides, that's not a regular rule. You invented it just now. I saw you writing it in your book."

"It's the oldest rule in the book," said Roody.

"Then it ought to be Number One," said BoJo unequivocally.

Roody-Doody turned pale and shut his notebook hastily. BoJo had outmaneuvered him.

"No more questions of this witness, your Honor," said Roody gloomily.

"Counsel for the Prosecution, do you have any questions for this witness?" asked the Judge.

"No, your Honor. This witness is not material to the case against the Defendant. Though he could have many similar charges to answer as and when he may be brought to trial himself . . ." responded Attorney O'Bama, chillingly.

BoJo gulped, looked around sheepishly and tried to make himself very inconspicuous, though that was extremely difficult considering his now towering size.

"SENTENCE THE DEFENDANT NOW!" shouted the Queen.

"I must remindeth the court that it is VERDICT first and then SENTENCE," said the Judge as patiently as only a 269-year-old man can.

"There's more evidence to come yet, please your Majestic Very High Royalness," said the White Rabbi, jumping up in a great hurry. "This writing pad has just been handed to the Court and it may be evidence."

"What's on it?" said the Queen sharply. She just wanted to get on with the fun of sentencing the Trumper.

"I haven't opened it yet," said the White Rabbi. "But it seems to be a note, written by the prisoner, er sorry, Defendant to - to somebody."

"It must have been that," said Roody, "unless it was written to nobody, which isn't usual, you know." That may have sounded crazy to most people but was entirely logical to Roody's arcane way of thinking.

"Who is it directed to?" asked Attorney O'Bama.

"It isn't directed at all," said the White Rabbi. "In fact, there's nothing written on the outside. It just says, 'Aboard Air Force One' in small letters on the top of the cover sheet."

He opened the note pad as he spoke, and said "It isn't a letter, after all: it's a just a few lines of strange words that don't seem to make any sense. Some in a foreign language, I think."

"Are they in the Defendant's handwriting?" asked Attorney Clingfilm.

"No, they're not," said the White Rabbi, "and that's the queerest thing about it. It's all in upper-case letters, like someone was 'shouting' when Twatting."

The jury all looked puzzled – "Who does that a lot?" - was going through their minds.

"Whoever wrote it must have imitated somebody else's handwriting," said Roody. "Maybe it was the Acting Chief of Staff, Mick Malarkey, who wrote it to fool everyone." Roody was obviously trying to throw the scent off his client.

"YES!" said the Queen.

"Please your Majesty," said Malarkey, "I didn't write it, and they can't prove I did. There's no name signed at the end."

"If you didn't sign it," said Roody, "that only makes the matter worse. You MUST have meant some mischief, or else you'd have signed your name like an honest man."

There was a general clapping of hands at this: it was the first really clever thing Roody had said that day.

"That PROVES his guilt," said the Queen.

"It proves nothing of the sort!" said BoJo. "Why, you don't even know what the words are about!"

"Herald, please read them," said the Judge.

The White Rabbi was going to put on his spectacles but then realised that the letters had been written very large, with a 'Sharpie' so that they were easy to read for someone with poor eyesight, but who was too vain to wear spectacles in public. So, who could that be?

"Where shall I begin, please your Honor?" he asked.

"Begin at the beginning," the Judge said gravely, "and go on till you come to the end: then stop."

"Er, OK, your Honor," said the White Rabbi and began to read.

I WANT NOTHING
I WANT NOTHING
I WANT NO QUID PRO QUO
TELL ZABAGLIONE
TO DO THE RIGHT THING
THIS IS THE FINAL WORD FROM
THE PRES OF THE U.S.

"That is very strange," said the Judge. "Why would someone write down those words in that way? Please share a photo of the note with the Jury as Exhibit H."

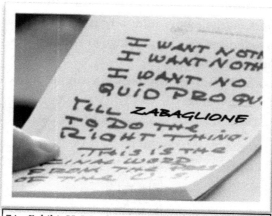

74.   Exhibit H: Word Soup = A Recipe For Disaster

"That's the most important piece of evidence we've heard yet," said the Queen, rubbing her hands. "So now let the Jury . . ."

"If any one of them can explain it, I'll give them a £1.00," said BoJo, who had grown so large in the last few minutes that he wasn't a bit afraid of interrupting her. "I don't believe there's an atom of meaning in it."

The Jury all wrote down on their iPads and Tablets, 'She doesn't believe there's an atom of meaning in it,' but none of them attempted to explain the meaning of the words on the notepad.

Everyone was really confused by what was written on the notepad, not only by the words themselves but also by thoughts of who would write them and why. So, everyone was talking to each other, the Jurors were looking at the photo and there was a general hubbub of noise all around the Rosy Garten.

At the Counsel for the Prosecution table, Atty. O'Bama and Atty. Clingfilm were also deep in conversation, trying to figure it out. No one was taking any notice of the kid in the Navy uniform. He had his earphones in, staring at the screen of his cell phone as usual, still playing Fortnite.

All of a sudden, the battle scene in Fortnite faded, his screen went blank and then the face of former Vice President, Joe Bidet appeared.

"WTF!" the kid thought and tried pressing all the keys to shut it off.

"Ethan," said Joe; "your mission, should you choose to accept it, is to bring this lying, racist, misogynistic, narcissistic m*ther f*cker down. And I mean, down! As usual, should you fail and be disbarred, terminated, court martialed or suffer any consequences as a result, the Secretary and I will disavow all knowledge of your actions. This message will self-destruct in five seconds."

There was a soft 'phut' as wisps of white smoke puffed out of his cell phone and the screen melted.

MISSION IMPOSSIBLE – ETHAN T. CRUZ
https://www.youtube.com/watch?v=UGFylgTrdr0

The kid looked around to see if anyone had noticed, but everyone was too busy talking about the words on the notepad to have seen anything. So, he quickly stood up and addressed the Judge.

"Your Honor, I have a few questions for the Defendant, if I may?"

"What're you doing?" hissed O'Bama.

"Sit down, NOW!" ordered Hillarious.

"I got this!" he said and then turned back to the Judge. "May I, your Honor?"

"Hmmmmmm! Weeeeell! Aaaaaaah! I thinketh there is no reason not to allow it. OK. Proceedeth," said the Judge, finally.

"Thank you, your Honor!" he said and faced the Trumper. "The Defendant shall return to the Witness Box!"

"I OBJECT!" chimed Roody-Doody.

75. Lieutenant Ethan T. Cruz

BANG! BANG! BANG! "OBJECTION OVERRULED," responded the Judge instantly.

"I thought I was dismissed!" said the Trumper as he was dragged back to the Witness Box by the Navy Seals. He obviously had no desire to be cross-examined by a young kid, way less than half his age.

"I still have a few questions yet," replied the kid. "Sit down!"

"Mister President!" said the Trumper.

"What's that?" said the kid.

"I'd appreciate it if you would address me as 'Mr. President' or 'Sir'. I believe I've earned it." said the Trumper in a very supercilious tone.

"The Prosecution Counsel shall address the Defendant as 'Mr. President' or 'Sir'," ordered the Judge.

"I don't know what kind of an organization you're running here," the Trumper snidely remarked to the Judge.

"The Defendant shall addresseth this Bench as 'Judge', 'Your Honor' or 'Mister President'. I'm quite certain that I hath earned it! Taketh your seat, Mr. President." responded the Judge very firmly.

"Anyway," said the Trumper turning to the kid; "who the hell are you to be wanting to question me some more? Standing there in your fancy, blue, Navy uniform with all those shiny brass buttons."

"My name is Lieutenant Ethan T. Cruz of the U.S. Navy's Judge Advocate General's Corps (JAG). I am here because, not only are you the President, but you are also the Cummerbund-in-Chief of the U.S. Military, including your, er, new branch the 'Space Force'." There was a ripple of laughter around the Rosy Garten. "Therefore, JAG has some jurisdiction over your activities, especially where they may be criminal."

"Herrummpfff! Ethan T. Cruz? What does the 'T' stand for?"

"It's Tomasito. But most people just call me Tom. Tom Cruz . . ."

"That sounds a bit Spanish to me. Are you Mexican?"

"Yes, I am, on my father's side and proud of it. Seeing you wearing that 'MEXIT Forever!' sweat-shirt reminded me of all the Mexicans who have got out of Mexico and made it here, despite <u>your</u> border patrols, fences, walls and many of their kids being locked in cages. So, thank you for wearing that 'Freedomista' shirt, sir . . ." Cruz said with a cheeky grin.

"It's NOT my shirt!! Someone gave it to me when I came to the court this morning because they took all my clothes away from me last night," ranted the Trumper. "Judge, I object to being questioned by this kid. He is Mexican and will be biased against me!"

"You mean he will be biased against thee in some racist way, in the same way thou are biased against him – even though thy sayest that thou are the least racist person thou knowest?" asked the Judge, pointedly.

"Well, er, yes for him, but no for me," he tried to weasel out of it.

"OK. Thou can have Atty. O'Bama instead," offered the Judge.

"No, no, no. NOT O'Bama!! I will stick with the kid!" the Trumper quickly replied, assuming that the kid wouldn't be very good at it.

"It's Lieutenant Cruz, if you don't mind. I believe I have earned it."

"Hhherrruummphhh! So, what do you wanna discuss now, Lieutenant? My favorite color?" the Trumper asked snarkily.

"No, Mister President. It's undoubtedly 'red'. It's the color of the Ripofflican Party, the color of the ties you wear nearly every day and the color of your face when you get angry – which is very often. Sir . . ."

"So, it's red. What of it?" asked the Trumper.

"Oh. Nothing really. It was just something that was 'ex parte', sir."

"I don't get it. What do you mean?"

"Sorry, I somehow thought you were an expert at Latin. I assumed you had studied it at Wharton or one of your expensive prep schools."

"Well, I do pick up legal terms easily as I have sued a lot of people over the years. I really have it up here," he said, pointing to his brain. "I am a very stable genius, you know. Many people ask me 'How come you know so much about the law?' And I tell them I just 'get' it. Maybe I should have been a lawyer instead of a President!"

"OK, sir. So maybe you can help me here as I'm just starting out as a lawyer, and I've been given some notes about this case, part in Latin."

"Sure, I can!" said the Trumper, his ego getting the better of him.

"Well, sir, let me read them for you. 'As you are an *amicus curiae* and that you have good *ad hoc* relationships with many *bone fide* world *dictatoribus*, you may be able to consult with them to find the *corpus delicti* as to whether *de facto* the *actus reas* which you undertook *ex parte,* namely yourself, and which you did *in camera* at the Oral Office, was *quantum meruit* for President Zabaglione to try to *perspicio* the son of your *adversarius rei publicae* who will suffer *in loco parentis* and if you were either a *pellicientes ingenium* or in a *mens rea* that would be an *expurgatio* as to your *efflagitatio postmortem* for a *quid pro quo'.*" Cruz slickly rhymed off, to the absolute bewilderment of everyone.

"WHAT!?!" exclaimed the Trumper.

"Oh! Sorry Mister President, I thought you said that you were an expert at Latin. You said you had lots of legal experience, given that you spent so much time suing people – and in those seven bankruptcy hearings too and all those class action suits from your tenants . . ." teased Cruz. "It's just a statement about your involvement in this case and how it may be resolved to everyone's satisfaction."

"Hhheerrrummph! Yes of course. It means, er, er. 'As I am an *amicable creature* [175] and that I have good *pawn shop* [176] relationships with many *dog and bone* [177] world *bus drivers* [178], I am able to consult with them to find the *delicious corpse* [179] and to see whether *the factory* [180] where the all the *actors* [181] were, and I undertook *one part* [182], namely myself, and which I did on the *TV camera* [183] at the Oral Office, it was a *huge quantity* [184] for President Zabaglione to try to *perspire* [185] on the son of my *public advertizer* [186], who will suffer like *his crazy father* [187] and if I was either a *genuine pelican* [188] or a *real man* [189] that would be an *esplanadetion* [190] as to my *flogging a dead horse* [191] for *a few quid to a professional* [192]." the Trumper bumbled his way through the paragraph.

"Ahh, er, thank you Mr. President. That's aah, very good. It's almost there. Not quite but almost," said Cruz with a beaming, irresistible smile.

---

[175] AMICABLE CREATURE: Amicus curiae - friend of the court
[176] PAWN SHOP: Ad hoc – another group
[177] DOG AND BONE: Bona fide - in good faith
[178] BUS DRIVERS: Dictatoribus - dictators
[179] DELICIOUS CORPSE: Corpus delicti - body or proof of the crime
[180] THE FACTORY: De facto - in fact
[181] ACTORS: Actus reas - the act of doing something
[182] ONE PART: Ex parte - on behalf of one party
[183] TV CAMERA: In camera - in chambers / in private
[184] HUGE QUANTITY: Quantum meruit - as much as he deserved
[185] PERSPIRE: Perspicio - investigate
[186] PUBLIC ADVERTISER: Adversarius rei publicae - political adversary
[187] CRAZY FATHER: In loco parentis – in the place of his parent
[188] GENUINE PELICAN: Pellicientes ingenium – unstable genius
[189] REAL MAN: Mens rea - the mental state
[190] ESPLANADETION: Expurgatio - justification, excuse
[191] FLOGGING A DEAD HORSE: Efflagitatio postmortem – demand to death
[192] A FEW QUID TO A PROFESSIONAL: Quid pro quo - Something for something

"For the benefit of the court, I would like to submit as Exhibit I, the translation of the statement on this case and its possible resolution," Cruz said and handed the Jury and the Judge a print-out of the full English translation.

> As you are a *friend of the court* and that you have good *special group* relationships with many *genuine* world *dictators*, you may be able to consult with them to find the *proof of the crime* as to whether *in fact* the *acts* which you undertook *on behalf of one party,* namely yourself, and which you did *in private* at the Oral Office, it was *as much as he deserved* for President Zabaglione to try to *investigate* the son of your *political adversary* who will suffer *in the place of his parent* and, if you were either an *unstable genius* or in a *mental state* that would be a *justification* as to your *deathly demand* for *something in return for something (quid pro quo)*

As the Jurors passed around the written translation, they either giggled, smiled, chuckled, covered their mouth with their hand or simply laughed out loud. They had all been part of the Congress's Impeachment Inquiry as witnesses, so they knew the full story. This was just a short, sharp, succinct summary – with a punch line at the end. That was what made them all react, as it was funny to them – especially after what they had all been through before, during or after the inquiry.

The Judge, of course, fully understood the Latin when Cruz had read it out at first. But he also smiled a knowing smirk when he read the translation.

The Trumper was watching the responses of the Jury and the Judge and he was starting to boil. He was beginning to realise that his version of the translation was way off track, and he had undoubtedly made a fool of himself – which he really hated. Despite his bluster and superficial bravado, he was really sensitive about being laughed at by anyone, for any reason. Suddenly, his 'valve' burst, and he barked across the court.

"WHAT'S GOING ON? WHAT DOES IT SAY ON THAT PAPER? I WANT TO SEE IT!"

Cruz handed him a copy, knowing that reading was not the Trumper's favourite pastime and that it would take him a while to get to the 'punch line' at the bottom of the page. Cruz had done it on purpose as he wanted to start getting under the Trumper's skin and make him angry.

The Trumper was reading the page, his lips moving silently as he read the words, slowly one by one. It was almost painful to watch and reminded Cruz of watching and listening to the Trumper read from Teleprompter speeches in a slow stumbling fashion like a dyslexic, autistic, five-year old with onset dementia.

Eventually, eventually, the Trumper reached the end of the page and it slowly dawned on him what it meant.

"WHAT IS THIS?" he shouted angrily. "You are saying I am an UNSTABLE genius and I am in a MENTAL STATE? What do you mean and why are you saying that?"

"Well, Mister President, in my legal opinion the only way you can avoid being proven guilty and suffering the consequences of that verdict – and the sentence that accompanies it – would be to plead diminished responsibility due to insanity," opined Cruz.

"YOU WANT ME – ME - McDONALD J. TRUMPER – TO SAY THAT I AM INSANE, CRAZY, COOKOO!?!"

"Yes, sir, I do."

"NO WAY JOSE!"

"My name is NOT Jose, sir. Its Lieutenant Cruz, sir . . ."

"Well, I am NOT doing that for you or for anyone!"

"OK, sir. That is your prerogative. Your choice. But if you choose to ignore the opportunity to make that plea, the trial will continue, cross-examination will re-commence, a verdict will be reached by the Jury and you will be sentenced accordingly. Do you understand, sir?" asked Cruz.

"Whatever!"

"Good," said Cruz.

He then took three documents from his briefcase at the Counsel for the Prosecution's table and approached the Judge.

"In that case, I would like to submit as Exhibit J, a copy of the Voting Record for the Senate at the President's Impeachment Trial."

Cruz gave a copy of the Voting Record to the Judge

"I would also like to submit as Exhibit K, a copy of the so-called 'Transcript' of the telephone conversation between President Trumper and President Zabaglione on 25 July 2019."

Cruz handed the Judge the Transcript, who looked quizzically at it.

"And finally, I would also like to submit as Exhibit L, the 'Miller-Lite Report' which concluded that while there was no proof of collision with Russia, it also did not exonerate the President and his campaign in relation to benefitting from activities undertaken by the Russians to help him get elected."

Cruz gave a copy of the Miller-Lite Report to the Judge.

"I don't understand," said the Judge. "You're admitting evidence for (1) the vote at the Impeachment Trial which acquitted the Defendant. (2) the Transcript of a telephone call that the President says is 'perfect' and (3) a crime that apparently was not committed, according to Miller-Lite."

"But we believe crimes were committed in all three instances, sir," Cruz advised the Judge with a confident expression.

"In the case of Exhibit J, the Senate Voting Record, we will show that the Defendant, his Administration staff and Moscow Mitch McConman, colluded together to get the Ripofflican Senators to all vote unanimously to acquit the Defendant, whatever the evidence to the contrary may show during the trial. Inside the Ripofflican Party this was referred to as a 'Code Red'.

Cruz then turned and said to the Jury, "The Prosecution will be calling Bolt-On the Walrus and Mick Malarkey as witnesses because both of them were in the room during the President's call to Ukraine."

"OBJECTION, your Honor," shouted Roody-Doody. "Bolt-On the Walrus was not on the list and Mr. Malarkey has already testified."

Atty. Clingfilm immediately stood up and said, "Rebuttal witnesses, your Honor, called specifically to refute testimony offered under direct examination." She had started to realise where Cruz was heading and was quick to support it.

"I will allow the witnesses," said the Judge.

"This is ridiculous!" said the Trumper, shaking his head.

"Mister President, a moment ago . . . ," Cruz started to say but was interrupted by the Trumper.

"Check the Transcript for Christ's sake!" he said angrily.

"We will get to the Transcript in just a minute, sir," replied Cruz, calmly and the Trumper stared at him with an exasperated expression. He really was not used to being spoken to or questioned in that manner. People were generally a combination of scared and deferential to him. Partly, because they knew how pettily vindictive he could be to anyone who disagreed with him and, partly, because there was an automatic attitude of respect to any person who held the position of President of the Trumperland, however misplaced that respect may have been in the case of the Trumper.

"A few weeks ago, you said on many occasions on TV that President Zabaglione was very clear about what you said in the call," asked Cruz.

"That's right," replied the Trumper.

"And Zabaglione was clear on what you wanted?" emphasized Cruz.

"Crystal!" said the Trumper.

"Any chance that Zabaglione would ignore the order, sorry, request?" said Cruz looking unconvinced.

"Ignored the order, er, I mean, request? asked the Trumper in disbelief.

"Any chance he 'forgot' about it?" asked Cruz, digging deeper.

"No," said the Trumper flatly.

"Any chance, after the call, that Mick Malarkey left the Oral Office and said, 'The old man is wrong!'?" Cruz asked, raising his eyebrows questioningly.

"No," said the Trumper, shaking his head from side to side.

"When you told Roody-Doody Joolianose to get the 'Three Amigos' to put pressure on Zabaglione to do the investigation into the Bidets, any chance they ignored him?" probed Cruz even further.

The Trumper looked at Cruz condescendingly for a long time before speaking.

"Have you ever served in government, son?"

"No, sir," Cruz answered.

"Have you ever served in Congress or the Senate?"

"No, sir."

"Have you ever had to make political decisions that could affect your career or the careers of others?" asked the Trumper putting on his 'Presidential' voice.

"No, sir."

"I expect people to follow my orders, as the President, or they get fired. It's that simple," explained the Trumper. "Are we clear!!"

"Yes, sir," Cruz answered quietly with a trace of a smile in his face.

"ARE WE CLEAR!!" barked the Trumper.

"Crystal," replied Cruz with a slight nod of the head and continued to hold that expression and that trace of a smile.

"Mister President, I have just one more question before I call Mick Malarkey and Bolt-On the Walrus to testify . . . If you gave an order that no military funding was to be released. . . And your orders are always followed. . . Then why did everyone else on the call think it was wrong?"

He paused and then continued, "Why would it be necessary, (1) to do a huge cover up; (2) say publicly that there was no pressure on Ukraine to do anything for your political benefit; (3) bury the Transcript in the deepest, safest, most secure server normally reserved for top secret covert operations and then; (4) finally, make sure that the Senate had a unanimous vote to acquit you at the Impeachment Trial?" asked Cruz, softly, but with a significant expression of disbelief on his face.

The Trumper was silent for several seconds. Furrowed his brow. Took one of his, now famous, deep snorting breaths and then looked directly back at Cruz.

"Zabaglione was a sub-standard, weak, President. I didn't want to transfer the military aid till he rooted out corruption in his country," the Trumper said very slowly and deliberately, as though he was thinking of each word just before he spoke it.

"That's not what you said! You said you weren't transferring the money because you wanted Zabaglione to 'do you a favor, though'! You said you wanted him to do an investigation into the Bidet's! . . .And, in the written statement that you read you said it was because the Bidet's were your political adversaries! You said you wanted the son to suffer to upset his father. . . ." and Cruz turned away from the Trumper.

"I recall what I said!" the Trumper responded angrily.

"I can have the Court recorder read back to you . . ." said Cruz pointing at the Carpenter.

"I know what I SAID!!" retorted the Trumper, getting visibly angrier by the minute. "I don't have to have it read back to me like I've got dementia!!!"

"Why the TWO ORDERS . . . Mr. President?" Cruz pointedly asked.

The Trumper stared at Cruz for several seconds, obviously considering what to say next, his brow furrowed, you could almost see the cogs turning slowly in his brain, his mouth set in a thin pouty line.

"Sometimes men take matters into their own hands . . ." he said eventually.

Cruz moved across the court to be closer to the Witness Box.

"You made it clear earlier that your men never take matters into their own hands! Your staff follow orders, or someone gets fired!" Cruz said softly, but vehemently, right in the face of the Trumper.

"So, Malarkey shouldn't have said what he said at that press conference, should he, Mister President?"

"You snotty little bastard!" slowly growled the Trumper, staring angrily at Cruz.

"YOUR HONOR, I WOULD LIKE TO ASK FOR A RECESS!" cut in Roody-Doody, fearing the likelihood that his client might say something he would later regret and that Roody would not be able to defend.

"I would like an answer to the question, Judge!" Cruz responded quickly.

"The Court will wait for an answer," the Judge replied, watching the face of the Trumper contort and grimace as he did so.

"If you gave an order to Roody-Doody Joolianose, to make sure that the 'Three Amigos' put the squeeze on Zabaglione to dig up dirt on the Bidet's," Cruz almost whispered, staring straight into the eyes of the Trumper. "Why did it have to be covered up???"

The Trumper just stared back at Cruz.

"Mister President?"

"Moscow Mitch McConman ordered the 'Code Red' for all the Senators to vote to acquit you because that's what you told Moscow Mitch to do!!!" snarled Cruz, right up close to the face of the Trumper.

"And, because it went bad in the cover up and the Congress hearings when a few good men - and a few good women too - gave real evidence of what had happened despite your gag orders, you cut loose Bolt-On the Walrus, Mick Malarkey, Perrier, Sunderland, Volkswagen, Vindalooman and even his brother!" barked Cruz.

At this point, Roody-Doody was stood up, protesting. "OBJECTION, YOUR HONOR!" And the Judge was saying, "That will be all Counsel!" But Cruz was unstoppable!

"You doctored the Transcript! You buried the originals! You lied about your reasons for holding back the military aid! You lied about phone calls to Sunderland! You lied about firing Ambassador Sonovabitch from the Kyiv Embassy!"

"Consider yourself in Contempt of Court!" said the Judge, but Cruz was not listening.

"I AM ASKING YOU, MISTER PRESIDENT, DID YOU ORDER THE CODE RED?" shouted Cruz across the court.

"You don't have to answer that question," the Judge advised the Trumper.

"I'll answer the question," snarled the Trumper to the Judge.

"YOU WANT ANSWERS?" the Trumper shot at Cruz.

"I think I'm entitled to them! "

"YOU WANT ANSWERS!!?? Repeated the Trumper angrily.

"I WANT THE TRUTH!!

"I CAN'T HANDLE THE TRUTH!! " the Trumper blurted out unexpectedly.

"Son, we live in a word that needs walls and those walls have to be guarded by men with guns, who do it even though they are 'losers' and 'suckers'. But who is gonna build that wall? And who's gonna pay for it? You! You, Lieutenant Cruz. You and your Mexican family!"

"I have a greater responsibility than I could ever possibly have fathomed and I'm really not up for it. You weep for President Zabaglione and you curse me and the 'Three Amigos'! You have that luxury. You have the luxury of being a smart-ass and thinking you know things that you think I will never ever know. Sonovabitch's firing, which you think was tragic, probably saved lives. Russian lives that didn't get blown away with our American Stingers . . . ."

"And my existence, while grotesque and incomprehensible to you, saves Russian lives!"

"I can't deal with the TRUTH, because deep down - in places I can't talk about at parties – I want to be on that wall. . . I NEED to be on that wall."

"I use words like HONOR, CODE and LOYALTY. I use those words as the backbone of a lifetime spent scamming people. I never HONOR my word or my debts, I always talk in CODE when I want one of my fixers to do something illegal for me, and I expect 110% LOYALTY from everyone that works for me – or they get fired."

"You use them as a punch line to hit me with!"

"I have neither the time nor the moral fiber to learn how to tell the TRUTH to a man who rises and sleeps under the very blanket of FREEDOM of SPEECH that I cannot abide. And then be questioned on the reasons as to why I can't abide it!"

"I would rather that you just said 'F*CK YOU' and went on your way. Otherwise, I suggest you pick up your cell phone and go back to playing 'Fortnite'. Either way, I DON'T GIVE A DAMN WHAT YOU THINK YOU ARE ENTITLED TO!!!"

Cruz had been standing, silent, in the middle of the court while the Trumper ranted and raved at him. But then he moved closer to him in front of the Witness Box.

"Did you order the Code Red??" Cruz asked, tight lipped.

"I did the job I needed to do!"

"DID YOU ORDER THE CODE RED!!" shouted Cruz.

"YOU'RE GOD-DAMNED RIGHT I DID!!"

There was a complete hush in the Court and the entire Rosy Garten. You could have heard the buzzing of the bees, but they had stopped buzzing too, such was the impact of the Trumper's words.

Lieutenant Cruz slowly walked back to the center of the court, turned, to face Judge James Madison, smiled his famous smile and said,

"No more questions, your Honor."

Cruz sat down at the Counsel for the Prosecution table, muttered, "Mission accomplished", pulled a new cell phone from his bag, put in his earphones and was instantly engrossed in playing 'Fortnite' once again.

The moment that Cruz sat down the court erupted in a deafening babble of noise as everyone spoke at once. It was like a turkey market with everybody going "Gobble, Gobble, Gobble, Gobble!"

O'Bama and Hillarious just looked at each other in amazement and then looked at Cruz, but he was already back in his virtual world of 'Fortnite'.

The White Rabbi was shouting, "Silence in Court! Silence in Court!" but no one was taking any notice whatsoever.

The Carpenter was banging on his desk with his hammer but was being ignored too.

BANG! BANG! BANG! went the Judge to no avail.

"OOORRRDDDEEEERRRR!! OOOORRRDDDDEEEERRRR!!" shouted Berrrccoww and the hubbub finally subsided to a low murmur.

"Silence in Court!" shouted the White Rabbi in his squeaky little voice and looked around, glaring at everyone as though to imply that he would punish anyone who spoke – even though he wouldn't and couldn't do anything of the sort.

O'Bama and Hillarious quickly assessed the situation and had come up with a game plan.

"Your Honor," said Hillarious, for once smiling as she spoke. "The Counsel for the Prosecution moves that the confession of the President to the charge of initiating the 'Code Red' in order to have a unanimous acquittal at his Impeachment Trial provides complicity in the other offences that my co-counsel, Lieutenant Cruz put forward. Namely, that the true and original verbatim transcript was buried so that others would not be aware of the Defendant's actions in the Zabaglione 'Quid Pro Quo' and his comments about the importance of saving Russian lives are a real indicator of his need to 'pay back' for them helping him win the 2016 election. I also believe that my cross-examination of the Defendant on the indictments in Charges No. 5 and No. 6, Charges No. 9 and No. 10 and Charge No. 26 were proven beyond a reasonable doubt. Further, that, in combination, the charges brought to the court's attention in detail show the overall attitude, moral laxity, propensity for lies and deception, complete disregard for the law and failure to even follow the basic principles set forth in the Constitution – your Constitution, your Honor – such that there is an implied guilt across all the 100 charges!"

"Thank you for your summation, Attorney Clingfilm. Members of the Jury shall taketh note of what has been presenteth by the Counsel for the Prosecution and likewise by the Counsel for the Defense," said the Judge. "Attorney Joolianose, would you like to maketh your closing remarks?"

"Yes, your Honor. Thank you," said Roody-Doody and scrambled through the big pile of papers on the table looking for his summation notes but couldn't find them. Eventually, the Trumper gave him the piece of paper he was looking for – which was right in front of him.

"Idiot!" muttered the Trumper, showing his disdain for his once-favourite lawyer. Loyalty only went one way with the Trumper.

Roody-Doody stood in front of the Jury and started to read, "Gentlemen of the Jury!" and one of the ladies on the Jury coughed.

"Er, er, Ladies and gentlemen of the Jury. You have heard all the evidence presented at this court today. But in the end, it is up to the conscience of your hearts to decide. And I firmly believe that, like me, you will conclude that President McDonald J. Trumper is in fact totally and utterly GUILTY!" and he started to sit down next to the Trumper at the Defense table.

"IDIOT!!" hissed the Trumper. He grabbed the paper Roody was holding and turned it over to the back of the sheet for the final part of the sentence.

"Aah, er . . .GUILTY of NOTHING MORE . . . than trying to do his DUTY under very difficult circumstances . . . !"

"NONSENZE! OFF VIZ HISS HEADT!!" shouted the Queen.

"Let the jury considereth their verdict, then cometh the sentencing," the Judge said, for the umpteenth time that day.

"NO, NO!" said the Queen. "Sentenze firzt - ferdickt aftervardz."

"Stuff and nonsense!" said BoJo loudly. "The idea of having the sentence first is one of the craziest things I've heard in this crazy place!"

"Holdt yourse tongkue!" said the Queen, turning purple with rage.

"I won't!" said BoJo, feeling very brave as he was now an incredibly tall person compared to everyone else and gaining height by the minute.

"OFF VIZ HISS HEADT!" the Queen shouted at the top of her voice. But nobody moved, mainly because they weren't sure who she meant. Was she still talking about the Trumper or about BoJo?

Some of the crowd, including the Terminator, looked up and shaded their eyes against the sun to try and judge how tall BoJo was getting.

The Terminator, being a practical, come-down-to-earth-from-the-future-kind-of-cyborg-guy, realised that whatever the Queen might have meant, there was no way he could reach high enough to chop off BoJo's head. And the Jury had yet to deliberate on the guilt – or unlikely otherwise – of the Trumper. So, the Terminator decide to wait. After all, he was a cyborg, so he wasn't growing any older.

BANG! BANG! BANG! went the Judge. "I hath been handed this note from the Queen which sayeth 'The Jury will useth the 'Survey Monkey' app on their iPads and Tablets to vote on whether the Defendant is guilty or not in accordance with the questions so listed'. The Bench hath no idea whatsoever what a 'Survey Monkey' is, nor an 'app' and hopes that the members of the Jury do so and likewise are in possession of 'iPads' and 'Tablets' – whatever they are, also. The Bench thanks the Queen for supporting the efforts of the Court by providing this piece of clever wizardry and providing the questions for the Jury."

The following questions came up on their screens.

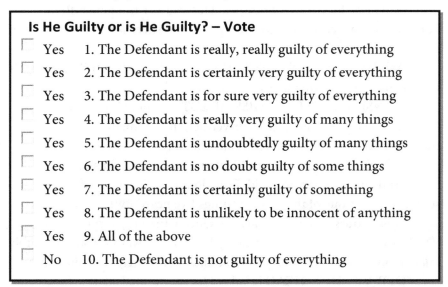

		Is He Guilty or is He Guilty? – Vote
☐	Yes	1. The Defendant is really, really guilty of everything
☐	Yes	2. The Defendant is certainly very guilty of everything
☐	Yes	3. The Defendant is for sure very guilty of everything
☐	Yes	4. The Defendant is really very guilty of many things
☐	Yes	5. The Defendant is undoubtedly guilty of many things
☐	Yes	6. The Defendant is no doubt guilty of some things
☐	Yes	7. The Defendant is certainly guilty of something
☐	Yes	8. The Defendant is unlikely to be innocent of anything
☐	Yes	9. All of the above
☐	No	10. The Defendant is not guilty of everything

"Well," said BoJo to himself, as there was no one as tall as he was to speak to, "how are you going to get out of that one, Mr. President?"

"I OBJECT!" shouted Roody-Doody, for want of something better to do.

"SHUTZ ZA FACKZ UPZ, Roody-Hoodys," responded the Queen in no uncertain terms. "Likez usuals, youse arez vay too latez."

"Aaaah," said the Judge. "The Jury will considereth their verdict in the case of McDonald J. Trumper versus The Crown. There will be no talking, no collusion, no cheating, no copying, no gerrymandering, no voter suppression, no SuperPACs, no ballot box stuffing, no social media campaigns, no hacking by the Russians. Just a plain and simple vote."

And with that final instruction from the Judge, the Jury set about voting, each of them trying to cover up their screens from the Jurors on each side of them – as if it really mattered given how the questions were stacked in favor of one result.

"The Jury shall submiteth their votes on the 'Survey Monkey' to the Clerk of the Court," ordered the Judge. "Proceed!"

"Clerk of the Court, do thou have the results of the vote?"

"I do sir!" said the Carpenter and took the print-out to the Bench. He figured, quite rightly, that the Judge would be more comfortable with a piece of paper rather than a new-fangled iPad or Android Tablet.

The Judge read the results. Nodded his head and gave the paper back to the Carpenter. "Please ask the Foreman of the Jury to read the verdict."

The Carpenter went over to the Jury Box and gave the print-out of the verdict to Lieutenant Colonel Alex Vindalooman. He had been unanimously voted in as Foreman of the Jury because he had been vindictively fired by the Trumper from his position as Director for European Affairs at the National Security Council. And the Trumper fired his twin brother too – even though he had nothing to do with the Impeachment Hearing or his brother's testimony.

76.   Do not worry, Dad. I will be fine for telling the truth . . .

So, everyone on the Jury thought that it would be fitting for Vindalooman to be the Foreman and read the verdict. And so it was . . .

He cleared his throat, coughed and said, "The results of the Jury vote are as follows:

10 YES VOTES: The Defendant is really, really guilty of everything

1 YES VOTE: All of the above

1 NO VOTE: The Defendant is not guilty of everything

The Defendant is therefore pronounced GUILTY AS CHARGED ON ALL ONE HUNDRED COUNTS!"

There was about twenty seconds of total silence in the Court and the Rosy Garten as everyone digested the decision that meant finally – finally – the Trumper was being held accountable for so many of his past transgressions. And then suddenly, the whole place erupted with sound.

"OFF VIZ HISS HEADT! " ordered the Queen with glee.

"YEEEEEEHAAAAAHHHH! " shouted Vindalooman.

"OOONNCHH! OOONNCH!" went Bolt-On the Walrus.

"Excellent . . . . result for the . . . rule of law!" said O'Bama.

"Lock him up!" said Hillarious.

"Gottcha yo' sumbitch!!" said the Sheriff.

"Jolly good show!" said Berrrccoww.

"WAKA! WAKA!" went all the Saffas.

"President found guilty!" went all the Flake Press to their live feeds.

"I OBJECT!" said Roody-Doody, but no one was listening.

"Victory Royale!" said Lieutenant Cruz, but no one was sure if he was referring to winning the game on 'Fortnite' or the case.

"OH . . . MY . . . GOD!" said Moscow Mitch McConman.

"Get over it!" said Mick Malarkey.

"Silence in Court!" said the White Rabbi, but no one heard him.

"Haaawaayyy the lads!" said Fiona Hillbilly.

"That was worth a $1 million!" said Gordon 'Egghead' Sunderland.

"Oh, dear. My hair really is a mess!" said Kurt Volkswagen, who had made the mistake of making the one and only 'No' vote, not realising it was a double negative and therefore a 'Yes' for guilty.

"OH SH*T!!!!!" said the Trumper as it slowly, ever so slowly, dawned on him that he wasn't going to get away with it this time.

77. That's Not Fair! I am Not Supposed to be Accountable for Things I Do

The Trumper was definitely NOT a happy teddy. "How could this be? Me guilty?" he thought to himself. "The one and only McDonald J. Trumper is actually going to be sentenced for doing something that I never, even in the tiniest part of my brain, thought might be in the slightest bit wrong. And would never admit to, even if it were."

"OOOORRRDDDEEERRIRR!! OOOORRRRDDDEEERRRRR!"

Finally, finally, the noise in the court subsided to a loud murmur.

BANG! BANG! BANG! "Silence in Court for the pronunciation of sentence," said the Carpenter.

While all the noise and comments had been flying back and forth, the Judge had been trying to figure out the best and most appropriate sentence for the Trumper. He was, without a shadow of a doubt, totally guilty. But he was also the husband of the Queen. What to do?

"The Jury hath pronounced the Defendant guilty on all counts," said the Judge. "Therefore, this Court sentenceth the Defendant to be punished at the pleasure of Her Very Royal Highness, the Queen of Queens!!" Which was a very clever side-step for the Judge and left the fate of the Trumper entirely in the hands of the Queen. So, he couldn't be blamed for being too harsh or too lenient with his sentence.

As soon as the words were out of his mouth a complete and absolute hush fell across the Court and the entire Rosy Garten. Everyone's mouth dropped open and they all turned to look at the Queen in anticipation of what she would say.

They didn't have to wait long. The Queen visibly preened herself, stood up on her dais, seemed, inexplicably, to grow another six inches taller (she slipped on her stiletto heels, hidden under her long gown), put her hands on her hips and glared at the Trumper with a look that could have melted the polar ice cap faster than anything the Trumper could have achieved, even with his total assault on climate change.

"OFF VIZ HISS BLADDY HEADT! " shouted the Queen with a huge smile on her face. "MIZTER TERNIMATOR, HE ISS ALLS YOURZ!!!"

The whole Rosy Garten erupted with cheering and clapping and people throwing their hats, and anything else that could get their hands on, into the air and 'Whoop, whoop whooping'. The only ones in the audience that were not happy were Roody-Doody Joolianose, Moscow Mitch McConman and his cohort of Ripofflican House of Cards. He looked just about as glum as a Mock Turtle can possibly look. And that is really glum. His hangers-on, the usual suspects - Cory Guardrail, Lyndsay Graham-Cracker, Chuck Assisgrass, Ken Johnnedy, Paul Randy, Jerry Moron, Marko Jackrubio, Jim Jordache, Devon Creamteas - each one of them had a face like a wet weekend.

The Trumper himself had slumped when he heard the Queen give the sentence. The only thing keeping him from falling on the floor was the fact that his Navy Seals were holding him up by his cuffed wrists.

The Terminator walked slowly over to the Defense Counsel table and said, "Vell, Mister President! I toldt you I vuld be back. And here I am!"

"I OBJEC . . ."

BANG! BANG! BANG! "SHUT UP ATTY. JOOLIANOSE. The Queen hath passed sentence and thou hath no authority to object. Unless of course thy want to taketh it up with the Queen directly?" said the Judge with a condescending smile.

"Er, er, er. No, your Honor. Thank you all the same," he replied.

The Navy Seals lifted the Trumper to his feet and that seemed to spark him into a little bit of life. It wasn't much life, just about what you might expect if Frankenstein had tried to start up his monster using a couple of U2 Duracell batteries instead of harnessing the power of lightening.

"BUT, but, but Melonia! This is me, the McDonald!"

"HA! Finaliez andt at lastz, youse gott my bladdy namez correck!! Itz MELONIA!!! Notz Melanomia, Millimartini, Meelymenia, Moliltoff, Melovania, Melamine, Mealymania, Melbania, Melamenia, Moldovia, Millipedia, Milomummia, Minniemousia, Melaminia, Millynoma, Millymona, Millemiglia, Mellamonia, Mellynoname or even Molybdenum, or any ozzer variationz. ITZ MELONIA!!!"

"BUT . . ."

"SHUTZ UPZ! Youse haff been calling me za wrongk namez effer sinces youse had zat shenaniganz viz zat prawn starz. Andt I haff neffer correckedt youse justs tzo see hows manies timezz youse vud gett itz wrongk! Andt ontoppazat youse neffer effer paidt ME za $130,000 venn I schleppt viz youse. Andt I desserff it! Tvice ass mucht! Tzo I amz ferry, ferry pizzed offz!"

"BUT . . ."

"SHUTZ ZA FACKZ UPZ!! McDoonnaldt youse ares za ultimate compbinationz off an *ASKHOLE*[193] andt a *COCKWOMBLE*[194] !!!"

"Yes, dear . . ."

"Misterz Traminator! He iss allz yourz. Takez himz outta my sightz!"

---

[193] ASKHOLE: Someone who asks too many stupid, pointless or obnoxious questions.
[194] COCKWOMBLE: A person, usually male, prone to making outrageously stupid statements and/or inappropriate behavior while generally having a ridiculously high and misguided opinion of their own wisdom and importance. Any one you know??

"Ja, Ma'am! Let's go Mister President. Time to go valkies!!"

They started to walk across the Rosy Garten, the Trumper still sandwiched between the Navy Seals and with the Terminator alongside. The Trumper was still in deep shock. He just could not believe this was happening to him.

He turned to the Terminator and said "You know, this is like Karmageddon! It's like when everybody, including the Queen, is sending off all these really bad vibes, right? For some reason no one believes me when I say I didn't do all those things. Lots of people have been saying that Climate Change is for real, even though I have been relaxing hundreds of environmental restrictions. And, like, the big hoax that the Dimocrats pulled with this coronavirus thing, turned out to be a real global pandemic after all. Then the Stock Market collapsed and it's like, a serious bummer for my chances of re-election in November."

"Ach, dontcha vorry about it, Mister President. Pretty soon you won't need to be worrying about re-election. Or anythink else for that matter. For you, it's soon going to be time for 'Hasta la vista, Baby!' "

POSTSCRIPT

This needs no explanation . . .

BOHEMIAN RHAPSODY – TRUMPER AND BFF PUTITIN
https://youtu.be/i05gKtHWjGY

Please, please, do not let him go!

POST POSTSCRIPT

On a more serious note.

Jeff Daniels starred as Will McAvoy, a news anchor, in a TV series called 'The Newsroom'. It was written by Aaron Sorkin, who also wrote the multi award-winning TV series 'The West Wing', a political drama about the White House. In July 2012, one episode featured a panel debate with university students. The panel was asked the question, "Why is America the greatest country in the world?". Will McAvoy's answer was incredibly prescient, as he could have been talking about the political quagmire in which we find ourselves today.

As you listen to what he has to say it's one of those phenomenal moments when you forget that it's an actor and a script. It feels like he is a real news anchor giving his heartfelt opinion.

And the answer he gives could be equally applied to either America or the United Kingdom.

THE NEWSROOM – JEFF DANIELS
https://www.youtube.com/watch?v=wTjMqda19wk

What did Aaron Sorkin know in 2012 such that he was able to predict a situation so accurately in 2020? And can someone please get him to write a TV show script for the next couple of years so that we know what is coming and can either brace ourselves against it or embrace it with open arms!

23

BE CAREFUL WHAT YOU WISH FOR!

Just as the Trumper and his entourage of guards was passing by one of BoJo's now very large feet, the Queen looked over in the Trumper's direction and remembered that she had also sentenced BoJo due to his earlier insubordination to her.

"OFF VIZ HISS HEADT!!" she ordered and pointed in BoJo's direction. Unfortunately, once again, she confused everyone as to whether she was talking about BoJo or the Trumper, because he was just shambling along in front of BoJo when she shouted. So, as before, everyone froze and looked at each other shrugging their shoulders.

"Who cares about all of you?" said BoJo, as he had grown to his full size by this time and felt like Gulliver in Lilliput. "You're nothing but a crazy, tin-pot, Trumperland dynasty and a Ripofflican House of Cards!"

Much to BoJo's surprise, at this, the whole Ripofflican House of Cards rose up into the air and came flying down upon him like a swarm of Murder Hornets. He gave a little curse, half of fright and half of anger, and tried to beat them off. But, in trying to do that, it was creating havoc on the ground in the Rosy Garten as he was staggering around, flailing his arms in the air and around his face to get rid of the swarming Ripofflican House of Cards. Unfortunately, he was not taking any notice of where he was putting his gargantuan feet. So, all the people were running amok around the garden, trying to avoid being stamped on.

Suddenly, everything swirled around in his mind and he found himself lying on the grass in the park, with one of his aides standing over him waving away some bees that were trying to get to the flower bed next to his head. There were lots and lots of bees in the flowers and the sound reminded him of the buzzing of the swarming Ripofflicans, like Murder Hornets, at the end of the trial of the Trumper. "What a trial!" he thought.

"Wake up, sir!" said the aide. "It's Harrison, sir. What happened?"

"Er, umm, er, thank you Harrison. I, er, think I tripped when my foot went down a rabbit hole," said BoJo. "I must have fallen and banged my head and passed out for a few minutes."

"But sir, you have been missing for hours. We have been looking all over for you, all day! We were looking along your usual jogging route. This place was called Wonderland Park, but it was closed to the public years ago. So, we didn't think to come in here as the gate is usually locked. But today its open for some reason. No idea why," said Harrison.

"Why was the park closed to the public?" asked BoJo.

"Oh, I am not really sure, sir. Some odd stories from kids playing here about seeing animals that talked and weird people and creatures that spoke in riddles. The kids all seemed to love it and would come here all the time. But some of the parents got spooked by it so the Guildford Council padlocked the park gates many years ago. One story I heard was that some guy called Charles Lutwidge Dodgson used to come here in the mid-1800s, sit on the bench over there and write children's books with all sorts of unbelievable, crazy plot lines," explained Harrison. "Probably just an old wives' tale or an urban myth!"

"Oh, er, really!" said BoJo. "That's, er, interesting. But you are probably right. Old wives' tale for sure. Er, yes, yes, er, herrummpphh!!"

Most dreams that you have when sleeping at night are really vivid, but you can't usually remember anything about them when you wake up. But BoJo could remember absolutely everything about his adventure in the dream he had just had about Trumperland.

But then he thought, "Or was it a dream?" BoJo wasn't exactly sure. "Oh, but it must have been. It was such a curious dream! Golly gosh! I daren't tell anyone about it or they'll think I'm just as crazy as the Trumper."

"But sir, we have been looking for you all day because a huge crisis has just hit the world headlines. There is some new virus – called coronavirus actually – that has suddenly started spreading across the globe like a plague." said Harrison.

"WHAT!??!" shouted BoJo, not believing his ears. This was what they must have been talking about in Trumperland. But how could that be? It was a dream and he did not know anything about any virus when he started his run earlier that morning.

"Yes sir. It's some kind of flu-like virus but much more contagious and much more deadly. They are already predicting that millions will get it and hundreds of thousands will die," explained Harrison.

"WHAT!!!??" said BoJo again. "We have to get back to Number 10 immediately."

"Yes sir," said Harrison. "Your car is waiting at the park gates and there is a change of clothes in there so you can look, er, er, shall we say – presentable – when you arrive as there are sure to be lots of press hanging around for a statement."

BoJo looked down at his baggy sweat-shirt, old tennis shorts and joggers and said "Herummpph. Aaah. Yes, you are right. I need to change. And when we get back to No. 10, you need to pack for me, pronto. I need to have 12 days in my country retreat at Chevening House with my number one girlfriend, Carrie On-Regardless."

"But sir! What about the coronavirus crisis?" asked Harrison. "It's ultra-urgent!"

"Oh, piffle-paffle! Coronavirus can wait. Nothing is going to happen. A few days at the start of it – whatever it is – won't make any difference," said BoJo grumpily. "I have a bigger crisis than that. I need to tell my ex-wife and the kids that I am going to marry Carrie now that she is already preggers with the next bouncing baby BoJo. I need some time to get my game plan sorted out as its likely to precipitate World War 3."

They hurried out of the park without even noticing that, oddly, the path was made out of yellow bricks. BoJo got in the back of his armoured, custom-built Jaguar XJ and they set off for London.

He started to get changed in the back of the car and pulled off his sweatshirt, but as he did so, he suddenly noticed the old, faded printing on the front. It said, 'MEXIT Forever!' ...

"Whoah! WTF!" he thought. "How can this be?" He looked at the sweatshirt again but, sure enough, it said, 'MEXIT Forever!' on it.

"No, no, no, no!" he said quietly to himself. "This can't be right!! Just carry on like everything is normal, Boris. Yes! Normal! Just do what you do best – smile a lot and tell everyone that everything will work out fine in the end. And we just need to get MEXIT, er, I mean BREXIT done!"

"Aah, Harrison!" said BoJo. "What is the Trumper's middle name?"

"The 'J' is for John, sir. Why?"

"Oh, nothing. I just wondered," BoJo lied. "You're sure? Really sure?"

"Yes sir. Absolutely! 100%. Check it on Wikipedia if you like."

"Phew!!," he thought. "I hope the Carpenter just screwed up!"

So, he carried on getting changed and felt in his shorts' pocket for his cell phone. There hadn't been any signal all the time he had been in Trumperland as he had been wanting to call someone – anyone – to help him get out of there. But there was just no connection. So, he was expecting lots of messages now that he had a signal again.

He pulled out the phone. There were no missed calls – which was odd - and he noticed that there was only one WhatsApp message on it from an unknown number. So, he swiped the screen to check it out.

It just said, "Wear a mask. Stay safe. Don't be like my idiot husband. Queen Melonia."

He dropped the phone and grabbed his testicles just to make sure that they were still there, and he wasn't just dreaming it all. It was a slightly reassuring, if somewhat foolish gesture. But that that was exactly BoJo's public persona. A slightly reassuring, if somewhat foolish gesture.

As he was sitting there, holding his testicles in the back of the Jaguar, he started to remember what he had been thinking when he ran into the park earlier that morning, which was "Bah, humbug! I wish UK had a presidency, like the US, then I wouldn't have to deal directly with all those other Ministers in the House and the Speaker shouting 'ORDER! ORRRDERRRR!'. And I could just cite Article II, like the US President, and do whatever I want."

And that brought back the memory of catching his foot in the rabbit hole and falling over as it went dark, very dark, along with a clap of thunder and a deep echoing voice that had said, "BE CAREFUL WHAT YOU WISH FOR!"

Then there was the same thing coming from Bolt-On the Walrus. "Be careful what you wish for!" Plus, the quote from John Lennon. "Reality leaves a lot to the imagination!".

"Maybe they were right," BoJo reflected. "The Trumper stuff was a bit like seeing myself in a looking glass. But, I don't want to be like him because that didn't end well, and I don't want to suffer the same fate! Maybe, I should change tactics and become a real 'Man of the People'? But I am not so sure I could ever force myself to do that. Hmmmmnn!"

As the car cruised along the busy A3 back to London, BoJo stared out of the window and was lost in thought about many things.

That phrase 'Be Careful What You Wish For!' kept rolling back into his mind as he was trying to decide what would be his best course of action for the future.

It was warm in the back of the car with the sunlight shining through the windows and there was the familiar, embracing smell of the soft, quilted, Connolly leather seats. BoJo was starting to feel relaxed and drowsy and, as he did so – inexplicably - a quotation from 'Alice in Wonderland' by Lewis Carroll, meandered through his brain.

It was something said by the Dormouse. "She generally gave herself very good advice (though she very seldom followed it)".

"Hmmmmnnn," BoJo thought as he gradually let his heavy eyelids slowly close. "Maybe I should ask Dominic Cummandgo for his advice. He is always good with things like this. I hope he is at No. 10 when I get back and not up in Durham at his father's estate . . ."

24

MEANWHILE PART 11 – BACK IN TRUMPERLAND

Meanwhile...

Meanwhile, as BoJo was drifting off to sleep, things started to come to life once more in Trumperland.

The gate to the park had closed itself and the padlock and chain carefully threaded themselves around the bars like a snake and locked with a rusty 'click'.

The long grass rustled as the White Rabbi hurried by and the Walrus splashed his way through the Big Pond. There was the rattle of cups and saucers as the March Hare and the Dormouse shared their never-ending drinks of covfefe, while the Mad Hater wheeled and dealed on his hat sales. The shrill voice of the Queen continued to order her unfortunate guests to their own executions. The distant wail of the Sheriff's police siren echoed as he chased the Bandit once again – while the Tweedle twins continued to argue and fight about who was dumbest, even as they were trying to catch sight of the Cheshire Pussy when it faded in and out of view. The Carpenter was once more cracking open oysters with his hammer, while Humpty Trumpty balanced precariously at the top of his ladder behind his hologram wall. The Gryphon continued to confuse everyone with his convoluted Yoda-like speech patterns while dancing tangos and fandangos. And all of that was mixed up with the distant sobs of Moscow Mitch, the very, very, miserable Mock Turtle.

And every now and then, you could hear from the trumpet-like mouth of the rabbit hole, someone with an extremely British accent try to calm everyone down so as to prevent their crazy activities in Trumperland from attracting too much attention from the rest of the world. It was only two words. But they were very, very loud indeed.

"OOOORRRRDDDDEEERRRRR!!! OOOORRRRDDDEEERRRR!!!"

Yes, life was getting back to normal in Trumperland. Whatever 'normal' was before, what it is now, or – perhaps - ever will be in the future . . .

And, you might ask, what happened to the Trumper? Well, he was on his way to be 'Terminated' when BoJo's gargantuan exit appeared to cause the Ripofflican House of Cards to collapse in a hornet's-nest frenzy and pandemonium ensued. Had he been 'Terminated'? Or had he succeeded in slipping away unnoticed in the anarchy, turmoil, riotousness, instability, lawlessness, strife and ferment that always seemed to follow the Trumper wherever he went?

No-one was actually quite sure what happened to the Trumper, much to the extreme anger of the Queen. Some people were even saying that the Ripofflican House of Cards had purposely caused the fracas to create a distraction so that their cult leader could escape. That was because, in the middle of it all, out of nowhere, a bunch of heavily-armed troops in full riot gear - many on horseback, but with no names, badges or insignia – rushed into the Rosy Garten and threw tear gas and flash-bangs at the previously peaceful crowd to create even more panic. Bill Barf's cavalry had come to the rescue in the nick of time! And who wouldn't put it past him to pull a trick like that?

It was somehow reminiscent of the comment the Queen had made to the Navy Seals when the Trumper was under house arrest, quoting what the former British Prime Minister, David Cameroon had said about BoJo. "The thing about the greased piglet is that he manages to slip through other people's hands where mere mortals fail."

The parallels between the Trumper and BoJo were evident once more and were very, very likely to increase as time went by . . .

78. Just a Reality Show Host Who Thinks He Can Make Up His Own Reality

A Fable-Parable-Fairy Story

THE EPILOGUE

This fairy story is just a snapshot in time and had to be curtailed at the very early stages of the coronavirus pandemic, otherwise it would have been very difficult to choose an end point. Neither the Trumper nor BoJo have done well in dealing with Covid-19, and many would say that they are amongst the worst-performing leaders in the world on this matter. On top of that, as I write this in late-September, the Trumper has an election coming. So, if I had let the story continue any longer, it would have opened up a very large can of worms that, at the moment, has no end in sight. Perhaps that means I will have to somehow revisit our two non-heroes/villains at some future point in time to see how the whole sad story shook out in the end.

So, I believe that those two need to be watched very, very carefully.

However, I wrote the first version of this Epilogue in mid-August 2020, saying that there was one immutable fact that we can all rely on – barring a revolution or a coup d'état – and that was that neither of them can stay in power forever. It was a 'soft' ending.

But, in the words of the late, great *Yogi Berra*[195], "It ain't over till it's over!"

---

[195] YOGI BERRA: Former New York Yankees professional baseball player and coach. Berra was well known for his pithy comments and witticisms, known as Yogism's. These very often took the form of either an apparently obvious tautology or a paradoxical contradiction. These included: "When you come to a fork in the road, take it." "You can observe a lot by just watching." "It's like déjà vu all over again." And many, many more.

Unfortunately, the words of the Trumper in the last few days have sent a chill down the spines of everyone in the world who values democracy. He has publicly declared – ahead of the election – that it's a 'hoax', it's 'rigged', he cannot guarantee a peaceful transition of power, that he should 'get rid of the (mail-in) ballots'. So, there would be no 'transition', just a 'continuation' of his presidency. Plus, any election disputes can be decided by the Supreme Court that he is trying to stack with one of his 'tame', right-wing judges in place of the recently deceased 'Notorious RBG'.

All of this means that real US democracy will be thrown out of the window, the votes of the American people ignored, and the result of the election decided by a Supreme Court that has a strong Trumper bias!

This situation reminds me of the EDSA 'People Power' Revolution in the Philippines in February 1986. Marcos had been in power for 20 years. In the election against Cory Aquino, he rigged the vote counting software so that when tabulators punched in numbers it went 'two for Marcos and one for Cory' instead of, say, 'one each'. The tabulators walked out and both candidates declared they had won, sparking off public dissent, the Secretary of Defense and top generals resigning, the majority of the Armed Forces and the Catholic Church backing Cory, plus millions of people holding a sit-in protest for days on EDSA, the main artery of the capital, Metro Manila. On Tuesday 25 February, both Marcos and Cory each had their own inaugurations as President! Yes!!

But Cory Aquino was obviously the peoples' choice and Marcos was under extreme pressure. At midnight – only a few hours after his inauguration – Marcos and his family were airlifted out of Malacañang Palace[196] by a US Air Force HH-3E 'Jolly Green Giant' Rescue Helicopter like the ones used in Vietnam. They flew to Clark Air Force Base north of Manila and then to Hawaii, where they lived in exile till Marcos died.

So, all of this tells you that your vote counts, people-power protests work, and the underlying structures of democracy, state, church, the rule of law and the armed forces can peacefully, and forcefully, combine to oust dictators and follow the will of the people. It really can happen!

---

[196] MALACANANG PALACE: The Philippine equivalent of the 'White House'.

I lived in Manila through the EDSA People Power Revolution as I was based there from 1981 to 2007. My house was 100 yards from EDSA, where millions were peacefully protesting, and about a mile from Club Filipino where Cory had her inauguration. So, I was right in the middle of it! We took food to the people doing the sit-in, we listened at home to 'Bomba Radyo', the unofficial 'rebel' radio station, as the commercial TV and radio stations had been shut down by Marcos. When we heard on 'Bomba Radyo' that Marcos had gone, we went out on ESDA at about 1:00am to tell the people – because they did not know at first - and we took bottles of whiskey to share a drink with them as a celebration. They had ousted a 20-year tyrant with no loss of life! Incredible!!

And, almost as amazing, was that fact that the following day EVERTHING was back to normal. I went onto EDSA at 7:00am and, as usual, it was heaving with cars and buses and everyone – including myself - just went to work as though nothing had happened. We had about 2,000 Filipino staff in our office and the chat was like:

"Oh, what did you do yesterday?"

"I was at the EDSA Revolution, where were you – blah, blah, blah?"

So, for those of you reading this before the election - and possibly in what might be very dark days between then and the 20 January Inauguration Day – don't despair if the Trumper pulls some crazy, illegal, unethical, hypocritical, unconstitutional stunts. It is possible to pull it all back and make it work again, for the good of the American people and, in fact, for democracy the world over. I have seen it happen.

It might mean millions of people doing sit-ins in Washington and in front of every State House in every state. It might mean mass defections from the US Armed Forces and lots of Vet protests. It could mean mass resignations from the DOJ and other key government offices. It could mean an about-face of the evangelicals and the church to drop their support of the Trumper. It could mean a sudden wake-up call to the Ripofflican Party to stop being the Trumper Cult Party and re-discover their principles.

It could even mean a group of US Navy Seals plucking the Trumper and his family out of the White House in a UH-60 Blackhawk Stealth helicopter and taking him to some safe haven to await whatever legal process is appropriate, like they did with Marcos many years ago.

They already have a game plan for that playbook. PROBLEM: (1) Authoritarian dictator using the presidency for his own personal benefit. (2) Disinformation campaigns. (3) Vote manipulation. (4) Refusing to step down for a smooth transition of power. (5) Unwillingness to abide by the will of the people. SOLUTION: (1) Extraction. (2) Take to safe haven. (3) Await due legal process – because justice matters

It's all the same as Marcos – except this time on US soil!

Can they do it if necessary? Will they do it? Do they have the cojones? I hope so, of it comes down to that!

Somehow, I don't think BoJo would go as far as the Trumper has done, but one way or another, both their terms in office must come to an end. So, hopefully, sooner rather than later, we can look forward to the time when life, the universe and everything will stabilise. It may not go back to being exactly the way it was – there are too many radical factors for that – but we can hope, and many will pray, that it will at least, stabilise.

And, therefore, we can all rise up and join together in singing the words to the much-loved song by Eric Idle of Monty Python's Flying Circus – *"Always Look on the Bright Side of Life".*

ALWAYS LOOK ON THE BRIGHT SIDE OF LIFE – ERIC IDLE
https://www.youtube.com/watch?v=JrdEMERq8MA

A wonderful song and very uplifting in these dark and troubled days – even if he was *'a very naughty boy'* [197].

TSB – 25 September 2020

---

[197] A VERY NAUGHTY BOY: Check out the original of the song as the finale of the movie, Monty Python's Life of Brian. It's on YouTube. It's a classic.

The End

(Well, except for a few other bits and bobs)

APPENDIX A: LIST OF MUSIC

A.   SONGS IN THE BOOK – with Text Box plus QR Code and URL

1. *Back in the USSR* - Beatles – Ch. 6 – The Cheshire Pussy
2. *It Wasn't Me* – Shaggy– Ch. 7 – Meanwhile Pt. 3 – The Pee Pee Tapes
3. *Another Brick in the Wall* – Pink Floyd – Ch. 8 - Humpty Trumpty
4. *Bohemian Rhapsody* – Wayne's World – Ch. 9 – Meanwhile Pt. 4 – Austin
5. *Sympathy for the Devil* – Rolling Stones – Ch. 10 - The Mad Hater . . .
6. *Kung Foo Fighting* – Celo Green – Ch. 11 – Meanwhile Pt. 6 – KFF
7. *Get Over It* – Eagles – Ch. 13 – Meanwhile – Crimes in Crimea
8. *Just One Lifetime* – Sting & Shaggy – Ch. 14 – I Am the Walrus
9. *Alice's Restaurant* – Arlo Guthrie – Ch. 14 – I Am the Walrus
10. *Dueling Banjos* – Deliverance – Ch. 14 – I Am the Walrus
11. *I Am the Walrus* – Beatles – Ch. 14 – I Am the Walrus
12. *The Mock Turtle's Song* – Steely Dan – Ch. 16 – Moscow Mitch . . .
13. *The Day Democracy Died* – Founding Fathers – Ch 16 – Moscow Mitch . . .
14. *American Pie* – Don McClean – Ch. 16 – Moscow Mitch the Mock Turtle
15. *Waka Waka (A Time for Africa)* – Shakira – Ch. 20 – To Kill a Mockingbird
16. *Smoke in the Water* – Deep Purple – Ch. 20 – To Kill a Mockingbird
17. *Guantanamera* – Celia Cruz – Ch. 20 – To Kill a Mockingbird
18. *Isn't it Ironic* – Alanis Morissette - Ch. 22 – A Few Good Men . . .
19. *Bohemian Rhapsody* – Trumper & Putitin – Ch. 22 – A Few Good Men . . .
20. *Always Look on the Bright Side* – Eric Idle – Ch. 24 – Meanwhile Part 11 . . .

APPENDIX B: LIST OF VIDEOS, MOVIES, TV SHOWS ETC

A.   VIDEOS IN THE BOOK – with Text Box plus QR Code and URL Link

1.   *Alice in Wonderland* - Queen of Hearts – Ch. 3 – Meanwhile Pt. 1 . . .
2.   *Fawlty Towers* – Basil & Sybil - Ch. 3 – Meanwhile Pt. 1 . . .
3.   *Wizard of Oz* – Yellow Brick Road – Ch. 8 – Humpty Trumpty
4.   *Archie Bunker* – Black & Women Presidents – Ch. 8 – Humpty Trumpty
5.   *Top Gear* – Caravan Race – Ch. 8 – Humpty Trumpty
6.   *Reservoir Dogs* – Quentin Tarantino – Ch. 8 – Humpty Trumpty
7.   *Hunger Games* – Jennifer Lawrence – Ch. 8 - Humpty Trumpty
8.   *Italian Job* – Michael Caine – Ch. 8 - Humpty Trumpty
9.   *Airplane* – Don't Call Me Shirley – Ch. 8 – Humpty Trumpty
10. *Trumper's Wall* – Jonathan Pie – Ch.8 - Humpty Trumpty
11. *Trumper's Best Words* – Trevor Noah – Ch. 8 - Humpty Trumpty
12. *Yes, Minister* – Why the EU? – Ch. 8 - Humpty Trumpty
13. *Austin Powers* – Mike Myers – Ch. 9 – Meanwhile Pt. 4 – Austin Powers
14. *Goldfinger* – James Bond – Ch. 9 – Meanwhile Pt. 4 – Austin Powers Up
15. *Coffee* - Dennis Leary – Ch. 10 – The Mad Hater's Covfefe Party
16. *Taxi Driver* – Robert de Niro – Ch. 12 – Tweedledumb & Tweedledumber
17. *Death Star Canteen* – Eddie Izzard – Ch. 12 – Tweedledumb . . .
18. *Risk* – Eddie Izzard – Ch. 14 – I Am the Walrus – Goo Goo G'joob
19. *Yes, Prime Minister* – You Lied – Ch. 14 – I Am the Walrus . . .
20. *Wall in Colorado* – CNN – Ch. 14 – I Am the Walrus – Goo Goo G'joob
21. *Yes, Minister* – Conscience & MOM – Ch. 15 – Meanwhile Pt. 7 . . .
22. *Vice* – Christian Bale & Amy Adams – Ch. 15 – Meanwhile Pt. 7 . . .
23. *Mar-a-Lago* – Trumper & Schleppstein – Ch. 15 – Meanwhile Pt. 7 . . .
24. *Room Next Door* – Randy Dandy – Ch. 15 – Meanwhile Pt. 7
25. *Room Next Door* – BoJo & Brexit – Ch. 16 – Mitch the Mock Turtle . . .
26. *Nobody Does it Better* – Trumper – Ch. 16 – Mitch the Mock Turtle . . .
27. *Room Next Door* – BoJo Election Special – Ch. 16 – Mitch the Mock . . .
28. *HIGNFY* – BoJo & Tony Bland – Ch. 16 – Mitch the Mock Turtle . . .
29. *Burn After Reading* – Brad Pitt – Ch. 16 – Mitch the Mock Turtle . . .

APPENDIX C: ATTRIBUTIONS

Key: (W.C) = Wikimedia.Commons

Wikimedia Commons is a media file repository which makes public domain and freely-licensed educational media content (images, sound and video clips) available to everyone. All users are allowed to copy, use and modify any files freely as long as the terms specified by the author are followed. This usually means crediting the source and author(s) with appropriate attributions. The list below includes all images in this book.

1. Dumb & Dumber: Pinterest by all-hat-no-cattle.blogspot
2. Blind Man & Lame. 1596: By Johann Theodor de Bry (W.C)
3. Alice in Wonderland. 1893: IA Library of Congress (W.C)
4. (a) Lewis Carroll. 1863: By Oscar Gustave Rejlander (W.C)
   (b) Ian Hislop. 2020: Permission given for use by Ian Hislop
5. (a) Boris Johnson Caricature 1. 2019: By DonkeyHotey (W.C)
   (b) Grey Sweatshirt. 2013: By Bizzie, Minneapolis (W.C)
6. BTIF Project. 2009: US Federal Government (W.C)
7. Rudy Giuliani. 2011: Caricature by DonkeyHotey (W.C)
8. Seventy-Two Virgins. 2005: Amazon.com by Boris Johnson
9. Moscovitch APC. 2015: US Army TRADOC (W.C)
10. (a) Greenland Panorama. 2007-09: By Kim Hansen (W.C)
    (b) Trump Tower. 2017: By NeONBRAND (W.C)
11. Trump Playing Golf. 2019: By 首相官邸ホームページ (W.C)
12. Purple Cat in Tree. 2020: Licensed from Adobe Stock Photos
13. (a) Cheshire Cat in Tree. 1866: By John Tenniel (W.C)
    (b) Donald Trump Caricature 1. 2016: By DonkeyHotey (W.C)
14. Cat's Grin. 2016: Photoshop caricature by DonkeyHotey (W.C)
15. Melania Trump Caricature. 2016: By DonkeyHotey (W.C)
16. Humpty Trumpty. 2019: Permission given for use by USAUnify
17. Trump Baby Blimp. 2018: By Loco Steve, Bromley (W.C)

18. (a) Baby on a Stick. 2018: By Alisdare Hickson (W.C)
    (b) Overcomb. 2017: By Paul Graham Morris, Edinburgh (W.C)
    (c) Humpty Trumpty. 2019: By Cyndy Sims Parr (W.C)
19. BMW Isetta + Caravan. 2015: By Lothar Spurzem (W.C)
20. Caravan Migrants. 2018: ByProtoplasmaKid (W.C)
21. Mexican Standoff. 2012: Martin SoulStealer (W.C)
22. Irish Backstop. 2017: By AmanoYukki (W.C)
23. (a) Brexit Bus. 2016: By Gizmodo/Google
    (b) Winding Road. 2013: By Rob Stoeltje, Loenen, NL (W.C)
24. (a) Battersea Power Station. 2005: By Albion (W.C)
    (b) Baby Trump Blimp. 2018: By ChiralJon (W.C)
25. Demonstrator. 2020: By Skunkhaus (W.C)
26. (a) Dr. Evil 2 (Impersonator). 2007: By Edans (W.C)
    (b) Kim Jong-un Caricature. 2017: By DonkeyHotey (W.C)
    (c) Donald Trump Caricature 2. 2018: By DonkeyHotey (W.C)
27. (a) Mad Hatter's Tea Party. 1865: John Tenniel (W.C)
    (b) Grey Sweatshirt. 2013: By Bizzie, Minneapolis (W.C)
    (c) Boris Johnson Caricature 2. 2019: By DonkeyHotey (W.C)
    (d) Donald Trump Caricature 3. 2020: By DonkeyHotey (W.C)
28. (a) Mad Hatter. 1865: By John Tenniel (W.C)
    (b) Donald Trump Caricature 4. 2015: By DonkeyHotey (W.C)
    (c) Flames. 2005: By MarcusObal (W.C)
29. Tweedledumb & Tweedledumber. 2019: By Doc Ivan (Twitter)
30. Igor, Rudy & Lev. 2020: By US Government Employee (W.C)
31. Mick Mulvaney Caricature. 2019: By DonkeyHotey (W.C)
32. Nancy Pelosi at WH. 2019: By Shealah Craighead (W.C)
33. (a) John Bolton Caricature. 2011: By DonkeyHotey (W.C)
    (b) The Walrus & the Carpenter. 1865: By John Tenniel (W.C)
34. (a) The Walrus on Briny Beach. 1865: By John Tenniel (W.C)
    (b) John Bolton Caricature. 2011: By DonkeyHotey (W.C)
35. Trump Mini Statue. 2017: By Odditymall
36. All The President's Men. 1976: Movie poster on Wikipedia
37. (a) Jeffrey Epstein. 2006: Palm Beach Cnty Sheriff Dept. (W.C)
    (b) Palm Trees. 2004: Kristine, St. Augustine, USA (W.C)
38. All The President's Men. 1974: Book cover on Wikipedia
39. Rage. 2020: Book cover on Amazon.com

A Fable-Parable-Fairy Story

DISCLAIMER

The QR codes herein provide links to material specifically available on YouTube. All such material has been posted there by others, not the author, and the views expressed therein are not necessarily those of the author. The author is merely indicating to the reader that the said material has some relationship, however tenuous, to the storyline. The reader is in no way obligated to follow any of the links provided in this book. The author does not claim to hold the copyright to any of the songs, movies, TV or radio shows, clips from performances of bands, artists, comedians, presenters and others in the entertainment field, including photographs, comments, quotations, extracts of lyrics, books, websites, social media or any other forms of stored or transmitted information. All such material is freely available to the general public via YouTube, Wikimedia Commons, Wikipedia, Google, Facebook, Twitter and other similar social media sources for everyone's information and enjoyment. Where such images have been used from sites such as Wikimedia Commons, the author has taken, in good faith, the statements therein, that such images are free of copyright and available for use in publications. Other sources, such as blogsites, Facebook, Twitter etc. are taken to be for public viewing and that images thereon may be sourced accordingly. Where specific permissions were required, these were requested. Attributions for all images are included in the above list.

A Fable-Parable-Fairy Story

CPSIA information can be obtained
at www.ICGtesting.com
Printed in the USA
BVHW041018081020
590605BV00014B/369